As the end of a worldwid[e] ... considers the lessons they have ... test.

In the face of a crisis that sweeps the entire planet back to the age before electricity, the Brannings face a choice. Will they hoard their possessions to survive—or trust God to provide as they share their resources with others?

#1 bestselling suspense author Terri Blackstock weaves a masterful what-if series in which global catastrophe reveals the darkness in human hearts—and lights the way to restoration for a self-centered world.

As the Pulses that caused the power outage are finally coming to an end, thirteen-year-old Beth Branning witnesses two brutal murders. She narrowly escapes from the killer and runs away in terror. If she tells anyone what she saw, he'll find her and kill her. But if she doesn't, her silence could cost her life.

Meanwhile, as Deni's ex-fiancé returns to Crockett with a newfound faith and the influence to get things done, Deni is torn between the man who can fulfill all her dreams and Mark Green, the man who inhabits them.

As the world slowly emerges from the crisis, the Brannings face their toughest crisis yet. Will God require more of them than they're prepared to give? How will they keep their faith if he doesn't answer their prayers?

TERRI BLACKSTOCK (www.terriblackstock.com) is the bestselling author of Last Light, Night Light, True Light, the Sun Coast Chronicles, Second Chances, Newpointe 911, and Cape Refuge suspense series, and other books. With Beverly LaHaye, she wrote Seasons Under Heaven, Showers in Season, Times and Seasons, and Season of Blessing.

Books by Terri Blackstock

TERRI BLACKSTOCK

#1 bestselling suspense author

DAWN'S LIGHT

aRESTORATIONovel

BOOK FOUR

ZONDERVAN®

ZONDERVAN.com/
AUTHORTRACKER
follow your favorite authors

We want to hear from you. Please send your comments about this book to us in care of zreview@zondervan.com. Thank you.

ZONDERVAN®

Dawn's Light
Copyright © 2008 by Terri Blackstock

This title is also available as a Zondervan ebook product.
Visit www.zondervan.com/ebooks for more information.

This title is also available as a Zondervan audio product.
Visit www.zondervan.com/audiopages for more information.

Requests for information should be addressed to:
Zondervan, *Grand Rapids, Michigan* 49530

Library of Congress Cataloging-in-Publication Data

Blackstock, Terri.
    Dawn's Light / Terri Blackstock.
        p. cm. — (A restoration novel; bk. 4)
    ISBN 978-0-310-25770-7
    1. Regression (Civilization) — Fiction. I. Title.
PS3552.L34285D39 2008
813'.54 — dc22

                                  2007051419

Published in association with the literary agency of Alive Communications, Inc., 7680 Goddard Street, Suite 200, Colorado Springs, CO 80920.

Interior design by Beth Shagene

Printed in the United States of America

---

08 09 10 11 12 13 14 • 23 22 21 20 19 18 17 16 15 14 13 12 11 10 9 8 7 6 5 4 3 2

This book is lovingly dedicated to the Nazarene.

Acknowledgments

THE RESTORATION SERIES HAS BEEN THE MOST DIFFICULT series I've written, mostly due to the amount of research involved. So many people have helped me with that, and I've attempted to acknowledge them in each book. For this book, I want to give special thanks to Bill Buchanan, for his electrical engineering expertise and his patience with me as I asked a million questions about how electricity works. A novelist himself, Bill understood what I was trying to accomplish and helped me think through the technical aspects of my story. Thanks, also, to his wife, Janet, for lending another set of eyes to the manuscript.

Special thanks to Dave Lambert, who's been editing my books for years, and always challenges me to take my writing to the next level. He edits with deep thought and insight into my characters and plot, and forces me to rewrite and rethink until the book is worthy of shelf space. I'm also thankful to Karen Ball, who acquired this series and helped edit it. Karen has a way of drawing the best out of her authors. Sue Brower has championed me at Zondervan for years. I owe so much of my success to the decisions she's made, and for that I'm very grateful. And thanks to Karwyn Bursma and Bob Hudson, for all they do to get my books into your hands.

And I can't end this series without a huge thanks to Beth Runnels, Gayle DeSalles, and Ellen Tarver, who've all assisted me in various aspects of my work. Each one of these ladies is uniquely talented, and they all provide me with services that make my life much easier.

Finally, thanks to my readers who have hung in there with me through all four of the Restoration novels. I pray that God will use the books to strengthen, challenge, and bless you.

ON MAY 24, CIVILIZATION AS WE KNOW IT COMES TO AN END. Plumbing doesn't work because the water treatment plants run on electricity. Trucks and trains don't run, so stores run out of food. Generators are rendered useless. In this major meltdown of life, people are stranded where they are, with no transportation, no power, and no communication. Crime runs rampant as evil fills the void, and desperation becomes the only moral guide many people recognize.

Eventually, word makes its way to Crockett, Alabama, that the event was caused by a star—a supernova named SN–1999—which is emitting electromagnetic pulses every few seconds. With no assurance of when the star might burn itself out and allow them to rebuild, people are left with a choice: will they hoard what they have until it all runs out, or will they share with those around them who are in need?

The Brannings, an upper-middle-class Christian family, who pride themselves on their righteousness, respond like everyone else at first: they hole up at home, hoarding their food, paranoid that interacting with others will force them to share the few provisions they have. The children are angry that their lives have been disrupted. They're bored without visual and audio entertainment. Deni, the twenty-two-year-old, is frustrated that she won't be able to get to Washington to start her new job and be with her fiancé, who lives there.

When Doug Branning finally comes to grips with the fact that this is not going to end soon, he breaks down before God, realizing that he's not equipped to function without technology. How will he support his family? How will he provide food? How will they survive? As he struggles to find answers, he begins to realize that God has a purpose for him and his family through this trial. People around him have great needs—physical and spiritual. The Brannings begin to understand that they have much to learn, and much to give.

When Deni's eyes open to the true character of Craig Martin, her fiancé, she breaks her engagement. She's begun to fall in love with Mark Green, a high school friend who lives in her neighborhood. But Mark is the son of a convicted killer, and when a neighbor is shot by an unknown assailant, people assume that Mark committed the crime. He's thrown into a dark and broken prison system. Deni and her family help to find the true killer and clear his name. As they do, Deni sees Mark's noble acts of forgiveness toward those who persecuted him, and falls more deeply in love with him.

The blackout continues for a year, and the Brannings learn to work together to survive, until God gives them their ultimate test …

Branning, Doug—forty-eight, father of four and husband to Kay Branning. He's a successful stockbroker who's never known failure until technology come to an end and he's forced to provide for his family and protect them from the dangers surrounding them. Although the circumstances of life threaten to defeat him when the power goes out, he manages to find the character and strength to do what needs to be done. He commits to studying the Word of God and becomes the pastor of a home church for Christians in his neighborhood.

Branning, Kay—forty-five, Doug's wife, mother to Deni, Jeff, Beth, and Logan. She was a spoiled soccer mom before the outage, living in a 4,000-square-foot home with all the bells and whistles, and driving a brand new Expedition. Now she faces a daily struggle to feed her family and help those around her who have less than she does. She takes much pride in being a good mother who protects and nurtures her children

Branning, Deni—twenty-three, Doug and Kay's spitfire daughter. Just before the outage, she graduated from Georgetown University in Broadcast Journalism and landed a job as an intern at the NBC affiliate in Washington, D.C. She was engaged to Craig Martin, an attorney who worked for a prominent U.S. senator. Just before the outage, she comes home to Crockett, Alabama (a suburb of Birmingham), to take care of some wedding planning. When the power goes out and transportation and communication are shut down, along with all electronics, she feels trapped. And when she and her little sister happen upon two murdered neighbors, her depression escalates. Other murders follow these, and homes around them are pillaged. Deni becomes desperate to get back to Washington to be with her fiancé. The father of a high school friend offers her a ride east in his horse-drawn wagon, and she leaves secretly. But it isn't long before she realizes she's thrown herself into the arms of a killer. She finally calls out to God for help and begins to recognize his provision in her foolishness. Her father, whom she believed to be weak, moves heaven and earth to find and rescue her. But when things get violent, she is forced to kill her tormenter in self-defense.

Branning, Jeff—seventeen, Doug and Kay's son. He was the star pitcher on his high school baseball team, a true jock and a popular kid at school. But he wasn't used to hard work, and he didn't much like it. He's a Christian kid but has moments of rebellion. Saddled with a lot of adult responsibilities since the outage, he finds the weight of the world on his shoulders as he tries to help protect his family from the evil surfacing around them.

Branning, Beth—thirteen, Doug and Kay's daughter, who looks up to her older sister. She's with Deni when they find her teacher and her husband murdered. She's sensitive to the needs of those around her. To help the children of the neighborhood cope through the outage, she begins to write and produce plays that become major events for the families of Oak Hollow. But the violence that she's witnessed over the last year has taken its toll on her, and she lives in fear of the Next Terrible Thing.

Branning, Logan—ten, Doug and Kay's youngest child, who was raised on Play Stations, computers, DVDs, and television, and finds their new way of life boring and unfair. But he's enjoying spending more time with his dad now that Doug is home most of the time.

Green, Mark—twenty-three, Deni's friend from high school and a neighbor in Oak Hollow subdivision. He's in love with Deni and helps convince her that her fiancé is not the right man for her. He's good looking, strong, inventive, skillful, and a strong Christian. He skipped college and went to work in construction. He's disliked in the neighborhood because his father was a convicted murderer. When a kid in the neighborhood is shot, Mark is accused and thrown into a broken and violent prison system. When the prisoners escape after killing two deputies and wounding the sheriff, Mark stays behind to help them. He's released when the other deputies walk off the job. But when he returns home, some of the neighborhood men beat him. His charges are finally dropped, and he winds up going to work as a volunteer deputy to help protect the community. When he has to care for the prisoners—including the men who beat him—he learns that forgiveness is not a emotion, but a choice. With the help of God, he manages to perform acts of mercy toward his enemies and, in doing so, proves to Deni and her family when he's made of.

Martin, Craig—twenty-eight, Deni's ex-fiancé. He's an attorney who graduated at the top of his class from Georgetown University Law School. He works for a U.S. senator and considers himself a mover and a shaker. When the Pulses began, Deni didn't hear from him for weeks. He finally showed up to see her but had an aversion to the hard work they were doing to help the community. Deni almost agreed to go back to Washington with him, but at the last moment, she changed her mind and broke off the engagement. He's been writing her ever since, begging her to marry him.

Caldwell, Brad—the Brannings' next-door neighbor and Doug's best friend. He's a good man, but not a Christian. An attorney who has a strong sense of justice, he set up a "neighborhood watch" in Oak Hollow and took the protection of the subdivision personally. An African American, he was initially blamed for the murders and robberies in the neighborhood and was beaten up and almost killed. He's the father of two boys and the husband of Judith Caldwell.

Caldwell, Judith — wife of Brad, a nurse, who begins to attend Doug's house church with her two boys, even though her husband won't attend with her.

Caldwell, Drew and Jeremy — Brad and Judith's sons, nine and seven, who are friends with Logan. Both children are traumatized when their father is beaten up, so he pretends he's fine to keep them from worrying.

Horton, Chris — twenty-two, Deni's best friend from high school, a nurse.

Rowe, Amber — twenty-five, the Brannings' other next-door neighbor. Her husband left her two weeks before the outage with three children under three, and she's having a terrible time managing. The Brannings try to help her as much as they can.

DAWN'S LIGHT

one

BETH BRANNING SAT ON HER BIKE A BLOCK UP THE STREET
from Alabama Bank and Trust and watched the hungry mob
waiting in the rain. The violent May thunderstorm pounded
and cracked like special effects on a Hollywood set, drenching those who waited to get their money. If her parents saw
her they would freak. It was no place for a thirteen-year-old,
they would say.

Even from a block away, she could feel the tension and
thrill of those who would go from poverty to plenty in a matter of minutes. Armed deputies surrounded this bank and all
the others in Crockett, along with the few running vehicles
in town — sheriff's department patrol cars, ambulances, fire
trucks. Clearly, they expected violence. The banks had been
closed since the power outage began a year ago, crushing
the economy and leaving even Beth's family poor. With the
poor and homeless so desperate, no one with cash would be
safe today.

The newspaper warehouse was on the other side of
Crockett, so she turned her bike around, careful not to tip
the bike trailer she pulled. Rain or shine, she had to deliver
papers. Raindrops pricked her skin, soaked her softball jersey, and made her shiver. It would take longer to prepare
her stacks today, since she'd have to wrap the papers in
plastic to keep them from getting wet. She might as well
get it done.

As she turned the corner onto a less populated road, a bolt of lightning flashed in front of her, thunder cracking instantly. Her heart kicked through her chest.

People got struck by lightning riding bicycles all the time. A great-uncle of hers had been fishing in a boat when lightning struck him dead. She had to get to shelter. She looked around for a safe place to wait it out, and saw the Cracker Barrel up ahead. It, too, had been closed for a year—since the power outage began—but its rustic porch would shelter her until the storm passed.

She pulled her bike onto the parking lot and rolled it up toward the porch, wishing they'd left their famous rocking chairs out. Lightning burst and thunder crashed again, making her jump.

Her clothes were soaked, and beads of water ran from her long blonde curls into her eyes. She shivered, wishing she'd listened to her parents. There were probably tornados coming, and the winds would pick her up and blow her away, like Dorothy and Toto.

Leaving her bike and trailer in the rain, she sat on the porch floor. Hugging her wet knees, she heard a sound from somewhere behind the building. A garbled cry, a muttered curse.

"Don't shoot!"

She sprang up and crept to the end of the porch.

"Please ... I'll give you the money!"

Her breath caught in her lungs as she peered around the side of the building.

Two men—one on his knees, facing her. The other stood behind him, holding a revolver to the kneeling man's head.

Beth's knees went weak, and she crouched, making herself smaller. The man with the gun wore a black raincoat with the hood pulled up. She couldn't see his face. But the one on his knees looked young—no more than twenty-five. His wet hair strung into eyes squeezed tightly shut.

She watched, frozen, as the gunman bent and pulled a stack of bills out of the other man's pocket. He shoved it into his, then cocked the pistol against the back of his victim's head.

The gun went off .... the victim thudded forward.

Beth's scream drew the killer's cold gaze.

Get away! Get help! She lunged for her bike, picked it up. Her necklace caught on the handlebars, breaking the chain. The cross pendant fell, and the bike tumbled into the mud. She heard pounding footsteps behind her—no time to right the bike. She would have to run.

As she leaped over it, the gun fired again. Hot wind whizzed past her calf, and she fell over the bike, flipping quickly onto her back to defend herself. She screamed again as the killer came closer, aiming for her chest.

She raised her hands to cover her face. "I won't tell!" she squealed. "I didn't see anything! Please ..."

His eyes were piercing, death staring her down. His finger curled over the trigger.

Lightning exploded again, hitting a nearby tree. Thunder cracked like an axe ... or another gunshot. From the edge of her vision, she saw movement. A man with a chest-long beard and a dirty T-shirt came out of nowhere and tackled the killer, knocking off his aim.

Beth scrambled to her feet and grabbed her bike. She heard the grunts of the two men wrestling for the gun as she leaped onto the seat. Standing on the pedals to move the weight of the trailer, she felt the bike's tires slide in the mud.

As she reached the street, the gun went off again. She looked back. Her rescuer had fallen. The killer leaped over his body, aimed his gun at her.

Her bike slid again, and she fell. He fired again, missing.

She righted the bike and pumped the wheels, putting distance between them before he pulled the trigger again.

"You say a word, and I'll kill you and your family, *Beth*," he shouted after her. "I know where you live!"

Shivering, she realized her name was on the back of her jersey. Why had she worn it? Why had she even come out today? He must know her family—her father and mother, her sister or brothers. Flying for her life, Beth rode toward home, praying the man wasn't following her.

two

KAY BRANNING HAD MADE UP HER MIND — IF SHE HAD to fight for her cash, she could do it. She'd waited a year to get her hands on her family's assets, and even though the banks were only authorized to give out two percent of each account's holdings each month, that would still net them nine hundred dollars today. And given the collapsed economy — and the rock-bottom prices — nine hundred dollars was almost a fortune.

Thieves were expected to come out of the woodwork today, but no guns were allowed inside the ropes surrounding the bank's property, except those held by law enforcement officers. Before Kay and the rest of the bank's customers could even get into the line that snaked Disney-style through the parking lot and out into the street, they went through a pat-down for concealed weapons. Thankfully, Kay's husband, Doug, was an armed deputy standing guard over the crowd, so at least the Brannings had a shot at getting their money home safely. Others had family members waiting outside the perimeter, armed and ready to escort them home.

The doors had opened two hours before, though Kay had stood in line for three hours before that. Already, thirteen people had been arrested trying to smuggle weapons past the ropes. Thirteen bank robberies averted. So far, no bullets had been fired, but the day was young.

Kay stood under her umbrella watching the door, waiting for those in the bank to clear out so another group could go in. Hank Huckabee, her neighbor, came out smiling like a lottery winner.

Deni, Kay's twenty-three-year-old daughter, stood near the sheriff's van, juggling her umbrella and her notepad as she interviewed a man who'd just given the teller a bloody lip. He sat in handcuffs with the other lawbreakers in the van, whining out his story as if Deni were the judge. Deni was too gutsy for her own good, but Kay knew better than to interfere in her daughter's work. Deni would kill her if she pulled mother rank. Instead, she caught Doug's eye, mouthed, "Your daughter," and gestured toward the van.

Picking up on her concerns, Doug stepped closer to the van. But Mark Green—Deni's boyfriend who was also a volunteer deputy—had beaten him there. He stood with his department-issued rifle ready, not intruding on the interview, but making sure that Deni was safe.

Doug winked at Kay, and she nodded that Deni was fine. They could count on Mark to keep her safe.

"You are *not* getting this money!"

Kay turned at the sound of the anxious voice. Her next-door neighbor Amber Rowe stood two rows away in the roped-off maze, shoving her estranged husband away.

"You can't have it, Mike! It's not fair. I have three children to support!"

"It's my money. I earned it."

Kay might have known the jerk would show up now, after abandoning Amber and their three babies a year ago, right before the outage. He'd moved in with another woman, and since then had done nothing to help his own family survive.

"I earned it too—raising your babies!" Raging indignation tightened her wet face. "You don't have any paperwork! They won't let you have it."

"I'm your husband," he bit out. "*Your* paperwork is my paperwork."

"I'll fight you for it! So help me—"

Kay caught Doug's attention again, and gestured toward Amber.

Kay could tell from Doug's expression that he took Amber's situation as personally as Kay did. Kay and Doug had spent the last year helping the abandoned family survive. They'd both considered hunting the deadbeat down and dragging him back home. But they'd figured Amber had enough children to care for.

Doug crossed the parking lot to the man who had once been their neighbor. Taking his shoulder, he said, "Hey, pal. Long time no see."

"Don't start with me, Doug," Mike said, shaking him off. "I just want my money."

Doug nodded. "So how do you want to split it?"

Mike's lips stretched tight over his teeth. "I'm not splitting it. I made every penny of it. She hasn't earned a cent."

"Sounds fair," Doug said. "By the way, you're up to date on your child support, right?"

Mike stiffened. "I don't have to pay child support. We're not divorced."

"Does your girlfriend know that?"

Mike bristled and looked around at the disapproving stares. "Why don't you stay out of this? It's between me and my wife."

"Why?" Doug asked, getting nose to nose with him. "I'll tell you why, my friend. Because Kay and I have been helping your wife take care of your children for a year now. You remember your children, don't you? Three toddlers with a dad who abandoned them during the worst crisis in history?"

Mike's teeth came together. "She threw me out *before* the outage," he said, as if that made it better.

Amber's jaw dropped. "*What?* I did not!"

Mike's declaration ignited something in Kay's heart. She knew the real story. Amber would have forgiven him and taken him back at any point along the way. Kay had even kept the children twice while Amber suffered the indignity of going to Mike's girlfriend's house and begging him to come back. He'd refused.

And now he was here, trying to take the money Amber needed to feed her children. No, that wasn't going to happen.

Amber was crying now. "I *never* threw you out. I needed you despite what you'd done, and everybody knows that."

Doug took Mike's arm. "Come on, pal. Let her get the money, and you two can negotiate later."

Mike's teeth came together. "Don't make me hurt you, Doug."

"I'm sorry," Doug said. "Did I hear you right? Are you threatening a law enforcement officer?"

The line moved up. Kay was almost to the front—the next group to go in. If she could just get Amber into the bank to withdraw her money before Mike could get to the window ... Ninety-eight percent of their account would still be there to fight over in court. But almost a hundred people stood in line between Kay's place and Amber's.

Kay called back, "Amber, come up here."

Amber looked at her. "I can't, Kay. I'll lose my spot."

"You're taking *my* spot."

Rain pounded harder, a stark percussion to the day's events. "I can't do that."

"Amber, get up here *now*!" Kay cried.

Amber scurried out of the line, her umbrella clashing with those around her, and ducked under the ropes.

The man who'd waited hours behind Kay protested. "She can't bust in front of the rest of us!" he shouted. "Lady," he said to Amber, "I feel for you, having a dog like that for a husband, but nobody is cutting in front of me. I've been here for five hours!"

"It's okay," Kay said. "I'll go take her spot. We're trading."

Mike stepped over the ropes, pushing between people to follow Amber. "I'm coming with her!"

Doug blocked him. "My wife only gave up one spot. You heard the man. No one else in front of him."

Mike shoved him. "You're crazy!"

"Oh, I wish you hadn't done that." Doug pulled his handcuffs off his belt. "You've just assaulted a sheriff's deputy." He snapped a cuff on Mike's wrist. Mike jerked his arm back, and Doug twisted him around. "And there you go, resisting arrest."

The people in line around them applauded as Doug dragged Mike to the sheriff's van, where several others in handcuffs waited.

But Amber was still upset. "How could he *do* that? Doesn't he care anything about his children?"

Kay put her arm around her and pulled her hood up to keep the rain off. Amber was young enough to be one of Kay's children, and she'd done a valiant job trying to keep food on the table. She'd worked alongside the rest of them, planting food in their front lawns, raising rabbits and chickens, and chopping wood.

"Don't worry about him. Doug will stall him until you get the cash, and then you can ride home with us. Doug will escort us. Nobody's taking your money."

Amber's distressed gaze followed Mike to the van. "I don't want him in jail, though. He's my children's father."

"Hush now," Kay whispered, forcing Amber to look at her. "They probably won't hold him long."

"Maybe I *should* give him some of it. I don't want him to hate me."

It was clear that Amber still loved her husband. The pain of his abandonment had run deep, and she hadn't gotten over it. "You can decide that later," Kay said. "Or let a judge decide. But right now, you need to go in there and get your money."

"But now *you'll* have to wait hours longer to get your own money. It's not fair."

Impatience sharpened Kay's tone. "Mike getting your money—that's what wouldn't be fair. I can handle a little inconvenience."

As soon as Kay was sure she'd calmed Amber down, she followed the line back to take Amber's place. Her gaze scanned the hundreds of people in a line that snaked through the parking lot and across the four lanes of highway in front of the bank. She hoped she got her money before dark.

Lightning flashed and thunder cracked a few seconds later. Of all days to have to stand in the elements.

She wished she'd told the kids not to deliver their papers today. She'd rather they were hunkered inside, out of the storm.

The line moved forward, and she watched as the guards at the door let the next twelve in. Amber got inside. Kay glanced at the sheriff's van. Mike was still trying to talk his way out of the handcuffs.

three

"YOU ARE *SO* LYING, DUDE. AND IT'S NOT EVEN FUNNY."
Jeff Branning sat backward in a straight-back chair, arms
folded on the back.

His friend Zach had been lying on Jeff's bed, arms
crossed behind his head. But now he sat up. "I'm not lying,
man. My dad would know."

Jeff got up, shaking his head skeptically. "So he told you
the Pulses are getting weaker? Are you sure he wasn't yank-
ing your chain?"

"He was dead serious."

"But how did he know?"

"He heard it from the government, where else?"

Jeff went to the window and looked out into the rain.
Zach's dad *was* an electrical engineer. He would know about
the strength of electromagnetic pulses.

He turned back to Zach. His friend still looked weak
from his injury a few months ago—but he wasn't crazy. "So
does he think the supernova burned itself out?"

"Not yet. But it will soon. That's what pulsars do."

"That's what they keep telling us." Jeff had read everything the library had on these stars, and the truth was, most
of them burned themselves out after only a few months.
SN–1999 had stolen an entire year of their lives. Could the
end really be in sight?

He looked at Zach, listened to the whistling sound of his
friend's breath. No, Zach wouldn't have made the story up.

But his father, Ned, could have been repeating a rumor. Jeff turned back to the window and peered up at the cloud-thick sky. If the star was burning out, things could go back to normal. Lights would come back on. There would be more cars on the streets. They'd have telephones again!

"That would be awesome," Jeff muttered. "TV and computers, man. Video games."

"Girls."

"We can get girls now."

Zach grinned. "Yeah, but we wouldn't have to work so hard. We could call them on the phone. Take them out in cars. Dude, if we could plug in amps, we'd be like real rock stars."

Jeff doubted their little acoustic band would take them that far.

He glanced down at the street in front of their house, and wondered why Beth wasn't back yet. He and Logan had delivered all their papers and gotten back half an hour ago. Maybe the storm had slowed her down. Or worse, maybe she'd taken a side trip to the bank to see all the drama.

Little twerp. That was just like her. If his parents saw her there, they would blame him for letting her do it. He hoped she got home soon before he had to go looking for her.

four

BETH RACED HOME, LOOKING OVER HER SHOULDER FOR THE killer. She couldn't see him, but she knew he was there. And even if he wasn't, he knew her name. It was a small town. He could find her.

She would be dead now if it hadn't been for the man who'd come out of nowhere. He'd looked homeless — dirty, unshaven — but he was a hero. Because of her, he was probably dead. The horror of that moaned up in her chest.

She had to tell someone so that the killer would be caught. But his words echoed in her mind: *You say a word, and I'll kill you and your family!*

Could he really do it? Would he know how to find her from just the name on her shirt?

What if he was following her? He may have had a bike behind the building. She glanced back and didn't see him, but he could still be there, just out of sight in the pounding storm, watching to see where she lived.

Rain burned her eyes; fear seared her lungs. She thought of going somewhere else to throw him off. Where? Her mind raced, frantic. She couldn't lead him to other innocent victims. And if she just stopped, he might decide to kill her now. She wanted to be in her house, with her big brother to guard her. Maybe she could get there before the killer caught up to her.

Her heart raced as she turned into Oak Hollow subdivision and sailed up the street to her house, fifth on the right. The garage wasn't open. She'd have to use her key to go in the front door, which would take longer. No, too risky. She turned into the driveway and rode through the mushy yard around the house, to the patio. She jumped off her bike, letting it clatter to the concrete. Bolting to the back door, she banged on the glass as she dug for the key in her wet jeans pocket.

Her ten-year-old brother came to the door and made a face through the glass.

"Open it!" she cried.

Logan saw the terror on her face and opened the door. She lunged inside.

"What's wrong with you?" he said.

Beth locked the bolt and ran to a front window. She saw no one.

"You're dripping on the floor. Mom's gonna have a meltdown if you don't get a towel. Hey, you're bleeding."

She was shivering—her teeth vibrating. She glanced at her leg. She must have skinned it when she fell over the bike.

"Did something happen?" Logan asked.

"No," she said, turning around. She crossed her arms, trying to stop shivering, and pushed past him.

Jeff, her sixteen-year-old brother, was coming down the stairs, Zach behind him. "Did you finish your deliveries?"

"No." She started up the stairs.

"Then where were you?"

"Just ... out."

Jeff looked insulted. "You went to the bank, didn't you?" he yelled after her. "You had to go see all the hoopla."

His voice was distant, hollow, little competition for the pulse hammering in her ears. She dripped across Deni's carpet and looked out the window, up and down the street.

She still couldn't see him.

Numb, she went to her room and got some dry clothes. She changed in the bathroom, leaving her wet, muddy clothes on the floor. Wrapping herself in a blanket so she'd stop shivering, she went back to Deni's room and sat in the dormer window, watching the street and waiting for the killer to come for her.

five

An hour and a half after she swapped places with Amber, Kay found herself back at the front of the line. It had rained the entire time, and her clothes were soaked through. But losing her spot in line had been worth it. Amber had gotten her cash, then had given her husband a hundred dollars to appease him. Doug had finally let him go with a warning to stop harassing Amber. He'd gone — with a threat to hire a lawyer and get the account put in his name. Doug hoped it *would* wind up in court, he'd said. Any sane judge would see the situation and rule in favor of Amber.

"I'm up!" Kay said as she reached the door. "I can't believe it."

Doug grinned as he gave his rifle to Mark and came to join her. Thankfully, the couple behind her didn't protest this time. "Sure you don't want to give up your spot to someone else?" Doug teased.

"I had to do it! That horrible man was going to clean her out. Those poor babies. What kind of parent would put himself and his girlfriend before his children?"

He put his arm around her and kissed her cheek. "That's why I love you."

"Really?" she asked. "*That's* the reason?"

"That and the fact that you make a mean corn mush."

The warmth of their laughter was welcome after such a long, wet day.

The guard opened the door and called for the next twelve in line. Kay and Doug stepped into the building, out of the rain, trying not to slip on the wet marble floor. Her heart pounded as the tellers counted out the cash to the ones in line ahead of them.

"Get the papers ready," Doug said.

Kay pulled her backpack off and unzipped it. She'd wrapped the papers in a plastic zipper bag she'd had in one of her suitcases, so they wouldn't get wet. Their latest bank statement from a year ago, their checkbook, an envelope full of deposit slips, their Social Security cards, and both of their driver's licenses.

When their turn came, she wiped her wet hair out of her face and stepped up to the teller's window. She felt like Elaine on *Seinfeld*, confronting the Soup Nazi. What if she misspoke or misstepped and was turned away?

But the frazzled teller studied their documents, then said, "How do you want it?"

Kay handed her an index card with the amounts on it. "Five hundreds, fifteen twenties, fifteen tens, and ten fives."

The teller counted it out like it was no big deal. But Kay wanted to do cartwheels. As Doug took the stack of money and stuffed it in his vest pocket, she threw her arms around him. He lifted her off the floor and kissed her neck. "We're back, baby," he said, laughing. "We're back!"

"Hey, outta the way," the man behind them complained.

The man's sharp tone didn't bother Kay, but she let Doug go, and they moved out of the way. "You hold on to the money," she told Doug. "I'm scared to carry it home."

"Okay." He stuffed the stack of bills into a shirt pocket under his bulletproof vest. "I'll take a few minutes to escort you home."

A horn blew, long and urgent, as they stepped out of the bank. The mob turned to see the sheriff driving up, the mayor as his passenger. Sheriff Wheaton, grinning like a teenager with a new car, kept pushing on the horn, even though there seemed to be no emergency.

The mayor got out and stood on the running board. With a megaphone to her mouth, she yelled, "Ladies and gentlemen, I just got word—the Pulses have stopped!"

A Super Bowl yell went up from the crowd, and Kay turned to Doug. "Did she say what I thought she said?"

"I think she said the Pulses are over."

They stared at each other, dumbfounded. "Do you think it could be true?"

Part of the crowd rushed to the van, surrounding them as the sheriff high-fived people through the window.

"How do you know?" someone yelled.

The mayor put the megaphone back to her mouth. "First, I got word from the conversion plant that the Pulses were getting weaker. A little while later, I got a telegram from Washington! The White House confirms it. SN–1999 has burned itself out! The Pulses are finally over!"

Screams of joy erupted again, and the wet mob that had been angry and impatient only moments before was now jubilant.

Doug grabbed Kay's face and kissed her, like a GI the day World War II ended. Giggling like teenagers, they worked their way through the crowd, hugging their friends and neighbors, celebrating the beginning of the end.

six

BETH'S HAIR WAS DRY BY THE TIME SHE SAW HER PARENTS, along with her sister, Deni, and Amber Rowe, as they turned into the neighborhood on their bikes. From her perch at her sister's upstairs bedroom window seat, she saw the grins on their faces, and knew they had gotten their money. Still, her father wore two guns to keep them safe—his rifle hanging from a sling, and his department-issued gun holstered on his hip.

She hugged her knees as they turned into the driveway. Then her eyes gravitated back to the entrance of Oak Hollow. Had anyone followed them? Was the killer just biding his time? Waiting until her parents got the money before he killed them all? The first murder she'd witnessed had been for money, after all.

She heard her parents come into the house, and a roar erupted from downstairs. Her throat closed. Had he come?

Then she realized that it wasn't the sound of fear that she heard. Her family was cheering. She went to the stairs, and moved down one step at a time. "No way! No *WAY!*"

KAY HAD NEVER SEEN JEFF SO EXCITED. HE WAS LITERALLY air-boxing on tiptoes, his face red with excitement.

"Zach was here a little while ago, and he *told* me the Pulses were getting weaker. I almost didn't believe him! Are you kidding me?"

Logan ran to turn the light switch on. When the bulbs didn't light up, his grin faded. "You're right, no way. Where are the stupid lights?"

"It's too soon," Doug said. "Our power grid is still down. They have to rebuild some things before we get power again." He messed up Logan's hair. "But it's coming, kiddo. It's coming."

Kay saw Beth coming from the staircase, her face filled with trepidation. "Did you hear, Beth? The Pulses are over!"

Beth's eyebrows lifted. "Really? It's not a hoax?"

"Really. We heard it from the mayor who heard it from the White House."

Kay would have expected Beth to squeal with excitement, but her reaction was somber. "That's great. Can we get the security system working again?"

What a thing to ask! Kay just looked at her. "Of course, eventually. And we got our money! Nine hundred dollars. We're rich again, guys." Kay almost sang the words, dancing as she did.

Beth's smile faded. She walked into the foyer and looked out the glass door.

Kay followed. "What's the matter, honey? Aren't you excited?"

Beth didn't look at her. "Yeah, I am. Were there a lot of muggings?"

"A few," Kay said. "But your dad gave us plenty of protection on the way home. And his uniform didn't hurt." She looked out the window, following Beth's gaze to the neighborhood entrance. "Are you expecting someone?"

"Like who?" Beth asked in a dull voice.

"Like maybe Jimmy?"

Jimmy was the former sheriff's son. He'd been coming over a lot for the last three months, and Kay was sure Beth had a crush on him. But today his name didn't bring a smile to Beth's face.

"No, I'm not waiting for Jimmy." She turned and went back toward the stairs.

"Honey? Is there something wrong?"

"No," Beth said. "I just don't feel good." She headed back upstairs.

Kay went back into the living room and looked at Jeff and Logan. "Anybody know what's going on with Beth?"

"I don't know," Jeff said. "But she went out to deliver her papers and was gone a long time."

Logan piped in. "And she didn't deliver them"

Deni swung around. "What? We needed those delivered."

"I think she went to see all the drama at the bank," Jeff said. "But she's in a real bad mood, so she's not talking."

Kay shot Jeff a look. "You should have delivered the papers together today."

"Logan and I did. But she wanted to go on her own."

"You should ground her, Mom," Logan said. "If I did that, you'd ground me."

Doug met Kay's eyes, trying not to smirk. "Thank you for that advice, son."

"Seriously," the ten-year-old said. "What are you gonna do to her?"

"Don't worry about it," Kay said, starting up the stairs.

She found Beth sitting at the window in Deni's room, hugging herself and staring out the window. "So where did you go?" Kay asked.

Beth looked back at her. "To the bank," she said. "I know I shouldn't have. I'm sorry. You can ground me. Make me stay inside for a month." Tears filled her eyes, and she crushed her lips together. "I should have done what you said. I'm sorry, Mom."

Kay sat beside her and pulled her into a hug. Beth was trembling. Was she that afraid of her punishment? "Well, at least you're all right. Did the weather scare you?"

Beth nodded and buried her face in Kay's wet shirt, but she didn't speak. Kay just held her. "It's okay, honey. We're home now."

Beth dropped the blanket she was wrapped in, and Kay saw the scrapes on her legs. "What happened?"

"I fell." The words seemed to upset her more, and her face twisted.

"Well, we need to clean it." She pulled Beth up and led her into the bathroom, where her wet clothes lay in a muddy heap on the floor. She found the hydrogen peroxide and got a washcloth out of the cabinet. "Sit down."

"Mom, you're all wet."

"Yeah, it was awful out there. Some day for the banks to open, huh?" She dabbed hydrogen peroxide on the scrapes. "Did anyone stop and help you when you fell?"

"Yes ... no." She took the cloth out of her mother's hand. "I don't want to talk about it. Let me do it."

Kay surrendered the cloth and looked into her daughter's face. Something else had happened. Something Beth wasn't telling. "Honey, why are you crying?"

Beth met her eyes, and for a moment, Kay thought Beth would tell her. But then she pulled back into herself. "I don't know. I just was embarrassed, I guess. And I didn't get the papers delivered to my newspaper boxes. I didn't even pick them up."

Kay frowned. It made sense. Falling in front of others would be humiliating to a thirteen-year-old girl. Maybe she'd done it in front of some of her peers. And Beth took her job delivering newspapers to the boxes around town very seriously.

"Well, it's too late now," Kay said. "People will live without their papers. It's a day to celebrate. We're not dirt poor anymore, and the Pulses have stopped."

She got a towel out of the cabinet and wrapped it around her wet shoulders. She couldn't wait to get out of these clothes. "It'll take a while for things to be up and running again. But now the restoration can begin. I can't even imagine having electricity again. Television, computers, a car! Think of it, Beth. When the grid is repaired, they can reopen the schools. The buses will run again. We won't have to work like slaves all day just to eat. The stock market will reopen and Dad can go back to work. Planes will fly." She threw her head back and laughed, giddy. "I can color my hair and grow it out again! I can get my nails done! We can go to McDonald's!"

For a moment Kay thought that might evoke a smile, but Beth only looked sadder. "Beth, how can you not be excited?"

"I am excited, Mom. But it's not going to help us today."

Kay's joy faded. When had her thirteen-year-old become the stoic voice of reason? The Beth Kay knew would have been asking a million questions, running around trying things out, rushing out to tell all her friends. Had all the things Beth had seen in the last few months begun to hurt her? Was she more traumatized by the violence around them than Kay had realized?

Maybe Beth needed a counselor.

"Honey, why don't you lie down and take a nap? Maybe you'll feel better when you wake up."

Beth just nodded and went back into Deni's room. Taking her place on the window seat again, she looked out the window.

"I'm going back downstairs now," Kay said. "Call me if you need me."

Beth didn't turn from the window. Her tears were still wet on her face.

seven

HE WASN'T CUT OUT FOR CRIME.

He stood in the bathroom of the Exchange Club Baseball Field, holding his breath against the smell. He hadn't come in here to use the facilities, since they didn't work anyway. All he wanted was the mirror.

He had to get this goatee off before that girl identified him. He stared into the smudged mirror and used fingernail clippers to cut the whiskers as close to the skin as possible. It was a pitiful way to go about this, but he didn't have any scissors, and to get a razor he would have to go home.

He couldn't believe how stupid he was. All to cover a lie to his wife.

He'd had a whole year to break the news to her about their money. And it would have been smart. At a time when they had no access to their bank accounts anyway, he could have told her the truth: that he'd lost the money at the black-jack tables, and they didn't have a penny to their name. Before the Pulses, the bank had been planning to foreclose on their house. The Pulses had bought him some time, so he'd never broken the news to her.

If only he'd come clean, he could have made her see that they'd been given a second chance—that despite his weakness, they were no worse off than anyone around them. But no, he had kept it to himself. And now he had to make it right.

He was not a killer. He was a man who solved problems. He had never set out to kill two people. Now he would have to kill three.

How had this happened? He would rather have an angry wife than a murder rap hanging over his head. It had all seemed so simple when he'd planned it. He hadn't expected anyone to be around, especially with the rain.

But the plan had gone awry, and now he faced the real possibility that he might be caught. He could never survive in prison. Never.

He left a little pile of hair clippings in the sink, then went back over what he'd cut, trying to get it even closer. It wasn't a close shave, but he could drag a razor over it when he got home.

He ran his hand over his chin and shook his head. He wasn't fooling anyone. His face was tanned dark—except for the area that had been covered by the goatee, which was now pasty white. He kicked the ceramic tile on the wall. He'd just become the poster boy for the term *stupid*. Why hadn't he just told the truth? Losing money to a gambling debt was much more tolerable than killing two men.

It was getting more and more tangled, more and more out of hand. He was losing control. But what was he supposed to do now?

One crime led to another. If he could just find the girl, shut her up, it would be the last crime he would ever commit.

He wasn't a criminal. He wasn't a killer. He told himself that over and over, trying to believe it.

eight

As conservative as Kay typically was when rationing their food supplies, she decided to sacrifice two chickens for dinner that night, since they now had the money to replace them. As always when they killed one of the rabbits or chickens from their flock, they did it across the street, in their deceased neighbor's yard, so Beth wouldn't see. She treated the animals like her pets and had a hard time handling the fact that they were raised for food.

Kay and Deni cooked some beans and potatoes, and they sat down to a feast. Before they ate, they each thanked God for providing for them through the outage, for ending the Pulses, and for allowing them to get the cash out of the bank.

Doug's voice wobbled in gratitude as he ended the prayer. "Lord, you've shown us that everything we have is from you, and we're in control of none of it. That's been a good lesson to learn, and we thank you for it. Thank you for how much closer you've brought us through this season. Thank you for the time we've had to spend together. Now, please help us as we decide how to spend this money. In Jesus' name we pray. Amen."

The family echoed "Amen," and began to dig in.

For a moment, conversation ebbed as everyone ate. But Kay noticed that Beth only picked at her food. She constantly looked out the back window, her eyes scanning the street between the houses behind them.

"Beth? Don't you want to eat?"

"I am," she said, and took a bite.

"What are you watching for out the window?" Kay asked.

"Nothing."

"She's waiting for Jimmy Scarbrough," Logan said, putting his hands over his heart. "She can't stand to be away from him."

"No, I'm not," Beth snapped. "Shut up, why don't you?"

"Did you two have a fight?" Deni asked.

"No. We're just friends, anyway." She looked back at her little brother. "Get a life."

"Come on," Doug said. "No bickering. We're celebrating. Now let's talk about how we're going to spend this money."

"Dad," Jeff cut in, "there's this dude who lives over by the post office who has this killer guitar he wants to sell, and my birthday's coming up, so I thought—"

"Jeff, we can't spend it on a guitar," Doug said. "We have to be smart with it."

"But we've been smart with all of the FEMA disbursements," Jeff said. "You never let us spend any of that on what we wanted."

"We spent it on things that would help us make more money," Doug said. "Like the flour and yeast for the bread we sold. The chickens that produced eggs. The rabbits that multiplied and gave us food."

Kay poured him some water. "And the knife sharpener that we bought for you, Jeff, so you could sharpen razors. That made us a little extra money. Your dad's idea made you an entrepreneur."

"But even when I made money, you didn't let me spend any of it on things I wanted. Now we can get nine hundred dollars a *month*. We're practically rolling in dough."

"We're not rolling in dough." Doug shot Kay a weary look. "We have to keep working as a family to survive. So no guitars. What will help the whole family?"

"A car." Kay set her fork down and folded her hands. "I want a car."

"Yeah!" Logan cried.

"Can we get a car for nine hundred dollars?" Deni asked.

"We might if there were any available," Doug said. "But there aren't. And no gas to put in them."

Kay wouldn't give up. "I figure they'll allow people to get car loans again soon, so with a small down payment we could afford it. And prices are so low now that we could probably get one really cheap. Relatively speaking."

"Actually," Doug said, "I think it'll be just the opposite. They'll be so expensive that only millionaires can afford them. No, it'll be a long time before that'll be a possibility, guys. I'll keep looking on converting the Expedition. That'll happen before we can buy a new one."

Deni shook her head. "I bet you're wrong, Dad. The government has to figure out a way to get cars back on the road. If they want to help the economy recover, they have to give us transportation."

"They'll come up with a bus system before they'll have enough cars for the public to buy."

"Dad, you're so negative," Jeff moaned. "This is supposed to be fun."

Doug grunted. "I'm just trying to be realistic. I'm a stockbroker. I know how the economy works. We have nine hundred dollars. This is not a bad thing. But let's think of things that we can afford to get right now."

"A refrigerator would be nice," Kay said.

"Yes, and that might be possible when the power comes back on. I could be wrong, but I don't think our refrigerator has solid-state parts, so maybe it'll still work."

"Really?"

"And if not, I'm sure those will be popping up for sale. They won't be that hard for manufacturers to make. So what else?"

"Coffee?" Kay asked. "I want a crate of instant coffee."

"Sugar!" Logan cried.

Doug smiled. "We'll see."

"Hair dye?" Deni asked, smirking.

"Yes!" Kay almost shouted. "Hair dye. Doug, please. If it's available, you've got to let me get it. I'm so sick of this gray."

Doug chuckled. "Kay, you don't have that much gray. And if you ask me, wherever we go, you're the best looking dame in the joint. Isn't she, guys?"

Jeff rolled his eyes. "Yeah, Mom, you're a real Miss America."

Kay punched him. "Thanks a lot."

"I'm not kidding," Doug said. "Your mom has come through this looking great."

"He's right, Mom," Logan said. "There are some real hags around here. Most of the ladies have white stripes on the tops of their heads where their roots have grown out, and without makeup, they'd scare small animals. Gag me. I hope they spend *their* money on hair dye and makeup."

Jeff laughed, almost choking on his food.

"And you, Deni," Logan added. "It wouldn't hurt to start fixing yourself up a little more. Then maybe Mark would finally ask you to marry him."

Deni threw her napkin at Logan. Everyone laughed.

Everyone except Beth, who appeared to have checked out of the conversation. Her eyes were still on the window.

nine

SATURDAY MORNING, MARK GREEN WAITED FOR DENI TO leave home before showing up at her house. He'd checked the work schedule at the sheriff's department to make sure Doug wasn't working today. If he'd timed his visit right, Doug and Kay would both be home.

Beth came to the door with her brother's rifle. "Hey, Sparky," he said, shaking off the rain and stepping inside. "What's up?"

"Nothing." As she closed the door, she glanced through the etched glass.

"Have you been able to work up any enthusiasm about the Pulses ending?"

She finally looked him in the eye. "Are you making fun of me?"

His smiled faded. "No, I was just teasing you. You're not going to shoot me with that thing, are you?"

"Not unless you give me reason to."

There. A hint of her sense of humor. Or was it? There was no twinkle in her eye, none of the usual shyness or admiration, none of the spirit that made Beth who she was. He decided to leave her alone. "Hey, are your folks home?"

"Yeah, they're here. Mom!" she called out. "Mark's here."

Kay came out of the kitchen. "Come in, Mark. Deni just left."

Mark went into the kitchen and looked through the window. Logan and Jeff were out back feeding the chickens in the rain. "I didn't come for Deni. Actually, I was hoping to talk to the two of you alone."

Doug, who sat at the kitchen table with his Bible open, looked at Kay and winked. Slowly, he closed his Bible. "All right, then. Why don't we go into the study?"

Mark's heart rate sped up as he followed them in. They suspected why he was here. He could tell by the hint of smiles on their lips, the way they avoided his eyes, the way they hurried into the study without asking why.

Doug took the chair behind his desk, and Kay sat in one of the Chippendale chairs. He took the other one. He'd sat in here a few months ago, when he'd talked his way through the mystery surrounding the break-in at his house. He'd grown close to Doug that night. He remembered their conversation the next day as they'd searched for his brothers. Doug had told him that he would like it if Mark and Deni got married. *I might as well just lay this out on the table, Mark. You're the kind of man I want for my daughter. A man I would consider it an honor to call my son.*

It hadn't been the right time then, not when Mark was struggling to clear his own name. He hoped Doug still felt that way. And he wasn't sure how Kay felt.

"So what's this about?" Doug asked, breaking the ice. "Did you come to talk to me about investments?" He clearly knew that wasn't it.

Mark glanced at Kay. Her eyes were round with anticipation. "In a way. I've kind of been thinking about what I want to do with the rest of my life."

"And?"

He wasn't ready to jump into the question just yet, so he cleared his throat and took the roundabout route. "I was thinking about using some of my money to get into the solar energy business."

Doug's eyebrows came up. "That's a great fit for you. You've already helped so many people with your solar ideas. And after things are back to normal, most people will want to ensure that they never find themselves without electricity again." He grinned at Kay. "This kid's got some sense."

Mark smiled. "Want to partner with me?"

Doug scooted to the edge of his seat now, his expression growing serious. "Are you seriously asking me?"

"I have enough to get things started alone if I have to. But with your help, I think we could really make a go of it."

He could see the wheels turning in Doug's eyes. "It would be a great investment. I suppose I could do it on the side if I go back to my job. What about the sheriff's department?"

"I'll keep working there until they rebuild their force. But I don't want to do it forever. I hope to have a family to support."

The smile returned to Kay's lips. "Oh?"

She knew why he was here, and the expression on her face told Mark how she would take it. "And that's what I really wanted to talk to you about."

Kay's eyes shot to Doug's. Her smile widened a little.

"Deni and me, actually. Our future."

Doug leaned on his desk. "Go on."

He cleared his throat and took a deep breath. "You know I love your daughter. Secretly, I've had a crush on her since high school, but this last year, I've fallen in love with her."

"I think the feeling is mutual," Kay said softly.

"Well, I wasn't so sure before, what with Craig still writing her and everything. And you know, Doug, that I was worried what would happen when things went back to normal. I didn't know if she'd still want what I could give her." He looked at his hands. They were sweating. "But we've been through a lot together, Deni and I. And over the last three months or so, she's managed to convince me that maybe she does want what I have to offer."

Silence fell between them, but Doug's and Kay's expressions told him they were rooting for him. So he went on.

"But I'm excited about the solar business, and I think I can make a good life for her if I work hard." Mark cleared his throat. "So I've come here today to ask your permission to ask Deni to marry me."

Kay threw her hands over her mouth and laughed, and Doug came around the desk to shake Mark's hand and pull him into a hug. Mark felt the love in his embrace, and he turned to Kay. She had tears in her eyes. He hoped they were tears of joy. "I've told you before, Mark," Doug said, "I've dreamed of Deni marrying you."

"You'll make a wonderful husband," Kay said. "And a terrific father for our grandchildren. Welcome to the family!"

Mark laughed. "Not so fast. I have to ask her first."

Kay bounced up and down. "Go after her," Kay said. "Ask her now. She's at the newspaper office."

"No, I want to do it right. Make it real romantic. Get down on one knee, the whole shebang. And I have a ring. I used some of my gold coins to buy it. I think Deni will like it."

"Okay, but don't wait too long," Kay said. "I can't hold this in for long."

"I'll do it this week. Don't tell the kids," Mark said. "I don't want it to slip out."

Kay pulled him back into a hug and kissed him on the cheek. He hoped Deni would be as happy about this as Kay was.

ten

THE KID COULD RUIN EVERYTHING. HE HAD PLANNED IT out so carefully, and the thunder and rain had been icing on the cake, masking the sound of the gunshots and washing away any evidence he might have left. Too good to be true.

Except now there was a witness.

It was all his wife's fault. If she hadn't constantly threatened to leave him and take their baby, he wouldn't have felt such pressure to cover for his gambling losses. Infidelity, she'd accused, even though she didn't have any real evidence. Just hunches, and that wasn't enough to hang a divorce on. Or so he'd convinced her. He'd managed to keep her—and his baby—living with him for now.

As long as she thought their money was trapped in the banking pipeline, she didn't have any reason to suspect he'd lost it all. But the moment they'd received news that the banks were reopening, he'd known it was the beginning of the end. Her suspicions about infidelity, along with the knowledge that he'd gambled away their life savings, would surely send her running home to mama.

Several sleepless nights and a few conversations with a confidant who'd given him the perfect target, and he'd come up with the plan. He would simply take someone else's money. His wife would think he'd made the withdrawal out of their own account. It would buy him a month—until the next withdrawal date.

He'd found the spot behind the Cracker Barrel, hidden from the road. He figured if he could intercept his target walking home this way, he'd use his gun to force him behind the building. Then he could kill him and take the money—solving several problems with one bullet.

And then the kid had shown up and seen the whole thing. He should have never let her get away. He should have killed her right there while he had the chance, but that homeless guy had come out of nowhere. Now he had two murders on his hands, and a kid who could identify him.

He had to be the stupidest man in Crockett.

She'd complicated everything. He'd had to retrieve both bodies. That was a wrinkle that he hadn't expected. If all had gone according to plan, he would have left the body there, and it would look like a simple robbery on a day when that was expected. But now that someone could ID him, he feared what might happen if the bodies were found.

Oh, what a tangled web ... The old cliché his mother used to quote played like a bad song in his mind. If she could only see him now.

He'd never meant to be a killer. Not until a few days ago.

To cover for his crime, he'd gone back in the storm with his rickshaw, loaded both bodies, and covered them with a tarp. If anyone had seen him riding home, they'd probably been so distracted with the rain, their newly recovered money, and the Pulses ending, that they hadn't given him a thought.

It had been too wet to dig a grave for them, so he'd hidden them in a shed until the ground dried. This morning he had finally been able to bury them while his wife and child weren't home.

Now that the bodies were hidden, he might be okay. If the girl did talk, the authorities wouldn't believe her without evidence. Maybe his threats had kept her quiet so far. If they hadn't, he would have known—there would have been news of the murders, and people would be looking for the bodies. But there had been nothing.

He looked down at the cross necklace he'd found on the porch floor. Maybe he could use this to find the infamous Beth.

He had seen her ride east, up Tungsten Road. That meant she lived in one of those ritzy subdivisions halfway out in the country. There were probably ten neighborhoods in that area. How many blonde Beths of that age could there be? All he had to do was go ask around.

He could pretend he was looking for her so he could return her necklace. And when he found her, one more problem would be solved.

Then, with any luck, he could get back to his life.

eleven

"MY KINGDOM FOR A WASHING MACHINE." DENI STOOD in her bedroom closet, searching for a top that had come through the Pulses unscathed. With all the hand washing with well water, nothing kept its color, and all the whites looked dingy.

Beth leaned in the doorway of her closet. "Your *kingdom?*"

"It's from Shakespeare, sort of. Never mind. Hey, maybe we can get our washing machine fixed. Or a new one, or whatever. I wonder when the water will be back on. Probably not before the electricity, since the pumps in the pipelines have to work. Well water has ruined my clothes."

"Where are you going?"

"I don't know. Big date, but Mark hasn't told me where." She pulled out a red top that she hadn't worn since before the Pulses started. Holding it up to herself, she shook her head. "Man, I've lost so much weight that nothing fits. Maybe I have time to take it in a little. Wish I could have gotten home earlier, but I had so many stories to cover for the paper. Going from a weekly paper to a daily one is killing me."

Beth straightened. "What kind of stories? Murders?"

"No, but lots of muggings. There are some seriously upset people who had their cash stolen yesterday."

"But nobody was killed?"

"None reported. Hey, did you get your papers delivered today?"

Beth hesitated, so Deni turned around.

"I got Jeff and Logan to do mine today."

"Then you're sure they all got delivered? Because I'm working too hard for people not to read it. Why didn't you do it?"

"I don't feel very good."

"Yeah, we're all sniffing and coughing after being out in that storm all day yesterday." She pulled her blouse on, buttoned it up. "So how do I look?"

"Fine," Beth said. Deni turned and realized she wasn't even looking. She was staring out the window.

BETH WATCHED THE STREET, STILL EXPECTING TO SEE THE KILLER. Why hadn't the murder been reported? Could that mean the victims had been found—alive? The thought had never occurred to her. She should have gotten an ambulance to go and see about them. Guilt twisted her stomach.

She went back to the walk-in closet. "Was anybody hurt in a mugging yesterday?"

Deni dug through her jewelry box for some earrings. "Several people. A few were hit in the head. One was stabbed, but he survived."

"Were any of them shot?"

"I don't think so." Now she looked fully at Beth. "Why?"

She'd asked too many questions. She made a paintbrush out of her hair and whisked it against her chin.

"I don't know. I was just thinking that a lot of bad stuff might have happened."

"A lot of bad stuff *did* happen. Thank goodness it didn't happen to us this time."

"Yeah, thank goodness," she whispered.

Beth went down to the kitchen. Her mom's glance lingered a little too long, as if she were searching Beth's face for a clue to her mood. She came toward her and kissed her on the forehead like she was checking for fever.

Her father came out of the bedroom. He'd just changed from his deputy uniform to a pair of shorts and a pullover shirt. He carried his shoes on two fingers. He'd lost his middle-aged paunch since the Pulses, and all his hard work chopping wood and stuff had made him muscular. But he looked tired today.

"Tough day?" Kay asked.

"Yeah, really tough." He pulled out a chair and dropped into it. "So did I hear Deni saying Mark was taking her out tonight?"

Kay wiggled her eyebrows and shot him a knowing smile. "That's right."

Beth didn't know what the big deal was. Mark and Deni were always together. "Why was your day tough? Did you catch any criminals?"

"A couple. This one guy robbed his next-door neighbor. They'd lived by each other for twenty-five years, and that night he broke into the house while they were sleeping and stole his neighbor's money out of his pants pocket. Got caught, thank goodness."

Beth carried the plates to the table. "So ... did you find any bodies or anything?"

Kay turned and shot her a surprised look. "Beth, what a question!"

Beth shrugged. "I just wondered."

Doug pulled his shoes on. "No. Thankfully, I don't think anybody was killed. A few minor injuries, but it looks like most of the robbers weren't from around here. I mean, think about it. They wouldn't want to be recognized. So they go to the surrounding towns as their banks open, rob them, then disappear back where they came from."

Beth was baffled. Why would two murders not be reported? Could it be that no one had found the bodies yet? Wasn't anyone looking for the two men?

"Are there, like, any missing persons reports out?"

Kay's frown cut deeper. "Why do you ask that, sweetheart?"

"No reason."

Kay came to the table, and stroked Beth's hair. "Honey, go call Jeff and Logan to dinner."

Beth looked cautiously out the back window. She saw her brothers at the back of the yard. No way she was going out there. With her luck, the killer would pick that moment to ride by on the street behind them. She opened the door, staying hidden behind it, and yelled for her brothers.

WHILE THEY WAITED FOR THE KIDS TO COME, KAY TURNED BACK to Doug. "I'm worried about her," she said in a low voice. "She won't so much as step outside. She wouldn't deliver her papers today, and she never misses that. Since the paper hired her, she's taken her commitment seriously. I asked her to go to the well for water, and she started crying. And this new fascination with murders and kidnappings ..."

"Well, she's been through a lot in the last year. We all have."

"But she's sensitive, honey. Maybe she's been more traumatized than we've realized. Maybe she needs to see a counselor."

He looked in the direction she had gone. "I was wondering the same thing. But where will we find one? It can't be just anybody."

"I can ask around."

"I doubt there are many of them working these days. The demand for counselors is probably about as great as the demand for stockbrokers."

"People still need help."

"Yeah, but who's willing to spend hard-earned money on counseling when they can barely scrape together enough to buy food?"

"We have some money now. If we can find a counselor, maybe we can afford it."

Doug nodded. "We'll have to. But I want whoever it is to be a Christian. I don't want someone who doesn't understand the basic principles of life to be poking around in her psyche."

"You read my mind," she said, bending over to kiss him. She touched his face, her fingers lingering on his stubble. "Do you think she'll be all right?"

"Of course," he said. "But let's try to make this happen as soon as possible."

twelve

KAY COULDN'T WAIT FOR LIFE TO GO BACK TO NORMAL. The days never seemed to end for her, with so much to do. She longed for conveniences she'd once had: Pop Tarts and granola bars for quick breakfasts, a drive-thru hamburger for lunch, and microwaved meals or frozen food for supper. Paper plates for easy cleanup, and four ladies from a cleaning service who swarmed through the house like a SWAT team once a week to do the deep cleaning.

Tonight she'd fed her family corn tortillas from the bags of agricultural corn feed she'd gotten with a previous FEMA disbursement. From the older neighbors in Oak Hollow, she'd learned a dozen ways to cook with corn. It had grown unappetizing, but the family had learned that food was for energy and not for entertainment.

Now that the kitchen was cleaned up and the floor scrubbed of all the mud and dirt that were tracked in daily, Kay went outside to the side of the house, where she'd hung her laundry to dry. She found Judith there, pulling down her own family's clothes. Her friend's brown skin glistened in the humidity.

"Girl, it took you long enough," Judith said. "I was beginning to think you were gonna leave these all night."

"It's not even dark yet," Kay said. "I can cram a hundred more things onto my to-do list between now and dark. What on earth did we do with our time before?" She sighed and glanced at Judith's nursing scrubs. "How do you do it?

Working full-time *and* coming home to all the stuff you have to do?"

"We make do."

When they'd opened the new hospital in Crockett, Judith had taken a nursing job there. The need was so great that she'd agreed to put in eight to ten hours a day. Amber Rowe, Kay's other next-door neighbor, babysat her kids for her.

Judith's husband, Brad—a lawyer—had recently become district attorney in Crockett. He, too, worked long hours. Though they were all busy, Kay and Judith had grown close over the last year.

"So how's our Beth doing today?" Judith asked as she folded a pair of jeans that were as stiff as cardboard.

"Not good. Still acting strange." She filled her in on Beth's paranoia and her morbid questions.

"Sounds like it could be post-traumatic stress disorder," Judith said. "I'm no psychologist, but she's sure been through enough to have it. Remember how she sulked around for days after she saw Mark beaten? How she took the rabbits into her room to protect them? Maybe it was manifesting itself even then."

"But she seemed better in the last few weeks."

"Does she have bad dreams?"

"Yes, but don't we all these days?"

"That's the thing. We all have reactions to trauma. Some negative reactions are normal. But PTSD has lingering symptoms. People with it sometimes have flashbacks. Sometimes they have anxiety attacks as they relive the event."

"*Which* event?" Kay's mind raced through all the traumatic things the family had been through in the last year. No wonder she was asking about murders and missing persons. Her sister had been a missing person, and then little Sarah—one of the children they were caring for—was kidnapped. Doug had been shot in their own home, and Zach—Jeff's best friend—was almost killed. Then Mark was beaten half to death before Beth's very eyes.

It was a wonder they weren't all losing their minds.

"Do you know she hasn't even gotten excited that the Pulses have ended?"

Judith dropped her last armful of clothes into the basket. "Now that *is* bad. Sometimes patients with PTSD can't think about the future. They have a sense of doom."

"We were thinking of finding her a counselor."

"Great idea. Do you know Anne Latham over on Bayor Street?"

"Not very well."

"Well, get to know her. She's a family therapist, or she was before the outage. Maybe you can get her to counsel Beth. I hear she was pretty good, back in the good ole days."

Armed with hope, Kay made a note to talk to her soon.

Before she could head back home, Kay saw Mark walking up the sidewalk. He'd dressed up a little for his night with Deni. With his jeans, he wore a white button-down dress shirt. He grinned as he came toward her.

Kay grinned back. "Big date tonight, huh?"

"Got that right. She in a good mood?"

"From what I can tell."

She thought of asking Mark if tonight was the night for the big proposal, but she decided to stay out of it. When the time was right, Mark would propose. She led him into the house, and called up to Deni.

What she wouldn't give for a working camcorder and the ability to go invisible tonight!

thirteen

DENI TOOK ONE LAST LOOK IN THE MIRROR AND GAVE HER-
self a thumbs-up. At least the three-quarter-length sleeves
covered her T-shirt tan. She slathered on some lip gloss, wondering where Mark was taking her. It wasn't like they could
go out to dinner or a movie. But Mark had promised her a
memorable night in celebration of the burned-out star.

She bounced downstairs and found him waiting like a
prom date in the living room. He held a bouquet of pansies,
the stems wrapped in tin foil.

"Mark, are those for me?"

He grinned. "I know they're corny. But I wanted you to
have them."

She took them and breathed in their scent. Mark's eyes
had that Cary Grant glint, like he had a secret.

"You look like a movie star tonight," she said. "Like one
of those hunka-hunka heartthrobs who can't go out without
paparazzi."

"Wow. So do you," he said, laughing. "You ready for
the red carpet?" He pulled her close and pressed a kiss on
her lips.

She slid her arms around his neck and rose up on her
toes.

"Go ahead and tell me," he said with a grin. "You love
me, don't you?"

She laughed softly against his lips. "How could I not?"

He stroked her hair and smiled.

"So where are you taking me?"

"How about a boat ride?"

"That sounds fun."

He pushed off from the couch. "Well, let's go, then. My yacht awaits."

His yacht, she knew, was a patched-up rowboat that hung in his garage. But that was yacht enough for her.

As they went to the door, they heard a car outside. She looked through the glass. It was a white Malibu, one she hadn't seen around before. "Is that car coming here?"

Mark opened the door, and they both stepped out onto the porch as it pulled into their driveway. The driver got out. Deni watched as he came around the car. "Hi, babe," he said. "It's me!"

Deni caught her breath at the sight of her ex-fiancé.

fourteen

"CRAIG?" HIS APPEARANCE WAS SO UNEXPECTED THAT Deni froze. "What are you doing here?"

He held out his hands, presentation-style. "I'm moving here!"

"What?"

"I'll tell you all about it, if I can get a hug."

He looked like she remembered in the days before the Pulses—the young VIP in a tailored suit, hair cut short and jaw clean-shaven. But somehow those polished good looks didn't appeal to her now. She didn't need this twist in her relationship with Mark.

When she didn't step off the porch, he stepped up and hugged her.

Deni glanced apologetically at Mark. Craig followed her gaze.

Mark's posture straightened as he shook Craig's hand. He was a good four inches taller than Craig. "Nice to see you again," he lied in a cool voice.

"You too." Craig's tone was just as cool. Turning back to Deni, he said, "I was just appointed as a regional advisor for the Department of Energy, to work on the Alabama Recovery Team." A self-conscious grin took over his face. "Man, you look gorgeous."

Mark looked at the ground, his jaw popping. The scar on his forehead seemed redder. Deni took Mark's hand, laced her fingers through his. "Mark and I were about to go out. He's taking me for a boat ride."

The tension in Mark's jaw seemed to melt, and he looked up. Craig met his eyes. Challenging.

"Nice night for it." Craig glanced toward the door. "Hey, I've been driving since the wee hours. They deployed us as soon as they knew the Pulses had ended. You think your parents would mind putting me up for a few days?"

No, she thought. That would be absurd, having her ex-fiancé living in her house while she dated someone else. "Wouldn't you rather be in Birmingham? Surely your office won't be in Crockett."

"Actually, it is. I convinced them to set up here."

The words spoke volumes, and Deni knew this wasn't an arbitrary decision. He had come here for her. Hadn't her rejection of his train ticket to Washington been enough to convince him she wasn't interested?

Apparently not.

"You've always liked grand gestures, babe," he said in a low voice, as though Mark wasn't there. "How about this one? I could have worked in any state or stayed in Washington at the DOE. But I came here."

Mark took a step toward him.

Deni stopped him. "You shouldn't have, Craig. I'm with Mark now. I told you in my letter."

"Find another place to stay," Mark bit out.

Craig ignored him. "Come on, Deni. I hardly know anybody else in town. There aren't any hotels open. Do you want me to sleep in my car?"

"No, I don't want you sleeping in your car. But you should have worked something out before you came."

"I thought we were friends," he said. "I figured your family would be glad to see me since I'm going to help get their lights turned back on."

Deni's heart jolted, and her defenses fell. "You are?"

"Of course. That's our main goal. And if I'm here, you can bet this part of town will be among the first to be restored."

He had her. She swallowed hard as visions of a refrigerator, overhead lights, television, and computers flashed through her brain. Could Craig really do that?

Of course he could. He'd worked for Senator Crawford for two years and knew a lot of people in government. He could get things done.

She looked at Mark, saw the trepidation on his face.

"I'll ask my parents," she told Craig finally. "Maybe you can stay for a day or two."

fifteen

MARK HUNG BACK AS DENI WENT TO THE FRONT DOOR and leaned in, calling her parents. He was amazed at the arrogance of this guy.

The line about sleeping in his car really got to Mark. He'd be happy to show Craig a nice bridge he could sleep under. And all the promises about restoring power — as if Craig had the pull to get the Brannings' house restored first.

But it was Deni who'd have to convince Craig she wasn't interested. Mark could see that she didn't want to be rude to the man who'd once meant so much to her. And Craig was pushy. When she'd hesitated about putting him up, he'd laid guilt on her. He knew her too well.

As anger warmed Mark's face, he fumbled in his pocket for the ring. What timing.

She turned back to both of them. "Let's go on in and let Mom and Dad know you're here."

Mark didn't want to. He wanted to take Craig to the lake, launch him in a canoe without a paddle, and let him swim back to shore. Mark knew Craig wanted him to leave, so he stayed.

As he passed Craig, he looked down at him, hoping his rival felt small. Craig didn't look pleased, which pleased Mark immensely.

It was his only consolation.

Kay heard Deni calling from the front door and her heart leapt. "He must have asked her!" she told Doug.

Doug laughed. "That boy doesn't waste any time." They raced each other to the door.

Deni didn't look like a blushing bride-to-be. Instead, she had a bad-news look on her face. Her ring finger was still bare. "Guess who's here," she said.

"Who?" Kay asked.

Deni opened the door wider.

Kay almost choked at the sight of Craig Martin.

"What the devil are you doing here?" Doug blurted.

Craig's smile twitched. Kay snapped a smile on her tight face. "Craig, it's great to see you. Are you passing through?"

"No," he said, giving them stiff hugs. "I'm staying."

Kay's eyes moved to Mark, stepping in behind Craig, looking as if he'd like to hurt him. Was the ring in his pocket?

How could this happen, tonight of all nights?

Kay swallowed hard. "Staying where?"

Deni cleared her throat. "He wondered if he could stay here for a couple of days."

Craig told them about his job, and Kay's heart sank deeper. This wasn't a weekend thing. He was digging in. Staking his territory.

Kay heard Beth coming down the stairs. When she appeared in the foyer, she took one look at Craig and said, "Uh-oh."

Kay shot her a scolding look and laughed nervously. "That's not a very nice greeting, Beth."

Beth looked at her mother. "But he lives in Washington!" Catching herself, she turned back to Craig and muttered, "It's nice to see you."

Mark caught her eye and winked.

Craig slid his hands into his pockets. "I'm here to get things up and running again."

"What things?" Beth asked.

"Electricity, communication, transportation ..."

Kay caught her breath. "Really?"

"Yes." Craig seemed relieved that he'd gotten her interest. "I just need a place to stay for a few days until I can find a place to live."

Kay froze, and she felt Doug doing the same. Mark sent signals with his eyes. Kay wanted to say no, that there wasn't a place anywhere in Crockett where he could find an empty bed.

"Mom? Dad?" Deni asked, rattling them back to the moment.

Kay realized she was being rude. Her mind raced for an alternative. "Maybe you could rent one of the empty apartments at Sandwood Place."

"No way," Craig said. "I've been to that place. I'm not living there. I can afford something much nicer. I just need time to look."

"But they're nicer now. The residents are really keeping it cleaner now that they know what to do. And some of the people have moved out and gone to live with relatives, so there are vacancies."

"Sorry. Not interested."

Doug sighed. "Well, what about Eloise's house across the street?"

He didn't bite. "I'll find something soon. I just need a couch to sleep on until I have time to look."

Mark finally spoke. "My father's house is vacant."

Kay almost laughed. The house Mark inherited wasn't exactly habitable.

Deni shot him a stern look. "Mark, it's all burned out. No one can live there until it's repaired."

Kay fought her grin. Mark seemed to like the idea of Craig living in a burned-out house.

"Thanks a lot, Mark." Craig's tone was sarcastic. "But if I get this area's power on first, I'd like to be able to use it."

Hope sprang to Kay's heart. "You mean we'll have electricity before everyone else?"

"This region will," he said. "Call us selfish, but we'll need a communication center, office equipment. We'll start with Crockett, of course. And this neighborhood will be on my priority list."

Before Kay could respond, Beth said, "He can have my room for a couple of days. I like sleeping with Deni."

"All right." Kay's voice sounded weak, hollow. She lifted her chin, hoping to sound more gracious—but what would this do to Mark and Deni? "You'll sleep in Beth's room, Craig."

Mark looked at the floor. Kay hoped he'd forgive her.

"Great," Craig said. "And Doug, there's something I wanted to talk to you about."

Doug's face was still tight, guarded. "Yeah?"

"It's about Christianity. I don't know if Deni told you, but the events of the last year have done a lot to humble me. And it woke me up to a lot of things. Including the existence of God." He paused, as if the words were thick in his throat. "I began to read the Bible, and its truth resonated with me. After a lot of soul-searching, I gave my life to Christ."

Boy, he was shoveling it on thick. Kay didn't believe him for a moment. But Deni seemed to. Her smile seemed victorious.

Doug's smile was thin, fragile. "That's wonderful, Craig," he said. "Our prayers for you all those months ago were answered."

They were still standing in the foyer. She should invite him in, Kay thought. Offer him some food. Where were her manners?

Craig went on. "I haven't yet been baptized. And I was thinking that maybe you could baptize me tomorrow. You still do church, don't you?"

Doug shot her a glance. "We sure do. We can baptize you in the lake during tomorrow's service. I'd be honored."

Kay tried not to look bitter, but she felt like a child fighting the urge to stick her finger down her throat. This guy was a piece of work! Using Christianity—one of the main things that had made Deni break up with him—to win her back.

Craig was no fool, but he clearly thought the Brannings were. And Deni seemed to be buying it. If only Mark had already put that ring on her finger.

sixteen

MARK STAYED AT THE BRANNINGS' WELL INTO THE EVE-
ning, though he barely said a word. As Craig ate too much
of the Brannings' food, he talked about the reconstruction. The family crowded around him as if he were the
conquering hero. As he talked to them about the Alabama
Recovery Team, Mark slid his hand into his pocket. His
index finger found the ring. He wished he could get alone
with Deni.

But the magic he'd expected for the evening was gone. He
wanted her undivided attention when he proposed. Tonight
clearly wasn't the night.

He sat on the couch next to her, channeling all of his
angry energy into his shaking foot. Now and then, Deni
would touch his knee to stop him. He'd quit for a while, but
within minutes, his leg went at it again.

Finally, when it was pushing ten, he realized that he
needed to go. He couldn't very well stay all night, just to
keep Craig away from Deni.

Deni walked him out onto the porch and closed the door
behind them. "Mark, I'm so sorry," she whispered. "But
please don't worry."

Mark breathed a silent laugh and looked out into the
darkness.

"Seriously," she said, "this is no big deal. He'll be here
a couple of days and then move into his own place. That'll
be the end of it."

"Deni, you can't be serious. He's here to sweep you off your feet. He won't give up after a couple of days."

"He'll have to. I'm not in love with him."

Mark's heart softened, and he felt a little hope again.

She stepped toward him and slid her arms around his neck. "I'm in love with you."

Mark's fears melted as he kissed her, and his heart ached for the words to tell her what she meant to him. But there weren't any—the ring said it all. Maybe now was the time to pull it out of his pocket, drop down on one knee, and ask her to marry him. But how would it be when she went inside and couldn't celebrate with her parents out of sensitivity for Craig's feelings? How would it be when Mark went home, leaving Craig there to tamp her joy and put doubts in her mind?

No, this wasn't the time.

Their kiss broke, and she looked up at him. "I don't want you getting all insecure over this. I didn't ask him to come."

"I know."

"And it's a good thing that he's a Christian now, right?"

"Yeah, if he's sincere."

Her arms slid down to his chest. "You don't think he is?"

Mark didn't want to say that straight out. "I'm just saying it's possible that he's telling you what you want to hear. Removing the obstacles you had about marrying him."

"Yes, it's possible. But what if it's true?"

"Then that's great. The angels are celebrating."

"Will you?"

Mark looked away from her into the night. Could he celebrate having *this* brother in the kingdom of God? Maybe, if Craig left Deni alone.

His thoughts disturbed him. "I hope so," he said. "What kind of Christian would I be if I couldn't?"

That seemed to satisfy her. "Are you coming to church in the morning?"

"Have I missed a Sunday yet?"

"No. I just thought ..."

"I'll be there." His tone was a little too sharp, but he wasn't sure what she wanted from him.

Her brown eyes were so pretty, so deep ... Did Craig know her depths, or did he think of her simply as the potential trophy wife he'd wanted her to be before?

"I'm sorry we missed the boat ride," she said. "Maybe we can do it soon."

"Tomorrow night?"

She thought for a moment. "Maybe we should see how it goes."

So that was how it was going to be. Craig's presence would dictate when she could go out with him. He let her go and slid his hands back into his pockets. "I hate this," he said. "I won't lie to you."

"I know," she said. "But you're going to have to trust me."

seventeen

"Can I stay home from church today?" Beth's question stopped the breakfast conversation about Craig and his baptism.

Her parents exchanged a look.

"Why?" her dad asked.

She pushed the egg around on her plate. "I don't feel good. It's hot and I want to stay home."

"Don't you want to see me get baptized?" Craig asked.

Beth started to say no, but she'd be chastised for her rudeness. Instead, she shrugged, squelching the urge to tell him to stay out of it.

Her mother sighed. "Beth, I don't know why you haven't wanted to leave the house all week, but you can't hole up in here refusing to face the world."

Jeff finished his eggs and dropped his fork with a clank. "Yeah, it's time you got back to delivering your own papers. I have enough to do. Come clean, Sis. Did somebody make fun of you? Are you embarrassed about something?"

Beth wished it was that simple. She picked at her food, wondering if admitting that would make them let her stay home. But no, she knew better. They would lecture her about having to face her fears, not letting words get her down. Sticks and stones, and all that. They would never dream that it was an angry killer she feared and not her friends.

Now it was Deni's turn. "You have agoraphobia, you know. The fear of leaving your house. You're turning into a recluse."

"No, I'm not. You don't know what you're talking about." She got up from the table and took her plate to the water bowl beside the sink. "Do I have to go, Dad?"

"Yes, we're all going."

Beth washed her plate and went upstairs, wishing Craig wasn't staying in her room. She would love to close herself in there alone. As it stood, she only had Deni's room.

She went into Deni's bathroom and stood in front of the mirror, trying to see what the killer would remember about her. If he saw her out in public, sitting at the lake in her church congregation, would he know her? She'd been wet the day of the murders, but he still could have seen that she was a blonde, and that her hair was naturally wavy. He'd seen her blue eyes, and might remember that.

Terror seized her, and her chest grew tight. If he'd followed her far enough to see her neighborhood, he *would* come to church. He would find out who her family members were. And then he would follow through on his threat.

She couldn't let that happen. If she left the house, she would have to disguise herself.

Going back into Deni's room, she dug through her sister's dresser for a pair of scissors. Finding them, she went back into the bathroom. She studied her reflection, touching her hair. It was her favorite thing about herself. Jimmy was always trying to touch it, as if he couldn't get enough of its softness. He would tell her she had a bug in it, then pick at it, trying to free it. Or he'd help her cool off her neck by lifting it up. Once he'd swept it behind her ear.

But it didn't matter. This hair could get her killed. She took a strand, lifted the scissors, and snipped. Six inches fell onto the sink.

But that wasn't enough. It would have to be really short, like a boy's. She took another strand and cut it shorter, this time above her ear. Her stomach began to burn, but she couldn't stop now.

She snipped and snipped, rounding it over her ears, whacking it off in the back. She hated bangs, because her hair was too curly to hang smoothly over her forehead. In the days before the Pulses, she could straighten it with a flatiron, making it lie down silky and smooth. Now it was just curly. She cut the strands long enough to push behind her ears. The bangs kept falling into her eyes, so she almost cut them shorter. But hiding her eyes was a good thing.

When she'd finished, she had a pile of hair clippings on the floor and in the sink. She studied the finished product. It looked awful. The blunt edges stuck out too thickly—not smooth and feathered as if a professional had cut it. But it was the best she could do. She wished she had some hair dye, so she could color it brown.

Tears came to her eyes as she gathered up the discarded hair. She pulled a makeup travel bag out of the cabinet under the sink and stuffed some of it in. She would keep it to remember. She zipped up the bag and cleaned up her mess. Then she went to her own room and stuffed the bag into her top dresser drawer.

Tears filled her eyes, but she blinked them back. Biting her lip, she went to the closet. Craig's suits and dress shirts hung there with her clothes. Since they had church outside by the lake, they didn't dress up. Still, her parents wanted her to wear something other than her everyday work clothes to set the day apart. She chose an outfit that didn't stand out—a brown pullover shirt and a pair of khakis. If anyone's eye skimmed the crowd, she wouldn't be the one who caught their attention. And if they did notice her, they'd think she was a boy.

She went back to Deni's room and dressed, then put on an old pair of sunglasses.

She gazed at herself in the mirror. She wouldn't recognize herself. Neither would the killer.

Her breathing was still shallow. She tried to slow it down, taking deeper breaths. But fear trembled through her.

Finally, she forced herself to go downstairs and get this over with. Deni was on her way up. She froze, midstep. "Beth! What . . . have . . . you . . . done?"

Beth pushed past her.

"What is it?" her mother asked, coming to the stairs. She looked up and sucked in a breath.

Beth managed a weak smile. "Like it?"

"*Beth!*" Her mother took a step up and grabbed her shoulders. "Why did you do this?"

She held her eyes wide to fight the tears. "It's hot. I wanted something different."

"But Beth, why didn't you ask me?"

"It's *my* hair," she said. "I didn't think you'd care."

Now the whole family was there, standing around the stairs, looking up at her like she was a freak.

Logan laughed. "Oh, man, that's bad."

Jeff chimed in. "You look like you got tangled in a lawn mower."

It was true. She felt the corners of her mouth shaking. Tears rimmed her eyes.

Her mother's face softened. "Honey, it just needs a little work. Let's go see if we can fix it."

"Come on, guys," Doug said. "Let's let the girls work."

Beth returned to the bathroom, and Deni and her mother followed.

"Mom, she needs a professional," Deni said under her breath.

Kay tried to smile, but she wasn't pulling it off. "I've been cutting the boys' hair. I can feather it a little. Make it a little thinner at the bottom."

A tear rolled down Beth's face. She wiped it with the heel of her hand, sniffed. "I'm sorry, Mom."

"It's okay, honey. The main thing is that you like it."

It didn't really matter if she liked it. That wasn't the point. Her hair was a small price to pay to protect herself and her family.

eighteen

"WHAT IS WRONG WITH HER?" DENI WHISPERED WHEN she and her mother returned to the kitchen. Craig was still eating. Doug was washing his plate in the bowl of water on the counter.

"I don't know, but I'm getting concerned," her mother said. "I was talking to Judith, and she thinks Beth might be showing signs of post-traumatic stress disorder."

Deni shook her head. "If anyone had that it would be us, not her. She's just been an observer. She hasn't actually had anything happen to her."

"Everything that's happened to us has happened to her too," Doug said, glancing toward the living room. "She's young and takes things hard. Remember how she got after Mark was beaten?"

Craig set down his water. "Mark was beaten?"

"Don't look so gleeful," Deni said.

"I'm not gleeful. Who did it?"

"It's a long story. It doesn't matter. The point is that Beth was really upset by it."

"Mark too, I'll bet," Craig said. "Is that where he got that scar on his forehead?"

"And a broken arm and collarbone," Jeff said.

Craig's eyes narrowed. "No kidding? I'd think he could defend himself better than that."

"He did," Doug clipped. "Otherwise he'd be dead."

Deni jerked Craig's glass out of his hand and went to wash it. "You know, I really don't want to talk about this."

He got up and followed her around the counter. His contemplative look rattled her. He was probably fantasizing about Mark getting lynched.

He leaned against the counter, crossing his arms. "When I was working for Senator Crawford, we worked on a bill about PTSD for veterans who fought in Iraq. I know a few things about it. If I can help—"

Deni drew in a long-suffering breath and looked at her mother. She was wiping the counter, practically ignoring him.

"Thanks, Craig," Kay said. "I think we'll go with a counselor."

It was rude, but it put him in his place, and Deni almost couldn't blame her mother. Still, when she saw the flush on Craig's face, she felt a little sorry for him.

nineteen

MARK HAD NO INTENTION OF GIVING UP HIS SEAT NEXT to Deni when they assembled for church that morning. But neither did Craig. So they both stood nearby, waiting for her to sit so they could grab the seat next to her.

Mark had to admit what he was doing was lame, like some love-struck high school kid, but what else could he do? No way was he going to let people think Deni was back together with Craig. Already, neighbors who'd heard of his work on the recovery team were treating him like a celebrity.

Chris Horton, Deni's best friend, came through the small crowd and greeted Craig as if he were a long-lost friend. She and Deni talked for a moment, then Chris caught Mark's eye, puckered her lip in a mock pout, and slipped away from Craig's fan club.

"Okay, what's going on?" she whispered as she reached Mark. "What's Craig doing here?"

Mark wanted to roll his eyes, but others were watching, no doubt whispering about his rival, waiting for him to reveal his true feelings. Instead, he gave Chris an exaggerated smile. Through his teeth, he whispered, "He rode in on his white steed yesterday, ready to rescue his damsel in distress."

"I heard it was a Malibu."

"Steed, Malibu, same difference."

Chris looked thoroughly entertained. "And you're thrilled about it."

He tilted his head. "Couldn't be happier."

"Don't worry, Mark. You know she loves you." Chris glanced back at Craig. He had shaken enough hands to win an election. "He is really cute, though."

Mark's fake smile crashed. "Traitor."

She flashed him a teasing grin. "If you want me to, I'll sit next to him. It isn't everyday there's an available man around here."

"It's your big chance. Go for it."

As Chris ambled back toward Craig, Mark ground his teeth. What was it women saw in that polished facade of his? His charm was as rehearsed as a presidential candidate's.

He swallowed back his distaste. He was going to have a hard time worshiping today. As the guitar music at the front signaled the people to take their seats, he looked toward the lawn chairs.

Beth was sitting at the end of a row, her hair chopped as short as a boy's. He almost didn't recognize her. Her eyes were hidden behind sunglasses too big for her face. She sat hunched over, hugging herself.

He sidestepped down the row and took the seat next to her. "I like your hair, Sparky."

"No, you don't." She usually smiled at the nickname he'd given her after the first time she'd sparkled on stage. Today, her frown had a tight hold.

"I do. It's a nice look for you."

"Okay, whatever." Clearly not buying it, she looked over his shoulder to the street.

He set his arm on the back of her chair. "Seriously, what's wrong?"

"Nothing." Her answer was final.

"Is it Craig?"

She rolled her eyes. "No, that's what's wrong with *you*."

He couldn't help chuckling. "Well, you've got me pegged." She didn't respond. Her glance strayed to the street again. "Are you expecting someone?"

"No," she said, jerking her gaze back.

"Jimmy, maybe?"

"No! Why do people keep asking me that?"

Something was really bothering her. All playfulness faded from his tone, and he leaned down to her ear. "Hey, you know if you need to talk, I'm here, right? If something were wrong, you could come to me."

Beth looked up at him with those doleful eyes. Her lips parted, and she started to speak. But as Jeff stood up at the front with his guitar and began leading them in a praise song, that vacant, distracted look returned to her eyes.

"You know that, don't you?" he asked her again.

Her voice was softer now. "Yeah, I know." She swallowed hard.

He started to sing the praise chorus, but Beth remained quiet.

Deni slipped down the row and sat beside him. Craig plopped down on the other side of her, and Chris followed him.

Deni slid her hand into Mark's, drawing his attention back to her. Relief and pride warmed his tense muscles, reminding him that she was still his girl.

FOR THE LAST SEVERAL WEEKS, DOUG HAD BEEN PREACHING through the convicting book of 1 John. But Mark was too preoccupied to be convicted.

We know that we have passed out of death into life, because we love the brethren. He who does not love abides in death. Everyone who hates his brother is a murderer; and you know that no murderer has eternal life abiding in him. We know love by this, that he laid down his life for us; and we ought to lay down our lives for the brethren.

Mark wondered if Craig could even follow the theology. Could the pompous narcissist grasp such concepts? The man who had refused to work to help the poverty-stricken apartment dwellers a year ago didn't strike Mark as someone with a great capacity for love.

Yes, Christ could have changed Craig, if he'd really given his life to him. But Mark doubted seriously that Craig's Christianity was real. Surely he was donning the robes of belief for the sake of winning Deni back. His desire for baptism was all an act.

Mark prayed it wouldn't work.

Mark brooded through the sermon, arguing with the voice in his heart that said he should welcome Craig into the family of God. As the service ended and the congregation crowded around the water's edge to watch Craig's baptism, Mark stood at the outskirts. Doug waded into the water, and Craig followed, all arrogance gone from his face. Deni stood back with Mark, her arm through his. "Be nice," she whispered.

Anger pulsed through him. *Be nice?*

He wondered if Doug had any compulsion to drown him. If Mark were in Doug's place, he might.

With that thought came a rush of guilt, but he quickly shoved it down.

He listened to Doug's prayer over Craig, watched him go down into the water ...

"Baptized with Christ in death ..."

And come up wet ...

"Raised to walk in newness of life."

He saw Craig wipe the water from his eyes, saw the trembling of his lips, the sincere look of submission ...

Doug hugged him, and as Craig slogged out of the water, shame began to burn in the pit of Mark's stomach. What if Craig wasn't acting? What if he really had come to Christ after his breakup with Deni?

Was Mark *judging* Craig or simply discerning? There was little Craig could do to convince him it was real ... even if it was.

Dripping wet, Craig took the towel Kay had brought for him. Wiping his face and wrapping it around his shoulders, he walked into the crowd of well-wishers.

Mark swallowed the bitterness in his throat. He could at least *act* happy about the supposed conversion. He planted his feet as

Craig worked his way through the crowd. When his rival came close, Mark extended his own hand.

"Welcome to the family," he forced himself to say.

Craig wiped his wet eyes. "Family?"

Deni smiled. "He means you're brothers now. Brothers in Christ."

Craig studied him, as if he didn't know whether they were James and John ...

Or Cain and Abel.

And Mark wasn't so sure himself.

twenty

THE KILLER HADN'T SHOWN UP FOR CHURCH. WHILE THE baptism went on, Beth wandered to the message board at the edge of the lake and read every scrap of paper that had been stapled, taped, or pinned there. There had to be a missing persons report. If the man who'd saved her life had been homeless, as he looked, he might not have been missed—even though he was a hero. But wouldn't the other man's family be worried about him? Wouldn't *someone* be looking for him?

She swept her bangs back, felt them curling up in the heat. All the man would have to do was come here and ask anyone for a blonde girl named Beth. Everyone knew about her because of the plays she'd put on in the neighborhood. She'd made herself too famous to all of her neighbors. Short hair or not, anyone could point him right to her front door.

She looked from one face to another. There were no more than thirty-five people here—she would certainly recognize the killer if she saw him again, wouldn't she?

Unless he wore a disguise.

No, she knew everyone here. No disguises.

Maybe he wasn't going to do anything. He was just trying to scare her into keeping her mouth shut.

She looked toward her father, dripping on the bank. She should tell him. He could figure out who the killer was from her description and lock him up. Then it would all be over.

But if he didn't find him, and the man knew she'd talked ...

Would it matter? Didn't he want her dead either way?

Her friend Cher came over and touched her hair. "Beth," she whispered. "I didn't know that was you. Did you get your hair cut for the play?"

She thought of saying yes, that she was casting herself in one of the boys' roles. But that wouldn't fly. She had enough boys who wanted a part.

Her heart sank as she realized that the next play would call attention to her. The killer would find her for sure. It was way too public.

She touched her hair. "No, I just got sick of the heat. And I've changed my mind about the play this summer."

"But, Beth, you already wrote it!"

"I know, but I'm too busy to help with it," she whispered. "I don't have time."

Cher looked crestfallen. "The little kids will be so disappointed. They're all looking forward to it."

"I can't help it. They'll find something to do."

Cher looked stunned. "What's wrong, Beth? I haven't seen you in a week. You're acting different."

"I told you, I'm just busy, delivering the papers and all."

"It's not like you have to go from house to house. You're just filling up the news racks."

Beth wasn't in the mood for this. She wanted to go home and hide in her room. "Look, if you want to do the play, go ahead."

Cher looked as if Beth had just broken off their friendship. "Are you mad at me?"

"No. I just don't want to do it, that's all."

Cher sighed. "Okay, then … I guess I'll lead it. It won't be as good, but at least the kids won't be disappointed."

"Good," Beth said, trying not to cry. "I'll get Logan to bring you the script."

"You can't even bring it?" Cher asked.

Beth looked at her best friend, knowing she was hurting her. She wondered if she could trust Cher to keep the secret if she told her. Of course she wouldn't. If Cher told *her* a thing like this, Beth would definitely tell her parents.

She had never felt more alone.

"I have to go," she said. "The baptism's over."

Cher went back to her family, and Beth went to give her polite congratulations to Craig. While she waited for everyone to hug him, her thoughts went back to the message board.

She would have to check the other boards around Crockett, see if anyone had posted a missing persons report anywhere. If she could find out who the dead man was, then maybe she could at least find a way to notify his family.

They deserved to know. She wished she could do something for the man who had saved her too. He might have a family somewhere who missed him and wished he'd come home. Maybe they'd prayed for him for years, while he lived on the streets.

If only they knew he'd given his life to save her. But she didn't know his name, or anything about him. She wasn't even sure he was dead.

"Beth? Beth!"

Beth shook out of her thoughts and saw her mother, looking at her like she'd gone off the deep end. "Are you okay?"

"Fine," she said. "Just thinking."

Her mother put her arm around her, kissed her head. "Let's get home, okay?"

Beth almost felt safe as they crossed the street and headed for home.

twenty-one

THERE WERE PAPERS TO DELIVER, AND BETH KNEW SHE had to deliver them. Since the killer hadn't shown up yet, maybe he didn't really know where she lived. Maybe that had just been a threat to keep her quiet.

Or maybe her silence was what had kept her alive so far. He could be watching her now, waiting for one sign that she'd ratted him out to her parents—determined to kill them too, if he had to.

Would he see her when she went to do her job? When the *Crockett Times* had converted from a weekly to a daily newspaper, the Brannings had seen a way to earn extra money. Her brothers were doing the hard work of delivering papers door-to-door, each of them with a large route. Lots of adults had applied for those paper routes too, but Harriet, Deni's boss, had favored her family because of all the work Deni did for them.

Beth had committed to fill all the coin-operated news boxes around Crockett each day. Some of them hadn't been filled Friday, and yesterday Jeff and Logan had done it for her. They wouldn't do it today.

She hoped her haircut was enough of a disguise to keep the killer from recognizing her. She donned her brother's baseball cap and sunglasses and dressed in clothes that a boy might wear. She hardly recognized herself.

She consoled herself with the thought that she could take the opportunity to check message boards while she was in different parts of town. Maybe she would see a missing persons poster that would tell her who the dead men were.

She went out to get on her bike. Would the killer remember that it was silver? That was a common color, so it wasn't likely to call attention to itself. The bike trailer stacked with newspapers would certainly be identifiable, but there were lots of newspaper deliverers around Crockett, and they all had trailers. In fact, almost every family had at least one.

Still, she felt a little sick as she biked out to the garage behind the newspaper office, where she always picked up her papers. She could usually get her deliveries made in the two hours after lunch. It had worked out well when she was going to school in the mornings. Now that school was out for the summer, she had time to do family chores in the mornings, then the newspapers in the afternoon. All her money went into the family fund.

She reached the warehouse and pulled her bike in. Delbert, the old man who oversaw the papers, was tying up a stack.

"Hey, Delbert," she said, getting off her bike.

The man looked at her like he didn't know her. "Hello, young fella. Can I help you?"

She pulled her glasses down and looked at him. "It's me, Beth."

He gasped and began to laugh a wheezing, phlegmy laugh. "Beth? I didn't recognize you, darlin'. You look ... different."

That was good, she thought. She saw Delbert every day. If *he* didn't recognize her, then surely the killer wouldn't.

"You runnin' from the law or something? You look like a different person."

She put the glasses back on. "Can't a girl get a haircut?"

"Sure can," he said, still chuckling. "But that ain't a haircut. That's a scalpin'."

She took the cap off to show him it wasn't so bad.

"You're still a cute li'l ole thing," he said in his grandfather tone. "Just took me by surprise, that's all."

Satisfied that her disguise was serving its purpose, she loaded her papers into her trailer and set out to fill her boxes. Then she rode her bike from one newspaper box to another, stopping at the message boards that were usually near them. At each one, she stopped and read the papers stuck haphazardly all over the boards, looking for word of the missing men.

At the third board she came to—the one in Magnolia Park—she saw it. A fresh handwritten flyer with an old snapshot stapled to it and the word *Missing* at the top of the page. It was the first man she had seen shot in the thunderstorm—the one on his knees. Her heart pounded as she read his name—Blake Tomlin. He was twenty-eight and he lived in Magnolia subdivision—the neighborhood adjacent to the park.

She pulled a pen out of her pocket and wrote the address on the palm of her hand. The flyer said he was twenty-eight years old, married with one son, age two. Her heart dove to her stomach. Had his wife thought he'd taken off like Amber Rowe's husband, overcome by responsibility and high on the cash he'd just withdrawn from the bank? She must be crying her eyes out, and that poor baby was probably wondering where his daddy had gone.

And his parents—what were they thinking? Were they angry at him for abandoning his family, or did they even know he was missing yet? What if they lived far away, like her grandparents, and hoped to see him when they had a car running again?

She got back on her bike and looked up the street, trying to figure out where the missing man's house was. She spotted it just a little way down, easily visible from the park.

Instead of turning back onto the road beside the park, busy with carriages and bicycles and horses pulling wagons, she rode toward Blake Tomlin's house, then slowed as she rode past it.

It was a nice house in a quiet neighborhood. The garage door was closed, and there was no activity in the yard. Tears burned in Beth's eyes. She should go to the door right now and tell Blake Tomlin's wife that her husband had been shot in the Cracker Barrel parking lot, the day before yesterday.

She thought of how tragic that would be for his wife. But it could be just as tragic for Beth's own family. She had to keep quiet, to keep anyone else from getting killed. Besides, no one would believe her without the bodies. All she knew of the killer was that he had a goatee. He'd been wearing that hood, so she didn't even know what color his hair was.

If she told them anything, a gang of police would descend on her, insisting on the whole story. And it wouldn't bring Blake Tomlin or the homeless man back.

She went back to the park. Setting her kickstand, she left her bike and sat on the swing. She could see the Tomlin house clearly from here.

A few children played around her, swinging and sliding, their parents watching from benches. Minutes ticked by, and she knew she should get back to the warehouse and reload for her last few racks. But she couldn't seem to tear herself away.

After fifteen minutes or so, she saw the Tomlin garage door roll open. She stopped swinging and held her breath as a young woman a few years older than Deni walked out with a broom and began sweeping. Beth's throat grew thick, and she swallowed. When she got to the end of the driveway, the woman stopped and looked toward the intersection.

She was watching for her husband to come home, Beth thought. Just like Amber Rowe, wondering how her marriage had gone so terribly wrong.

But Mrs. Tomlin's husband hadn't abandoned her like Amber's had. The poor woman had no clue that her husband lay dead.

A boy of about two toddled down the driveway to join his mother. Beth's hand came to her chest, as if it could calm her pounding heart. The little boy would never know what had happened to his dad. He would grow up thinking his father didn't love him, that he had just walked away.

Beth was going to cry, and that would call attention to herself, so she got back on her bike and rode away. Wiping her eyes, she glanced around to make sure no one was following her. It was time to go back to the warehouse and reload. She had a few more boxes to fill, and then she could go home.

On her way back, she found herself just blocks from the Cracker Barrel, where it had all started. Curiosity and horror drew her back to the site. She rode past it without stopping, but she slowed enough to look where the second man—the man who'd saved her life—had fallen. From the street, she saw no sign that he'd ever been there. Riding along the curb, she peered behind the Cracker Barrel. There was no sign of Blake Tomlin's murder, either.

For a moment hope fluttered in her heart, and she imagined that neither was dead, after all. That they'd both been wearing bulletproof vests. That after she'd ridden away, they'd both gotten up and gone home.

But if that had happened, why was there a missing persons sign for Blake Tomlin? Maybe he'd come to, confused and disoriented. Amnesia. Yes maybe he had amnesia, and was wandering around trying to remember his name.

But a chill came over her as she remembered the gun firing right through his head, the man dropping to the ground, blood mingling into mud. People didn't survive things like that. Even if he'd some-how crawled away, someone would have seen him and called for an ambulance. Deni would surely have done a story on it, and her father would know if it had been reported to the sheriff.

Beth finished her route, her mind racing with possibilities, but the one that loomed largest was this: the killer had come back for the bodies, and only he knew where they were.

twenty-two

KAY WAS IN THE KITCHEN WHEN BETH CAME HOME AND shot through the room with Jeff's baseball cap pulled low over her face.

"Beth, where were you? I thought you were in your room."

"I was delivering my papers," she said.

Kay smiled. That was a good sign, wasn't it, that Beth wasn't hunkering in her room today? Beth pulled the cap off and Kay saw the sweat soaking her daughter's short-cropped hair. She'd never worn her brother's cap before. What was that about?

She may have gone out, but she still wasn't behaving normally.

"Honey, I want to talk to you," Kay said.

Beth was already on her way out of the kitchen. She turned back. "What?"

"Sit down."

A look of fear came over Beth's face, as if she'd been caught at something.

Kay frowned as Beth came to the table and pulled out a chair. "Honey, is there something you want to tell me?"

Beth sat down slowly. "Like what?"

"Like some secret you've been keeping."

Beth's gaze darted out the window, where her father and brothers were working in the yard. "No, I don't think so."

Disappointed, Kay sat down across from her. "Beth, you haven't been acting normal lately, and I'm worried about you."

"You don't have to worry. I'm taking care of everything."

"Taking care of everything? What are you talking about?"

"Just … there's nothing to worry about, okay?"

She wasn't making sense. "Honey, I want you to do something for me. I know you've been busy working on the new play you wrote, and you'll be starting casting for it this weekend. I don't want to take any of your free time for this, because the Lord knows, you need that. But I've been talking to a counselor about you and some of the stuff you've been through lately."

"What stuff?" Beth's eyes locked back onto hers.

"Just some of the trauma. Some of the things you've witnessed."

"You told her that?" Beth sprang up. "I didn't see *anything*. You shouldn't have told her I did."

The outburst surprised Kay. It was as if they were having two separate conversations. "Beth, calm down!"

Beth burst into tears. "Mom, I don't want you going around talking about me!"

"I'm not going around talking about you, Beth. I talked to a counselor about sitting down with you and letting *you* talk. It was confidential."

"What does that mean?"

Kay sighed. "It means she won't talk about it to anyone else. She's a professional. She has to keep these things to herself."

Beth's tensions eased somewhat. She looked down at the palm of her hand, studying something she'd written there.

Kay took her hand and read it.

"Whose address is that?"

Beth pulled her hand away. "Just somebody who wants to subscribe to the paper." She changed the subject. "About the counselor. I guess I could talk to her, but I don't know what you want me to say."

"She just wants to see if she can help you. You've seemed depressed lately, honey."

"I don't want people discussing me behind my back."

"We won't. But a lot has happened in the last year. Things are better now. We can see light at the end of the tunnel. Everyone's so excited, but you just still seem so depressed."

Tears welled in her eyes. "I just ... I don't want the family to be hurt—"

"You're not hurting us, honey. We're hurting *with* you. We want to see you get through this." She touched Beth's perspiring face, made her look at her. "Will you talk to her? Her name's Mrs. Latham and she lives a few blocks over."

"Benny Latham's mom?"

"Yes, I think so."

"He's been in some of my plays," Beth said. "I know her. She's nice. She helped make some of the props when we did the Christmas play."

"Oh, good." Maybe this would work out better than Kay thought, if Beth already had a relationship and a sense of trust in the woman who'd be counseling her. "Now that school's out, when will you be rehearsing the play? We'll work the appointments around that."

Beth propped her chin on her hand. "I've decided not to do the play."

"What? Why not? You've already written the script."

"I have too much to do, what with the papers and all. I gave the script to Cher. Logan ran it over to her last night. She'll have to do it without me." She got up. "Can I go to my room now?"

Kay tried to hide her disappointment. "Well, yes. Sure."

Kay watched Beth leave the kitchen. What was going on? Beth loved entertaining. She loved writing scripts, directing, casting. Giving the children something to think about other than the hard work they did all day. It was an outlet for them and provided a much-needed source of refreshment for the neighborhood.

Beth loved the accolades she got from handling so much herself. Everyone had been so proud of her when she started this. So what had happened? It had to be PTSD. The aftereffects of the trauma they'd all faced were draining the life out of her. Her child needed help, and soon. Maybe she could catch Anne Latham at home tonight and set up a session for tomorrow.

twenty-three

SHE HAD TO COME OUT SOONER OR LATER. THE KID NAMED Beth who'd seen him kill Tomlin would show her face at some point, and when she did, he'd take care of her. He'd been looking for her since that Friday, riding the streets of the neighborhoods on the east side of Crockett—the direction he'd seen her go. Occasionally, he would ask kids in the neighborhoods if they knew a girl named Beth—blonde hair, shoulder length, about eleven or twelve years old. Most of them refused to talk to him. With all the crime these days, people were on their guard.

But a few kids who'd bought his friendliness had given him some answers.

They didn't know any Beths in Broadmoor subdivision, and in Bradford Terrace there was one, but she was six. There were two Beths in Pecan Grove—but he'd seen them both. One was a red-haired sixteen-year-old. The other was four.

There were still several other neighborhoods, with miles between them, at intervals down that long country road. He turned into Oak Hollow, trying to look as if he belonged there. People were out working in their yards, pulling up weeds in gardens in their front yards, planting food. There was money in this part of town. He bet all of them had had cash to withdraw from the banks. And they hadn't had to kill anyone to get it.

He rode around the neighborhood, skimming the heads of the children he saw, looking for his Beth. He came to a well where several neighbors stood talking. Stopping and balancing his bike with his foot on the curb, he said, "Hey, guys. Wonder if you could help me. I saw this kid over at the produce stand the other day, and she dropped this necklace. The chain must have broken. I tried to catch her when I saw it, but she was already gone. It looked kind of expensive, so I wanted to return it. Name on the back of her jersey said 'Beth.'"

One of the women stepped toward the bike and looked at the necklace. "It's nice of you to return it. Most people wouldn't."

He smiled. "Well, you know. It was probably a gift from somebody."

"We have four Beths here, at least," one of the boys piped up.

His dad clamped a hand on his shoulder, shutting him up. "Why don't you just give us the necklace, and we'll see which one it belongs to?"

He breathed a laugh. "How will I know you got it back to her?"

"You'll have to trust us, pal."

He slipped the necklace back into his pocket. "No, thanks. I'm not even sure she lives in this subdivision. Just tell me where the Beths live, and if I find the right one, I'll return it myself."

The child clearly enjoyed being an authority. "There's Beth Crebbs, Beth Owens, Beth Branning—"

His dad pinched his shoulder. He should have known. It was a mistake talking to a group with adults among them.

"Come on, guys. The little girl probably wants her necklace. You probably know her. Cute thing. Blue eyes, long blonde hair. Eleven or twelve, maybe older. Just point me to her house. I'll give it to her parents."

The woman shook her head. "I don't really feel comfortable naming names. Either give the necklace to us, or keep it."

He gave up and decided to come back when he could catch the kids alone.

He rode out of the neighborhood, intent on coming back tomorrow. At least he had one thing going for him. She clearly hadn't told the police about him yet, or there would be descriptions of him in the papers and on message boards all over town. And Blake Tomlin was still considered missing—not dead.

Beth Crebbs, Beth Owens, Beth Branning. He repeated them over and over in his mind. He'd look up those three last names when he got home and located his phone book. It would have addresses. Then he'd be able to find her.

twenty-four

THE STACK OF FILES ON MARK'S DESK AT THE SHERIFF'S department seemed to be growing, no matter how fast he worked. A group of inmates they were holding in the jail were being transferred to the county prison today, and their paperwork had to be up-to-date and in order. The job had fallen to Mark and Doug, but Mark feared it wouldn't be done in time.

"I never worked so hard in my life," Doug muttered as he closed one of the files and tossed it into the transfer box. "Stockbroking was a piece of cake compared to this."

"Yeah, and it paid better." The truth was, any pay would be better than the salary they took home here. They had volunteered for the job with no expectation of pay at all. But now that they'd been at it for a few months, the sheriff had put them on the payroll. Sometimes the county could pay them—sometimes it couldn't. Mark had learned to expect nothing, and when a paycheck came, it was like found money. His satisfaction came from knowing that crime wasn't allowed to go unchecked, though there was only so much this tattered group of untrained deputies could do.

Mark finished a file and opened another. "So ... has Craig found a place to live yet?"

"No," Doug said. "He seems to be dragging his feet."

Mark glanced up at him. "You know why."

"Yeah, I know. But I don't want to throw him out. He's a new Christian—I don't want him to think he can't count on the body of Christ when he needs us."

Now Mark couldn't concentrate on the file in front of him. He brought his eyes up to Doug. "You really think that's real? The whole Christianity bit?"

Doug met his eyes. "I've talked to him, and I think it is. But whether he's sincere is between him and God. It's not our job to judge him. It's our job to disciple him."

"Fine, but do you have to do it with him living in your home? Can't the guy afford a place to stay?"

"He can, and I'm sure he'll find a place soon. I'm still pushing him to rent Eloise's house."

Mark didn't want him living across the street from the Brannings, either. If Craig had to live in Crockett, let him move across town.

He punched holes in a stack of loose papers, shuffled them so the judge's ruling was on top, followed by the police report and the affidavits signed by witnesses. Another file completed.

His mind wandered back to Craig and his newfound Christianity. Doug was right. He had no business judging the sincerity of another Christian. Salvation didn't turn people into perfect replicas of Christ. Sanctification took time and discipleship.

Maybe he needed to cut the guy some slack. Mark had been kinder to the men who had beaten him half to death. He'd found forgiveness in his heart for them—had even cleaned out their cells and scrubbed their filthy toilets, so they wouldn't have to live like animals during their incarceration. But bitterness toward Craig had taken deep root and was infecting his every thought.

Doug's sermon the other day came back to him. *We know that we have passed out of death into life, because we love the brethren.* He had heard it through his bitterness, applying it only to Craig, and not to himself. But he was called to love too.

Craig didn't need any toilets cleaned. But as Doug had pointed out, he did need discipleship.

If he extended an olive branch and offered to do a Bible study with Craig, would he accept? Maybe he'd be too proud to back down from a challenge.

It would certainly kill two birds with one stone—he would be able to test the sincerity of Craig's Christianity and, of course, follow the Great Commission to make disciples.

His bitterness seemed to lift as his goal came into sharper focus. Yes, he'd extend the invitation tonight, right after work. Then he'd see what Craig Martin was really made of.

twenty-five

BETH HAD NEVER FELT MORE AWKWARD. IT WAS WEIRD HAVing Benny Latham's mom examining her thoughts, trying to figure out if she was losing it. Maybe she should just save them all the trouble and admit that she was. Thankfully, the counselor had decided to let her mother sit in with them for this first session, so Beth didn't have to do all the talking.

They'd paid for her time with a basket of eggs. Her mother thought it was a fair exchange to keep Beth from going crazy.

Mrs. Latham's voice was honey-smooth, like a kindergarten teacher. Her brown hair was cut in a chin-length bob, and she wasn't old enough to have gray roots. "I want to talk to you, Beth, about some of the upsetting things you've dealt with in the last year. I'd like for you to tell me which ones stand out as the most important ones in your memory."

Beth didn't know where to start. "Finding my teacher and her husband dead, I guess. Deni disappearing. Little Sarah getting kidnapped. Dad getting shot."

"Do you have a problem reliving the events in your mind? Playing them over and over?"

"Sometimes. I try not to think about them, though. Sometimes I can't control it. I have dreams about them."

"You want to tell me about those dreams?"

Beth really didn't want to. She was tired and jumpy. She still wasn't sure she hadn't been followed over here. "Do I have to?"

Mrs. Latham exchanged looks with her mother. "Of course not. Only if you want to."

"I don't."

"Okay." She said it like it was just fine with her. "Beth, sometimes traumatic events can create lasting effects in our bodies. Do you have any physical symptoms? Stomachaches, dizziness, sleeplessness?"

"Headaches," she said. "I have headaches. I have one right now."

Mrs. Latham seemed glad. She made a note of it, nodding. Beth looked around the room, trying to focus on the way she'd decorated. Ben was clearly the star of the home. There was an entire wall devoted to his T-ball career, a picture of him with a red, white, and blue Uncle Sam suit on. School portraits from preschool to third grade.

A piano sat against the wall, the primer music open to "Mary Had a Little Lamb." And over the couch was a framed mural that Ben must have painted. Either that, or it was by one of those crazy earless painters who made millions from their colorful blobs creatively slathered on canvas.

Mrs. Latham put the notebook down. "Beth, let's get off the subject of the bad things that happened and just talk about you. What do you want to be when you grow up?"

"I don't know," she said.

"Well, you're a very good playwright, a great director, a great actress. Do you see yourself doing something in the performing arts?"

Beth shrugged. "Not really. I think I'm over that." From the corner of her eye she saw the shadow of someone walking past the window. She jumped.

Mrs. Latham looked out. "That's just my husband, Beth. Did he startle you?"

Her heart was racing. "No. I'm okay."

"She's very jumpy," Kay said. "Lots of things have been startling her lately."

Mrs. Latham studied her. Beth imagined her turning pages in the textbook of her mind. "Page 133, 'Patient Jumping Out of Skin.'"

"Beth, are you expecting something bad to happen?"

Beth brought her gaze back to the counselor. "Maybe."

"Tell me about that."

She'd said too much. "Bad things do happen a lot."

"But aren't you excited that the Pulses have ended? Don't you look forward to having electricity again? Technology? TV?"

She wished they could pull the window shades. Perspiration was breaking out on her face, prickling under her arms. "Yeah, I guess. If they ever do happen. But that's a long way off."

She felt bad for the counselor. She was probably frustrating her. But she feared if she spoke too much, she'd start crying. And then she couldn't stop.

"I like your haircut," Mrs. Latham said. "It's pretty. It looks nice on your face."

Beth touched her hair. "Thank you."

"Do you like it?"

She hated it, almost as much as she hated the reason for it. "Not really. It'll grow back."

"Why'd you cut it?"

She looked at her mother. Had she discussed this with Mrs. Latham beforehand? Her mother clearly thought it was a symptom of her going off the deep end. She wondered if Mrs. Latham's textbook had a chapter for random haircuts.

"It was hot," she said. "It always looked stringy and dirty." There. That sounded normal, didn't it? Did she sense in her words that she was trying to disguise herself so a killer couldn't find her? Maybe Mrs. Latham wasn't that tuned in to the human mind.

Mrs. Latham finally sent her outside to wait for her mother. Beth figured she was boring her to death. She sat in the shadows of the garage, watching the street for the killer who might be looking for her, trying to figure out which house she lived in. By now, he may already know.

Maybe she should go to the police. Maybe if she did, they could find the killer and lock him up before he came for her. Then again, maybe he hadn't come because he was a man of his word. A killer with a conscience. He'd said that he would only kill her and her family *if* she talked.

Her silence could be saving her life and the lives of those she loved.

And no amount of counseling could change that.

INSIDE THE LATHAMS' LIVING ROOM, KAY WIPED TEARS. "I'M sorry she wasn't more forthcoming. I know you didn't get much from her."

Anne looked at her notes. "Actually, I got more than you think. Kay, I think your concerns about post-traumatic stress disorder are well-founded. Beth is showing several of the symptoms."

"She is?"

"Yes. She has physical symptoms, a sense of gloom, she's unable to think about the future because she seems to have the sense that she won't be here. The dreams she has of these traumatic events, her inability to concentrate or focus. Her jumpiness, as if she's living in a state of fear. Lack of interest in the things she used to be interested in. Detachment from the excitement over the Pulses ending."

"So what can we do to help her?"

Anne closed her file. "Kay, this is considered an anxiety disorder, so there are some medications that might help her. Dr. Morton could take my recommendation and put her on something if we decide that's the best approach. But first, I'd like to have a few more sessions with her alone. See if I can get her to talk about the things that have traumatized her, and maybe we can retrain her thinking so that she can cope with these things. Meanwhile, just reinforce her confidence in her skills and her talents, invite her friends over to get her mind off these events, try to get her to loosen up and have fun."

"Okay, I'll try."

"And try to get her focused on the future. On the rebuilding and the good things she has to look forward to."

Kay wasn't quite satisfied. "What about her cutting her hair? Would PTSD make her do that?"

"It could, though I can't quite put together why she did that yet. Maybe she just wanted a change."

"Not like that. Not my prissy little Beth. To just chop it off like that, without any warning ..."

Anne thought that over. "It is disturbing. I'll keep trying to get to the bottom of it. But PTSD does sometimes cause strange behaviors." She looked at her calendar. "Why don't we get together next week?"

Kay made the appointment, then walked outside, wondering if she was doing the right thing. Did Beth really need counseling? Did she need medication? Or simply more prayer? Maybe she just needed for Kay to spend more time with her.

The idea of taking a job with the recovery team fled from her mind. No, Beth needed her. And so did Logan and Jeff.

She found Beth sitting in the garage, staring out at the street. The dismal look on her pale face only reinforced what Anne Latham had said.

Beth needed help. And Kay would do whatever it took to get it for her.

twenty-six

DOUG HAD RESISTED KAY'S DESIRE TO USE SOME OF THEIR precious cash to buy instant coffee, but she had won, and as he sipped it at the kitchen table early Monday morning, he remembered what a luxury it was. He had to sip it black, since he'd put his foot down about buying sugar, but the scent and taste and warmth on his tongue brought back memories of life before the outage. Would life really go back to normal?

Sleep was a rarity when he worked the night shift at the sheriff's department, then got up to chop wood, hunt, and work in the garden that would help feed them for the next few months. And then there were his sermons that had to be composed, and people in his church who needed attention and care. In his spare time, he worked on converting the engine in his Expedition, anxious to get it running again when he had fuel to put in it. There was so much to be done and not enough time.

It was five a.m., and no one was up yet, so he sat under the light of an oil lamp, trying to formulate what he was going to say to Craig about finding a place to live. The young man had made no effort to find a place yet.

Eloise's house sat empty, completely furnished. When she died, her son had encouraged Doug to rent it out if he wanted. The neighborhood did use her backyard for raising rabbits, and someone had stolen siding off of the back of her house, since lumber was so hard to come by. But other than dust and cobwebs, the interior of the house was in good shape. He would have to be firm with Craig and insist that he walk over with him to look at it.

He heard someone coming down the stairs and looked up to see Craig, fully dressed and ready for work, carrying a big bag on his shoulder.

"You're up early."

Craig's eyes looked sleepy. "Yeah, I wanted to be ready for my first day of work today. There's an awful lot to do." He looked around the kitchen. "Is that coffee I smell?"

"Yeah, want some?" Doug got up and got the pot he had boiled over a fire on the grill outside. He got Craig a cup and filled it.

Craig took it and breathed in the scent. "Wow, this is great. Just what I need. I miss Starbucks."

"Yeah, me too. So what have you got in that bag?"

Craig took a seat at the table and set the bag in another chair. "Plans and schematics and pages of documents I've been reviewing about the power substations, the refineries, and the strategic petroleum reserves. That kind of thing."

Doug was fascinated. "I can't even imagine overseeing something like that. I'd be completely overwhelmed."

"I am, a little," Craig admitted. "But we're taking things a step at a time. The first job was to find a place to set up our offices. Saturday one of my team members found and rented the building that Champland Insurance used to have."

"I know that building. Over by the conversion plant?"

"That's right. Since we'll be working closely with the plant, it was convenient. We got it complete with all their office furniture."

"So I guess Champland Insurance won't be bouncing back."

"Not anytime soon. The insurance industry bottomed out after the Pulses started."

"So where are you going to start with the recovery?"

Craig sipped his coffee. "Actually, the recovery effort has been going on since the Pulses began. Several U.S. departments have been working together with the White House to do as much advance rebuilding as possible."

Doug heard his bedroom door, off the kitchen, open. Kay came out in a pair of shorts and a T-shirt and padded barefoot into the room. "Morning. You guys want some eggs?"

"Sounds good," Doug said. "Craig was just telling me about the recovery. That the work started at the beginning of the Pulses."

That got Kay's attention. "So they're all ready to get the power turned back on?"

"Well, not exactly," Craig said. "After the Pulses ended, Congress called an emergency session to implement funding for the recovery teams and approve plans for rebuilding. Once that was done, the recovery teams started work on getting the power trucks running, so they'd be ready to move when we were ready."

"What about fuel tanker trucks?" Doug asked. "You can't run the power trucks if you can't transport fuel."

"Exactly. They've been converting the fuel tanker trucks. Our goal is to get fuel in here so we can black start some of the power generators."

Kay cracked some eggs into a bowl and stirred them up. "What is black starting?"

"Good question," Craig said. "Frankly, I'd never heard the term before a year ago."

"I know what it is," Doug said, glancing at Kay. "Years ago, people who'd studied electromagnetic pulses recommended that changes be made within the power industry, so that in the event of a nuclear bomb in our upper atmosphere or an E-bomb that caused an electromagnetic pulse, there would be a way to generate electricity. Who would have predicted that we'd have millions of EMPs and that it wouldn't be man-made? That it would have come from a star?"

"No one. But fortunately, the power companies did listen to the recommendations, and they divided their power grids into islands, so that if one area went down, the others could keep going." Craig took a roll of paper out of his bag and unrolled it on the table. "Here are the ones in this area."

Doug leaned forward, studying the map.

"Each one provided electricity for local load areas," Craig went on. "Black starting those islands meant using small generators to jump-start larger generators. Those could then start the main power station generators."

Doug nodded. "And the generators that will black start them require a lot of fuel."

"Yes," Craig said. He was clearly in his element, and Doug couldn't help being impressed at his knowledge and passion for his task.

Kay stopped stirring and came to the table.

"The problem was that it isn't just electricity that has to be restored," Craig said. "Every silicon chip within those stations has been destroyed. So before we can even get the system black started, we have to do some significant rebuilding of the control circuits within the stations themselves."

Kay looked crestfallen. "That could take forever."

Craig smiled. "Not quite. But it's an overwhelming job for all of us leading the recovery. It's the first time in the history of the country that the government has been forced to deal with disaster in every county of every state simultaneously. It's not as if people from the north can rush down and help the ones in the south, like they often do after a disaster. And no other countries are any better off. Everyone is struggling. The only ones who aren't are the ones who don't depend on electricity. The Amish, for instance. They were all set up for something like this."

"I used to think they were crazy," Kay said. "But now I think they're brilliant. They didn't miss a beat after this disaster, did they?"

"Nope. They went right along with all they were doing. And they became the experts that society looked to to learn how to do things. Up in Pennsylvania, they actually began doing workshops to teach people how to live. They've been a big help to people in that area."

"So how are you going to get fuel to black start those stations?" Kay asked. "Is it even possible?"

"Yes, we have strategic petroleum reserves that have almost a billion barrels of crude oil stored. The mechanical pumps to get it through the pipelines have been rebuilt, so they're ready to go. But first, we have to get the refineries back online."

"Oh, my word," Kay said. "There are so many steps. I'd go crazy if I were you."

"Yeah, it's tough. I'm more of an instant gratification guy. It's going to take truckloads of patience to work my way through this. But we'll do it one step at a time."

She set down the bowl of eggs. "And you're in charge of all this?"

"Not completely. We have teams in every region, with state directors. I'm one of a handful of people in charge of the central Alabama region. It's a real team effort. We have to get the power to the refineries so they can refine the crude oil. Alabama's resources will first go toward powering the refineries in Saraland, Mobile, Atmore, and Tuscaloosa. Saraland has the largest capacity. They produced 80,000 barrels a day before the Pulses. They'll be first to get their power on."

Doug looked up at Kay. "So that means we'll have to wait a lot longer."

"Maybe not too much longer," Craig said. "But there are a lot of unknowns right now."

Doug smirked and winked at Kay. "Want to move to Saraland?"

"I also have to hire people to recruit and hire all the workers, assign them to areas where their experience and expertise can be used, and coordinate the labor. So tell everyone you know that we're hiring. We'll set up tables at the next FEMA disbursement in a couple weeks to hire people. But we'll be starting to hire even today. We'll make sure it's in the papers, so word should get around quickly."

Kay got the eggs and started for the door to cook them on the grill. "Trust me, word will spread like wildfire. This is America. People will want to help."

"The power companies will be hiring back all their employees, so those already trained will be higher up in the hierarchy, and the newcomers will work under them. It's funny. The blue-collar workers are the most valuable people around right now. White-collar folks are pretty much useless."

"Tell me about it," Doug said. "Not a real high demand for stockbrokers these days."

"What about the mechanics and engineers you've already drafted?" Kay asked.

"They'll be at the forefront of the recovery. Especially the engineers and electricians. We'll leave the mechanics in the conversion plants to keep converting vehicles that we can use. We'll add to that carpenters and construction workers, architects, communications workers, computer techs, and a whole host of occupations that will help us recover. Even if the applicants are not experienced, there are things they can do to help with the effort. We're also getting the National Guard units involved. We're fighting a war here, but this time it's not against people." He finished his coffee and gave Doug a look. "You could come to work for us, Doug. You too, Kay."

Doug leaned back in his chair. "I'm pretty busy with the sheriff's department, not to mention preaching."

"But are you getting paid?"

He got nothing for preaching, since he diverted his congregants' tithes toward helping the people around them. And the sheriff's department had put him on the payroll, but often the payroll wasn't met. "Not regularly. But they need people to enforce the law. Somebody has to do it."

"We'll be paying a dollar an hour for the average workers, a little more for the more experienced ones. It's not much, but in our economy, that'll go a long way. It'll infuse money back into the infrastructure and get more cash flowing."

Doug had to admit that it sounded good. Forty dollars a week *would* go a long way. And if Kay and Deni did it too, that would be 480 dollars a month. A year before, that would have been laughable. But today it was a fortune.

Still, he had made a commitment to the sheriff's department. Paycheck or not, he had to do it.

Kay sat down at the table, full of questions about what kind of job she could get. While Craig tantalized her about a position in the offices, Doug took the eggs out and began to cook them on the grill.

What would it be like if Kay took a job there? What would happen to Logan and Beth? He didn't like the idea of Jeff being left unsupervised all the time, even at sixteen. Beth and Logan definitely needed someone at home. But if she wanted to do it, he supposed they could work it out.

Though he hated what the Pulses had done to society, he had to admit that he loved what they had done to the family. The lack of technology had drawn them all closer. Instead of leading separate lives, watching television in their bedrooms, playing video games and staring at computer screens, they gathered each night in the same room. Communication in the form of telephones and email were dead. But it felt as if communication in his family had blossomed to life. It was moving to see the kids working hard at their own jobs and giving their pay to the family. A year ago, the idea of helping support their family would have been laughable.

And his relationship with Kay was closer than ever. They'd never enjoyed each other so much. Laughter and conversation had become as easy as breathing. He dreaded the distance his job would create when the power was restored.

The restoration effort was important, yes. But the restoration of his family had been an unexpected blessing. He didn't want to upset that balance and closeness they'd found. He'd have to pray about what to do. He hoped Kay would pray, as well.

He glanced back through the window. Craig was in deep conversation with Kay. Craig would need an awful lot of prayer as he helped lead this effort. No wonder he hadn't had time to think about a place to live. Maybe providing him a place to sleep wasn't such a bad thing, after all. It was something they could do for the recovery effort.

He decided not to broach the subject of moving out. Maybe he should give him a few more days.

twenty-seven

DENI GOT HOME FROM THE NEWSPAPER AFTER DARK AND saw Craig's Malibu parked in the driveway. Next to it sat Mark's bicycle, chained to the lantern on the front lawn. What were Mark and Craig doing here together? This had to be awkward.

She opened the garage, pulled her bike in, and stepped into the kitchen. Her mother was buzzing around preparing for dinner. "Mom, what's going on?"

Kay chuckled. "Just our latest mini-drama. The ongoing saga of your love life."

She didn't appreciate her mother's humor. "Are they *together?*"

Kay pounded her bread dough with her fist. "Yeah, Mark came a few minutes ago. I told him you weren't home, and he said he didn't come to see you. He wanted to talk to Craig."

"And you said *yes?*"

Kay rolled her eyes. "Deni, we're talking about two grown men. They didn't need my permission. It's not my job to keep them apart. Besides, you think Mark's going to attack him or something? That's not his style."

Deni looked into the living room. "Where are they?"

"Upstairs."

Her heart sank. She turned back to her mom. "Did Mark look angry?"

"Not really. He was actually very pleasant. If you're worried about it, go up and see what they're talking about."

"What do *you* think they're talking about?" she whispered harshly.

Kay shrugged. "Maybe they're flipping a coin."

Deni caught her breath. "Mom!"

Kay abandoned her bread and came closer. "Deni, it's not up to them; it's up to you. You know who you want. And if it's Mark, you need to encourage Craig to get his own place."

"So what do you want me to do?" she whispered. "Pack his bags for him? I've been busy all day. I haven't had time to find him a place to live."

"You've been in love with Mark all these months, honey. You've been happier than I've ever seen you."

"And nothing's changed."

"Well, it will if Craig has anything to say about it."

"He doesn't. But I don't think Mark should badger him. What's he gonna do? Try to convince him to live in his dad's burned-out house?"

Kay smirked. "Maybe he'll invite him to stay with him."

"Yeah, that'll be the day." Deni went through the living room and looked up the staircase, trying to listen. She heard nothing—no yelling or crashing. Slowly, quietly, she went upstairs.

She saw Beth in her pink bedroom, lying on the bed, curled up with her knees to her chest. She glanced into her own room, and there were Mark and Craig, standing and talking in quiet voices, tense, like wolves about to tear into each other.

Neither had seen her, so she slipped into Beth's room, and stood at the door, listening.

"What are you doing?" Beth asked, sitting up.

Deni glanced back at her. "Shh. Mark and Craig are in my room," she whispered. "I want to hear what they're saying."

Beth pulled her feet under her. "Deni, what did you work on today?"

She waved her hand at Beth to silence her. She could hear Craig's voice, calm and low.

"I'm not going to negotiate with you over Deni. All's fair. May the best man win."

"Deni?"

"Please!" Deni whispered. She watched Beth lie back down, then stepped closer to the door.

IN DENI'S ROOM, MARK STOOD WITH HIS BACK TO HER DORMER window, his arms crossed as he looked at Craig, wondering if he always spoke in lame clichés. Deni hadn't mentioned that. "I didn't come here to talk to you about Deni," Mark said. "I came here to make you an offer."

"An offer?" Craig asked. "What have you got that I would want?"

"A little knowledge," Mark said.

Craig let out a hard laugh. "Um, I seem to remember that you don't even have a college education, and I graduated from Georgetown University Law School. I doubt seriously there's anything you can teach me."

The barb stung. Mark hesitated, wondering if he should even go ahead with his plan. "I'm not here to one-up you, man. In the education department, you have me beat hands down."

"Then I can't wait to hear."

Mark let his arms drop. "It's about Christianity."

Craig's hard expression softened somewhat. "Okay."

"I thought maybe you'd like to do a Bible study with me. There's a lot to learn, and it can be confusing for a new believer sometimes. It helps to have somebody to do it with."

Craig almost laughed. "Oh, I get it. You're gonna rub my nose in the fact that I'm brand new at this. That there's something you know that I don't."

Had Craig forgotten that he'd just been the one to rub his nose in his education? "The ground is level at the foot of the cross," Mark said. He almost winced at his own cliché, but it was true. "What I mean is, it doesn't take any special insight or education to be a Christian. All you have to do is surrender your life to Jesus in faith, and you've done that."

"Yes, I have." Craig's tone was still defiant.

"But one of the Proverbs says, 'As iron sharpens iron, so one man sharpens another.' That's what I was thinking we could do. Sharpen each other." He smiled. "Spiritually speaking."

Craig just stared at him, as if searching for a catch. "So this is not a joke? You really want to do a Bible study?"

"That's right. You up for it?"

"And this has nothing to do with Deni," Craig said.

Mark thought of denying it, but it wouldn't be entirely true. "Well, if you want to know the truth, it has a lot to do with Deni. I figure she's going to wind up with one of us, and whichever one it is, we could both do with a little Christian growth."

Craig's eyes narrowed. "You've got to be kidding."

"I'm not. Like you said, may the best man win. The choice is Deni's. But either way, she deserves a godly Christian man. If you're the one who wins, then I want you to make her happy."

"So you're going to teach me."

"I thought we'd learn together. But if it makes you uncomfortable—"

"I don't need you telling me how to make Deni happy," Craig said. "And I don't want you testing me to see if I'm a sincere Christian."

"I'm trusting that you are," Mark said. "But if that threatens you, then let's forget it. I don't want to make you feel that way."

"Oh, I'm not threatened," Craig said, taking a couple of steps toward Mark and raising his chin. "In fact, I think it's a great idea."

His eyes showed neither joy nor delight, but a glint of competition. He reached out to shake Mark's hand. Mark obliged.

"Let's do it," Craig said. "When do you want to start?"

"How about first thing in the morning? My house, say, six a.m.?" He could see that the early hour didn't appeal to Craig, but he didn't back down.

"All right. What do we start with?"

"Let's each read the book of John before we get together tomorrow."

"The whole book?" Craig asked. "In one day?"

"Sure. It's only twenty-one chapters. But if you need more time, we can just go over what you do get done."

Craig's lips were tight. "I'll get it done."

"You'll enjoy it more when you see the whole picture instead of taking it piecemeal. So I'll see you at six in the morning, at my house?"

"No problem."

Mark turned to leave. As he did, Deni stepped out of Beth's room, surprising him. She was smiling, but her eyes were narrowed like Craig's, as if she didn't quite trust him. "What are you doing?"

His heart ached at the sight of her. He grabbed her hand, pulled her against him, and pressed a kiss on her lips.

Craig stepped out of the room, hands in his pockets. "How was your day?" he asked in a cool voice.

Deni pulled back and let Mark's hand go. His heart sank. Not a good sign.

Her expression was tight as she looked at Craig. "My day was fine. How was yours?"

"Great," Craig said.

Tension rippled around them. Mark thought of leaving, but he detested the idea of leaving her here with Craig, as if this was where he belonged. So he just stood there.

Beth came out of her room. "Deni?"

Deni didn't even look back at her. "What?"

"I was just wondering," Beth said. "I went out today and saw on one of the message boards that some guy named Blake Tomlin was missing. Did you report on that?"

Deni turned toward Beth. "Yeah, we got that report. My gut feeling is that he got his cash and took off for greener pastures."

Beth's cheeks flushed. "That's pretty judgmental. What if something happened to him?"

She shrugged. "It's possible."

"It could be like when Jessie Gatlin went missing. You should write about it so people will be looking. Someone might know what happened to him."

"We'll see. You really love a good mystery, don't you?"

"No, I don't," Beth said. "I just feel sorry for his family." Cutting off the conversation, she went into Deni's room and sat on the window seat.

twenty-eight

MARK HAD GONE HOME BY THE TIME CHRIS CAME BY THE house. Instead of her nursing scrubs, she wore a pair of jeans that were a little too baggy for her small frame, and a bright aqua blouse that brought out the blue in her eyes. "I hope I'm not interrupting supper," she told Deni. "Your family's probably celebrating with a five-course meal now that they have some cash, huh?"

"We did that the other night." Deni led her to the kitchen where she was washing dishes. "My parents can't agree on how to spend it, so we had the usual—corn tortillas. And it took all of five minutes to choke down, so don't worry about it."

"It's better than nothing. Keeps a little meat on your bones." Chris lowered her voice. "So where is he?"

Deni scrubbed a plate in the bowl of sudsy water on the counter. "I assume you mean Craig?"

"Yeah. He's staying here, isn't he?"

"Yes, he is, unfortunately. He's upstairs."

A smile lit up Chris's eyes. "Well, what are we waiting for? Let's go up."

Deni scrubbed the last few forks, rinsed them in the second bowl, and stacked them in the dishwasher to dry. "Wait a minute. Is that why you're all spiffed up? Did you come over here to see him?"

Chris giggled and brought a finger to her lips. "Of course I did," she whispered. "Since you don't want him—I might."

Deni just gaped at her.

Chris leaned on the counter. "You don't care, do you?"

"No, I just ..." She grunted. "Weren't you one of the ones try-ing to convince me he was a jerk?"

She smirked. "I don't recall using that word."

"No, but you really didn't think he was right for me. Why is he suddenly right for you?"

"Because he's changed. And I'm lonely." She shrugged. "I don't want to *marry* the guy. I just want a little male companionship."

Deni dried her hands. "Okay, whatever."

Chris just looked at her. "You're not okay with it, are you?"

Deni's mouth fell open. "I'm fine with it." She glanced through the living room to the stairs, hoping he wasn't listening.

Chris slid her hands back into her pockets. "You know what? Never mind. Just forget I said anything."

Deni felt like a jerk. Why *shouldn't* Chris go out with him? It would get him off Deni's back. "No, Chris. Really, I don't mind. He's just not good husband material. I don't want you to get hurt."

"You sure you don't still have feelings for him?" she whispered.

Deni almost choked. "Yes, I'm sure!"

Chris grinned. "Because if you do, can I have dibs on Mark?"

Deni shoved her. "What is wrong with you? No, you can't have Mark!"

"Great," Chris teased. "What self-respecting guy is going to commute by bicycle to see me? If I don't take your cast-offs, then where will I be?"

"Mark is not my cast-off. And neither is Craig."

"Don't worry about it. I'll just die a spinster."

What a drama queen. Chris had at least a dozen guys after her; she just didn't like any of them. "A *spinster?* Chris, you're twenty-three. Don't make me kill you." She headed for the stairs. "Come on, let's go up."

She led Chris up the stairs and found Craig in Beth's room, paperwork laid out on her desk.

"Wow, all this looks really important," Chris said as they stepped inside.

Craig looked glad to see her. "Hey, Chris. How are you?"

"Great." She looked over his shoulder. "So is any of that telling you how to get our power back on?"

"Actually, it's telling me where I need to deploy the people I hire to work at the power stations."

Chris dropped onto Beth's bed. "Well, it's good to know somebody's working on it. You couldn't by any chance have it on by Wednesday, could you?"

He laughed. "No, I don't think so. Why Wednesday?"

"Because I've decided to throw a Supernova Burnout party. Wednesday's my day off from the hospital."

Deni dropped into the lime-colored easy chair next to the bed. "But Oak Hollow's already giving a party."

"So sue me. You can never have too much celebration. This'll be at my house, for everyone in their twenties—married, single—just to get together, relax a little, and have a little fun. Oh, and I was thinking about getting your brother's band to play, just to give us a little background music."

"Sounds like fun," Deni said.

"Good," Chris said. "What about you, Craig? Are you too busy to come hang out with friends?"

Craig flashed Chris that charming smile of his. "I'll make time."

Chris's eyes sparkled, and Deni shook her head. Her friend was way too obvious. "What can I bring?" Deni asked. "I have all the well water you could want."

Chris laughed. "Don't worry about the food. We have apples galore. We'll have apple pie, apple hors d'oeuvres, apple cider ... Do I sound like that guy in *Forrest Gump* with the shrimp?"

"A little." Deni had long envied Chris's family's apple orchards. "That'll be a draw."

"Then I'll put it in the invitations. I'm going to put a message up on the message board, and you guys tell anybody you see." She went to Craig and leaned over the desk. "So you see how important it is to get our power turned on by then?"

Craig grinned. "I'll see what I can do."

twenty-nine

DENI WAITED UNTIL TEN O'CLOCK FOR MARK TO COME back over, as he did every night that he wasn't working. But he never came. She realized with regret that she should have gone to him. He was clearly brooding about Craig and needed her reassurance. But it was too late to go out safely tonight.

Exhausted from a hard day's work for the newspaper, she decided to go to bed. She glanced in Beth's room. Craig sat at Beth's desk, reading by the light of the oil lamp, hunched over a Bible.

He turned. "Hey."

She paused at his door and leaned against the casing. "I was on my way to bed."

Craig got up then and came toward her. "I was hoping to spend more time with you tonight. Looks like you're as busy at work as I am."

She nodded. "Going from a weekly to a daily paper has really ramped up my hours. There are a lot of stories to write."

"I know the feeling."

"Yeah, I guess you do. But your work is a little more important right now."

"We could use your help. If you could come by tomorrow, see our setup and write about our hiring, it would help a lot." His voice was soft, intimate.

"Yeah, I've already been assigned that story. I'll be there in the morning." She glanced past him. "What are you doing?"

He looked back at the Bible. "Studying the book of John. Mark challenged me to read it before tomorrow."

"The whole thing?"

"That's right. I borrowed a commentary from your dad and I'm working through it."

She fought her smile. Mark wasn't going to make this easy. "You know, you don't have to do this with him. You could say no."

"Why would I do that?" He lifted his chin. "I can hold my own with him."

"I know you can, but it's not necessary. I don't know why he even suggested it."

"I do."

She wished the whole thing had never come up. What had Mark been thinking? "Well, John is pretty self-explanatory, right? You don't need commentaries for it."

He went back to the desk and sat down. "You sure? I got bogged down in the first chapter. The first verse, even. 'In the beginning was the Word, and the Word was with God, and the Word was God.' I don't get that."

She hesitated to engage with him on this. It was probably just a ploy to draw her in. Then again, how could she fault him for trying to understand God's Word?

"Well, John's talking about Jesus."

"Jesus?" Craig asked. "How do you figure that?"

She went into the room and leaned over the desk, pointing to verse one. "Look at the context of the chapter. Verse fourteen says that he—the Word—became flesh and dwelt among us. Who did that?"

"Jesus did."

"Right. It says we 'beheld his glory, the glory as of the only begotten of the Father.' Who was begotten of the Father?"

"Jesus again?"

"Yes. So if 'the Word' is Jesus, go back and read it like this: 'In the beginning was Jesus, and Jesus was with God, and Jesus was God.'"

Craig sat down and read back over the verses. It was as if a light came on behind his eyes. "Okay, I can see that now."

Satisfied, she turned and started out of the room.

"One more question," he said, stopping her.

"What?"

"So in verse six, the man named John who was 'sent from God,' he's the guy who's writing the book, right?"

She could see how he could be confused. "No, he's talking about John the Baptist. John, the apostle, is the guy who wrote the book."

"Two different Johns, huh? That's confusing." Craig sat back in his chair and swiveled around. "I graduated law school at the top of my class, and I have a photographic memory. But I can't get this. It's hard. And I *want* to understand."

Her heart softened toward him. He really did seem to be trying. Maybe it wasn't a ploy, after all.

"How do you guys know this stuff? Is it from going to Sunday school all those years?"

She smiled. "Partly. But most of what I've really understood about the Bible has come in the last year. Just keep reading. Chapter two is not so hard. It's about the miracles Jesus did, starting with his turning the water to wine. I really don't think you'll need a commentary for that. Read it out loud, and it'll come alive."

Craig turned the page and skimmed the chapter. "Okay, I see."

"Don't sweat it, Craig. This Bible study is not a competition with Mark. He's not like that."

He leveled his eyes on her, his lids heavy. "Yes, he is, Deni. We both have the same goal. He didn't invite me into this so we could become big buddies."

"He's not trying to make you look stupid."

"Then what *is* he trying to do?"

"Maybe he really wants to disciple you. You're a new Christian."

"Why would he care? I was clear about why I put in to work in this area. I came to get you back."

She met his eyes, and remembered why she'd fallen in love with him before. She also remembered why she'd fallen *out* of love. Mark's words to Craig played back through her mind—that he wanted to make sure that whoever won Deni was a godly man.

That sounded just like Mark. Craig might be five years older, but he wasn't that mature.

"But I'm gonna do this," Craig said, "and if he is in it to make me look like an ignorant jerk, well, I'll just pray that I learn something in the meantime. I really do want to learn this."

"Then pray, and the Holy Spirit will reveal it to you. It's all good news. Every discovery is going to excite you."

Craig turned back to the words, and she watched the light of the kerosene flame dance on his face as he read the opening verses with new eyes. He looked up at her. "Will you stay and finish going over this with me?"

She thought of saying yes, but this intimacy was a bit too disconcerting. It would be better to leave this to her father and Mark.

"I'm really tired," she said. "All you need to do is read it. Let the Holy Spirit teach you."

He opened his arms. "You sure? I could really use your help."

"You can always ask my dad if he's still up."

He sighed. "That's okay."

She thought so. She went to the door. "Well, good night. You have a lot of reading to do."

"Yeah," he said, and she heard the hollow melancholy in his tone. "Hope I can get it all done tonight."

thirty

MARK GOT UP EARLY AND SCRAMBLED SOME EGGS ON THE barbecue pit outside so he'd have something to offer Craig. As he did, he wondered about the night before. Had Craig gotten Deni alone? Had she felt those old feelings coming back? Had they talked tenderly into the night, remembering old times?

He was stupid to have stayed home pouting last night. He should never have given them time to be alone.

He sat down at the patio table. It was still dark out, and a cool breeze blew through his hair. He needed a haircut and a close shave. He should start tucking his shirts in and retire the work jeans with the hole in the knee. Maybe he should use some of his cash to buy a new car. If a Malibu impressed Deni, maybe he could get a Mercedes. A Sportster, with all the bells and whistles.

He must be crazy. He wasn't poor by today's standards, but he couldn't afford such a luxury. He was more of a V-dub kind of guy. Besides, if it took outclassing Craig to win Deni, then he may as well give up now.

He heard the knock on the front door, so he went through the house to let Craig in. Mark had to hand it to him. He was prompt.

Craig stood at the door with his Bible in hand. It looked brand new, hardly used. The silver on the edges of the pages still glistened. Mark shook his hand and brought him in. "I made eggs if you're hungry," he said. "And coffee."

"Coffee? How'd *you* get coffee?"

"I bought some instant with some of the cash I got out of the bank. It was a Mother's Day gift. She won't mind if we use a little."

Mark led him out back, where he'd lit two lanterns. The dark sky was beginning to recede. The fire on the barbecue pit still burned, providing a little more light. Soon the sun would begin to come up.

"So you live here with your mom?"

Mark didn't answer for a moment. The question sounded like a slam. He scooped the eggs out of the skillet and onto a plate, then set it down in front of Craig. "Yes, I live here with my mother and stepfather. Living is hard, these days. It takes a whole family pulling together to survive."

"Did you live with them before the outage?"

The fire was hot on his face. "Yes. I was saving up to buy a house."

"You were in construction work?"

"That's right." He was being interrogated, and he didn't like it. Turning the tables, he said, "So did you read John?"

"I did." Craig ate the eggs, sipped the coffee. Setting down his cup, he said, "I got a little bogged down last night, but Deni helped me through it."

Mark's stomach began to burn. He hadn't meant for this Bible study to be an opportunity for Craig to bond with Deni. There was an intimacy in Bible study that he didn't want her to have with Craig. He hoped they hadn't prayed together.

His throat felt too tight to speak, so he focused on his eggs. He filled his own plate, then sat down across from Craig. He took a rubbery bite. They were already cold.

They ate in awkward silence. When he finished, Craig set down his fork and folded his hands on the table. "Let's get real here for a minute, Mark. You're not fooling anybody."

Mark pursed his lips and stared into his mug.

"You don't want to do a Bible study with me. You just want to have the upper hand. You want to demonstrate how much more spiritual you are than me. This isn't about Jesus. It's about Deni."

Mark set his cup down and met his hard gaze. "If that's what you think, why'd you come?"

"Honestly? Because I didn't want Deni to see me backing down."

"So this newfound Christianity of yours. Is it real? Or is it just your latest tactic?"

Craig leaned toward him. "Try me."

This wasn't getting off to a good start. "It's not my job to try you. I have to assume that you're on the up and up. If you're blowing smoke, that's between you and God."

"That's right, it is." Craig leaned back. "But meanwhile, I do appreciate the challenge. I've never read anything like the book of John. When I became a Christian, I started at the beginning. I've read from Genesis to Proverbs, so far."

"Nothing in the New Testament?"

"Nothing but a passage here and there. I've been missing out. Maybe I should have read that first." He opened his Bible, glanced up at Mark. "So congratulations, you're biblically superior."

Mark really didn't like this guy. "I think that's an oxymoron, isn't it? You can't know and understand the Bible and feel superior about anything."

Craig looked smug. "Oxymoron? And here I thought you were uneducated."

Mark got to his feet. "You know, maybe this was a bad idea, after all."

"Maybe so," Craig said. "But what will we tell Deni?"

Mark imagined telling her that Craig was too much of a jerk. That he was too competitive to actually learn anything. That his arrogance was an obstacle too high to hurdle.

"We'll tell her the truth," he said. "That we couldn't get along. That the iron sharpening iron thing doesn't work when it's two rivals for the same woman."

"But does yours really need sharpening?"

"Of course it does," Mark said. "I have as much to learn from this Bible study as you do. I'm not teaching you, you know. I planned on just working through the book verse by verse, to see what God would show us together."

It looked as if Craig had finally run out of sarcastic barbs.

Mark pulled his chair back in and leaned on the table. "One of us is going to wind up with Deni. It won't hurt either of us to sharpen our biblical knowledge. Like I said, she deserves a godly husband."

"And you think that's what you are? Godly?"

Mark almost laughed. "Actually, if you judge me by the conversation we've just had, no, I don't. And you're not, either. We're a couple of giant egos trying to one-up each other. But if we come down from our lofty heights, maybe we could both learn something."

Craig stared down at his Bible, chewing on the side of his lip. For a moment, Mark thought he was going to get up and leave. He almost hoped he would.

But Craig threw him another curve. "All right," he said. "Let's start with chapter one."

thirty-one

DENI RODE HER BICYCLE TO THE CHAMPLAND INSURANCE building, which the government had purchased for the recovery team's command center. The parking lot was still full of stalled cars that had been there for the past year. Double-parked behind some of them, she saw Craig's Malibu, some other cars with government tags, and five power trucks.

She envied the drivers. If she could only drive again, she could accomplish so much. Half of her time working for the paper consisted of getting from one place to another.

A year ago, she'd felt like a little kid riding a bicycle. But she'd come to appreciate it. Her legs had grown stronger, and she could ride miles without getting out of breath. She could scoot around town fairly quickly on her ten-speed.

But she still longed for the privilege of driving again.

She got the chain out of her backpack and laced it through the door handle of one of the abandoned cars. Because the building hadn't been used since the Pulses began, they hadn't yet installed bicycle stands. Several other bikes were locked against cars, so she supposed no one would complain. It had become a good way to secure bicycles, since these cars weren't going anywhere.

As she padlocked the chain, she heard the hum of a generator somewhere in back of the building. Holding her backpack and digging through it for her clipboard, she stepped inside. The activity surprised her. It had been difficult to tell from the parking lot how many people were here, but now she saw about a dozen men and women sitting in the waiting area. Across the large, cubicled room, she saw a glass conference room where a roomful of people sat listening to a man who was writing and drawing on a huge dry-erase board. The days of PowerPoint presentations were long gone.

She wandered through the cubicles until she saw Craig talking to several men. She caught his attention and waved.

His face lit up.

What a strange thing, to have him react to her that way. Though she was over him, it did her heart good. She'd craved that attention from him for so many months when they were dating. Even the night he'd put the ring on her finger, he'd rushed off to work immediately afterward. She hadn't rated in the top five on his priority list.

He held up a hand for her to wait, then finished his conversation. He walked the men toward her, shook their hands, and said, "We'll see you at eight in the morning."

The men looked delighted as they left the building.

"Hey, babe," Craig said, leaning down to hug her.

She bristled at the word *babe*. "Don't call me that," she said, but she accepted the hug, patting his back platonically. "So do you have time for an interview about the hirings?"

"Of course," he said. "We have to get the word out ASAP." He glanced at the others waiting and said to them, "Someone will be with you guys in a minute."

He led her through the building. "Those were job applicants. They've already started showing up. And over there—" he waved toward the glassed-in conference room—"they're briefing the power company employees. We have our work cut out for us, but things are moving along."

He glanced back at her as she clicked her pen. "I'm really glad to see you here. Maybe I can lure you into working for us."

She smiled. "I have a job."

"Making what?"

Not much, she thought. She got a dollar a day, and occasionally her boss at the *Crockett Times* paid her in food—a jar of beans, a head of lettuce, a bag of peanuts. Her job was more a labor of love than a working wage. It was enough to help her family, but not enough to live on her own. But she didn't want Craig to know that. "I do okay," she lied.

"But you can do better than okay. We're starting our workers out at a dollar an hour."

"*What?*"

"Yes. Your parents didn't tell you?"

"I didn't talk to them much last night. A dollar an hour? Really?"

"You could get in on the ground floor, work here in the offices helping coordinate things. I could give you a nice title and a lot of responsibility."

She had to admit, it was tempting. "What kind of jobs are available?"

"We have a ton of things we're hiring for. But I've been thinking you would be excellent to head up our Communications Department. We need people to handle public relations, write press releases, answer questions from reporters, keep the public informed. That may not sound like much right now, but trust me, it's huge. And I'll need you to help me coordinate that and help me with job applicants."

She narrowed her eyes. "Are you serious about a dollar an hour?"

"For that job, it'll be more like $1.25 an hour. Come on, Deni. This is right up your alley. You love the excitement of this kind of thing. You'll know everything before anyone else does. And you'll be helping your country."

He knew her too well, and he was pushing the right buttons.

"Besides, it's a great résumé enhancer. A fast-track to the career of your dreams. After a job like this, you can write your ticket."

She looked around at all the activity. She would love to be a fly on the wall in that power company meeting. Her heart rate sped up at the thought of being in the government loop on matters so important to the nation. And the money—how could she turn that down?

"You're the one making hiring decisions?"

"That's right. And babe, I'm offering you the job."

She sighed. "If you quit calling me babe, I'll think about it."

He didn't let that get him down. "Think fast. I can't hold the job forever. We need someone yesterday."

She did want to take it, but first she should talk to Mark and make sure it was okay with him. Guilt surged through her at the thought of telling Harriet, her editor. What would the paper do without her?

"Let me think about it, at least for a few hours."

Craig shrugged. "Okay, but don't take long. Now for your article. What would you like to cover?"

"I was thinking I could write several articles. One on the hiring, of course. But I think our readers would really like to hear about what's involved in getting the power grid up and running. Are you going to have to rebuild the transformers?"

"Actually, no. Transformers are resilient because they're surrounded by breakers and all kinds of protective circuitry, so they probably weren't destroyed in the Pulses. It's the control circuits that have to be rebuilt."

He explained to her how things worked. She took careful notes, trying to understand so she could present it correctly in her article.

"Now do you see why I need someone to handle the PR?" he said. "It takes over an hour with each reporter, to explain to them how all this works and what we're doing to fix it. And that's just the electricity. There are a million other facets of our work that people are curious about. I don't have time to do this several times a day. And whoever takes this job is going to have to work really hard to get up to speed. We need to start now."

She was still writing, trying to get it all down before she forgot.

"Come on, Deni. Help me out. I need you here."

She stopped writing and looked up. "You know, if it weren't you asking, I'd snap this up. But I think it might be awkward working with you. I'm with Mark now, and I don't want to upset him."

"Mark." He said the name as if it were sour in his mouth. "He's a nice guy and all, but I just don't see you with him."

She breathed a laugh. "That's okay. *I* see me with him, and that's all that matters."

She saw the tension on his face as he looked beyond her. He swallowed hard. "Besides, if he cares for you, he'll want you to have this opportunity. Anyone would jump at it."

That was true. Still, she'd rather not commit to anything without consulting him first.

Then again, he hadn't consulted her when he'd taken the job at the sheriff's department. In fact, she had begged him not to do it. He'd ignored her wishes.

It had been the right thing, she saw now. The county needed him. But at the time it had felt like a betrayal. Putting himself in harm's way had frightened her to death.

Craig's eyes were still on her, waiting.

"I'll probably take it, Craig. I know it's a good opportunity, and I think I'd love it. But if I do, I need some assurances from you that it'll be just business. Strictly professional. I wouldn't be coming here for you. I'm coming *in spite* of you."

He set his hand over his heart. "You really know how to hurt a guy, don't you?"

She felt bad about that look in his eyes. "I'm not trying to hurt you, Craig. Really, I'm not."

He dropped his hands. "Don't worry about it. Just accept the job. I'll keep the 'babes' to myself, and I'll treat you like a colleague instead of the woman I'm desperately in love with."

If that was any indication of how things would be, they weren't getting off to a very good start. But she couldn't help smiling. "All right," she said. "When do you want me to start?"

thirty-two

KAY BALANCED FOUR GALLONS OF COOKING OIL — TWO ON each side — on her bicycle. The weight in her baskets was almost too much for her thin tires, but she hadn't wanted to buy less for fear that they'd run out.

The oil had become her secret weapon for keeping her family fed.

When the Pulses had first begun, she'd been worried about their nutrition. But over the winter months, as food had gotten more and more scarce, she'd realized her children were getting frighteningly skinny. Mrs. Keegon, one of her elderly neighbors in Oak Hollow, had suggested that she begin cooking more things in oil to boost their calorie intake. It had kept her family from looking like skeletons and provided the energy they needed to get all their hard work done. The extra oil had little nutritional value, but when you were trying to survive, good nutrition was low on the priority list. Keeping those hunger pangs at bay and giving her family fuel for energy was the number-one food priority.

Now that the winter months had passed, more produce was available at the stands along the roads. But those stands often ran out before she could get there. Since the banks had opened, she'd expected to buy more food. But the food supplies in the stores and stands had run out quickly, so she'd had to keep resorting to her tricks.

She had never worked so hard in her life.

Grocery stores hadn't been open in months, but produce stands were. She'd learned the value of buying bushels of field corn, which was used to feed horses. With the help of her elderly friends, she learned to use the corn to make hot cereal, corn patties, corn tortillas, hominy, dumplings, and corn bread. The queen of the microwave, who had ordered takeout more than she'd cooked in the pre-outage days, had finally learned to feed her family for pennies a day. She'd even made a little money selling the bread she baked.

She could also make tortillas with flour, water, and oil. It was cheap, and once she'd figured out how to fry food over the barbecue pit, it had been quick and easy, too. There had even been days when she'd gotten her boys to drink a tablespoon of cooking oil in warm water. That had boosted their calorie intake even more, enabling them to work without getting weak.

But she kept the calorie thing to herself. Her girls wouldn't like it, even though their clothes were so baggy that they hung off them. Hers were baggy too. Funny how she'd done cardio workouts three times a week before the Pulses, just to stay a size ten. Now she was probably a two, but she didn't like it. Her bony look made her face more wrinkled. She needed a little more padding to smooth the wrinkles out. Kay didn't mind looking forty-six, but she didn't want to look a day over it.

She heard a car behind her and looked over her shoulder. Mark honked his patrol car's horn and slowed beside her. "Hop in," he said. "I'll take you home."

Thankful, she got off her bike. Mark got out and loaded it on the bike rack at the back of his car. They'd outfitted all of the patrol cars with them, since the people they arrested often had bikes. They were too valuable to leave sitting somewhere. "Cooking oil, huh?"

"Yep. They were running out fast, so I grabbed all I could carry."

He secured the bike and opened the passenger door. "Sorry my hunting's been off lately and I haven't been able to bring you food. I haven't had much time."

She got in. "Oh, Mark. It's not your job to feed us."

"No, but I like to."

She watched him walk around the car and get in. "So how are you holding up with Craig here?" she asked.

He laughed. "I was going to ask you the same thing."

"You first."

He shrugged. "I'm fine. Don't like it one little bit, but what can you do?"

"I know. You still have that ring?"

He reached into his pocket and pulled it out. She took it and smiled at the quality of the stone. Deni was going to love it.

"You still going to give it to her?"

"Sometime. But not now."

"Why not?"

"Because if she's inclined to say yes, I don't want her to have to censor her excitement out of sensitivity for Craig's feelings."

Kay handed him the ring, watched him slide it back in his pocket. "Admit it, Mark. You'd love to rub his nose in it, wouldn't you?"

He turned into the neighborhood. "Maybe a little. But not enough to do it."

They saw Deni in the garage. She turned and waved.

Mark pulled into the driveway. The soft smile on his face as he looked at Deni melted Kay's heart. "Thanks for the ride, Mark. And listen—"

He looked at her.

"Don't wait too long. Craig's going to be here for a while. I don't want him to get a foothold."

"Has he got any plans to move yet?"

"No, but I'm going to go over to Eloise's tonight or tomorrow and start cleaning it up. It's just that his work is so important, and he doesn't have time to think about a place to live. We kind of feel like putting him up is something we can do for the recovery effort."

Mark drew in a long breath. "It won't hurt the guy to take his suitcase across the street. I'll help him."

Kay smiled. "I know, and we'll bring up the subject soon."

"Meanwhile, he's going to park himself here until somebody kicks him out, just so he can be close to Deni."

"Well, you just do what you can."

Deni came to the car, mirroring Mark's smile. Leaning down to Mark's window, she looked across the seat. "Mom, are you trying to steal my boyfriend?"

It was clear that Mark felt her pleasure. Kay got out of the car, wishing he would give Deni the ring.

thirty-three

BETH CHANGED HER DELIVERY ROUTE SO THAT THE NEWS-
paper box in Magnolia Park was the last one she delivered
each day. It put her there at about three o'clock, after which
she sat on the swing and stared at the Tomlin house, hoping for another glimpse of the widow who didn't know her
husband was dead. Her need to see Blake Tomlin's wife and
son outweighed her fear of the killer seeing her. Yesterday
she'd gotten a glimpse of them, along with an older couple
who looked like they might be his parents. They'd probably
come to town to search for their son.

The park was more crowded today than usual. Beth
watched the house, wondering how the Tomlins could stand
to be cooped up on a day like this, the curtains closed, and
no windows open. It must be hot in there, not to mention
dark.

Two women sat on a bench behind her, talking quietly
as their children played. On the breeze, their voices carried
farther than they knew.

"Blake wouldn't just take off like that."

Beth caught her breath and glanced behind her. Blake's
wife—the same woman she'd been watching from a distance—sat there with a friend. Beth hadn't noticed her
before because today the woman's big hair was tied up in
a ponytail. Beth's heart kicked through her chest wall. She
stopped swinging and listened.

"Maybe you're wrong," the friend said.

Beth twisted her swing to look at the woman. She was prettier up close than she'd been from a distance. Her gaze drifted to the toddler who sat in the sandbox only a few feet away from her, hammering a mound of sand with a shovel.

"Danny misses him so much," the woman said. "He keeps watching out the window for him."

"I'm sure he's all right. The jerk probably just got the money and ran with it."

Beth felt horrible for Blake's wife. Some friend.

"That's not true," the wife said. "Why do you say things like that?"

"Because I know him. I'm just saying that he's probably all right. Alive somewhere. Money does funny things to people. I knew a family once where a guy had a double life. A whole different family in another state. He traveled all the time."

"He does not have another family!" The woman spat out the words, and Beth stole a look at her again. Her face was red hot. "I need your support, Sharon. Not speculation about what a jerk my husband is. I'm telling you, something happened to him, and the police won't do anything."

"I'm sorry. I didn't mean to upset you. I was just trying to give you hope that he's all right."

He's not all right, Beth wanted to blurt. *He's dead. A man made him kneel and shot him through the back of his head, all for money.*

Tears sprang to her eyes, but she blinked them back. She watched the angry young mother get up and go to the sandbox. Pulling the little boy out, she said, "Come on, sweetie, we're going home."

For a moment, Beth wanted to cross the grass and tell everything, to undo the damage the other woman had done. But would telling Mrs. Tomlin that her husband had been murdered really make her feel better?

"Beth, is that you?"

Beth's heart jolted, and she swung back around. Jimmy Scarbrough had ridden up and balanced his bike with a foot. "Jimmy!"

He gaped at her. "Did you cut your hair?"

She looked back over her shoulder at Tomlin's wife. She had turned back and was looking at Beth. Great.

Beth went to pick up her bike and got back on it.

"Beth?"

She shot Jimmy an angry look. "*What?*"

"Why did you cut your hair all off? You look like a boy!"

She felt like crying. "I wanted to, okay? I don't have to ask anybody's permission to cut my hair if I want to."

She saw the hurt shock registering on Jimmy's face. She had never spoken to him that way. "Ex-*cuuse* me," he said.

She felt bad then. "I'm sorry. I didn't mean to jump down your throat."

He came closer. "I was looking for you. I followed your route."

There was a time when that would have thrilled her, but now she had other things on her mind.

"Did I make you cry?" Jimmy asked.

Beth shook her head and glanced back at the woman. She was holding her baby now.

"No, I'm not crying. I have to go." She took off on her bike, past a wagon being pulled by two horses, dodging a pile another horse had left in the road.

Jimmy would probably never speak to her again. Why would he want to, with her hair looking like this?

"Beth, wait up!"

She felt the tears falling down her face and quickly wiped them away. She pulled into an abandoned convenience store parking lot and balanced at the curb. Jimmy pulled to a halt beside her.

"I really didn't mean to hurt your feelings. I was just surprised. It looks cute, though. I like it."

Those tears rushed faster and her face twisted. "No, you don't."

"I do. Come on, what's wrong?"

She glanced back toward the park, hiccuping a sob. "I just ... have a lot going on."

"You want to talk about it?"

"No," she said. "I can't. If I do, somebody could really get hurt."

His face changed. "Wow."

She sat there blubbering like an idiot, wondering why she had even said such a thing. It was the most she'd told anyone.

But she needed to talk to someone. Could she trust him? He was the former sheriff's son, after all. He'd seen and heard a lot, and he was no stranger to violence. His father was still recovering from a gunshot wound that had almost killed him.

Jimmy got off his bike and laid it on the ground. He came and took her hand. "Sit down and talk to me."

She set the kickstand on her bike and let him lead her to the curb. They both sat down on the grass. She was still crying, so she hugged her knees and dropped her face into the circle of her arms.

He touched her back, patting her. "Beth, are you in some kind of trouble?"

She nodded. "I can't talk about it."

"Tell me," he said. "It can't be that bad. What did you do?"

The question threw her. "I didn't do anything."

"Then why are you in trouble?"

"Somebody else did something."

His eyebrows lifted. "Is it that guy who's at your house?"

Beth looked up at him. "Craig? How do you know about him?"

"Because I rode by your house a couple of days ago and saw his car. I saw Cher and asked her who it was. Has he hurt you?"

"No, not Craig. It's not him."

Jimmy knelt next to her, his gaze boring into her. "Then who?"

She wanted to tell him. She needed to talk it out, but if she told him what had really happened, he was bound to tell his father. Then *his* father would tell *her* father, then Sheriff Wheaton, and before she knew it the killer would know.

She dropped her face against her knees, unable to stop her tears. "It's that ... that lady back at the park."

"What lady?"

"That lady whose husband disappeared. I saw his missing person sign on the message board. I feel so bad for her."

He just stared at her. "That's it? You're upset about a woman whose husband left her?"

She knew it didn't make sense. "They have a little boy. He's like two years old."

"Do you know them?"

"No. I just see them sometimes in their driveway. They live across from the park."

"Oh. I see."

But he didn't see. He didn't see at all. She drew in a deep breath, knowing she'd said too much already. "I have to go home. My parents are gonna be worried."

He just sat there, watching her with a look of confusion. She imagined that he was thinking how weird and complicated girls were, that they would lose it over the pain of someone they didn't even know.

"I'm sorry about the lady," he said.

She nodded. "Me too." She got up and picked up her bike.

"Are you gonna be okay? You want me to ride home with you?"

"Yes," she said quickly. She would feel safer if someone was with her. "Would you?"

"Sure. I finished my paper route, so I'm good to go." He got on his bike and pulled out next to her. "So what do you think about the Pulses being over? I heard they were already trying to get the power back on."

Beth just nodded as he gushed about the future. She feared she wouldn't be here to see it.

thirty-four

"YOU SAID YOU WERE OKAY WITH ME TAKING THAT JOB."

It was true, Mark thought. When Deni had come to him all wide-eyed about the job, he had swallowed his objections and tried not to shoot her down. What did his opinions matter, anyway? It was already a done deal.

He watched her quietly now as she rolled a page into her typewriter, hoping that burning feeling in his stomach didn't translate to his face.

"But you're not, are you? You're not okay with it." She set her elbows on the desk and gave him her undivided attention. "Can we talk about this?"

"What's there to talk about? You did the right thing. I'd try to get hired myself if I wasn't already committed to the sheriff's department."

"I don't want you to worry about Craig. He promised it would be strictly business."

He let out a bitter laugh. "You know he lied." He dropped into a chair across from her dad's desk and put his feet up on the ottoman. He hoped he looked relaxed, even if every muscle in his body was rigid.

"Even if he did lie, it won't matter."

"You sure? He's pretty important. Power can be seductive."

"You have more power over me than he does. Mark, you have to trust me."

He did trust her. He trusted Craig too—to do everything in his power to win her back. Part of him wanted to tell her not to take the job. She might even listen and stay at the newspaper. But then what?

He couldn't hold her back. This was a great career opportunity, and why shouldn't she have it? If Craig weren't the boss, Mark would be rooting for her to take it. No, Mark never wanted to be the one who stood in the way of Deni's dreams. He just wished Craig weren't the one making them come true.

They heard hurried footsteps on the hardwood floor in the hallway, and Chris appeared in the doorway. "Oh, there you are." She was out of breath. "Deni, you've got to help me. The party starts in three hours and I can't get it all together!"

Deni got up. "But I have three stories to write, and I was hoping to wash up and change clothes."

"Please, Deni. You can't let me embarrass myself this way. You too, Mark. I need you both!"

Mark loved seeing Chris in a tizzy. It was quite amusing. "I can't help right now, Chris. I just came by here on a break. I have to get back to work."

She wadded the roots of her hair. "You're not going to ditch the party, are you, Mark? What if nobody comes? What if I'm left with a ton of apple hors d'oeuvres and candles galore, and I'm sitting there all by myself?"

"Don't worry, I'm coming," Mark said. "I'm working till seven."

"But it *starts* at seven!"

"I'll be there," he said.

Deni laughed and put her arm around her friend. "It's going to be fine. Everybody's talking about it."

Chris looked at her. "Really?"

"Yes, really. And I'll come over and help now, then I can come home to change after you've gotten a grip. I'll just stay up all night writing those stories, but don't worry about it."

"Thank you!" She grabbed Deni's hand and pulled her to the door.

Mark got up and followed them out. "Deni, I'll pick you up at seven."

She shook her head. "Don't worry about picking me up. I'll go a little early and meet you there." Pulling away from Chris, she stood on her toes and kissed him. "See you then. Be careful."

He couldn't help laughing at the two of them as he went back to his car.

thirty-five

BETH'S BEST FRIEND CHER WAS WAITING IN THE BRANNINGS' garage when she got home from delivering her papers. Beth's stomach tightened as she pulled in. She didn't want to talk, or something might slip out. She'd told Jimmy way too much already.

Cher sat cross-legged on the concrete, playing with a kitten that looked only a few weeks old. "Isn't she cute? I named her Freckles. She was from the litter that the Allens' cat had. My mom said I could keep her."

Beth got off her bike and sat down next to Cher. She picked up the gray tabby and looked her in the face, but the cat whined and scratched her, trying to get down. She thrust her back at Cher.

"You could get one if you wanted. They have three that haven't been taken."

"We have enough animals," she said.

"Rabbits and chickens don't count. They're for food."

"I don't know what we'd feed a cat. Anyway, I don't want one."

Cher let the kitten go and watched it romp across the garage. "Guess who I saw yesterday?"

Beth wasn't interested. She wanted to go in and lie down. "Who?"

"Jimmy. He rides by your house almost every day, like he's trying to get a glimpse. Does he ever stop?"

Beth shrugged. "Not really. But I did see him today."

"He really likes you. Aren't you excited?"

"He's okay." A man on a bike rode by and Beth's eyes followed him. It was just Jack Pratt's dad.

"Okay? Beth, what is *wrong* with you?"

She wanted to close the garage, to keep anyone riding by from seeing her. What if the killer came by and she was sitting here? "I have to go in," she said.

Cher got up and chased down her kitten. "You don't want to hang out?"

"Not really. I don't feel good."

"Are you sick?"

Irritated, Beth started for the door. "Maybe. I don't know. See you later, okay?"

Cher looked hurt again. She picked up her kitten and held it against her chest. "All right, I'll go. Come by if you want to hang out."

"I will." Beth opened the door and stepped inside.

"Oh, one more thing."

Beth turned back. "What?"

"There was this man looking for you."

Beth's lungs seemed to close, trapping her air. She stepped back into the garage. "What man?"

"Some man who had your necklace. You know, the cross one?"

Beth's hand came up to her throat. It was *him*. The chain had broken. Her chest hurt. She thought she might faint. "Did you tell him where I live?"

"I didn't see him," Cher said. "My dad and brother were at the well Sunday when he stopped and asked. My dad said he'd give it to you, but the man didn't trust him."

Beth sucked in air, unable to let it out. Panicked, she ran to close the garage.

"What are you doing? I was about to leave."

Beth slid the metal door to the ground with a crash. "Go through the house." Darkness was thick between them. Beth opened the door and stepped into the kitchen. "What did they tell him?"

"Who?"

"*The man!*" Beth began to cry. "What did your dad tell the man?"

"I'm not sure. He didn't give him your address, I know that. Beth, what's wrong?"

"I don't like people talking about me." She couldn't breathe out and began to get dizzy.

"Are you hyperactivating or something?"

Beth grabbed the counter, fearing she would fall.

Cher ran around it and grabbed a paper sack full of nails. She dumped it out and handed it to Beth. "Here, breathe into this."

Beth took the bag and breathed, blowing it up, sucking it back in … out … in …

She could breathe better now. Sweating, she pulled the bag down. "Did they give him … my last name?"

"Maybe," Cher said. "He can probably look it up in the phone book and find the address. Don't worry, I'm sure you'll get your necklace back."

She heard her mother coming in the back door. "Cher! It's good to see you, honey."

Cher turned to her with concern. "I'm glad you're here. Beth was having trouble breathing."

Her mother gasped, "Beth, are you okay?"

She was still breathing hard.

"I gave her that bag to breathe into."

"She was hyperventilating?"

Now her mother was all concerned, and Beth didn't want anyone hovering over her right now. She needed to lie down.

"Honey, what caused this?"

"Nothing." Cher was going to tell her mother about the man who was looking for her. Her mom would tell her father who would tell the sheriff, and then what? Her mind raced for a story. "I just … realized I lost my necklace. The cross."

"Honey, that's okay. It's no big deal."

Cher opened her mouth to speak. Beth grabbed Cher's hand, almost making her drop the kitten. "Cher has to go, don't you, Cher?"

Cher gaped at her, baffled. Still, she played along. "Uh, yeah. I told my mom I'd come right home."

Beth led her to the door, opened it, and waited for her to leave.

"You're acting crazy," Cher whispered harshly. "What is wrong with you?"

"I told you, I'm sick." As Cher stepped out onto the porch, Beth closed the door. She waved at Cher through the glass and watched her huff away.

Her mother came up behind her.

"Beth, honey, tell me what's going on."

"I just got hot," she said. "I need to lie down." With that, she ran up the stairs.

thirty-six

WHEN SHE WAS SURE THAT CHRIS HAD EVERYTHING UNDER control, Deni hurried back home to get ready for her friend's party. It had been warm today, and since she'd ridden all over town on her bike, she needed a bath. What she wouldn't give for hot running water.

Maybe her work with Craig would make that happen faster.

She did her best to clean up with cold well water.

She put her hair in a towel, then went to her room to finish cleaning up. She wanted to look nice tonight, and she hoped her hair would dry fast enough.

She dressed in a blouse she hadn't worn much in the past year, so it still looked fresh and clean. And she pulled on a pair of Beth's old jeans. They were too big for her thirteen-year-old sister now, but they fit Deni rather nicely. They were too short, but she folded them up, making them into capris. A girl did what a girl had to do.

Finally, a pair of pants that didn't have to be belted or safety-pinned to keep them from falling down. She stood in front of the mirror, feeling emaciated. She'd never imagined she'd think that of herself. But the winter had been tough, and she'd come out of it with an angular, anorexic body. In her early college years, she had worked hard for a skeletal body. Now food rationing had done the job that starving herself had failed to do. How stupid was that? Striving to look like you were starving to death? Why would anyone with plenty of food deny their hunger pangs?

That was just one of the things the Pulses had clarified for her.

She heard Craig's voice downstairs, and she stepped out into the hall as he came up. He looked tired and distracted. "Hey, are you coming to the party?"

He smiled at the sight of her. "What party?"

"Chris's party, remember?"

He hit his forehead. "Oh, yeah. I've been so busy, I forgot. Yeah, I'll come for a little while, but then I have to go back to the office. I was just taking a break."

"I was about to leave." She had run out of lip gloss, so she took some Vaseline and slicked it on her lips. It would have to do.

He leaned in the bathroom doorway, watching her. The intimacy in that struck her, and she turned away from the mirror.

"You look pretty," he said.

"Thank you." She moved to the door, but he didn't step out of the way. She looked up at him. "I ... need to get to my purse."

Finally, he moved aside. "Wait a minute and I'll come with you."

She went into her bedroom and stared down at her purse, wondering if she should tell him she'd rather go without him. The last thing she wanted was for anyone to think she was his date. But since they were both going to the same place, it would be absurd to make him wait ten minutes and walk there alone.

She waited for him downstairs, and in a few minutes he was ready. "Wanna take my car?"

She glanced at it as they stepped outside. "I thought you were supposed to conserve gas."

"I am, but it's not that far."

"We can walk."

"Sure? It's been a long time since you've ridden in one."

"Not really. Mark drives a patrol car. He gives me rides sometimes."

He smirked. "Good ole Mark."

She breathed a laugh.

"Are you ready to get started Monday?" he asked as they walked.

"More than ready. I can't wait. But I felt bad when I told my editor. She really depends a lot on me."

"Then she should pay you better."

"She pays me what she can afford."

"Then she can't afford *you*."

Deni looked up at him. "The job wasn't about money, you know. I loved what I was doing. I did it for free before she hired me."

"Yeah, but labors of love don't help you climb the employment ladder. You need some résumé enhancers. Some real work with real pay."

She didn't like the mercenary way that sounded, but she let it go. "So how are things going? Made any progress?"

"We're still hiring, trying to build our workforce so we can get the circuits repaired in the power substations. We've made some progress toward getting the refineries powered. I'm guessing some of them will have electricity in the next few days, if everything stays on schedule."

"And if they work, then we'll be able to get fuel?"

"That's right. It's the domino effect. You can't do one thing without the other."

Her excitement waxed again. She would be in on all of this. Participating in the recovery. Making things happen.

Chris's front door was wide open, and Deni heard laughter and voices inside. She led Craig in, smiling at the transformation the house had undergone in just the last hour. It glowed with candle-light, and Chris greeted everyone at the door. Her blonde curls were loosely pulled into a striking updo that gave her a look of sophistication and elegance. She looked polished and lovely. Deni was impressed.

As they walked into the living room, she felt Craig's proprietary hand on her back. She tried to walk faster, to put some distance between them, but he kept pace. She looked around, hoping Mark was there so she could quickly put to rest any appearance that she was with Craig. But Mark hadn't yet arrived.

Jeff, Deni's brother, was already there, playing guitar with his friend Zach, providing a nice musical ambience.

People stood in clusters, talking and laughing. Deni saw Amber, her next-door neighbor. She sometimes forgot that Amber wasn't much older than she. Raising three preschoolers alone made her seem so much older. She sat on a barstool talking to Will Truman and George Mason, two of the town's paramedics. Will had a girl with him that Deni didn't recognize, but George had his eyes on Chris as she flitted around greeting her guests.

Deni decided to see what she could do to help that along. She got a cup of water and held it like a cocktail as she joined them. "You guys clean up nice. Amber, I love your blouse."

Amber looked down at herself, as if she couldn't believe someone would compliment her. She was beautiful when she fixed herself up, but she still had that sad glint to her eyes that reminded Deni she wasn't finished grieving over her marriage.

"This is great, isn't it? Doesn't Chris look beautiful?"

George grinned. "Does she? I hadn't noticed."

"Liar," Will said. "You can't keep your eyes off her."

"If you're interested," Deni said, "you'd better snap her up. There are other eligible bachelors here."

Amber bit into an apple slice. "Are you back with that guy?"

Deni glanced back at Craig. Chris was introducing him around as though he were a celebrity. "No, I'm still with Mark. Craig's just a friend now."

"Must be weird having him staying with you when you two were engaged."

Deni sighed and lowered her voice. "It is, frankly. But it's just temporary."

Amber sighed. "Just be careful. You don't want to choose the wrong guy and wind up like me."

Deni winced. "Have you heard from Mike since the banks opened?"

"Oh, yeah," she said. "He served me with divorce papers. He's trying to get the courts on his side about the money. But Brad hooked me up with a pro bono attorney, so we'll make sure they know about his girlfriend—and the abandonment." Her eyes welled as she looked down at her glass. "Thing is, I really don't want a divorce."

"I know."

"But what can you do, if they just leave?" Amber drew in a breath and dabbed at her eyes. Looking through the crowd, she nodded toward Derek and Cathy Morton. "Hope someone can save *that* marriage."

Deni's gaze drifted through the crowd to Derek Morton, the doctor who lived in the neighborhood, and his wife Cathy. Cathy looked flashy in a gold lamé blouse. Deni had rarely seen her without her baby since it was born seven months before, but her eyes darted to and fro as if trying to catch another woman meeting Derek's eyes. The problem was, his eyes did rove. Hopefully no one here would return his interest.

Deni heard a knock at the door and turned to see Mark coming in. Her heart fluttered at the sight of him in a pair of jeans and a black T-shirt with a picture of a globe on it and an arrow that said, "You are here"—a stark contrast to the khakis and button-down dress shirt Craig wore. A smile lifted her face as she waited for him to meet her eyes.

Finally, they connected. He winked, and she went toward him, forgetting all about Craig. She took his hand and reached up to kiss him, and saw the pleasure in his eyes. "Where've you been? I thought you'd never get here."

"Hey, I had to make my entrance." He glanced across and found Craig, surrounded by people bending his ear about the recovery. "Seriously, I didn't want to come in uniform, so I went home to change." He leaned down to her ear and said, "What's with you coming with Craig? My mother said she saw you walking over."

"He was there and I was there, and we were coming at the same time. But don't worry. I'm with you. I'll make sure everyone knows it."

He checked out her face, and she hoped he saw the sincerity there. He was tanned dark, and his black hair was a little shaggier than normal. She loved it like that.

"You look great," he whispered against her hair. "Smell good, too."

The hairs on her neck rose. "Want a water cocktail?" she asked.

He grinned. "Make it a double."

"*And* apple hors d'oeuvres, which I helped make."

"And very skillfully from what I can see."

She took his hand and led him to the kitchen.

LATER THAT NIGHT, DENI MANAGED TO PULL MARK AWAY FROM THE others, and they sat outside on a bench at the back of the yard—now a vegetable garden. It wasn't as pretty as it had been in the pre-outage days, but it was quiet and more private than the noisy house.

"Finally alone," he said, sliding his arm around her and stroking her hair. "I was beginning to lose hope that would ever happen again."

"Nothing's changed."

"Everything's changed," he said. "Mr. Government Official rides back into town, bent on taking you back, and moves into your house."

"He really isn't there much. My mom has started cleaning up Eloise's house for him. He'll move soon."

"Won't happen."

Deni frowned. "Why not?"

"Because where he is, he has immediate access to you at all times, he can watch what you're doing, and he can undermine our relationship."

She sighed. "Mark, he has a lot more on his mind than me. Hey, you never told me how your Bible study with him went."

He breathed a laugh. "It was more like a chess match, if you want to know the truth."

"Chess? What do you mean? Did you two butt heads over the Bible?"

"No, we butted heads over you. He accused me of asking him to do this Bible study just to make him look bad to you."

She tilted her head. "*Is* that the reason?"

"No. I honestly thought it would be the right thing to do. But frankly, I don't like the idea of you—" He raised his fingers in air quotes—"*helping* him go over the book of John. I didn't intend for this to be more of a bonding time for you two."

"Mark, what would you have expected me to do? He was studying the Bible and he didn't understand it. This was all your idea, you know."

"I know. I've been kicking myself ever since."

"And here I thought you really wanted to disciple him."

"Oh, he doesn't need discipling," Mark said. "That would make me superior, and he can't let that happen."

"So you're not meeting again?"

"Next week."

She couldn't help laughing. "I don't get you two. If you hate each other, why are you doing it again?"

"We don't hate each other, Deni. We're just very competitive about you. The stakes are very high."

On some absurd level, she thought that was sweet. "Well, you don't have to be. I didn't pull *him* away from the party, did I? I've been missing you like crazy. I haven't seen enough of you lately."

"You just saw me a few hours ago."

"For half an hour." She leaned into him. "Not enough."

He wet his lips and looked down at her, and she saw the twinkle in his eyes, as if her words had done him good. She slid her hand down his face, and he took it and kissed her fingertips. "You give me goose bumps," he said.

His words delighted her. A soft breeze whispered through the leaves, and from the house she could hear the soft thrum of guitar chords. She could sit here like this for hours.

He kissed her, and she forgot about Craig and the infrastructure of the country, the Pulses, and the struggles. Instead she savored the feeling of perfect security, certain love, and the joy of Mark's arms around her.

WHEN THEY WENT BACK IN, THE DYNAMIC OF THE PARTY HAD changed. Craig sat in the easy chair usually occupied by Chris's father, and all attention was turned on him.

Chris sat on the floor at his feet, looking up at him with rapt attention.

"The third-world countries will probably have telephone service before we will," Craig was saying. "They used to get our outdated technology, so a lot of them are still using mechanical switches. The Pulses didn't affect those. Most of ours were converted to solid-state switches years ago. Those were all fried."

"What about the small towns that haven't been updated?" Max Lamb asked. "Some of them still have mechanical switches."

"Right," Craig said. "Those may actually have local phone service before we do here."

"What about long-distance service? I'd love to call my parents in Tuscaloosa," Amber said.

"I'm afraid long distance is going to take much longer than local service. And if any of you have those antique hand-cranked phones in your attic somewhere, you might want to get them down. Those will work well with a switchboard, and you'll have phone service faster. And rotary phones will be back faster than push-button phones."

"How do you keep up with all this?" Cathy Morton asked.

"With lots of help," he said. "No kidding. We have to hire thousands of people."

"Are you hiring nurses?" Chris teased.

"You laugh," he said. "But I'll need liaisons with the hospitals when we get to that point."

"We already have physical plant directors for that sort of thing," she said. "I would think you'd be working more with them. Not nurses."

"Once our workforce is up and running, we'll need an infirmary. Seriously, stop by and talk to us."

Chris shrugged. "I don't know. I think I'm probably best used where I am."

Deni was proud of her for not being seduced by Craig's sales pitch—even though Deni had been herself. She noticed a look pass between Chris and George Mason. The paramedic seemed to feel the same way. They were both called to do what they did, and they were sorely needed.

"So you don't want to get on the ground floor of serving your country in such an important way?" Craig pressed.

Chris had a playful look on her face as she looked up at him. "I am serving my country. I've been serving them throughout the whole thing."

"Well, yeah. But they don't pay you enough."

"Hey," she said, getting to her feet. "Last week, I got paid with four jars of honey. The week before, I brought home a goat. So I don't know what you're talking about, mister. I'm doing just fine."

Everyone laughed, and Chris changed the subject. "Anybody want pie?"

thirty-seven

Deni was initiated into the recovery team on FEMA Disbursement Day, after several days of preparation and training. She'd been given guidelines on what kinds of people they were looking to hire at that event, and she was among the staff that would take applications. Those with experience could be hired on the spot—others would need interviews. Coordinating the starting dates was one of her jobs. It would be impossible to process a thousand new employees on the same day, so the starting dates had to be staggered to best accommodate the needs of the teams.

The work leading up to the event was grueling, but she loved every minute of it. Her time with Mark had been severely curtailed, but she hoped that after the Disbursement and the initial rush of applicants, things would settle down. She was with Craig constantly, however, and was impressed with how competent he was at multitasking. His law school skills gave him the ability to take in a lot of information in a short amount of time and retain all of it.

Despite the women who seemed to flock there looking for jobs in the offices or the field, Craig still seemed to have eyes only for her. She had to hand it to him. He'd come a long way from the detached fiancé who hadn't even tried to contact her in the first months of the Pulses.

The morning of the FEMA Disbursement, Deni's wind-up alarm clock went off at three a.m. She'd worked until eleven the night before, getting the high school football field ready for the event. Now she had to get there early enough to beat the crowds and get her teams in place.

She heard Craig moving around in Beth's room as she got up. Where did he get his stamina? She was exhausted after only a week on the job.

She glanced back at her bed, hoping the clock hadn't awakened Beth. But the bed was empty.

She struck a match and lit the oil lamp. As shadows climbed the walls, she saw her sister sitting on the window seat in her dormer.

"Beth, what are you doing up so early?"

Beth's short hair had a cowlick in the back. "I couldn't sleep."

"Why not? I'd kill for another couple of hours."

Beth just stared into the night. "I was just thinking about the Disbursement."

"What about it?"

"I was wondering if Mom and Dad would let me stay home. I don't want to go."

Deni opened her closet door and started dressing. "You have to go, or you don't get your twenty-five dollars."

"But we just got all that money from the bank. Maybe we could do without it."

Deni pulled on the red polo shirt that said "Alabama Recovery Team" on the front and back. "Beth, that's a lot of money for the family, and you have to be there to get it. Why don't you want to go?"

"Because I hate crowds."

Deni shot her a look. "You've never complained about going before. You usually like all the drama."

"Not now. I just want to stay home. Can't you get my money for me? You work for the government now."

"No, I can't. I don't have access to the money." She sat down on the bed and pulled on her socks and sneakers. "You'll just have to buck up. They're going to make you go."

She went into the bathroom and washed her face, then brushed her teeth and hair. Then she put on the white sun visor she'd bought in Florida on her high school senior trip. She wasn't normally the visor type, but she hoped it would keep her from getting too sun-burned. She'd run out of sunscreen months ago.

When she came out, she saw that Craig was waiting for her. "Your chariot awaits, Madame."

She smiled and followed him to the car, glad she wouldn't have to ride her bike in the dark.

thirty-eight

As chaotic as each of the FEMA Disbursements had been, Beth thought today's was the worst yet. The new line for job applicants had complicated things, giving less room for the disbursement lines. Everything moved slower.

And to keep people from attacking the workers in an attempt to steal the cash, they'd put the tables up on raised platforms, with armed National Guardsmen around them. Only the families being served at each spot were allowed on the platform, so it kept a little more order.

She had worn her brother's T-shirt and a pair of baggy gym shorts, hoping she'd look like a boy. She hoped her disguise and sunglasses would keep the killer from spotting her. She stood in line now, perspiration dripping down her face in the hot June sun.

Beth scanned the crowd, looking for the face of the double murderer who'd changed her life. If he was from Crockett, he would be here today, to pick up his money. She knew he liked cash.

She sought out goatees and gray, beady eyes, heavy men shaped the same as the killer. Maybe he was lurking somewhere, waiting to steal someone else's money. He could even be waiting behind the Cracker Barrel again.

Guilt surged through her. Since she hadn't reported him for what he'd done, he was free to do it to someone else. But what was she to do? No doubt he knew her name and address by now. He could come at any time. He was probably just waiting to see if she told anyone.

The only reason she was still alive was that she'd kept her mouth shut.

"Are you okay, sweetie?"

Beth looked up at her mom and nodded.

"You're shaking. Why?"

Beth hadn't realized it. "Because it's hot."

"You don't usually shiver when you're hot."

She shrugged and leaned to look around her. Last night she'd dreamed that he had caught her, and she couldn't scream. Would she be able to scream now?

She stayed at the center of her family, hidden by the people pressed in around her. It was stifling, but it was safe. Maybe she could get through the day without him seeing her.

Finally, Beth and her mother and brothers made it to the front of the line, and Deni and her father took a break from their posts and joined the family to collect their own disbursements. There were only three families in front of them, and the Brannings were next to step up onto the platform. As they moved closer to the steps, Beth felt more vulnerable.

Beth followed her family up the stairs. She felt exposed, put on display, and it seemed as if the thousands of people in line were focused on her. As she got to the top of the platform, she stepped in front of her father and peered off to the side, out over the sweating crowd.

She saw a man with a goatee, a black baseball cap turned backward on his head. Though she couldn't see his eyes, he was the same weight and height as the killer.

Terror shot through her.

She leaped off the stage and ran through the crowd. Behind her, she heard her mother calling, "Beth? Where are you going?"

No, Mom, don't call my name!

"Beth!"

She bent low and ducked between legs and arms, worming her way to the other side of the crowd. Finally, she broke free near the bleachers of the football field, and ducked between two of the steps. Coming out behind the bleachers, she blasted toward the trees.

Hiding behind an oak, she looked back, breathless. No one was following.

Maybe it wasn't even him.

But what if it was? She had to get out of there.

Sweat burned her eyes and soaked her shirt. Her lungs filled like balloons, trapping air.

She spun and ran through a neighborhood, cutting through the yards. She could work her way home through the back streets.

She ran as fast as she could the five miles home, praying the killer wouldn't come.

thirty-nine

WHAT HAD GOTTEN INTO HER?

Kay stood at the edge of the platform, trying to see which way Beth had gone. "Doug, I have to go after her! Something's wrong!"

Already she had lost her in the crowd.

"We can't get out of line, Mom," Jeff said. "We're all the way up here!"

Kay bent over the table. "Stamp me. He has the papers."

The woman took her time taking the papers.

"Please, I have to go after my child."

The woman sighed and stamped her hand. Kay turned and ran down the steps and burst through the people packed tightly in lines.

Maybe it was the post-traumatic stress disorder kicking in with a vengeance. Maybe Beth was flashing back to some of the other trauma.

Kay squeezed and pushed through the people, and finally made it to where they'd locked their bikes. Beth hadn't had the key to get hers unlocked, so it still stood where she'd left it.

She spun in a circle, her eyes frantically searching the crowd for Beth.

What if something had happened to her? What had prompted her to run off the platform? Where had she gone?

She pushed back through the crowd, searching, calling out, "Beth!" Running up and down the snaking line, she searched for her child.

There was no sign of her.

Finally, she saw the family coming off the platform. She rushed to her husband. "Something's happened, Doug! I can't find her!"

Doug looked back at the platform. "We'll look for her here, and you go see if she went home."

Kay nodded and sliced through the lines again. She got back to the bikes and unlocked the chain, pulled hers out, then locked the others back together. She rode as fast as she could pedal down the long country road to Oak Hollow.

She should have brought a gun, she thought as she rode. Even though she had no cash on her, riding alone and unarmed was like riding through the valley of the shadow of death, knowing that bandits and thieves waited to take what wasn't theirs. *Dear God, let Beth be safe!*

Thankfully, she didn't run into trouble. She turned into the neighborhood and made her way to their house, threw down her bike, and opened the garage door. She pulled the bike in, then hurried inside. "Beth! Are you here?"

She saw dirty footprints on the kitchen floor. They hadn't been there earlier, and they were Beth's size. She must have come home.

She went from room to room, calling for Beth. No answer. Finally, she went into Deni's bedroom and saw the dirty footsteps across her carpet. She followed them to her bed.

But Beth wasn't in it.

Slowly, she lowered to her knees.

Beth was under the bed, shivering in a ball.

"Beth, what are you doing?" She pulled Beth out. Reluctantly she came, trembling. Kay pulled her into her arms and held her tight. "What happened, honey? Did someone hurt you?"

Beth shook her head and just stared at the doorway.

forty

"WHO ARE YOU AFRAID OF?"

Beth just shook her head. "No one."

Beth kept looking at the door, so Kay took her chin in her hand and made her look into her eyes. "Beth, I can't help you if you don't tell me the truth."

"I am telling you the truth." Beth's voice wobbled.

Her denials were knives cutting into Kay's heart. "Then why are you shaking? Why were you hiding?"

"I don't know ... all those people. I felt like they were staring at me—"

No, that couldn't be it. Beth loved to have people looking at her. That's why she did the plays. "You jumped off the platform and ran five miles home. That wasn't self-consciousness, Beth, it was fear."

"I saw a puppy," Beth muttered. "I thought somebody was going to step on it, so I jumped down to help it."

A puppy? "So where is it?"

"Where is what?"

"The puppy. Where's the puppy?"

"I ... it got away after I rescued it."

"But I didn't see you rescue a puppy, Beth. I saw you take off through the crowd like you were being chased." Frustration and her own fear brought tears to her eyes, and Kay's face twisted. "Beth, please don't do this to me. I have to know the truth. You're my child. I want to help you."

That only made things worse. Beth's upper lip seemed to swell as she let out another wail. "Don't cry, Mom. Please don't cry."

"I'm worried about you!" Beth reached for her then, and Kay clung to her, feeling as if some unnamed threat—real or imaginary—was pulling her child away. How could she stop it if she couldn't make her talk? Maybe she should get tough with her. Demand that she open up. Force her to spill her secret.

But Beth looked so fragile. "I'm just jumpy, that's all," she said. "I feel like things are getting worse. Bad things keep happening."

"But good things are happening too. Why can't you see that?"

"Because the terrible things are bigger."

Spoken like a victim of post-traumatic stress disorder. Wasn't this just what Anne Latham described? The events over the last year had piled one upon the other, until Beth felt crushed beneath the memories. Maybe this was all psychological. No physical threat. No logical explanation.

Beth needed anxiety medications, antidepressants. Were those even available now?

Eventually Doug, Jeff, and Logan made it home, relieved to find that Beth was here. Her behavior had been a reason for low voices and whispers, rather than laughter and mockery from her brothers.

Kay sat on Deni's bed, holding Beth in her arms as she cried. Her mind raced for answers.

But for the life of her, she didn't know how to help her child.

forty-one

BETH DIDN'T SLEEP THAT NIGHT. SHE LAY AWAKE IN DENI'S bed, staring at the ceiling and wondering where the killer was. For all she knew, he could be out murdering others, since he'd gotten off scot-free.

She thought of that conversation she'd overheard at the park. Blake Tomlin's wife, defending her husband and marriage to an insensitive friend. She was probably up tonight, as well, wandering the house and praying that her husband would come home.

Someone had to tell her. Beth got up and went to the window, looked out into the night. There must be some way she could let the woman know without alerting the killer. If she could just get a message to her, letting her know that her husband was dead.

It wouldn't make Mrs. Tomlin feel better, but at least she'd know the truth. A woman needed to know when her husband was dead.

Beth decided to go downstairs and write a note. She could slip it in the Tomlins' mailbox tomorrow.

She went into her dad's study and lit the lamp. Pulling a piece of paper out of his desk, she began to write her note.

I saw your husband murdered the day the banks opened. A man with a goatee killed him behind Cracker Barrel. He killed another man, too. I don't know what he did with the bodies.

I didn't want you to think he ran off. I can tell from his picture he was a nice man.

She looked at her scrawl, wondering if she'd said too much. What if Mrs. Tomlin called the police, and they called the newspaper, and the letter was printed? The killer would know that she'd described him. He would come after her for sure.

No, she'd write it over and leave that part out. Carefully, she drafted it again.

It was still pretty bold, but she told herself that she had to have courage. She wadded the first one and dropped it in the wastebasket.

Terror pulsed through her in jolts of adrenaline. She prayed over the letter, that it would help the widow somehow. What was that word they used for ending things? Closure? That was what Mrs. Tomlin needed and deserved. A little closure.

Weary, she went back to bed, where she lay awake for the rest of the night.

forty-two

WORRY FOR BETH INVADED KAY'S EVERY THOUGHT THE next day. Her daughter still seemed melancholy, like the weather that had turned rainy, and she looked tired, as though she hadn't slept at all. After her morning chores, Beth left to do her paper route, and Kay went into Doug's study to pray.

She often spoke to God curled up in an easy chair in a quiet part of the house, usually after reading her Bible. The act of delving into God's Word put her in a frame of mind to go to the Lord in humility, recognizing the amazing privilege of going through the veil and straight to his throne.

There were times, though, when she got on her knees.

Today, she knelt on the floor to cry out for the protection and deliverance of her child, from whatever bondage she was in. PTSD wasn't too big for God.

She prayed for a while, pouring out her fears and worries, and when she finished, she knew she'd been heard. She got up and sat on the floor for a moment, basking in the afterglow of intense prayer.

Her eyes fell on the wadded paper in Doug's trashcan, with Beth's unique handwriting. She pulled it out and unfolded it. And as her eyes moved across the lines, her heart slipped into a mournful percussion.

*I saw your husband murdered the day the banks opened.
A man with a goatee killed him behind Cracker Barrel. He
killed another man, too. I don't know what he did with the
bodies.*

Kay let out a strangled cry and brought her hand to her mouth.
Suddenly, everything came into focus.

*I didn't want you to think he ran off. I can tell from his
picture he was a nice man.*

Kay got to her feet, staggering beneath the weight of understanding, and ran through the house. "Doug! Jeff!"

But no one was home.

She burst into the garage and grabbed her bicycle. As she
launched onto the wet street, she begged God to help her find her
child.

BETH KEPT HER FOCUS AS SHE DELIVERED THE PAPERS IN THE
rain, intent on getting to Magnolia subdivision and putting that
letter in the Tomlins' mailbox. She tried not to let her mind go
beyond that one act—to the police who would inevitably be called,
the search for the body.

Would the killer honor the fact that she still hadn't told anyone
about him? Or would he come after her with a vengeance? Surely,
word would get out that she'd exposed the murders. He would
know that she was the one.

Fear made her reconsider. No, this was stupid. If she put that
letter in the mailbox, she might as well tell her father what she'd
seen. If police were to be involved, they needed the information
that would lead them to the killer.

She finished most of her deliveries, saving the one in Magnolia
Park for last, as she'd done each day. Since it was raining, the park
was empty. She pulled her trailer onto the grass and drew it in front
of the box. Unlocking the box, she took out the papers left over
from yesterday and put a fresh stack in.

She left her bike there and went to the swings. With a clear view of the Tomlins' house, she pulled the letter out and read it again. She thought of that woman who'd sat on that bench, trying to convince her friend that her husband wasn't a louse who'd abandoned his family. She thought of Blake Tomlin's face, the stark terror as the killer held a gun to his head. The homeless man whose face she hadn't clearly seen.

No one should die without a funeral, without anyone even knowing they were gone.

She felt like a coward for not acting sooner. Even so, she still didn't have the courage. So she sat on that swing, moving back and forth, staring at the house where the young family grieved without knowing why.

forty-three

He couldn't believe his luck.

The girl he'd been looking for sat on the swing as if waiting for him, right where he'd been told she'd be around three o'clock each day.

He'd had quite a time getting to her. He'd narrowed her down to four families in Oak Hollow with children named Beth. As he'd ridden through the neighborhood asking children if they knew her, he'd gotten the name Beth Branning.

Unfortunately, her father was a sheriff's deputy, which made his goal more difficult. And there was always someone around her house. Though it appeared that she hadn't exposed him yet, he knew it was just a matter of time.

He wasn't cut out for prison. He would die before going there. But he preferred that she die instead.

Then he'd learned of her paper route, and her routine of sitting on a swing and staring at the Tomlins' house. What better opportunity?

He waited in the trees beside the swings, watching her and wishing for thunder so he could get away with another gunshot. Maybe he should shoot her anyway; people in the neighborhood would assume it was thunder. It was raining hard enough.

But he couldn't take the chance.

She was small and frail. He could take her easily with his bare hands. He had the element of surprise on his side. She wouldn't even know what hit her.

forty-four

KAY HAD NO IDEA WHO BETH'S LETTER WAS INTENDED FOR. Was she headed somewhere now to deliver it? Kay couldn't be sure. she wasn't even sure there was another copy. Maybe Beth had thrown it away because she'd changed her mind.

Either way, her daughter was in trouble, and Kay had to help her.

She longed for a telephone so she could call 911. Instead, she flew through town, hoping to catch Doug at the sheriff's department before he headed out on patrol. She found two patrol cars in the parking lot. Abandoning her bike without locking it, she ran up the steps and into the building.

Doug was standing at the door to Sheriff Wheaton's office. He turned when she came in.

"Doug, Beth needs help!"

"What?"

Kay couldn't cry now. She had to stay coherent. "She's in trouble. She saw a murder, and right now she's delivering this to somebody!" She thrust the letter at him as the sheriff came out of his office.

Doug's face went white as he read it. "Oh, my God ..." He handed the letter to the sheriff and brought his hands to his head. "She could have been killed."

The sheriff read the note. "Do you think it's Tomlin? The guy who's missing?"

Doug cut across the room to a bulletin board. He pulled down a missing person poster with a snapshot stapled to it.

"Could be. She mentioned his picture. Maybe she saw one of the posters somewhere." He looked up at Kay. "She kept asking about missing persons, muggings." He scanned the information on the sheet. "It has the address."

Kay jerked it out of his hand. "I know where this is." She turned and headed for the door. "I'm going."

"I'll take you," Doug said.

Kay turned back to him. "No, you go to the newspaper office and get a list of the boxes on her route. Follow it and pick her up when you find her. I'll go to the Tomlins' street and see if she's left the note for them. If not, I'll be there when she comes."

Wheaton intervened. "I'll take care of the paper route. Doug, you take your wife in the other patrol car. Bring Beth back here. We need a statement from her."

Relieved, Kay followed Doug to his car, and they headed for Magnolia Park.

"She's probably all right," Doug said as he turned the wipers on. "She's done her route every day, and nothing's happened. We'll find her."

Kay hoped he was right. But she couldn't fight the anguish over what her daughter had been going through, and the fear that had kept Beth silent all this time.

forty-five

BETH SAW HIM FROM THE CORNER OF HER EYE, AND SHE turned. The man who'd kept her up nights, who had invaded her dreams, whose threat had kept her in terror. He barreled toward her, teeth bared like a rabid dog. A scream gurgled in her throat, weak and useless. She fell back off her swing and tried to get up.

He grabbed her and slapped a hand over her mouth, muffling her. The strength and bulk of his arms bound her as he pulled her from the swing set, toward the trees. She kicked and jerked, trying to remember everything she'd ever seen on television about fighting off attackers.

She bit his hand, heard him curse behind her, but he didn't let her go. She kicked backward, digging her heels into his shin, knocking her head back against his face. He dragged her to the edge of the park, into the trees where no one would see. She lifted her legs, trying to make the weight of her body loosen his grip, but it only grew tighter.

She bit his hand again, determined to draw blood. He jerked it away, and she choked out a scream.

"Shut up, you little fool!" He turned her around and grabbed her neck with both hands, his fingers cutting into her throat. Her hands came up to his, clawing and pulling, trying to break free. She struggled for breath as her vision grew blurry.

God, I don't want to die.

Somewhere in her consciousness she felt him lifting her, thrusting her back. Her head smashed into something hard ...

And she plunged into a nightmare of darkness.

forty-six

KAY WAS CALMER BY THE TIME THEY GOT TO MAGNOLIA Park. Doug was right. Beth had gone out every day and nothing had happened. She was probably fine, and they would pick her up and insist that she tell them everything. She would lead them to the killer.

But as they pulled onto Magnolia Drive where the Tomlins lived, her eyes scanned the park. There, next to the newspaper box, she saw Beth's bike and trailer.

"Over there!" she cried. "Pull over!"

Doug stopped his car at the curb and cut the engine. Kay jumped out. "Beth! Beth, where are you?"

Doug slammed his car door and headed toward her bike. "She wouldn't have left her bike like this. She has to be nearby." He cupped his hands around his mouth and yelled, "Beth!"

Kay went back to the curb and looked up the street for an address on one of the homes. She found one, then counted off until she saw the Tomlin house. Maybe Beth had gone to talk to the widow. Maybe she was in their house right now.

She turned to tell Doug, but saw him walking toward the swing. "Doug, maybe—" Then she saw the narrow trenches in the mud. It looked as if someone had been dragged.

Her chest grew tight, her lungs clamping shut.

Doug ran toward the trees. Kay followed on his heels, unable to breathe.

There she was. Lying in a heap in the dirt.

Kay let out a desperate scream as Doug fell to Beth's side.

forty-seven

HE HOPED THE KID WAS DEAD, BUT HE COULDN'T BE SURE. She was as light as a feather, and strangling her had been easy. He couldn't believe the strength behind his hands as he'd slammed her head against the tree.

Eighteen days ago, he'd had all the makings of a model citizen. Now he'd killed three people, one with his bare hands. Where had that come from?

Fear had overcome him, turning him into something he didn't like.

And then he'd heard the car, and someone calling her name. He'd left her there on the dirt and set out into the trees. The power outage was his friend today. If there had been cell phones and police radios, they would have cut him off as he came out on the other side of the trees. As it was, he was sure that whoever had come was more interested in the girl than in him.

He only hoped he hadn't mucked this one up. She had to be dead.

Then he could get back to his life, appease his wife and keep his baby. And no one would ever know what he was really capable of.

He would *become* a model citizen.

forty-eight

DOUG CHECKED HER PULSE AND SAW THE BLOOD POOLING in the mud.

"Is she dead?" Kay screamed, falling to her knees. "Oh, dear God, she's blue!"

"No, there's a pulse." He slid his hand under her head. His face twisted with anger as he looked toward the trees. "Her skull. It's ... caved in."

"Beth! Beth!" There was no response. "We've got to get her to a hospital."

He started to pick her up, but Kay tried to stop him. "We shouldn't move her. What if her neck or back is broken?"

"There's no time to get an ambulance!" He scooped her up in his arms. Her head lolled back, her mouth open. They ran to the car. "You drive, Kay."

Kay opened the door for Doug, and he slid inside. She made sure the door wouldn't hit Beth's legs. *Oh, God, what happened to her?*

Running around to the driver's seat, she slid onto the old bench seat and started the car. She turned on the flashing lights and flicked on the siren.

"Hurry, Kay."

She nodded and pulled onto the busy street next to the park. A wagon with four horses was going by, but she pulled out around him, almost hitting a bicycler coming the other way. She swerved to miss him, then laid on her horn to make people get out of the way. Couldn't they see this was an emergency? That someone could be dying as they took their time? Didn't sirens mean anything?

Next to her, she saw that Doug was holding Beth's nose and breathing into her mouth. "Has she stopped breathing?"

He didn't answer.

She ignored stop signs and drove through town. "I'll take her to Birmingham, to University Hospital."

"No, Kay." Doug's voice was hoarse, frightened. "She won't make it that far. Take her to Crockett Medical Center."

She didn't like that idea. Crockett Medical Center was a new hospital converted from an old nursing home. Surely they didn't have critical care or a trauma center. She glanced over at Beth. Her blood was dripping down Doug's arm into the stained fabric of the car seat.

Could the little hospital handle a trauma patient with a severe head injury?

She heard Doug's sudden intake of breath. "Her neck. There are scratches on it. It's bruising. No wonder she can't breathe."

Sweat soaked Kay's armpits, her chest, dripped from her chin. Another horse and wagon slogged along in front of her, and she blared the horn again. "Get out of the way!" she cried, swerving around him.

Not too much farther. She looked at Beth again. "Her neck … what does that mean?"

"I think she was strangled." The word broke in Doug's throat.

He touched Beth's face with his blood-covered hand. "Beth, wake up, honey. You've got to hang on. Please, don't leave us now. Wake up."

Kay turned the corner; the hospital building lay ahead. "Who did this, Doug?"

"I don't know," he said, "but we're going to find out."

The building that had once been Majestic Nursing Home was a three-story, L-shaped building, its front door in the corner of the L. She turned into the half-circle driveway at the door. The siren still blared, and she hoped it would draw someone out to help them.

Doug didn't wait. He opened the car door, slipped his arm back under Beth's legs, and got out. Kay ran beside him.

People were everywhere, sitting on benches outside the doors. Horses and carriages lined the parking lot, and a long bike rack sat on the grass, holding dozens of bicycles. Kay ran ahead and threw open the doors. As he brought Beth in, Kay yelled out, "Help! Someone, please help!"

The waiting room was full of the sick and injured, but none was as near to death as Beth. The nurse at the receptionist desk stood up, looking across the counter at the blood on Doug's shirt.

"We've got a severe head injury! Patient's not breathing—" Doug yelled, with all the authority of a police officer. "A blunt force injury with possible skull fractures, strangulation—"

Fully engaged, the nurse abandoned her post and called to the back for help, then ran around the desk.

The room seemed to close in on Kay, and she felt herself growing weak, sick. She fought the nausea rising inside her. Someone brought a gurney, but Doug couldn't let her go. "Her skull is smashed flat. I'm afraid to lay her down. It might do more damage."

Kay felt dizzy. She was going to faint. She went to a wall, tried to steady herself. The voices seemed to merge in her head, too many of them all at once. Pulling herself from her fog, she saw the doctor take Beth from Doug's arms, saw them rush her back through double doors ... away from them.

Doug stood with empty arms, his shirt and the front of his pants covered with Beth's blood.

"Where—where are they ... taking her?"

"To surgery, they said." Doug just stood there, shock bleaching the color from his face. "They can't do X-rays, CT scans. How will they save her?"

Kay took a step toward him. The fog closed in as she hit the floor.

forty-nine

THE BURGLARY REPORT AT CAMPORT AND SONS WELDING
Company had kept Mark busy for the last hour. In broad
daylight, while business thrived inside, someone took the
bike rack apart and stole all the bikes lined up there.

He'd spent the last hour trying to calm down the angry victims who had to walk home, and filling out the report, including a description of the man with the horse and wagon who'd
been seen on the street. Then Mark had driven around trying
to find that wagon, but the perpetrator was long gone.

He went back to the station to see if there was anything
new he should respond to. Maybe they'd have radios soon,
so they could get calls in the field and respond more quickly.
Telephones too, though wishing for them seemed almost as
futile as wishing for fairies right now.

The glass doors of the Sheriff's Department were open in
an attempt to keep air circulating in the hot, musty building,
but the temperature outside was pushing ninety. He wasn't
sure it helped.

He looked around at the empty squad room. Usually
there were three or four deputies here writing out reports or
running things by the sheriff or the chief deputy. Something
must have happened to send them all out at once.

A noise clattered in the small kitchen, so he went to the
door and leaned in. Harry Vickers, who'd also been recruited

as a volunteer, was dipping water into cups for the prisoners. "Hey, Harry. Where is everybody?"

Harry glanced back and saw him, then turned fully around. "You haven't heard?"

"No, heard what?"

"Deni's little sister, Beth, was attacked."

His jaw fell. "*What?* Is she okay?"

"Apparently not," Harry said. "They took her to the hospital. Sheriff Wheaton heard the siren and found them there. She's got a head injury, he said. They took her straight to surgery."

Mark couldn't believe no one had found him to tell him. "How long ago was this?"

"An hour, maybe less."

"Who found her?"

Harry told him all he knew—that Doug and Kay learned of the murders through some note Beth left, that they'd gone to Magnolia Park and found her unconscious and bleeding.

This couldn't be. Not Beth.

Mark's heart pounded in his ears. "Does Deni know?"

"I doubt it, unless her parents sent someone to tell her. Wheaton's first priority was to go to the crime scene and try to catch the perpetrator. He told me to send every deputy that came in straight there."

"I've got to tell her. She and her brothers should know." He started for the door. "If Wheaton comes back, tell him I'll be at the park soon."

He ran down the steps, almost slipping on the third from the bottom. In seconds he was in his car, pulling out without looking for anyone in his way. He drove to the recovery team's building, hoping to find her there. Leaving his car idling in the parking lot, he ran in.

Thankfully, she was in the front area, talking to some applicants. "Deni, come with me. Beth's been hurt."

Deni dropped her clipboard and followed him out without telling anyone she was leaving. "What happened?" she asked as she got into the car.

He ran through the story as he'd heard it.

"Take me to the hospital," she said as tears rushed to her eyes.

"First let's get Jeff and Logan. They'll want to be there too."

Deni couldn't speak. She only nodded. Mark turned on his flashing lights and headed for the Brannings'.

WHEN THEY PULLED INTO THE DRIVEWAY, DENI BOLTED OUT AND burst into the house. "Jeff! Logan!"

Logan came out of the great room. "What?"

"Beth's been hurt. She's in the hospital. We have to go."

Logan just stood there. "What happened?"

"I'll tell you in the car. Where's Jeff?"

"Out back."

Deni threw open the door and saw Jeff in the chicken coup, soaked from the rain. "Jeff, Beth was attacked. She's hurt really bad!"

Jeff came out and locked the coup. "Attacked? What do you mean?"

"I don't know. Come on, we have to get to the hospital."

She went through the few details she knew as they rushed to the car. As soon as the car doors slammed shut, Mark pulled out, his lights still flashing.

"Did you see her, Mark?" Jeff asked, leaning up on the seat.

"No. I don't even know the details."

"Where was she injured?"

"Her head, I think."

"Her *head?*" Worry cut deep between Jeff's brows. "Could she die?"

Deni looked back. "I don't know." But she did know. A head wound was serious. Beth could be dead already, for all they knew. And if she was living, how could they help her without X-rays and other technology?

She glanced at Logan, who sat quietly in the back. She could see from his pale expression that his mind was trying to grasp such a tragedy.

"She'll be all right, guys." Mark reached across the seat and held her hand for a moment. "We just have to pray."

Deni figured there was no time to waste, so she led her brothers in prayer for their sister as Mark's patrol car flew through town.

When they reached the hospital, they tumbled out of the car and hurried inside. Deni ran to the desk, cutting in front of those who stood in line. "Please," she cried to the nurse. "My sister was brought in—Beth Branning."

The nurse got a sorrowful look on her face. "Yes, she's in surgery."

That meant she was alive. Relief flooded through Deni. "Do you know where my parents are?"

The nurse looked as if there was something she wasn't telling. "Your mother wasn't feeling well so she was taken to exam room four."

Now her mother was sick? "What do you mean she wasn't feeling well?"

"She passed out."

Deni just stared at her. Was Beth's condition that bad? "Can we go back?"

"Of course." She handed the next person in line a form to fill out, then came around the desk. "It's just through these doors."

Deni turned to check on her brothers and saw that Mark had parked the car and come inside. The group followed the nurse through the doors and down a corridor. Deni saw the "Exam Room 4" sign sticking out from the wall.

"They're right in there." The nurse pointed, and Deni pushed past her and ran to the room.

She came to the door and saw her mother sitting on a gurney. "Mom!" All her emotion rushed up in her throat and she burst into tears. "What's going on?"

Before her mother could answer, she saw her dad getting up from a chair.

He was covered in blood.

fifty

MARK LEFT THE HOSPITAL AS SOON AS HE GOT THE WHOLE story from Doug and Kay. He raced to Magnolia Park, where he found the other deputies. The attacker was long gone, and most of the evidence had been washed away by the rain. There were, however, men's footprints with an unusual tread, and small trenches where Beth had been dragged from the swing. There were clear signs of a struggle. Neighbors had been canvassed, but none of them had seen a thing.

When Mark saw the letter Beth had written, he had murder on his mind. Whoever did this to Beth was going to suffer like she was suffering. He wouldn't rest until that happened.

When they felt they could learn no more from the scene of the crime, he and the sheriff went to search the yard behind Cracker Barrel where Beth's letter said Blake Tomlin and the other guy had been murdered. They found little more than discarded trash. But there was a Speedy Lube and gas station next door, closed since the Pulses began. Maybe there was someone there who'd witnessed what Beth had.

Mark crossed the Cracker Barrel property and knocked on the side door. No one seemed to be there. He tested the knob—locked.

He cupped his hands around his eyes and looked through the dusty window. On a table near the door, he saw a box of ammunition. No way anyone would leave it lying around, right inside a window where it could be seen. Ammo was too hard to come by. Maybe the killer had been here and feared going back after committing his crimes.

"I got something!" he yelled. "Over here!"

Sheriff Wheaton rushed over. "What is it?"

He pointed to the box of .38 caliber cartridges on the table.

"Looks like the killer was waiting for his victims inside here." He glanced at the door and windows. "No sign of breaking and entering."

Wheaton called the other deputies over. "Dust the doorknob for prints."

Without the Automated Fingerprint Identification System, a computerized database of fingerprints from all over the country, they would need to have a suspect to match them to. But it was a lead. Maybe they'd be able to locate the owner of the building. It was possible that he was the perpetrator. At times like this, Mark wished he had more training. Because of the way he'd been pressed into service back in February, he'd never had time for any real training, other than a few crash courses at night and some books on policies and procedures. Now he wished there was some kind of field manual for solving attacks on innocent girls.

But no one would have more passion about solving this case than he had. If it was the last thing he did, he would find Beth's attacker and make sure he paid for what he'd done to his little friend.

They located the name of the owner of the Speedy Lube on the business license framed on the wall, then found an old phone book on top of a dusty filing cabinet and got his address. "Graham Morgan," Wheaton said. "Let's go see if Mr. Morgan fits the attacker's description."

MARK'S HEART RACED AS THEY DROVE TO TRAVIS ROAD, WHERE the owner of the Speedy Lube lived. Wheaton was quiet as he drove, and Mark took the time to pray for Beth. They'd had no time to go by the hospital to get word on her condition. Was she out of surgery yet, or was this one of those all-day things as they tried to piece her skull back together?

He pleaded with God to save her. Memories of conversations he'd had with her about death and dying flooded his mind. She'd told him once that she was waiting for the Next Terrible Thing to happen. She'd been obsessed with the fear that she'd be the victim of some violent crime. He'd tried to calm her down, to remind her that God protected those who walked with him.

Why hadn't God protected her? She'd been witness firsthand to the violent trials Mark had experienced in his own life. Maybe Christians were doing a disservice to people, leading them to believe that God never allowed anything bad to happen to his children. It was a nice thought, but reality didn't bear it out. And when it didn't, how many fell away from the faith?

He should have counseled Beth better. He should have taken more time to explain things to her, instead of blowing it off and trying to make her feel better.

Now, what she feared worst had happened.

Please, God, heal her. Reach down and touch her head. Stop the bleeding in her brain. Stop the swelling. Heal her and help her to rise up and walk. Let this be something that strengthens our faith, instead of straining it.

The Morgan house was out in the country. Two cars were parked in the dirt driveway, covered with a layer of yellow pollen. The hoods were open and the engines had been removed. Morgan was probably trying to convert them himself.

"If he's a mechanic, he might be working for the government," Wheaton said. "We'll be lucky if we catch him at home."

Mark wished they'd taken time to get an arrest warrant. As it stood, this was simply a fact-finding mission.

But if the guy had a goatee, as Beth had described, Mark wasn't sure he could restrain himself. Then again, a guilty man would have shaved.

He kept his hand near his holster, in case he needed to draw his weapon. Wheaton knocked on the door.

"They're here!" It was the sound of a teenaged girl. Mark heard giggling behind her.

The door flew open. Four girls of about fifteen stood there. Their expressions crashed at the sight of them.

"Oh. We thought you were ... someone else."

Wheaton introduced himself. "We're looking for Graham Morgan," he said.

"My dad," she said. "I'll get him."

They watched from the porch as the girl ran to the back door and called for her dad in the backyard. The other girls began tittering behind her. From the giggling conversation, Mark gathered that they'd been expecting some boys.

The back door opened and a man with a full head of red hair, sunburned skin, and a full beard came in. He didn't appear worried or uneasy. "Come in, officers. What can I do for you?"

Inviting them in was a good sign, Mark thought. Most criminals preferred to do their answering at the door. And there hadn't been time for him to grow the beard—so he didn't fit the description.

"Are you the owner of the Speedy Lube and Stop and Go on Mulholland Drive?"

"Such as it is. Haven't been able to get a drop of fuel in a year, and the conversion plants are doing all the oil changes. Don't know if I'll ever get her open again."

That was more than they wanted to know. Mark's impatience tightened his chest.

"We're investigating an incident that happened behind the Cracker Barrel a couple of weeks ago. We'd like to search your building. We were hoping you'd come open it for us."

He frowned. "Why?"

"We have reason to believe the perpetrator may have been hiding inside. We saw ammunition on the table."

"Did somebody break in?"

"Doesn't look like it. May have been somebody you know."

Morgan got his keys and started for the van. "Well, let's get to the bottom of this."

MORGAN UNLOCKED THE SPEEDY LUBE FOR THEM, AND THEY went inside.

Careful not to disturb anything that might turn out to be evidence, Mark stepped into the car bay with the hydraulic lifts in the floor. Against the wall were dirty, empty shelves that had once probably held motor oil and air filters. The conversion plant had no doubt purchased all of Morgan's supplies.

Mark looked around on the oil-stained floor. There were some footprints. Could any of them belong to the killer? They had taken a cast of the footsteps near where Beth had been beaten. He remembered the tread on the killer's shoes—shaped like lightning bolts. The footprints he saw looked like a match.

They found the ammunition box they'd seen through the window. "Is this yours?" Wheaton asked.

Morgan shook his head. "That's not even the caliber I use."

"Can you tell us who has access to your place?"

He shrugged. "Well, I had two assistant managers who have keys. But they'd have had no reason to be here."

"We'll need the names and addresses of those men," Wheaton said.

"Sure," Morgan said. "Clay Tharpe and J. W. Cole. But they're nice guys. Family men, both of them. We've been buddies for a couple of years. They wouldn't do anything like that." He led them into his small office, found a Rolodex. "Here are their addresses."

Mark took the cards. The Tharpe address was in a neighborhood only a block away from the Speedy Lube.

"One more thing," Wheaton said as he jotted the addresses down. "Either of those guys have facial hair?"

"Tharpe has a goatee."

Bingo. Mark looked at Wheaton, and Wheaton nodded.

"Who's the victim, anyway?"

"We can't really discuss it."

The man swallowed and rubbed his sunburned face again. "Look, I don't know what happened here, but I can tell you that neither Clay nor J. W. would hurt a flea. Just wouldn't happen.

I know them too well. They're not perfect, neither of them, but they're not violent men."

"Well, if they're innocent, they have nothing to worry about," Mark said.

But if one of them was guilty, Mark might just give him what he had given Beth.

fifty-one

THE SURGICAL INTENSIVE CARE WAITING ROOM, WHERE THE Brannings were told to wait for news of Beth, was no place for a shell-shocked family. Because it wasn't a priority area of the hospital, the generator-powered electricity wasn't on in this room. That was fine with Kay, since she would rather they use all their resources in the operating room right now. But the dismal waiting room only had light from one corner window. She supposed it was a good thing that the room didn't get more sun, though, because the heat was already stifling. More sunlight would make it even worse.

Oh, for air conditioning.

Doug paced the room, wearing a set of green scrubs that a kind nurse had found for him. His bloody clothes were wadded in a bag at her feet.

The waiting room was full of others who'd been through the wringer. Vinyl recliners that made Kay's skin sweat were the only beds some of them had known in days. People who looked in bad need of a bath sat with numb expressions, staring into the air, waiting for word of their loved ones. Some of them probably hadn't eaten in days. Waiflike, some drifted around the waiting room, living for the few minutes every few hours that they could see their loved ones.

She begged God not to put Beth in the ICU, unless they let Kay stay with her. She couldn't stand the thought of putting her child's life in the hands of overworked and understaffed medical personnel, and the thought of Beth waking up alone was almost more than she could stand.

"Kay, I came as soon as I heard!"

Judith and Brad Caldwell rustled into the waiting room. Judith's face shone with perspiration, and her green scrubs were ringed with sweat, like all the others who worked here.

Brad wore a golf shirt and dress pants. Since he'd been appointed Crockett's prosecutor to replace the attorney who'd quit, he'd had to start wearing his nicer clothes. It was a far cry from the uniform he'd worn before, when he worked as a volunteer deputy. They'd all been glad to have him using his attorney's skills again.

Kay and Doug hugged them both.

"Judith, can you find out anything for us?"

"I already did. She's still in surgery. But she's got the best neurosurgeon we have working on her. He came from University Hospital. We got him when this hospital opened because his parents live in Crockett. He decided to move his family here so they could be closer to them."

"Well, that's a blessing."

"Girl, you have no idea."

Brad sat down near where Kay was standing. "Kay, I know you've had a rough day, but I need you to tell me what happened."

Kay sat and launched weakly into the story again. Her voice was hoarse from screaming at the park, but she pressed on, giving as many details as she could.

When she finished, Brad looked as angry as Doug. "Well, it's in the sheriff's department's hands now."

"Wrong," Judith said. "It's in God's hands."

Brad wasn't a believer. As many times as Doug and Kay had shared their faith with him, he'd remained uninterested in God. He encouraged his family to go to church, but he rarely joined them.

"Whoever's hands it's in," he said, "when they find this dude and put him in *my* hands, you better believe he's going down."

Judith looked at Kay. "You need to get somewhere where you can pray. I know just the place."

"I'd love that," Kay said.

194

DAWN'S LIGHT

Judith sprang up. "Get your stuff and follow me."

They all gathered their things and trailed Judith through the halls.

"There's a conference room where you can sit in more comfortable chairs and have a little privacy. I can't promise we'll have it all day, but it's empty now."

"Thank goodness somebody knows their way around this place," Doug said. "I'd never even been in it until today."

The hospital had only opened a month before, in response to the growing number of patients from Crockett who were having to travel long distances to get to the one open hospital in Birmingham. The government had given Crockett a grant to buy this old abandoned nursing home and have it converted into a hospital. It had taken months for it to be ready, but now that it was, the doctors around town who practiced from their homes had moved to the hospital.

Judith had worked for Derek Morton in their neighborhood until he'd moved, and then she'd gotten hired on here too. This was also where Chris worked.

They followed Judith into the conference room. It was dark, but there was an oil lamp in the corner of the room. Judith lit it and set it in the center of the table.

The glow was welcoming. Everyone sat down around the table, Jeff and Logan side by side, Deni and Kay opposite them.

Doug sat on the end. "Are you sure they'll know where to find us when the surgery's over?"

"Don't worry," Judith said. "I'm going to tell them where you are right now."

Brad lingered at the door. "You guys need anything?"

Kay shook her head. "No, thank you, Brad."

"You can come pray with us," Doug suggested.

Kay expected some cryptic remark, but Brad just shook his head. "No, I'll leave you guys alone."

They stepped out of the room, and Kay looked at Doug. His eyes were full of tears, and his lips trembled at the corners. He closed his eyes and took his wife's and son's hands. They joined hands around the table. Lowering his head, he whispered, "Lord, this room is a blessing. Thank you for this kindness."

He sank in emotion, but kept praying, lifting Beth up to the throne of heaven, laying her in the arms of God, begging him for healing. Even Logan, who usually prayed in halting one-sentence prayers, talked openly to God, appealing to the Creator of the universe to pull Beth from the edge of death.

fifty-two

CLAY THARPE'S HOUSE DIDN'T LOOK LIKE THE HOME OF A killer.

He lived in a neighborhood that Mark had helped build a couple of years ago, when he'd worked in construction. They were attractive little starter homes, built for families with young children. The subdivision was well kept. While most of the homeowners had made vegetable gardens out of their front lawns, Tharpe still had grass.

Mark supposed Tharpe's job at the conversion plant gave him enough cash to buy food. It was difficult for a man with one of the few full-time jobs available these days to find time to keep a garden.

The sheriff's department van had drawn a lot of stares as Mark and Wheaton drove up the street and pulled into the Tharpes' driveway. By the time they got to the door, a woman had already stepped out, holding a baby girl on her hip. She met them in the yard.

"I heard your van coming. What's wrong?" she asked as they got out of the van. "Has my husband been in an accident?"

"No accident," Mark said. "Are you Mrs. Tharpe?"

"Yes." She touched her chest. "Thank goodness. Every time I see a sheriff's van turn into this neighborhood, I'm just absolutely certain that Clay has been hurt. You know, people think all they do at the conversion plant is work on engines, but there's a million things that can go wrong. Just last week

Fred Tipton cut his hand off when he got it stuck in some kind of contraption he was working on, and Jerome Novak had severe burns when something he was working on caught fire." She extended her hand. "My name is Analee, by the way. And why are you here?"

She was a talker, Mark thought. That could work in their favor.

Wheaton spoke first. "Mrs. Tharpe, we came to ask you a few questions about your husband. I assume from what you've been saying that he's not home."

"That's right," she said. "He's at work. What's this about?"

"You mind if we go inside?"

She looked around at the neighbors who were watching from porches and sidewalks. "Sure, come on in."

Though they didn't have a search warrant for the house, being invited in at least gave them the chance to look around to see if there was anything lying out that might connect Clay Tharpe to Beth, or even the missing man, Blake Tomlin. The house was spotless. It looked like the Tharpes were neat freaks.

Mark saw a picture of a man on an end table—goatee and all. His stomach burned.

"So what's this about?" she asked, motioning them to the couch.

Wheaton sat, but Mark kept standing. "Could you tell us if you've seen your husband today?" the sheriff asked.

"Of course, I saw him this morning. I made him breakfast before he went to work."

"What about later on today? Say, around lunchtime."

"He didn't come home for lunch today. Occasionally he does, but a lot of times he takes his lunch with him. They've got so much work there he can't get away. Wouldn't be so bad if we could have some of the fruit of his labors. I'd kill for a running car again. I couldn't believe it when I heard the Pulses had stopped, and I started thinking that maybe that would happen soon. Now that we have the cash we need we can put it into a car as soon as it's available. That is if they're cheap enough, but they'd have to be, wouldn't they? Otherwise how could anyone afford one?"

It was hard getting a word in, but Wheaton tried again. "So he didn't come home for lunch today," he repeated. "Mrs. Tharpe, which conversion plant does your husband work at?"

She put the baby in her infant seat. "He works at the one on Alabaster Street in Crockett."

That helped. There were four in the Birmingham area, and Mark was glad they wouldn't have to drive a long way to interview the man.

"How long does your husband usually take off for lunch?" Wheaton asked her.

"If he comes home he usually has an hour, but like I said, most of the time he just eats while he's working."

"You mentioned you have some cash now. Did you get it out of the bank the day they opened?"

"Clay did. He didn't want me there with the baby."

"Did your husband work that day?"

The baby started to kick and grunt. She went to her diaper bag on the table and dug through for something. "No, he had the day off so he could go stand in line."

"Which bank was his account with?"

She pulled out a pacifier. "There it is. I'm sorry, what did you ask?"

"His bank."

"BankPlus. We used to be at Alabama Bank and Trust a couple of years ago, but they had this rude teller—"

"And he came home with the money?" Wheaton cut in.

She put the pacifier in the baby's mouth. "That's right. And you know the first thing I bought?"

Mark almost chuckled at the look of dread on Wheaton's face. "What?"

"A car seat for the baby. Now, I know I'm not going to have anything to put it in for a while, but I believe in positive thinking, you know? My neighbor was selling the seat at the swap meet, and I snapped it up. Little Star and I will be able to travel again, and I can take her to see her grandparents, can't I, Star?" She leaned over the child. "Isn't that right, precious? We decided to name her

Star since she was born during the Pulses. She's going to have a big impact on the world, aren't you, sweetie?"

Mark jumped in. "Mrs. Tharpe, do you have a picture of your husband that we could have? It has to do with an investigation."

She frowned. "What kind of investigation?"

"We can't really discuss it right now. But it would help us a lot if we could have his picture."

She glanced at the picture. It seemed a lightbulb had come on, and she had begun to realize that Clay could be in serious trouble. "I ... I only have that one. I don't want to give it to you. It's my favorite."

"We could bring it back. If we could just have it for a couple of hours—"

The doors seemed to shut. "No, I don't think so." She crossed her arms and the luster in her eyes disappeared. "Is Clay in some kind of trouble?"

"We just need to talk to him, Mrs. Tharpe," Wheaton said.

"He is in trouble, isn't he?"

Mark looked at the floor as Wheaton spoke up. "Thank you for your time, Mrs. Tharpe. If you change your mind about the picture, we'd appreciate your bringing it by the sheriff's department."

They started to the door, and Analee followed them out. "Do you want me to give him a message?"

Wheaton turned back. "Ask him to come by and see us. We'd just like to chat with him for a few minutes."

As they got back in the van, Wheaton glanced at Mark. "Well, there's one thing for sure. That woman has nothing to hide."

"I don't know," Mark said. "She got uncooperative there at the end. Sure would have liked having that picture." He slipped behind the wheel. "Going to the conversion plant?"

"That's right. Let's hit Alabaster Road."

As he drove, Mark yearned to be with Deni and her family. He should be holding her, comforting her, praying with her.

But since he'd first heard about Beth, Mark had been on a vengeful hunt for the man who'd attacked her. He wouldn't rest until he found him. Only then would he allow himself to succumb to his own grief.

THE ALABASTER ROAD CONVERSION PLANT WAS RUN BY NED Emory, who lived in Oak Hollow. He was the father of Zach Emory, who had been shot a few months ago, and Mark had been blamed. Though Mark had been found innocent and the real killers had been caught, Emory still seemed to dislike him.

For that reason, he decided to let Wheaton do most of the talking as they went in to find Clay Tharpe. The garage bays of the plant were open, letting a light breeze drift through. The sound of a hundred revving motors reverberated through the place, and men who'd been drafted for this purpose worked tirelessly over each one.

They stopped at the closest group of men. "Where can we find Clay Tharpe?" Wheaton yelled over the noise. One of the men pointed upstairs.

At the top of the stairs, Mark saw another group of men, heads together over something they were putting together. Mark searched the faces for a grey goatee. And then he saw Ned Emory. The plant manager came toward them, a look of dread on his face.

"What are you two doing here?" he asked.

Wheaton shook his hand. "Ned, I'm sorry to disturb you at work, but we're looking for one of your employees—Clay Tharpe."

"Tharpe? What for?"

"We want to ask him some questions."

Ned seemed to recognize the evasion. He looked down over the rail to the first floor, scanning the heads. "Well, I don't see him anywhere." He hollered downstairs. "Jessup, you seen Tharpe?"

Jessup looked up at him and yelled back, "He left early."

Mark looked at Wheaton. So much for Clay having work as an alibi.

They started down the stairs.

"You can talk to Jessup, his supervisor. He's not in some kind of trouble, is he?" Ned called down.

Wheaton and Mark ignored him as they headed toward the supervisor. "Mr. Jessup," Wheaton called.

The chubby man looked up at them. "Yeah?"

"You said Tharpe left early. What time would you say that was?"

"I guess around eleven o'clock," he said. "Told me he had a migraine headache that was killing him. I told him this was the last time I was letting him off."

"The last time?" Mark asked. "Has he been taking off a lot?"

"Yeah, he's been leaving early every day, coming back late from lunch. I'll put him on a task, and when I turn around, he's gone."

"Has he always been like that?"

"No. Just the last couple of weeks. Why? Has he done something?"

"We just want to question him about a situation that he might know something about."

"Well, I don't expect to see him again today. He'll milk this migraine for all it's worth. You might catch him at home, if he's really sick."

"We were just there. His wife thought he was here."

"Well, there you go. Now you see what I'm dealing with."

fifty-three

CRAIG HAD NEVER FELT MORE OUT OF PLACE. HE STOOD just inside the fence at the substation on Tambridge Road, observing the work being done to get the station back online, so that power could be restored to the Crockett area. He'd gotten word this morning through a telegram that one of the utilities that supplied electricity was back online, generating electricity again.

Craig thought it was a joke. After driving from one substation to the other, he'd finally found his transmission engineer, Butch Morris, whom he'd only known for a couple of weeks. He relayed the message. "Is this even possible this soon?"

"Sure, it's possible."

"But how could they have all their control circuitry repaired that quickly? I expected it to take weeks, if not months."

Butch took off his hard hat and finger-brushed his comb-over. "They had the parts already in place in some of the hardened warehouses, just waiting for the Pulses to be over. They probably started transporting 'em the day the Pulses ended. Wouldn't take many days to replace 'em and get 'em them generating again."

"So what does that mean to us?"

"It means that as soon as we can get our substations repaired, we can connect them to the transmission lines and get our areas back up. Problem is manpower. We don't have enough workers. We need more linemen. You're not hiring 'em fast enough."

"Trust me," Craig said. "If someone puts *lineman* or *technician* on their application, I put them right to work."

He let Butch go back to work and stood back, running through the crash course he'd taken about turbines and insulators and transmission towers. There was a time—before the outage—when he would have driven past a substation and complained that it was an eyesore to the community. He might have suggested that Senator Crawford write a bill about camouflaging them so they'd be more attractive. It would have been born of pure ignorance, since he'd had no idea that these were the stations that brought lights and heat and air conditioning, and powered the companies that pumped sewage or provided running water.

Now he saw those metal towers with all those unsightly transmission lines and all the machinery inside the fence with the words "Keep Out—High Voltage" on it as miraculous. And the workers milling around inside, with knowledge he didn't have, seemed like heroes.

They didn't return the admiration, however. He felt in their way, even though he paid their salaries.

As he got back into his car, hope and pride welled up inside him. Hope that it might not take as long as he thought to get the power restored. Pride that he'd had something to do with it.

He drove back through town, honking at pedestrians and bike riders in his way, wishing they'd get a clue that cars were back on the road. He longed for an air conditioner, but most of these old cars didn't have them, and even if he'd had one, he didn't have enough gas to use it. So he kept his windows down, hoping the warm wind would somehow stop the sweat from drenching his dress clothes.

As they came out of the conversion plant, Mark saw Craig's car pulling into the recovery team's parking lot. He hadn't been there when Deni had taken off, so he probably hadn't got word yet about Beth's attack.

He glanced at Wheaton. "Looks like Craig Martin's over there. I should go tell him about Beth."

Wheaton nodded. "We can take a minute to do that."

They pulled up behind Craig as he was getting out of his car. It did Mark's heart good to see Craig's dress shirt marked with huge sweat rings.

Craig got out and shot him a look. "You guys come to apply for a job?" he asked in that smug voice of his. "We pay better than the county does."

Mark bristled. "Everybody pays better than the county does."

He reached to shake Craig's hand. His nemesis took it grudgingly.

"I thought you might not have heard about Beth."

Craig reached into his car and got a towel, began blotting his face. "What about her?"

"She was attacked earlier today. Deni's with her at the hospital."

"Attacked? By whom?"

"By some guy in a park. We're trying to find him now. She has a severe head injury. She was in surgery when I left the hospital."

The full force of the news finally registered on Craig's face. "Which hospital?"

"Crockett Medical Center."

"How is Deni?"

Mark's jaw popped. Was he giving secrets to the enemy? "She's pretty upset."

"I'll get right over there. Thanks for telling me."

Mark had a sick feeling in the pit of his stomach as he walked back to the van. Craig would be there comforting Deni while Mark was out trying to find the killer. But it couldn't be helped. Clay Tharpe had to be caught. He just prayed that Craig didn't make any headway while Deni was especially vulnerable.

fifty-four

THE SURGERY HAD BEEN GOING ON FOR FOUR HOURS, AND Kay was going to jump out of her skin if she didn't hear something soon. Two hours ago, Judith had come to tell her that Beth was still alive and stable, but that was all she knew.

Finally, Kay heard their names called.

"Branning family? Is there a Branning family in here?"

"Here we are!" she shouted, and almost tripped over someone's feet as she tried to get to the door. The family was on her heels.

"Your daughter's out of surgery, Mrs. Branning. Dr. Overton would like to see you in the conference room."

"Is she still alive?" Kay choked.

"Yes, she is."

"What's her condition?" Doug asked.

"Dr. Overton would prefer to explain that to you."

Kay covered her mouth and sobbed into her hand. It was bad. If it weren't, the nurse would have been smiling, and she would have said that everything went well and that Beth would be waking up soon.

That's what they'd said when Deni had her tonsils out at age seven and when Jeff had tubes in his ears as a baby.

Doug put his arm around her. She felt him shaking, and she realized the same thoughts were going through his mind. Deni, Jeff, and Logan were quiet as they followed them down the hallway and back into the conference room where they'd prayed earlier. They filed in and sat around the table, stiff and silent.

Dr. Overton came in wearing a white coat over his green scrubs. He gave them a halfhearted smile, then closed the door.

"How is Beth?" Doug demanded before he'd even sat down.

Dr. Overton sighed as he sat down and opened her chart. "We did all we could to stop the bleeding," he said. "Her skull has multiple fractures from some sort of blunt-force trauma. From the shape of the posterior part of her skull, I think she was slammed against something." He looked across the table at Doug. "Do you know what that could have been?"

The rims of Doug's eyes reddened. "There was blood on a tree near where we found her."

Kay hadn't even seen it. She'd been so focused on Beth on the ground.

"Yes, that would be consistent with what we found. The fractures may be serving her well at this point. It's giving her brain some room to swell, reducing the pressure."

"Oh, dear God," Kay whispered. She'd never believed that a fractured skull would be a blessing. She couldn't believe it now.

"She was also strangled. She has bruising and swelling on her neck, which is making it difficult for her to breathe. There was no arterial damage, but her airways were compromised. We have her on a ventilator for now, with a tube that will help keep her airways open."

"Strangled!" Though Doug had used the word *strangulation* earlier, Kay couldn't get her mind around the cruelty that entailed. She covered her face now and sucked in a sob. "Who would do this to a child?"

The doctor looked down, and Kay wondered if he'd spent time asking the same questions. After a moment, he went on. "We do have generator power for certain important areas of the hospital, but we're limited in the things we can plug in. We will use generator-powered electricity for the ventilator, but we can't use it for other things, like the compression stockings that we would normally put on her to keep blood clots from forming because of inactivity. We will give her some graduated compression socks to help with that, but it would be a good idea to massage her legs and feet when you think about it to keep the blood circulating."

Kay could do that. It might be all she could do, but she could do that.

"Her Glasgow Coma Score was three."

"What's that?" Deni asked.

"It's the scale we use to evaluate a patient's neurological response on a scale of one to ten. Three indicates no response. Unfortunately, she's still unresponsive."

"But she's going to pull through, right?" Jeff asked.

The doctor studied the chart a little longer, but Kay had the sense that he was just buying time to frame his answer. "I'm afraid we can't say that for sure. She's in critical condition. We tried to stop the bleeding in her brain, but we have no guarantees that we got it all. And without the usual diagnostic and monitoring tools, it's almost impossible to tell for sure. With injuries like this, we usually put them on IV steroids and antiseizure medications. Unfortunately, we're having trouble getting those medications. It's a terrible time to have this kind of injury."

Kay frowned. "So ... what? We just sit here and wait? If she dies, we know you didn't get all the bleeding, and if she lives, we know you did?"

"No, it's not that cut and dried. There are things we're watching that will indicate whether she's bleeding. We'll have her in the surgical ICU for a while, and we'll be monitoring her to make sure she's stable. We've put a drain in her head, and we anticipate some bleeding. If it becomes excessive, that'll be a sign that she's bleeding somewhere else. We've also put in a feeding tube."

"Is she going to have brain damage?" Doug asked.

"We're hoping the damage to her brain was minimal. But she was without oxygen for several minutes until Doug started the mouth-to-mouth. That saved her life and may have minimized the brain damage from the strangulation. The blow to the head did cause significant damage, but it'll be a while before we can measure how much. Even if she recovers fully, it could take up to eighteen months for her to be completely back to normal."

"Is there even a possibility that she could wake up and be perfectly normal?" Kay asked.

"It's possible, but unlikely. Usually that improvement is gradual." Kay sank back.

"What are the chances she'll pull through?" Deni asked.

The doctor shook his head. "I don't like to give percentages, because I don't know. There are a lot of factors that figure in to this kind of thing. As advanced as we are in medical science, we can't account for miracles of healing. Are you people of faith?"

"Yes," Doug said. "We are. We're Christians."

"Good," Dr. Overton said. "So am I. And you should know that your daughter was bathed in prayer before I ever started operating on her today."

Kay felt new tears rushing up to her eyes. "Thank you, Doctor."

"I believe that prayer often changes things. But I want you to know that she's in a very dangerous position, and it could go either way."

The words echoed through Kay's mind as he finished going over the details of Beth's surgery. Kay's mind raced. Beth could die. She might never wake up. Her last conscious thought would be one of stark terror—her last sight, the face of her killer.

Kay had to get to her. She could coax her awake. She knew it. A doctor's care didn't hold a candle to a mother's love.

She would save her daughter through faith and sheer force of will. And if they tried to bar her from the ICU, she would beat down the doors until they let her stay with her child.

Finally, Dr. Overton got up to leave. He stopped at the door. As if he'd heard her thoughts, he said, "We'll allow two of you to stay in ICU with her at a time."

"Really?" Being kept from her daughter while she was in the ICU had been one of Kay's worst fears. "All the time?"

"With our technology limited and our monitoring equipment so lacking, we find that it helps to have a family member watching over the children. Another set of eyes and hands are helpful. But we ask that you wear a mask and gloves when you come into the ICU, and the scrubs we'll give you before you enter. We don't want any unnecessary germs being brought in there, and the precautions will help protect you against any bacteria in there, as well."

"Are they sterile paper scrubs?"

"No," he said. "We ran out of those a long time ago, and our shipments are few and far between. For now, we just wash the cloth ones with bleach. But as you can imagine, we don't have enough for people to come in and out for short visits. You have to take them off when you leave the ICU and put new ones on when you come in. After they're worn, they can't be used by anyone else until they're washed again. It's very important that we keep the germs out."

"Yes, of course," Kay said. "When can we see her?"

"Shouldn't be too long," he said. "Go on back to the waiting room, and we'll send a nurse to get you when we've moved her."

fifty-five

BETH LAY IN HER ROOM, SO SMALL AND BROKEN, WIRED UP like a robot being overhauled. Kay's oversized scrubs rustled as she crossed the room to her daughter. Her face was swollen, her eyes shut. There was a mask over her mouth and nose where a ventilator helped her breathe.

Kay wanted to tear them off, grab her up, and carry her out of this place. If she could turn back time for just a few hours, Beth would be back safe at home. Kay would never let her leave the house again. She would keep her daughter safe from killers. Hadn't she done that for thirteen years? Beth had never had a broken arm, an infected wound, or a cough that hadn't been doctored. Kay had seen to it.

Yet here she was, her skin deathly white, her breathing controlled by the ventilator. The back of her head was shaved and stitched and her skull was misshapen. They had laid her on her side, with pillows tucked around her.

Doug came around Kay and bent over Beth. The surgical mask they'd given him was soaked with his tears, and it looked like it would soon be useless. He pulled it down and kissed her cheek. "I'm so sorry, sweetheart," he said, stroking what was left of her hair. "Daddy should have known."

Kay pulled back the covers and searched Beth's body for other bruises. The marks on her neck were more visible now. She thought back to the day the Pulses stopped, when she'd come home and found Beth's wet clothes on the floor. She'd had scrapes on her legs then. Kay should have understood that her daughter was suffering. What kind of mother was she?

She kept looking down her arms, under her gown, her legs ... They had given Kay embolism stockings to put on Beth. Kay clutched the white socks in her fist. Then she unrolled them and pulled the sheet back from her daughter's icy feet. Her toes were turning blue.

"These won't work," she said. She'd been in the hospital herself for a hysterectomy five years ago, and they'd put pneumatic compression stockings on her calves to keep her from getting a blood clot. Now they had these useless tight socks instead.

Kay wrestled them onto her daughter's feet, careful not to hurt Beth or move her too much. The stockings were so tight that Kay thought they might cut off Beth's circulation rather than aiding in it. She struggled to pull the sock up to Beth's knee, then checked to make sure it wasn't cutting into her skin. Then she worked on the other one.

Doug was oblivious to what she was doing. He kept his face by Beth's. "Honey, can you hear me? You were injured, and we've got you in the hospital. They did an operation. You did good. You're a real trouper. We need for you to wake up and talk to us."

Kay was sweating by the time she got the stockings in place. Now what? What did her daughter need? She had to do something.

Water. She needed water. "Where can I get her some water?" she asked.

Doug looked at her. "She doesn't need water, honey. She's on an IV and she has a tube in her throat."

Kay looked up at the bag that was dripping vital fluids into Beth's veins. How could that help her? It wasn't dripping fast enough. She went around the bed and checked to make sure it was working at all. What if it stopped? Beth could die. Any one of a million factors could fail, and they would lose their daughter. She touched the bag, watched the tube, saw a drip form and creep toward Beth's arm. It wasn't good enough, Kay thought. They should be doing more for her.

Beth was barely a teenager. She was supposed to be leading her play rehearsal. She was supposed to be fussing over costumes and props. She was supposed to be singing the songs she'd written.

She felt Doug's hands on her shoulder, and she turned and fell against him. He touched her paper shower cap, held her close. The embrace brought Kay's heart to her throat, threatening to choke her. Despair shivered through her body. "Where was he, Doug? Where was God when this happened?"

She felt him sobbing into his mask, his shoulders shaking with each breath.

He didn't have the answer.

DENI WAITED OUTSIDE THE ICU DOOR FOR ONE OF HER PARENTS to come out so she could go in. The waiting room was filling up with friends and neighbors who'd heard about Beth. Brad Caldwell was still here, along with the Huckabees, and Amber Rowe had come after getting a sitter for the children. Jimmy Scarbrough and his parents arrived with tears. His father, Ralph, the former sheriff of Jefferson County, had lost fifty pounds since his shooting, and his breath was shallow from the long walk up the hall. But it was clear he was on the mend.

Other members of their church had drifted in to offer prayers and compassion.

Where was Mark?

Of course—he was out working, she told herself, trying to find Beth's attacker. Maybe by now they knew who he was. They might even have him in custody.

She hoped he'd be off the streets soon so he couldn't harm anyone else. Then Mark could come to be with her.

"Deni?"

Jimmy Scarbrough got up from his seat and shoved his hands into his pockets. His father got up, too, with great effort, and set his hand on his son's shoulder as they came toward her.

"What, Jimmy?"

He glanced at his dad, and Ralph nodded. Jimmy swallowed as he looked back at Deni. "I saw Beth at Magnolia Park a few days ago. I should have told you earlier but I didn't know ..."

Her eyebrows lifted. "Did you talk to her?"

"Yes. She was upset because of that lady with the missing husband. She was crying and I tried to get her to talk to me about it."

"Did she?"

"Sort of. She told me she saw them in their driveway sometimes, and I guess she felt bad for them."

The former sheriff stroked his son's hair. "Jimmy, tell them what she said about getting hurt."

Jimmy's eyes rounded. "Yeah. At first, she said she couldn't talk to me because somebody might get hurt. She wouldn't tell me anything else about that. Then we got off the subject and she told me about the lady. I forgot what she said about getting hurt ... until she did."

Deni's chest tightened. *Somebody* might get hurt? Did Beth think she was protecting the Tomlin family? Or their own family?

If only he had told them, maybe her parents would have pushed harder for Beth to tell them what was going on. "Did she say anything about witnessing a murder?"

He shook his head. "No, nothing. I should have made her talk to me." His eyes filled and the corners of his mouth edged down. "I wish I'd told your parents sooner."

Deni blew out a strong breath and pulled the kid into a hug. "You couldn't have known how important that was, Jimmy. We all had signs that we didn't pick up on. But I'll be sure and tell my parents. They'll want to talk to you about it."

He wiped his eyes, then went back to his seat. His father sat down next to him, his arm around him. She could see that Scarbrough's shooting—a tragedy that had almost taken his life—had turned into a blessing for the boy, as it had drawn them closer. She was glad. Jimmy would need him to get through this. She thought of the Tomlin family who had broken Beth's heart, mourning their loved one without even knowing he was dead. How long had she been watching them, carrying their pain?

If only they could find the body so the family could be notified and have some kind of closure.

She thought of Beth's fear over the last few days. On Disbursement Day, Beth had begged to stay home. Deni had found her sitting on the window seat looking out at the street when she'd gotten up, while it was still dark. Beth probably hadn't slept at all that night. Now it felt as if all the anguish Beth had endured had collected in the pit of Deni's stomach, making it impossible for her to stop crying.

Someone tapped on her shoulder, and she turned to see Craig. He opened his arms, and she fell into them. "I came as soon as I heard. I'm so sorry, baby."

He wasn't Mark, and she wasn't his baby.

But his arms did bring comfort.

fifty-six

MARK'S SHIFT ENDED, BUT HE HAD NO INTENTIONS OF abandoning his task. Clay Tharpe still hadn't been found. Mark had gotten word that Beth had survived surgery, and he longed to go to Deni. But minutes counted in a murder investigation. Tharpe was still free, and he probably knew by now that they'd identified him. They couldn't allow him to escape.

As the new shift came on duty, Mark walked into Wheaton's office. The sheriff usually worked from his Birmingham office, but since the attack, he'd hung around Crockett. Mark supposed he had a vested interest in the case, since Beth was the daughter of one of his volunteers.

"Sheriff. I've decided to stake out the Tharpe house all night."

"How?" Wheaton asked. "If you have a vehicle there all night, he'll see you as soon as he turns onto the street."

"I could camp out in their backyard."

Wheaton shook his head. "You can't do that, Mark. It's private property."

"Come on, Sheriff—you know he's the killer."

"I don't know any such thing, not for sure. And even if I did, it doesn't matter if he's Charles Manson. We can't go onto that property without an invitation or a search warrant."

"Then I'll sleep in somebody else's yard, somewhere that gives me a good view of the house. They won't see me."

"Again, you've got legal complications." Wheaton leaned on his desk, palming his elbows. "Look, you have to do this right or the guy'll get off on a technicality as soon as he's arrested."

"Not as long as Brad Caldwell is the prosecutor."

"Brad Caldwell is not the judge," Wheaton said. "And even Brad will have to go by the book so this guy doesn't walk."

Mark felt like Wheaton was playing for the opposing team. "Then what do you suggest?"

"Either you sit on the street, which is no good, or you could park at the school grounds a block away."

"But I won't have a good view from the school grounds. It's too far away. And in the dark—"

"There's nothing else you can do."

Mark dropped into the chair across from Wheaton's desk. "Why can't I talk to some of the neighbors, get them to let me use their house?"

"First, you'd have to tell them what's going on, and they're liable to tip the Tharpes off, especially if they're good friends. I don't have enough staff to send somebody with you, and if you're there alone, what are you gonna do when you see him? You can't very well arrest him alone and haul him in."

"Watch me."

Wheaton pushed his chair back and got up. "Mark, I know you're highly motivated to find this killer. I am too. But I'm not sure about this."

"I'll stay awake all night if I have to," Mark said. "I'll walk up and down the street."

"You're liable to get shot if somebody thinks you're a prowler."

Mark threw his hands up. "I'll take my chances. Whose side are you on?"

"Yours," Wheaton said. "I'm just being realistic, and I don't want to see one of my best men get killed."

"I won't get killed." Mark stood up and strode to the door. "I won't rest until I have this guy in custody."

"Just be careful, son."

THAT NIGHT, MARK PARKED HIS PATROL CAR BEHIND THE HIGH school, where no one from Tharpe's neighborhood would see it. From the corner of the parking lot overlooking the neighborhood, he could see candlelight flickering in Tharpe's windows. Leaving his patrol car, he ambled up the sidewalk, then lingered at their yard. Through the windows, he saw Analee walking back and forth with the baby, looking forlorn and upset.

If only he could get a warrant to search the house and the yard, to see if he could find any clues leading them to Blake Tomlin.

All of their evidence was circumstantial. No matter how Tharpe's disappearance after the attack looked, it wasn't enough to support an arrest. Neither was his previous employment with the Speedy Lube next to the Cracker Barrel. Yes, he fit the description in Beth's note, but that wouldn't stand up in court.

Mark walked up and down the street as the night grew darker. His eyes were growing tired and dry. He couldn't remember the last time he'd eaten. He could use a jug of water. Maybe he should just give up and go to the hospital.

But something told him that Clay would try to return home tonight. Mark had to be here when he did.

The candle went out in the Tharpe house, and Mark figured Analee had given up and gone to bed. He felt sorry for her. After he and Wheaton had interviewed her earlier today, Mark's gut told him she'd had nothing to do with the attacks. If that was true, she probably felt abandoned by a husband who seemed to have vanished.

He ambled back to the high school parking lot and sat under the roof overhang in front of the door, watching the street and wishing for a pair of night vision goggles. He prayed for Beth, begging God to save the kid who meant so much to all of them, and to help him bring justice to her attacker.

fifty-seven

DENI COULDN'T SUPPRESS HER YAWNS AS DARKNESS FELL over the waiting room. She watched with her head resting against the wall as a hospital orderly dragged a ladder in, climbed up, and tightened a lightbulb. Someone at the door flicked the light switch, and a dull yellow glow gave the room a more homey look. It wasn't enough to read by, but it would keep them from tripping over each other. Most of the visitors had returned home to take care of their own families, leaving only family members of the sick or injured.

Across the room, she heard sniffling as a family waited for word about their young son's surgery. He'd fallen out of a deer stand and broken his back, and Deni supposed he was in as much trouble as Beth. His family sat stiffly in the uncomfortable chairs. She had done the same earlier today. Now she and her brothers had settled in. Logan had rolled up a pillow and was sleeping on the floor. Jeff sprawled across two chairs, but he wasn't asleep.

Craig sat next to her, his foot jittering on the floor. The sound made her nervous.

She was thirsty. There were jars of water that someone had brought as a ministry to them. But she didn't dare drink. To go to the bathroom, they had to go outside to the Porta-Johns lined up behind the building. It just wasn't worth it.

Chris had come on shift and brought them some tortillas to get them through the night. It was much-needed sustenance.

But Deni needed more.

Where was Mark? She hadn't seen him since he'd brought her to the hospital earlier. He had sent her messages with some of the deputies who'd come by after their shifts. He was tirelessly hunting the killer, they said. He had taken Beth's attack personally, and God only knew what he would do when he came face-to-face with her attacker.

Mark's determination would result in an arrest, Deni was confident. She just hoped he didn't get killed in the process.

Her heart ached to see him. His presence calmed and comforted her. Even when he'd been the one in trouble, he always considered her comfort first and assured her that things would be all right. She wanted him to talk to Beth. Maybe her sister would respond when she heard Mark's voice. Beth had always had a special bond with him.

Not so with Craig. Though her ex-fiancé had remained by her side for the past few hours, forsaking his important work, her family hadn't invited him in to see Beth. His presence would add nothing. But Deni appreciated his being here. It was so different from the months following the Pulses, when he'd been indifferent and detached. Part of her drew satisfaction from his focused attention. The other part wished he'd go back to work.

Her father stepped into the doorway of the waiting room. He had aged ten years in the past few hours. Deep lines cut into his face, pulling his features down. His nose and the rims of his eyes were red, breaking her heart. He walked slowly, his hands limp at his sides, and his eyes looked distracted.

Deni got up as he came toward her. "Dad, is there any change?"

He rubbed his mouth. "No, no change."

"Is Mom alone?"

"Yeah. Why don't you go keep her company?"

Deni looked down at Craig. "I'll be back."

He slipped his hand into hers and squeezed. "Send a nurse to get me if you need anything."

She went into the ICU, changed into a fresh set of scrubs—bleached colorless from the frequent washings—and found her mother sitting beside Beth's bed, resting, her head beside Beth's leg.

"Mom, are you okay?"

Kay sat up. Deep half-moon shadows drooped under her eyes. "Yeah, honey, I'm fine."

Deni went to the bed and leaned over to kiss her sister. They had turned her to her other side since Deni had been in last. The back of Beth's head seemed more swollen than before. So did her face. Her skin was pallid and thin. Deni swallowed the thought that she looked like a corpse.

Her face twisted as she met her mother's eyes. "Mom, she's not getting better, is she?"

Kay just shook her head.

Deni pulled a chair up to the bedside and got close to her sister. "Talk to us, Beth. Please wake up." When there was no response, she turned back to her mother. "Has she done anything? Moved at all? A toe, even?"

"No, hon. Nothing."

There was no sign that Beth heard.

Deni's eyes followed a tube from Beth's head to a small bulb half-full of red fluid. "Maybe the anesthesia hasn't worn off. Maybe tomorrow morning she'll wake up and start chattering."

The look on her mother's face told her she doubted it.

Kay forced a smile and changed the subject. "Has Mark come up yet?"

"Not yet."

"Craig?" Her tone was a little cooler.

"Yeah, he's here. He's been great. He has such an important job and he's just sitting here with me."

"We need Craig out there," Kay muttered. "Maybe they could do more for Beth if we had power. And if we had an MRI or a CT scanner, we'd know what we were dealing with, and maybe the doctors could do something." Kay slid her fingers through her hair. "I never thought I'd have to watch my child suffer because of a stupid power outage."

"I know."

Kay began massaging Beth's leg. Deni scooted her chair down and started rubbing the other one.

Her mother's voice was hoarse as she spoke. "I should have been more thankful for all the medical marvels when things were working, but I took them so for granted. How dare I ever be depressed about anything when I had it so good? A car that ran, electricity, computers, telephones, drive-thru windows, medicine for anything that ailed. What more could I have wanted? I was spoiled rotten."

"No, you weren't, Mom."

"Yes, I was," Kay insisted. "Even right after the Pulses began, when we had a pantry full of food that we hadn't eaten, a freezer full of meat, neighbors to help us and give us advice, a lake and tools and an ax. I felt sorry for myself then. I wondered, 'Why us?' "

Deni thought of protesting again, but her mother just needed to vent.

"And in the winter months, I felt so sorry for us because we were almost out of food and everything was so hard. But we still had our family. We still had everybody healthy. We had fire to keep us warm, and Mark and your father and Jeff to hunt for us and bring us food. We had the solar oven that Mark showed us how to build. We had enough. God provided. Why couldn't I be more grateful?"

"You were, Mom. We thanked God all the time."

"Not really. *I* didn't. A week ago, even, I felt sorry for myself because I was tired. I didn't realize the sheer bliss of having my family safe and healthy."

"Mom, stop beating yourself up. You're not like that."

Kay looked fully at her daughter. "You don't know what goes on in my heart, Deni. My poor-mouthing to God must be a constant insult to him."

"Mom, God didn't do this to punish you for not knowing what you had," Deni whispered. "He isn't trying to teach you to be grateful by letting Beth's head get bashed in."

The words tripped in Deni's throat, and she couldn't help the thought that followed. Why *had* he let Beth's head get bashed in?

God could have prevented it. Tears burned her eyes. "Why didn't God intervene, Mom?"

Kay cleared her throat, probably searching for the mature thing to say. "He did intervene. We got there in time to save her."

"But why didn't he get you there in time to keep it from happening?"

She saw the conflicting emotions passing across her mother's face. When Kay's features dissolved into tears, she wished she hadn't asked.

Kay pulled a handkerchief out of her jeans pocket, wiped her nose. "Later, when we're able to step back and think this through, we'll see the ways that he worked. What Satan meant for evil, God meant for good."

Deni thought of the story of Joseph in Genesis. His brothers had been jealous and sold him into slavery. Later, after years had passed, Joseph had forgiven his brothers with those same words.

But she couldn't see any grand purpose in the attack on Beth. Clearly, her mother couldn't, either. Tears had sapped her strength. Deni stopped massaging Beth's leg and looked around for a glass of water. She saw the one she'd brought to her mother earlier, still sitting on the table beside Beth's bed. She handed it to Kay. "Mom, you need to drink this."

Kay smiled and took the glass, bottomed it. "Thank you, honey. You're giving me strength."

But her mother didn't look strong. She looked as though she hung on a fraying cord of hope. And soon it could break entirely.

fifty-eight

ANALEE THARPE WISHED SHE HAD GOTTEN MORE INFORmation from the police when they were there earlier. But the minute they asked for that picture of Clay, she'd known they weren't just there to ask him a few questions. Why would they want his picture if he hadn't done anything wrong?

She'd almost told them that Clay had shaved several days ago. He'd worn that goatee as long as she'd known him. His reason—that it was too hot for any hair on his face—seemed lame and ridiculous now. And why had he cut it off away from home? He'd come home with sprigs all over his chin.

Had he gotten rid of it because the law was looking for him?

She had expected him home long before dark. But here it was, eleven o'clock, and no sign of him.

Of course, that didn't mean he was in trouble. This was more of the same, really. He often came home late. And he'd been acting strange. He'd been jittery every day for the last week.

When she'd found the necklace in his pocket, he'd explained it away. "I saw a girl drop it at the produce stand," he'd told her. "I picked it up and tried to return it, but she was gone. Trust me. I don't even know her."

"Why do you still have it then?" she demanded.

"In case I run into her again. Don't go getting all jealous, now. If I had a girlfriend I'd be giving *her* a necklace, not the other way around."

That hadn't made her feel better. He'd had a lot of late nights at work for the past few weeks, and some of those times she had checked up on him and found that he wasn't really at the plant. When confronted, he always had some excuse—that he was sent to work on a car at some government agency, or that he'd been dispatched to run an errand. Funny that no one at work said that when she asked them where he was. She had threatened to leave him and take little Star home to her parents. Those threats always pulled remorse and apologies from him, and he'd straighten up for a while.

But the police wouldn't have come here for infidelity, would they? They wouldn't care whether he was faithful to his wife.

It had to be more than that.

She finally went to bed but lay awake staring at the darkness, listening to the sound of her baby's breathing in the bassinet next to her, wishing Clay would come home.

And then she heard the door. She jumped to her feet and grabbed the rifle as someone came in.

"Analee?"

She heard Clay's voice as he came through the house, and a combination of relief and anger burst through her. Setting the rifle back down, she ran to see him. "Where have you been? The police were here asking about you. Do you have any idea what I've been going through today? The baby was crying all day and I was worried—"

He set a hand over her mouth to stop her talking. "Analee, listen to me. We don't have much time."

fifty-nine

CLAY ALWAYS HAD TROUBLE GETTING HIS WIFE TO LISTEN to him. In fact, it was hard getting a word in. She spoke every thought that came into her mind, fully formed or not. But now she seemed speechless as he removed his hand from her mouth.

"I'm in some trouble," he said in a voice just above a whisper. He went to the window, looked out, then closed and locked it. "And it's my own fault. But I need you to listen to me and understand how it happened."

She followed him into the kitchen. He closed and locked the window there, and wished he could light a lamp so she could see the sincerity on his face. But he couldn't take that chance.

"Have you been hiding from the police?" she asked.

"Analee, just listen to me."

"I am listening."

"I lied to you," he said. "When we got your grandfather's inheritance, I told you that I'd put it in the bank, that it was safely tucked away in our savings account."

"Wasn't it?"

"No, it wasn't."

She stiffened, and in the moonlight coming in through a window, he saw her face hardening. "Clay, what did you do?"

He moved toward her, set his hands on her shoulders. "I got stupid."

"What do you mean, you got stupid?"

He pulled her to the couch, set her down. Then he sat on the coffee table, facing her. His breath was heavy, and he longed to wash his face and hands and change his clothes. What a long, foolish day it had been.

He drew his thoughts back to Analee. "I started to think that I could double it, if I could just get a winning hand at blackjack."

"Oh no. Don't tell me!" She shoved his shoulders. "You told me you'd stopped gambling. You promised!"

"I know," he said. "But I couldn't help myself. I just knew I could win and double the money. Maybe even triple it."

"You lost it, didn't you?" She said the words bitterly, tears glistening in her eyes.

"Yeah, I lost it."

She got up and walked away from him, turned back. "But I don't understand. You brought home cash the other day. It was two percent of what I thought we had. How did you do that if it wasn't in the bank?"

His throat was dry, and he couldn't make himself say it.

"What did you do, steal it?"

His silence arced like electricity between them.

"You did! You *stole* it!"

He walked around the couch. "I took it from somebody else who got theirs from the bank that day. It was a classic holdup. I pulled a gun and told them to give me all their money or else. And they did. It was no big deal."

"Armed robbery was no big deal?" Her mouth hung open. "Clay, what were you thinking?"

"I did it for you. That seemed better than telling you the truth. I knew if I did you'd leave me."

"No," she said. "Don't blame this on me!" Her eyes moved from side to side, as if she was going back over everything in her head. "No wonder they're looking for you. They asked for your picture. What if the person you robbed can identify you?"

"You didn't give that to them, did you? Analee, tell me you didn't."

"I didn't," she said. "But I had no idea that you had done something like that. Why couldn't you tell me about the gambling? I could have dealt with that."

He swallowed hard. "You have to understand, I did this for you. I couldn't bear to see you disappointed in me again. I didn't want to lose you and Star. I thought I could fix it."

Her hands came up to grasp her hair at the roots. "Clay, you have to go to the police. You have to turn yourself in."

"No, I can't."

"Why not? It's the only right thing to do. Besides, they already know. They were here!"

"I know they were. And they're watching the house now. I saw a patrol car over at the school."

"A patrol car? Watching us?"

"Don't worry. They didn't see me."

She was on the verge of hysteria, so he grabbed her shoulders and shook her. "Analee, listen to me. I'm not going to prison. Do you know how many people did the same thing that day? How much money was taken from other people?"

"It wasn't theirs," she shouted. "They should go to jail too!"

"It's payback for what the casinos did to me."

"The casinos didn't do it to you. You did it to yourself before the Pulses." She shook free of him. "Who *are* you?"

"I want you to come with me. We have to leave town tonight."

She shook his hands off of her. "I'm not going anywhere with you!"

"Please! Analee, what's it going to be like if you stay here and they come for me? You care so much what people think about you, and what they're going to think is that you're the wife of an armed robber. How will you feel if I'm in prison and you have to go about your life with everybody knowing that?"

She dropped her hands. "Why did you do this to me?"

"Honey, we can fix it. I can borrow a car from the conversion plant."

"Borrow? You mean *steal?*"

"Borrow. I've worked on enough of those cars to own half of them. We'll just take it and plan to bring it back sometime. I know where we can get some gas. We can get to your parents' house before daybreak." When she shook her head, he added, "They can see the baby for the first time. We'll surprise them."

"I don't want to bring my parents into this."

"Why not?" he asked. "With communication still down, the police departments won't even be talking to each other. Nobody's gonna know. We can tell them we just decided we wanted our family together. They've been trying to get you to come anyway. All those letters. They never have to know. We can start over there. And honey, I have the cash. I've still got it."

She began to sob and dropped onto the couch. "Why did I marry you? How did I miss the clues that you were like this?"

"You married me because you love me, and I'm *not* like that. I'm a good person. I did what I had to do to take care of you and Star. It'll be okay. No one will ever have to know what happened. I swear, I'll never be so stupid again. I've learned my lesson. Give me a second chance, so Star won't have to grow up being the child of a prisoner. She shouldn't have to pay for what I've done. We have to protect her."

Her face changed, and she looked at him. He knew he had broken through. If he could just get her to consider it, he could take her the rest of the way.

"No one got hurt," he whispered. "It was just money. When we get there, I'll send it back to the guy if you want me to."

"Then you know him?"

"Yes. I threw his wallet away, but I remember his name and address."

Her eyes rounded. "You would send it back? And we could start over without having to worry?"

"I promise you, sweetheart."

She considered him for a moment. "If I do this ..."

He had her. "Yes?"

"If I do this, there's not going to be any more gambling, even if the casinos open back up. Even if they come and beg you to play with them. I don't want to hear anything about gambling. Do you see how it's ruined our lives?"

"It hasn't ruined them," he said. "Honey, we can start over and pretend this never even happened. But we have to go *now*."

He reached out for her, and she didn't push him away. Her arms slid around him, and she wept into his shoulder. He'd won. She was going to give him that second chance, and soon they would be on their way out of town. He would be able to keep his baby, and still evade the police.

sixty

THE SOUND OF A BABY CRYING ALERTED MARK THAT something had changed in the neighborhood. He'd taken a break from walking to sit in the dark doorway of the school, forcing himself to stay awake as he waited for Clay Tharpe to come home.

He couldn't see his watch, but it had to be two a.m. He'd been here for hours. And the crying baby's voice drifted up on the wind.

He crossed the parking lot, walking slowly up the street. Maybe some child had woken in the middle of the night, and its cries were carrying through open windows. He scanned the street, looking for a light flickering on in one of the houses. None did.

As he neared the Tharpe house, he saw that the garage door was open. The beam of a flashlight moved inside the bay.

Drawing his weapon, he went behind the house on the opposite side from the garage. He crossed the back-yard—knowing this qualified as trespassing. But what was he to do? Let Tharpe walk?

Maybe it was just Analee, looking for something in the garage. But the garage had been closed half an hour ago. He was sure of it. Why would she have opened it?

He felt in his gut that Tharpe had come home—but why hadn't Mark seen him? He'd watched the house all night. Maybe Tharpe had anticipated that someone was watching the house. Maybe he'd even seen Mark's van and come up from behind the house.

As Mark moved through the yard, he glanced toward the windows. Everything was still dark. He reached the garage, flattened himself against the wall, and crept to the front. The baby had stopped crying, but he could hear movement, muffled voices—a man's and a woman's.

He was right. Tharpe was home.

He eased around to the edge of the garage opening, his weapon pointed skyward. In one movement, he stepped toward the open bay and brought his gun down. "Freeze!" he shouted.

Analee screamed, and the baby choked out a cry. But he couldn't see Tharpe. He moved the gun in sharp jerks, his eyes wide as he searched the darkness.

He heard a whoosh from the wall next to him. Something smashed into his head.

Pain burst white and broad, and he felt himself falling backward, his head hitting the concrete, the gun flying from his hand. Footsteps came closer, and he forced his eyes open and saw Tharpe standing over him with a two-by-four raised for another blow.

"Don't, Clay," Analee cried. "You'll kill him!"

"I got his gun," Tharpe said. "Come on, let's go."

Mark tried to pull himself out of his stupor as they rode out on bicycles. He rolled over, tried to get his knees under him, pushed himself up. Stumbling to his feet, he felt his head clearing. He touched his forehead; blood dripped into his eyes. He'd been hit in the head before ... and had a scar on the other side of his forehead to prove it.

It wasn't as bad as he thought. The fog was clearing. He looked up the street, saw the reflective lights on their bikes as Tharpe and his wife rode away, turning the corner.

Mark tried to run after them, but they'd gotten a head start. He made it to the corner, but they were too far away to catch on foot.

He turned back and ran for his van.

When had Clay come home? Why hadn't he seen him? Mark bolted across the parking lot at the school and around to his car. Jumping in, he stepped on the gas and turned the key.

It cranked, but wouldn't catch.

He tried again, pumping the accelerator. Tharpe knew car engines inside and out. He must have tampered with it while Mark was walking up and down the street. Now what? If he took the time to figure out what was wrong with the engine, they'd be long gone and he'd never find them. But he'd never catch up to them on foot, either.

Slamming the heel of his hand on the steering wheel, he got his flashlight and opened the hood. He wiped the blood dripping into his eyes on his sleeve, and saw that it wasn't the battery. The cables were still tightly clamped. He looked for the distributor cap and realized it had been removed.

He kicked the side of his vehicle, knowing he wasn't going anywhere in it tonight. He took off running as fast as his legs would carry him, hoping to at least see the direction the Tharpes were going.

sixty-one

CLAY AND ANALEE RODE AS IF THEIR LIVES DEPENDED ON it, not speaking as he led her up the streets that would take them to the conversion plant. Star had stopped crying. Soon they would have her in a car, and Analee could hold her as they made their way out of the state. He hoped he could find gas.

They turned onto Alabaster Street. The lights to the conversion plant were off, and it looked as though no one was there. He pulled onto the lot. Though they kept long hours here, from seven in the morning until ten at night, there was usually no activity in the wee hours.

Analee pulled up to the door and put her foot on the ground, balancing the bike. "Clay, you didn't kill him, did you?"

"No, I just surprised him and knocked him off his feet."

"Because you can't go around killing cops. I was with you. What if we get caught and they think I'm an accessory? What would happen to Star then?"

"I said I didn't kill him!" He went to the door and shook the knob, knowing he couldn't get in. They hadn't given him a key. He wasn't that high up in the hierarchy yet. But he knew how to get into the cars parked behind the place. There were a few already converted and waiting for pickup by government agencies. He could hot-wire one of those.

"Wait here," he said. "I'll come around with a car."

"I'm scared," she said. "I don't want to stand here by myself."

He came to her bike, unhooked the baby, and picked her up. As Analee got off the bike, he kissed Star and handed her to her mother. "All right, come with me. Just leave the bikes here. We won't need them anymore."

"But they're valuable. We'll need them in Huntsville. We can't do without them."

"Analee, work with me here!"

"But Clay, they'll identify us when they find our bikes. They'll know we're the ones who stole the car."

He hadn't thought of that. Sighing, he said, "This is getting really complicated."

"Then let's don't do it. Let's just go back. You can turn yourself in. We can pay the money back. Maybe they'll let you go after the restitution is paid."

That would be fine if it was just as he'd told her. But there was no restitution for murder, or for assaulting a police officer. He had no choice but to run. "I need you to stay quiet," he said. "I don't know for sure if anybody's here."

She shut up, and he led her quietly around the building. There were seven cars there that they had converted, but the keys to each were inside the building. One of them was a pickup truck. Maybe that was the one he should try.

"Okay, we can put the bikes in that truck."

She seemed satisfied at that, so they retrieved the bikes and rolled them to the truck. He put them into the bed. The truck was locked, so he found a crowbar and knocked the window out. He unlocked it, then dusted the glass fragments off the seat. "Get in."

They hadn't been able to bring the car seat for the baby, but it wouldn't have mattered. The truck was so old that it didn't even have seat belts, so Analee climbed in and held the child in her arms. Holding his flashlight in his teeth, Clay got under the dashboard and hot-wired the engine. It rumbled to life.

He pulled himself up into the driver's seat, looking to see how much fuel he had. Only an eighth of a tank, but that was enough to get them all the way out of town. Maybe he could get a little more out of the filling station next to the building.

He backed the truck out and pulled it around to one of the fuel tanks. He tried it, but the spigots were locked soundly in their cradles, so that no one could steal fuel.

Oh, well. Maybe he could go from one police station to another, siphoning gas out of their squad cars. It was risky, but they were the only ones he was sure had gas.

He got back into the truck and closed the door. The baby was already asleep in Analee's arms. Analee looked resigned to the situation they were in, and she was quiet—a rare occurrence. He hoped she stayed that way. He pulled the truck out of the parking lot and headed north.

sixty-two

MARK WAS DRIPPING WITH SWEAT AND OUT OF BREATH by the time he reached the sheriff's department. He burst through the front doors and cried out to the dozing deputy, "Give me the keys to your car. They got away!"

Billy London got to his feet. "What? Who got away?"

"Clay Tharpe." He saw the keys lying on his desk and went to grab them. "He took the distributor cap off my car so I couldn't go after him."

Billy followed him to the door. "Who's Clay Tharpe?"

"A murderer, that's who."

"The one who killed that little girl today?"

Mark swung around. "Killed? Don't tell me she's dead!" He grabbed Billy's arm. "Did Beth die?"

"No, I don't know. I just thought—"

"Did someone come tell you she's dead?" he screamed.

Billy fell back over a desk. "No, I haven't heard anything. I meant to say he *attacked* the little girl."

Mark let him go. He stepped back, adrenaline pounding through his heart.

"Man, get a grip. You should go home and get some rest."

"I can't," Mark said. "They're gonna get away. Then what good are we?" He looked down at the keys in his hand. "Look, if any of the squad cars come back in, tell them we're looking for a man and a woman on bicycles with a baby on the back."

"How will they know it's them?"

Mark wanted to slug him. Through his teeth, he said, "They'll be the only man and woman with a baby on bicycles at three in the morning."

Then he hurried out to the car parked haphazardly at the curb. He started the car and headed in the direction he thought the Tharpes had gone. His heart still hammered from his fright at the thought of Beth dying. "God, please don't let her die. Pull her through this, Lord. We can't lose her."

As he prayed, his eyes searched frantically through the night for the killer who had duped him.

sixty-three

By DAWN, MARK HAD GIVEN UP ON TRYING TO FIND THE Tharpes. He had searched every street in Crockett. The knot on his head where Clay had hit him with the plank had swollen. It hurt like an ice pick probing through his brain, and the skin was crusted with dry blood. He was hungry and thirsty and utterly exhausted.

When he finally came back to the sheriff's department at 7:30 a.m., he learned that a car had been stolen from the conversion plant. There was no doubt in his mind who had taken it. That explained how they'd gotten out of town without being caught, but he had no clues as to which way they had gone or what their destination might have been.

Wheaton and the rest of the guys on the daytime shift insisted that he go home and get some rest while they canvassed the Tharpes' neighborhood and talked to his coworkers. Maybe there were relatives nearby — parents, cousins, uncles, or aunts. Good friends who might live in other towns.

"We'll find them, I promise you," Wheaton said. "Tharpe is behaving like a guilty man, and these crimes won't go unpunished."

But Mark wasn't so sure. He sat on his desk, staring into space, trying to think of some way to speed up this process.

"Mark, I'm ordering you to take off and get some rest."

"I can't." He felt his emotions coming forth like a tsunami, rolling its deadly waves over his lungs, his heart, his throat. He was losing control, drowning. He rubbed his trembling mouth, closed his eyes.

Wheaton's voice softened. "Mark, go to the hospital. Be with your girl. She needs you."

His shoulders shook with his failure. "I wanted to take her good news."

"You tried. You did more than anybody else did. And it's not over. We'll get him."

Mark wiped his face and tried to toughen up.

"Take one of the patrol cars," Wheaton said, patting his back. "Get somebody to look at your head. While you're gone, we'll get a mechanic to replace the distributor cap on the van Tharpe vandalized."

Mark drove to the hospital and sat in the parking lot for a moment, trying to pull himself together before he saw Deni. The last thing she should have to do was comfort *him*.

He found the surgical ICU waiting room on the third floor. Families clustered in distinct areas all around the place, some of them sleeping, others talking quietly. They all looked like they'd been to the front lines in a war with death.

Across the room, Logan slept on a blanket on the floor, and Jeff was out cold in one of those plastic recliners. Deni sat next to him—and next to Craig. She was sound asleep, her head resting on Craig's shoulder. Craig's head was rolled on top of hers, and he, too, was asleep. Mark's throat closed up, and he thought of turning and walking away. But the fight in him rose again, and he resolved that he wasn't letting Deni go, not like this.

He stooped in front of her, touched her knee. She jumped.

"Hey," he whispered.

"You're here." Extracting herself from Craig, she fell into Mark's arms, and he rose higher on his knees and held her with all his strength. He felt her tears on his neck, breathed in the scent of her hair, basked in the comfort of her embrace.

"I wanted to come earlier," he whispered. "But I was out chasing Clay Tharpe."

"Is he the one who hurt her?"

"No doubt in my mind," he whispered against her hair. He pulled her to her feet. "Let's go sit somewhere else."

She glanced back at Craig. Her movement had awakened him, and Mark saw the challenge in his sleepy eyes. She took Mark's hand and pulled him to an empty area. "Mark, did you catch this guy Tharpe?"

He didn't want to worry her with the details. "Not yet. The department's still working on it. Tell me about Beth."

"She's still in a coma. She won't wake up." She noticed the bloody bruise on his forehead, touched it gently. "What happened to you?"

He forced a smile. "I'm working on a scar to match the one on the other side, so I'll look balanced."

She didn't find that funny. "Did somebody hit you?"

"Yeah, with a two-by-four, but don't worry about it."

Vengeance flashed in her eyes. "Was this the guy who attacked Beth?"

"Yes, I think it was."

Deni's eyes rounded. "I thought you hadn't caught him."

He sighed. "I had him, but he swung and knocked me off balance, and he got away." He touched her face, wanting her to understand. "I went after him. I've been looking for him for five hours."

There it was again, the tsunami, choking him, pulling at the corners of his lips, burning his eyes.

She pulled him back into her arms and held him, and he let the storm have its way. She didn't let him go.

He hated himself for his weakness, and hated even more the fact that Craig had witnessed it. He pulled himself together and wiped his nose on his sleeve. As he pulled out of her arms, his gaze collided with Craig's.

Deni seemed to notice. "I didn't mean to fall asleep on his shoulder," she whispered against his ear. "He was sitting next to me, and I must have slid over when I fell asleep."

"Do me a favor," he said, "next time don't sit next to him."

"I won't. Please don't be upset about that."

He shook his head. "No, we have plenty of other things to be concerned about."

He saw Doug coming into the room, looking exhausted. He smiled when he saw Mark. "Hey, buddy," he whispered so as not to wake the other families.

Mark got up and embraced him. Quickly, he told him about his night, and his close call with Tharpe.

"Valiant try, son," Doug said. "I appreciate that a lot."

"Get some rest, Mark," Deni said. "Just sit down and close your eyes for a minute. I'll be right here. We'll wake you if we hear any news about Beth."

Mark looked at Craig, met his cool gaze. No, he wasn't going to sleep.

But to appease Deni, he pulled out the footrest on his plastic recliner, and laid his head back.

sixty-four

MARK HADN'T MEANT TO DOZE OFF. WHEN HE WOKE, he realized that a couple of hours had passed. Deni wasn't there. Craig still sat in the chair he'd been in when Mark arrived. His clothes were rumpled, but he still looked like the professional he was. Thick stubble darkened his jaw and dark circles underlined his eyes.

Mark lowered his footrest and pushed his hand through his hair.

"Didn't mean to nod off. Where's Deni?"

Craig looked like he didn't want to answer. "She went to relieve her mother for a few minutes, while Kay cleans up."

Mark said nothing else. The two of them sat in silence, seats away from each other, waiting. Finally, he saw Doug coming through the door. His eyes were wet. "How is she?" Mark asked.

"The same." He motioned back to the door. "Go in and see her if you want. Deni's in there alone right now."

Craig's mouth fell open. "I thought it was just family."

Doug looked down at him, then back up at Mark. "Mark is family."

It was all Mark could do not to strut after that. He headed to the ICU, told the nurse whom he was there to see, and she gave him a set of scrubs. He pulled them on, fixed the mask over his mouth and nose, and found some gloves, hoping he wasn't dragging any germs in with him. When he'd done everything the nurse told him to do, he went into the room she pointed to.

Deni got up and kissed him. "You're awake."

"Yeah," he said. "Sorry I nodded off." He walked to the side of the bed, and tears rimmed his eyes as he looked down at his young friend. He'd never seen anyone look this bad before. Her face was swollen, her head shaven and bandaged. He thought of Clay Tharpe with his hands around her throat, smashing her head against a tree trunk. Mark could feel his blood pressure rising. His hands shook as he reached down and stroked Beth's arm.

"Talk to her," Deni said. "Maybe she'll hear you."

He leaned over, putting his face close to Beth's. His voice wobbled. "Wake up, Sparky," he said. "A lot of people out here are really worried about you. We need you. Get better. You can't let this beat you. And just so you know, I'm on the trail of the man who did this to you. He's never gonna hurt anybody else. We'll get him. Don't you worry."

Still, there was no response.

Mark wanted to race out of the building with his sights set on Tharpe like a guided missile, and do to him what he'd done to Beth. "It's not right," he said through his teeth.

Wiping his face, he looked around the room. "Let's get her some books and read to her. She must be bored to death, lying there like that. If she's the least bit aware—"

"Do you think she is?"

"I heard about a guy who was in a coma, and he knew sign language. He communicated with his mom that way."

"But I've asked her to move a finger if she can hear me, and she doesn't."

"Still. It might stimulate her brain, help her to come to. What books does she like?"

"She loves the Chronicles of Narnia."

"Are they at home? I could go get them."

"That would be great," Deni said.

He leaned back over the bed. "You hear that, Sparky? We're gonna filibuster you until you snap out of it."

He kissed Deni, then left her there. He ripped off the mask and gloves and took off his scrubs. Dropping them into the laundry bin, he headed out of the ICU, determined to make Tharpe pay for what he'd done.

sixty-five

By the time Mark returned to the sheriff's department, Wheaton and the dayshift deputies had finished questioning Tharpe's neighbors and coworkers.

Wheaton had listed all of their leads on a big dry-erase board in the back room. "We found out that both of his parents are dead," Wheaton said as he sat on the table opposite the board. "But it turns out that his wife has parents who live up in Huntsville. And the neighbors said she's been real homesick for them since the Pulses began. They haven't seen her baby yet."

Mark's brows came together as he studied the board. "Any other relatives?"

"The neighbors didn't know of any, so I guess there aren't any important ones. I think Huntsville's our strongest lead."

"Did the guys at work have anything to offer?"

"Oh, yeah. They were so ticked about him stealing the car that they were ready to spill their guts. Couple of them said that a few months ago he'd put in for a transfer to one of the Huntsville plants. Ned Emory confirmed that, but he didn't agree to the transfer."

Mark took in the other notes on the board. Under "Huntsville In-Laws," Wheaton had written, "Infidelity." Mark pointed to it. "What's this about?"

Wheaton crossed his arms. "One of his coworkers told me that Mr. Tharpe wasn't always faithful to his wife. He has a weakness for pretty women. And he has a gambling addiction. The same guy was Tharpe's gambling buddy. Said that before the Pulses Tharpe lost their life savings. He kept it from his wife."

How could that fit into the murder and assault? Was the robbery of Blake Tomlin to make up for the lost money? Maybe that was his motive. "Can we go to Huntsville and bring him back?"

"Brad Caldwell gave us a green light for the arrest after he heard about Tharpe assaulting you. The prosecutor wants the guy locked up as much as we do."

"Did anybody have the address of the parents in Huntsville?"

"Yep," Wheaton said. "Turns out their next-door neighbor had it from a couple of years ago when they'd gone home for a week. Left the phone number and address in case of emergency."

"What are we waiting for?" Mark asked. "Let's go to Huntsville."

sixty-six

THE OLD VAN WAS IN SERIOUS NEED OF A FRONT-END ALIGN-
ment, and whenever they increased their speed over fifty
miles an hour, the steering wheel shook and shimmied. It
was a gas guzzler and got about ten miles to a gallon, less if
they were in town. But they had brought along another tank
of gas that they hoped would get them there and back without having to stop and search for another source.

It took them two and a half hours to get to Huntsville—
much too long as far as Mark was concerned—but Wheaton
didn't appreciate backseat driving. Billy London rode shot-
gun, constantly fidgeting and glancing at the speedometer.
The horses and wagons and bicycle trailers on the highway
continually got in their way.

After what seemed an eternity, they got to the Huntsville
exit. Pulling off into the parking lot of a closed convenience
store, they tried to figure out where they were. After a few
minutes, they had the place mapped out and were on their
way to Clay Tharpe's in-laws.

They drove to the neighborhood, aware that once they
turned onto the street their engine would alert every resident
there.

Wheaton decided to park on the next block over. "He's
not gonna come without a fight, so let's move quietly and
cover the doors and windows before we let them know we're
here. Once we've apprehended him, we can go back for the
van."

They locked the van, then took off on foot to the next street over. Drawing their weapons, they fanned out around the house. While Sheriff Wheaton and London went to the door, Mark covered the back, watching the windows and doors, expecting Tharpe to make a quick exit. He heard the pounding on the door, heard Sheriff Wheaton calling out "Po-lice!"

Suddenly the back door flew open, and Tharpe lunged out.

"Hold it right there!"

Tharpe froze.

"Hands behind your head!"

Tharpe did as he was told, but his eyes shifted from side to side, looking for escape. "I want my lawyer!" he shouted. "I'll have you arrested for stalking. First, my house, now this!"

Keeping the barrel of his Glock aimed between Tharpe's eyes, Mark moved closer. "On the ground!"

Tharpe knelt, hands still behind his head. "Look, I know you're chapped about the two-by-four, but you scared me. It was self-defense."

Mark pulled his handcuffs off his belt and got behind Tharpe. He pressed the barrel of his pistol against Tharpe's head and snapped a cuff onto one wrist. Before he could get the second one on, Tharpe swung around suddenly and grabbed the gun.

Rage shot through Mark's head, pounding in his temples, as he struggled to overpower him. Tharpe's grip around Mark's wrist was strong—the same grip that had almost killed Beth. Mark threw the weight of his body into loosening Tharpe's grip. Inches from his was the face Beth had seen before she fell unconscious.

Vengeance exploded in Mark's brain, and he slammed his head into Tharpe's face. Pain blasted through his busted forehead, but he felt Tharpe's nose crunch. The killer let the gun go and brought his hands to his face. Mark knocked him to the ground and wrestled the other cuff on. Tharpe screamed like a little girl.

His wife came out wailing, her shocked parents behind her. "He didn't do anything! Please—"

Mark jerked the man to his feet as Wheaton and London came around the house.

"Let him go!" Analee cried. "We've got a baby! He'll pay the money back."

Mark was breathless as he recited Tharpe's Miranda rights. When he finished, he said through his teeth, "You're under arrest for the attempted murder of Beth Branning, assault of a police officer, evading arrest, and grand theft auto, just for starters." Mark wanted to add that he was charged with the murder of Blake Tomlin and some other unnamed person that Beth mentioned in her note, but they didn't have the bodies yet. Brad had sent instructions to haul him in on the other charges first.

"I was just trying to save my family," Clay said. "I stole the car but I was going to bring it back. I wasn't going to keep it. I didn't attempt to murder anybody. I don't even know what you're talking about."

"There's a little girl dying in the hospital."

Clay spat at him. Mark grabbed his face in his hands. "I'd kill you with my bare hands," he said through his teeth, "but instead I'll find the bodies of the two men she saw you murder and let the state do it for me."

"You're not going to find anything!"

"Watch me," Mark said. "We found you, didn't we?"

London got the van, and Mark took pleasure in throwing Tharpe in, then climbing in next to him to make sure he didn't go anywhere. His wife insisted on coming with them. She said tearful good-byes to her worried parents, then bringing the sleeping baby, she got into the van.

Wheaton turned around and pointed at her. "You can ride as far as we can get without you saying a word."

Analee just swallowed. "I have the right to free speech. I'm still an American, you know. I think you should know that my husband is innocent. He couldn't kill anyone!"

Wheaton almost came over the seat. "What did I tell you?"

"Okay," she said. "Not another word."

They were all silent as they drove back to Crockett. It wasn't until they arrived that Mark unclenched his fists. Relief shot through him as he got Tharpe behind bars and slammed the door.

Then he stormed back to the front. "Sheriff, we have to search his house and yard. There are two bodies we haven't found yet."

"We don't even know that for sure," Wheaton said.

"Beth had no reason to lie about it, and she wrote it in that note. He moved the bodies somewhere. I say we start with his yard, since it isn't that far from the Cracker Barrel. His yard is fenced in. He could have buried them without being seen."

He'd forgotten that Analee was sitting across the room. She got up and shoved her chin into the air. "I *welcome* you to search my yard," she said. "There's no one buried there. My husband is not a killer."

"Fine, then we don't need a warrant. Let's go," he said to the sheriff.

Wheaton tagged several of the men. "Come on, we've got work to do."

sixty-seven

THE THARPES' BACKYARD WAS PLOWED AND FILLED WITH a vegetable garden—which surprised Mark, since the front yard wasn't plowed. Rows of cabbage, carrots, and radishes filled the yard in healthy soil. The garden had been well-tended, so it was difficult to tell where graves might have been dug. But Mark walked along the rows, looking for plants that might be freshly planted, or dirt that had recently been turned.

Analee chattered nonstop. "My husband is a fantastic father and a great husband. He would never hurt a fly."

Mark stooped and checked one of the younger plants.

"Please don't pull up my plants and don't step on them. That's our food!"

Mark wished she'd go check on the baby. He looked at the dirt that looked a little darker than the rest. No, this couldn't be it. There was crabgrass here, and it was mature. He got up and walked on.

Near the back of the yard stood a portable shed. Wheaton was already at the door, shining his flashlight around inside. It was possible that Tharpe might have stored the bodies there temporarily, but he wouldn't have left it there. It had stopped raining the afternoon of the murders. He would have been able to dig a grave that night if he'd wanted to.

Mark walked behind the shed. The dirt did look freshly turned there, even though some vegetables had been planted. Something was wrong, though. These plants weren't as neatly planted as the rest of the vegetables. He stooped and examined the young plants. They were cucumber plants—he had them in his own yard. But they needed full sun, and between this shed and the fence, these plants would be in the shade for most of the day.

If there was a grave here, this could be the place. Mark stood up and looked around. If he had been the killer, he would have dug the grave behind the shed. It would have kept Analee from seeing what he was doing. He could have hidden the bodies in the shed until the rain stopped and the ground had time to dry a little, then dug behind here to bury them. Analee would have thought he was simply working in the garden.

"Sheriff, over here," Mark said. The sheriff came out of the shed and London joined him behind it. In a low voice, he said, "These are cucumbers. They need sun. Either he's ignorant about plants, which doesn't seem to be the case, or he planted them here just to cover something else. They look freshly planted. Look at the soil."

The sheriff agreed. "London, get me my shovel."

London crossed the yard and got the shovel leaning against the house.

"What are you doing?" Analee asked, following him. "You're not going to dig up my plants, are you?"

"Just a few of them," Wheaton said. "Ma'am, I need you to go back in."

"No! I have a right to see what you're doing to my property!"

Wheaton looked up at her. "Do you want to prove your husband's innocence? If he didn't do anything, then you have nothing to fear."

"But my plants!"

"If we don't find anything, you have my word we'll put them back."

Grudgingly, she headed back in. But Mark was sure she was watching through the window.

Wheaton took the shovel and stabbed the blade into the ground, tossed aside the dirt. Summer sun beat down on Mark's neck and sweat dripped from his chin. His heart raced as Wheaton dug the blade in again and again.

The dirt was soft, easily giving way. Mark and London stood still, watching as Wheaton's hole got bigger, deeper. He was digging too slowly, so Mark stepped up. "Here, let me."

Wheaton surrendered the shovel and wiped his face.

Mark thought of Beth's note, the two men she'd seen murdered. The image of her lying swollen and dying on that hospital bed drove him to dig faster. They were there—the certainty made the hairs on his neck rise.

He rammed the shovel into the dirt and felt his blade hit something. "There's something there." He dropped the shovel and went down on his knees, digging gingerly with his hands, trying not to disturb any evidence he found. He felt the object, dusted the dirt away.

It was a shoe. He looked up. "Here we go."

Wheaton knelt next to him. "Let's see what else is there." They both dug with their hands around the shoe. Some denim cloth emerged.

When they reached the man's twisted body, Mark sat back. Some inexplicable grief broadsided him, and he fought back tears. Beth was right.

As Wheaton uncovered the second body, Mark covered his face with his dirty hands, and thanked God that justice would be done.

ANALEE FELL APART WHEN THEY BROUGHT HER OUT TO SEE THE dead men her husband had buried. "Why would he do that?" she cried. "I don't understand. He told me that he gambled our money away before the Pulses, and when the banks opened he was going to be found out. So he had to rob somebody. He didn't tell me he'd *killed* anyone. I never would have left town with him if I'd known that."

Mark believed her, but it didn't calm his anger. "Did he tell you that a thirteen-year-old girl witnessed the murders, and that he tried to kill her?"

She put her hands over her ears. "No, I can't believe he could do something like that."

"You want to come to the hospital and see?"

Wheaton held up a hand warning Mark to calm down. "Analee, now that you've seen what your husband is capable of, we need you to come to the department and make a statement."

She was trembling and unsteady, sobbing hard. "Okay," she said finally. "I'll tell you whatever you need to know."

sixty-eight

KAY'S HANDS ACHED FROM MASSAGING BETH'S LEGS. HER daughter still lay there like a rag doll. Was she already gone? Had her soul departed at the park that day? Was her brain still working?

She rubbed her tired eyes and picked up the Bible from the table. They'd been reading it aloud, hoping to banish the spirits of darkness and death that hovered over the place. They had started at Genesis and had read straight through, a segment at a time. Doug had left it open to Psalm 55. " 'My heart is in anguish within me,' " she read aloud, " 'and the terrors of death have fallen upon me. Fear and trembling come upon me, and horror has overwhelmed me.' "

She stopped and swallowed, then forced herself to go on. " 'I said, "Oh, that I had wings like a dove! I would fly away and be at rest. Behold, I would wander far away, I would lodge in the wilderness. Selah. I would hasten to my place of refuge from the stormy wind and tempest." ' "

Oh, if she *could* run away. If she could only shrug off this heavy mantle of despair and fly away to a time beyond now. A time when there was no pain.

"Mom?"

She turned her weary face. Jeff stood tentatively just inside the room. "Dad said for me to relieve you. Mark is here with some news about Beth's attacker."

Her attacker? The only good news would be that he was dead.

She straightened Beth's covers, stroked her hair, kissed her cheek. "Okay, I'm coming. Read to her, sweetie."

As Jeff took her place, she walked through the valley of death—what the intensive care unit had become to her—and took off her scrubs. Her muscles ached with fatigue as she scuffed out of the place and went to the waiting room.

Mark sat with Deni and Doug, a black bruise across his forehead. He looked even more battered than she felt. "Did you find the man who did this?" she asked.

"We did," Mark said. "We have him in custody."

Custody. It sounded so benign, like a child in the presence of loving parents. He may be behind bars, but he was healthy and safe ... in one piece. Not broken like Beth. "What's his name?" Her voice sounded raspy and hoarse.

"Clay Tharpe."

Kay sat down and looked at her hands. She folded them into a church and steeple, all the people shivering and hunkering inside. "Has he confessed?"

"No," Mark said. "But we found the two bodies where he buried them."

She looked at Doug, saw the anguish on his face. As if to hide it, he rubbed his jaw. She feared he would rub off the skin.

"Did he come without a fight?" Doug asked.

Mark's hand came up to his forehead. "No, he didn't. I had to break his nose to subdue him."

Somehow, it helped to know the man had an injury of his own. She hoped he'd go through the rest of his life disfigured.

KAY SAT FROZEN FOR A WHILE IN HER SEAT IN THE WAITING room, staring at the wall and wondering what this man—this Clay Tharpe—looked like. Was he a hulk or a skinny coward? Could you look at him and see evil, or did he have a face people trusted?

She fought the compulsion—the desperation—to see him face-to-face.

The Israelites had it right, when they assigned a blood avenger to take the life of their relatives' murderer. She imagined herself being the one who turned his evil back on him.

When Deni touched her hand, she jumped. "Mom, are you all right?"

"Yes. Fine."

"I thought you'd be more relieved that they found him. Aren't you glad?"

Glad? No, glad wasn't the word she would have used. "Yes, I'm glad," she said anyway.

"I thought ... well, I expected you to react a little ... differently. You haven't said much."

Kay forced herself to focus. "Did you? What did you expect me to do? Cry? Scream? Put my fist through the wall? Laugh? Dance? *What?*"

Deni shrank back, clearly hurt at her mother's tone. "I thought you'd be glad," she said in a weak voice. "That's all."

"I told you I am." She got up, unable to sit here any longer. "I'm going out to the bathroom."

She left them in the waiting room and headed outside where Porta-Johns sat lined up in a row. But something compelled her to walk past them. She needed exercise to burn off the vengeance in her head, to sweat away the poison of hatred. She walked past the post office and the boarded up trophy shop, past the Dunkin' Donuts that hadn't cooked a donut in a year, past the high school that had no kids. She walked without calculating the number of blocks ... though her mind had decided on her route.

She turned up Fremont Street and crossed its intersection with Monroe Boulevard. The sheriff's department sat at the end of the road, blocks separating it from other buildings. Somewhere within those walls sat the barbaric animal who'd hurt Beth.

She knew what she had to do.

Long, purposeful strides moved her along the street, up the steps to the front door, through the glass doors. There was no one in the front room. She heard voices in the sheriff's office, but whoever it was hadn't heard her come in.

Perfect.

Her heart whipped against her chest wall as she crossed the room to the steel door separating the offices from the jail cells. Quickly she opened it and slipped into the dark, muggy room. It was ten degrees hotter than it was outdoors, and the place smelled of urine and body odor.

She caught the door so it wouldn't slam with that crashing metallic sound meant to frighten first-timers. There were fewer than ten men scattered throughout the five cells. She searched the dimly lit room for someone with a broken nose.

Several of the men made catcalls and lewd suggestions as she walked from one cell to the next, searching for that misshapen nose. Finally, she saw a man with two black eyes and a crooked, swollen nose. He looked more like a victim than a criminal. He could have been the guy down the street.

But she knew better. "Are you Clay Tharpe?" she demanded through her teeth.

He got off his bunk and came to the bars. "Yeah, why? Are you my public defender?"

Her hands clenched into fists. Her lips were tight, thin. "No, I'm Beth Branning's mother. You know her. She's the child you tried to kill."

A muscle on his face twitched. "I don't know what you're talking about."

The denial turned her fire up a notch. "I'll see to it that you never hurt anyone ever again. If they let you out, I'll kill you myself."

He stepped back from the bars, holding out his hands as though she could come through them. "Look, they've got me all wrong. I didn't do what they say. I was set up."

The jail door screeched opened, and she heard Wheaton's booming voice. "Kay, how'd you get in here?"

"She's threatening me!" Tharpe shouted, his voice echoing over the concrete room. "These guys heard her."

"You hurt a kid, man?" one of his cell mates yelled.

Wheaton stormed through the room. "Kay, you come out of there, right now."

Kay wouldn't budge. She took hold of the bars. "You'll be repaid," she shouted. " 'They band themselves together against the life of the righteous, and condemn the innocent to death.' " Wheaton grabbed her from behind as she went on quoting the passage she'd memorized from Psalm 94, her volume rising. " 'But the Lord has been my stronghold, and my God the rock of my refuge. He has brought back their wickedness upon them and will destroy them in their evil!' "

Wheaton dragged her from the bars, but she wouldn't stop.

"The Lord our God will destroy you, Clay Tharpe! And if *he* doesn't, *I* will!"

Wheaton forced her past the other cells as the inmates began to yell.

Then she realized how she could accomplish it. She could turn his cell mates against him. Didn't they say that prisoners turned on those who abused children? "You men—how can you stand to be in the same cell with him?" she shouted to his cell mates. "He slammed my daughter's head against a tree trunk, and strangled her! Are you going to let him get away with it?"

She heard some of them yelling across the cell, curses rising up to echo off the walls. Clay Tharpe screamed out as the two others in his cell came at him. Wheaton got her to the door and pushed it open. The door slammed behind her, its power quaking through her.

"You shouldn't have done that, Kay."

Her chest rose and fell as she tried to steady her breath.

"You're making my job harder," he said.

Her face twisted as grief flooded over her, pulling her under its deadly power.

Wheaton's voice grew gentler as he put his arm around her and pointed her to the front door. "London, go check on the prisoners. I'm giving Kay a ride back to the hospital."

sixty-nine

THE POSITIVE IDENTIFICATION OF ONE OF THE DEAD men—Blake Tomlin—gave Mark a sense of completion. The other body had no identification—just a backpack with items that appeared to be scavenged from the garbage. Did he have family anywhere? Was there a mother somewhere praying for her son? Friends who would mourn him if they knew he was dead?

The man must have a story. A reason that he dug through garbage and had no one to report him as missing. Even the homeless had mothers ... siblings.

They might never find the homeless man's family, but they could notify Melissa Tomlin and hopefully give her some kind of closure. Mark and Sheriff Wheaton took the time to change clothes, then went to the Tomlin house in full uniform—not the usual T-shirts that said "Jefferson County Sheriff's Department." The dread was obvious on her face as she invited them in.

She introduced Blake's parents, whose faces were anxious ... but hopeful. If only they had better news.

Melissa's parents were there, too. They introduced themselves as Scott and Katherine Anthony. Her father had an expression of sad anticipation. Her mother busied herself with their toddler.

"He's dead, isn't he?" Melissa asked.

"No, he can't be." Blake's father sat stiffly on the couch.

Wheaton sat on the edge of his chair, staring down at his cal-
loused hands. "I'm afraid you're right, Mrs. Tomlin. We found his
body today."

His mother let out a long wail and collapsed against her husband. They reminded Mark of Doug and Kay, weeping for their
broken child. He looked away, wishing he could give them privacy
in their mourning.

Melissa's father rushed to her side to hold his daughter, but
the young woman didn't respond. She didn't move a muscle. Not
a twitch changed her expression. It reminded him of the moments
before a tornado hit. "Where?" she asked. "Where did you find
him?"

"In the backyard of a man named Clay Tharpe. We have reason to believe he murdered your husband on the day the banks
opened."

"The day he went missing." Now he saw a breach in her wall,
a tiny crack before the spillway broke. Her eyes closed. "I thought
he just left with the money. That he didn't love me."

Mark admired the stoicism on her delicate features as she held
the tears back. He had expected her to fall apart. This must be agonizing. Which would be worse? Feeling abandoned by her husband,
or knowing he hadn't come home because he was dead? Beth must
have wondered the same thing.

Blake's mother was inconsolable. Melissa's parents looked more
concerned with her.

"Is this man in jail?" Melissa's father asked.

"Yes, we arrested him today."

Melissa cleared her throat. "My husband ... where is he
now?"

"We took him to the ..." Wheaton paused, took a deep breath.
"To the morgue. We need you to come and identify the body."

She looked at her father, shook her head. "I can't. I can't do it.
Daddy, tell them." Then it came. The break in the dam. She fell
into her father's arms. He held her face pressed against his chest,
stroking her hair.

"I'll do it." Blake's father's chin trembled. "He's my son."

Yes, that was better. If they could spare her that pain ...

Wheaton stood up. "Mrs. Tomlin, I'm so sorry. But I need to ask—did you or your husband know a man named Clay Tharpe?"

She looked back at them. "No, I ... I don't think so."

He told them about Beth and her note, but the details didn't help.

Mark cleared his throat when Wheaton finished. "Do you have a pastor for the funeral?"

Melissa didn't answer, but her mother-in-law spoke up. "Yes, we'll use ours."

He nodded, wondering why he'd asked. It wasn't as though he could get Doug to leave his child's bedside and conduct the funeral of the man whose murder she'd seen. Maybe they were Christians and wouldn't have to grieve as those who had no hope.

Wheaton promised them justice and got up. As Mark followed him to the door, he said, "I'll pray for you, that God will show you his presence and comfort you."

Even in her mourning, Blake's mother seemed to appreciate his words. Melissa didn't seem to hear.

"Thank you for coming." Blake's mother had come to her feet. She was a small woman with curly hair and glasses, and she looked gaunt and pale and grief-stricken. He'd seen that look many times before ... sometimes in his own mirror.

She sniffed. "I appreciate your finding him and arresting him. At least he can't hurt anyone else."

Mark's chest was heavy as he followed the grieving father out to the van. He felt that burning feeling again—that sick feeling of unrest. There was no way to assuage it now. His work was done. He'd gotten Tharpe behind bars and notified the victim's family.

If only he could do something for Beth.

He didn't get in the van. "I'm going to take off now, if it's okay," he said to Wheaton.

"Sure, son. You need a break. Go home and get some rest. Want me to give you a ride?"

"No, that's okay. I'm going to the hospital, and it's not that far."

Wheaton slid his hands into his pockets. "Thanks for helping me do the dirty work. And look after Kay. Make sure she doesn't pop into the department anymore. She probably needs a doctor to sedate her."

Mark knew she didn't need anything of the sort. What Kay needed was for her daughter to wake up.

seventy

KAY'S OUTBURST AT THE JAIL HAD NOT MADE HER FEEL BETTER. When she came back to the hospital, Doug tried to calm her. The pressing weight of stress was getting to them all, so Doug asked Craig to take the family home. Deni stayed at the hospital to sit with Beth.

Kay refused to leave, but Doug insisted.

"Doug, I'm not going. I've prayed for a miracle, and I expect it to happen. I want to be here. And even if it doesn't happen tonight, if she's at all aware, she'll know I'm not here. What if she needs me?"

"She loves Deni, too. Deni will be here. But you're exhausted, Kay. You have to come home and rest. There might be even tougher days ahead. We need our strength."

Kay finally agreed, but only after explaining it to her comatose child.

As they drove, her heart raced at the thought of what she'd done at the jail. She hated Clay Tharpe. She had never hated anyone so much in her life.

She didn't like that consuming emotion. It burned inside her like acid, its poison seeping through her cells and altering her organs. Her heart wouldn't stop sprinting. Her stomach rebelled. Her lungs seemed constricted. Her head ached.

Thankfully, Craig went back to work after dropping them off. The four of them went into the house, and the boys scattered to their rooms. Kay collapsed on her bed.

"Are you okay?" Doug asked, standing over her.

"Who cares if I'm okay?" she asked. "It's Beth who's not."

"You won't be any good to Beth if you don't take care of your-self." He sat down on the bed next to her, started to massage her shoulders. "You want to talk about what happened?"

"I told you what happened. I wanted to look into the face of the man who did this, so I did."

Her face was buried in the pillow, but she felt him lying down next to her. She was cold, but his strong hand on her back was warm. It brought her comfort, though she didn't want it. "Well, I wouldn't have recommended it, but in retrospect, it was a pretty gutsy thing to do."

She had expected him to chastise her. She turned to her side fac-ing him. "It wasn't gutsy. I snapped. If I could have gotten to him, Doug, I might have killed him."

"I know the feeling."

She rolled to her back, rubbing her eyes. "I might have gotten him killed, anyway."

"How?"

She looked at the ceiling. "I incited his cell mates to hurt him. I told them he attacked a child."

Doug was silent for a moment. "And what did they do?"

"I don't know. They were yelling at him, cursing, when the sheriff took me out. Tharpe looked so smug and safe in there. I wanted him to fear for his life and know what it is to have someone attack you. To have his head smashed against something."

Doug stroked her arm. "I know."

She pictured what might have happened after she left. He had probably been cornered, intimidated, terrorized, injured. Did he feel like a tough guy now? Did he still feel like he had the upper hand? Did he know even an ounce of the fear that Beth had felt that day?

Her joy at the possible outcome struck her. Shame came in its wake, indicting her for her hatred, for her violence, showing her something ugly and terrible about herself.

Her shoulders began to shiver, her arms to tremble, as the real-ization fell over her. Look where her thoughts were taking her. Look what she had become.

"Oh, dear God. What have I done?"

Doug sat up. "What do you mean?"

Kay got off the bed, stepped into the shadows, and turned back to her husband. "I'm like him."

"No, you're not. You're nothing like—"

"Yes, I am. I have the capacity to do what he did. I tried to do it today by inciting others to do my dirty work. But it was murder. I had the same violence in my heart that he has."

"You did it out of righteous anger. He did it for pure evil."

"I did it for *vengeance*. But vengeance belongs to God." Sorrow mingled with her shame.

Doug pulled her back to the bed and held her tightly. She knew he wasn't judging her. He was trying to help her with the olive press that was crushing her.

She thought of Tharpe in that cell, without a moment's peace, staying awake all night, afraid to close his eyes for fear of what might happen. Maybe Wheaton had moved him to a different cell.

"Clay Tharpe felt he had a reason for attacking Beth, and that reason was evil. But I could have done the same evil for a reason that was just as compelling. I worked it out in my mind. I premeditated it, just like he did."

"Kay, if that's what happened, then pray about it. I'll pray with you."

She closed her eyes, and tried to do that, tried to humble herself before the God of the universe. How would he answer her prayers for Beth if she had such hatred in her heart? "I can't," she whispered. "I'm so angry at God!"

Doug kissed her and slid his hand through her hair, to the back of her neck. "God can stand to have you beating against his chest. He can handle your despair."

"What about my guilt? Can he handle that?"

"He did already, when he became flesh and walked among us. Christ died because we have the capacity to murder if given the right motivation. He died because we can be consumed with our own vengeance. He died because he loves us anyway, and he didn't want the disease of sin and hatred to kill us. He wanted us to be free."

"He did the same thing for Clay Tharpe," she said bitterly.

She could see in Doug's face that he didn't like that any better than she did. "Yes, he did."

She looked into his eyes, searching for answers. "He wants us to pray for our enemies. But I can't, Doug. I can't do it. I can't even pray for myself."

"Yes, you can."

She squeezed her eyes shut, and felt as though God, her Father, picked her up and held her against him. She squirmed and kicked and beat against him, but he held her tight, anyway. She forced herself to pray for Clay Tharpe in high-pitched, halting words. "Lord, I know I'm supposed to forgive … but I need time. The best I can do right now is to ask you to undo the damage I did in that cell. Give them the wisdom to move him to a cell by himself. Let your vengeance be the one that prevails in this … not mine."

Doug picked up when she could go no further. "Father, we ask that you bring Clay Tharpe to repentance. Show him his need for a savior."

They lay together, bound in prayer, listening for God's voice. But there was only silence, and a momentary peace that lay over them like a goose-down blanket, comforting them into a shallow sleep.

seventy-one

DEAR DENI,

I had to go back to work. There's so much to do, and I'm not helping anybody by sitting here. Just know that I love you and I'm praying for you. I spoke to Beth's doctor about the medications he can't get, and I'm going to do my best to get them here, as well as find an MRI or CT scanner. It's the least I can do for my future sister-in-law. I love you, baby. Send someone for me if there's a change. I'll be back as soon as I can.

Love,

Craig

Mark read the note Craig had left behind and felt his throat closing up with anger. Future sister-in-law? Baby?

Deni's eyes rounded with hope, and that made him even angrier. "Do you think he'll be able to do that? Get the drugs that could help her, I mean? And the scanners?"

Leave it to Craig to make promises he couldn't keep. "The drugs are possible, I guess. But as for the scanners, I doubt it. Anything they had before the Pulses would have been destroyed. And without electricity and computers to build new machines—"

"Well, he wouldn't say it if there weren't a possibility, would he?"

Mark shrugged. "He said Beth was his future sister-in-law. You tell me."

She took the letter back, read it again. "Oh, that."

"Yeah, that."

He couldn't hold it against her. She was so distracted by Beth's coma, so tired and tense, that he couldn't blame her for not flaring up at the suggestions in Craig's letter. But *he* could do something about them.

The next day, Mark decided to head by Craig's office, to talk to him about arousing the Brannings' hope with promises to save the day. Craig may be important, but he wasn't *that* important. And while Mark was there, he might just talk to him about the terms of endearment he used for Deni. She wasn't Craig's baby.

She was his.

At least, he hoped she was.

Craig's office was crowded with employees now, everyone engaged with a sense of purpose, bent over tasks and hurrying from one place to another. A cheer went up, and Mark saw his archrival standing at a telegraph machine with several others who were clearly celebrating something.

He crossed the room. Craig spotted him, and his smile faded a little. "Mark, what is it?"

Mark should have realized Craig would think he was there about Beth. He quickly put that fear to rest. "Nothing. No change." He glanced over Craig's shoulder. "Am I interrupting something?"

"Oh, yeah," Craig said, his smile returning. "We just got a telegram saying the power grids that cover the White House and the Pentagon are back up. And we also got the areas around three of the Gulf Coast refineries back up."

Mark couldn't believe it. "Seriously? I didn't think it would happen that fast."

"They've been working on it the whole year of the Pulses," he said. "Our teams were able to black start some of the distribution plants."

"So how long before ours will come back on?"

"Sooner than we thought, I hope." He shook a few hands of his coworkers, then turned and led Mark to his office where it was quieter. "So what brings you here?"

"Your note." The muscles in Mark's face were rigid.

Craig sat down in his executive chair, put his hands behind his head. "Yeah?"

Mark looked down at him. "I don't think it's wise to make promises you can't keep, about getting scanners and drugs that aren't available."

"I wasn't making false promises," he said. "I truly do intend to try. It's complicated, because there are solid-state components to all of those scanners. But I'm thinking that MRIs might be available first, since their main components are magnets. The president and his family will be the first to have it available, so I'm sending telegrams to some of my colleagues in the Senate building, to see if they can tell me if any scanners were preserved anywhere, or what company might be working on rebuilding those things. If I can find that out, maybe we can get an idea of how long it'll be. I'm also asking Senator Crawford, my old boss, to check with some of his drug company lobbyists who live in Washington to see how we might get the drugs Beth needs."

"Sounds like a long process. Beth may not have that kind of time."

"I'm doing the best I can," he said. "Maybe God will be with us."

Mark slid his hands into his pockets. Maybe Craig *could* deliver. It didn't really matter who saved the day, as long as someone did.

He suddenly felt ashamed at his jealousy. Then he remembered the way Craig had referred to Deni. He thought of bringing it up, but it seemed useless ... petty. Deni wasn't Craig's "baby" unless she wanted to be.

"I'd really appreciate your prayers," Craig said.

Mark shook free of his thoughts. "Yeah. Of course."

"I feel a real sense of urgency to do everything I've been tasked with, and I want to do my best for Beth. I feel like I've been put here for such a time as this."

He'd been reading the book of Esther, Mark thought. No one had challenged Craig to, and he hadn't been forced into it. He was staying in the Word on his own. Maybe Craig really was a brother in Christ.

Mark swallowed his pride. "Hey, since yesterday was so crazy and we didn't get to do our Bible study, let me know if you ever want to start it back up. I promise it won't be a clash of the egos this time."

"Maybe when things get back to normal."

Mark couldn't help his relief that Craig was noncommittal. Maybe Mark would have time for the Lord to dig out the weeds in his heart before that time came.

Mark left the office praying that Craig would have the influence to help Beth and to get their power back on soon. Before, he'd considered the restoration of their power something that would make life cushy again. But now it could be a matter of life and death.

seventy-two

THREE DAYS LATER, MARK SHOWED UP AT CHURCH. IN SPITE of Beth's condition, Doug had decided to preach. He marveled at the strength of Doug's character to fulfill his role as pastor while suffering himself. It spoke volumes to all who were there. Brad had even come with his family to support Doug—a rare occurrence.

Even the wind seemed to silence as Doug began to speak. "I wanted to come and lead you in worship today, because ..." His voice faltered, and he looked down at his Bible, as if trying to compose himself. Mark watched, wishing he could help as Doug fought his trembling lower lip. "Because God is worthy of worship, in bad times and good ..." His voice broke off, and he looked at his Bible again.

Mark thought of going up to take over for him, but what would he say? The people who'd come didn't need a sermon. What they needed was to undergird their brother in Christ in prayer. He stood up. "Doug, why don't you let us pray for you today? Just let it be a prayer service."

Doug's tears fell as he nodded. "Good idea," he managed to say. "My family would appreciate that very much."

Doug wept as they gathered around him and lifted Beth and the family up in prayer. Over an hour later, when all had made their petitions to God, Mark looked up to see Brad standing on the outskirts of the small crowd, tears running down his own face.

As the crowd broke up with hugs and whispered encouragement, Mark crossed the grass to Brad. "I know it meant a lot to Doug that you came today."

Brad nodded and wiped his face. "I just don't get it."

"Get what?"

"How y'all maintain your faith when such horrible things happen. If prayer works, why hasn't it? Of all families, why wasn't this family protected?"

Mark's mind went blank. He wasn't prepared to answer. He stood there dumbstruck, silently praying that God would give him words reasonable enough to reach through Brad's intellect. "We maintain our faith because we know there's more. That this life isn't all there is."

Brad locked his gaze on him, as if he wanted to believe, but couldn't.

Mark thought of telling him about the sufferings of Christ when he took on flesh, that Christ intercedes for us, understanding the pain of our suffering. But Brad was a lawyer; his mind wouldn't be satisfied with that. Arguing Scripture with him wouldn't work when he didn't believe in Scripture. Telling about Christ's intercession wouldn't work when Brad didn't believe in prayer ... or in Christ, for that matter.

"We believe that there's a plan. That all things work together for good for those who love the Lord and are called according to his purpose." He realized glumly that he had quoted Scripture. He pressed on, trying to make a case that could stand up in Brad's court. "Brad, you know I've had my own share of suffering."

Brad's eyes softened. "Yeah, you have. And you still believe."

"Because it's not just about this life. God has taken me through everything he's taken me through to make me who I am. The horrible stuff that's happened has made me depend more on him. He's always come through."

"Come through?" Brad asked. "You call this coming through? Everything that's happened with your family? This, with Beth? That doesn't look like coming through to me."

Mark realized he was losing this argument. Mentally, he kicked himself for not being more prepared. He was supposed to be ready for these questions. Why hadn't he rehearsed them in his mind?

"We're not in charge, Brad. God is. Those of us who believe trust that he's working out our lives according to his plans. It's not always easy. Sometimes life just stinks. But we can hang on, knowing that someone bigger than us is in charge."

"That wouldn't give me any comfort," Brad said, "when that 'someone' allows cruelty. When good people are on their knees begging for relief, and nothing happens."

"We don't believe that nothing happens."

"Then you're kidding yourselves." With that, Brad crossed the street and headed home.

Mark let out a long sigh and watched him leave. Under his breath, he muttered a prayer of apology for handling things so poorly.

THAT NIGHT, AS MARK WALKED THROUGH THE JAIL FEEDING THE prisoners, he saw that Clay had a few bruises that Mark hadn't given him. Clay's cell mates had taken Kay up on her suggestion. Wheaton had moved him to an otherwise empty cell for his own safety.

When he saw Mark coming, Clay rushed to the bars. "Did my wife bail me out?"

Mark gave him a disgusted look. "You know you're being held without bond. You're not going anywhere."

"But that's not right. Others get bond!"

"You're a flight risk, Tharpe. And a danger to the community."

"No, I'm not. I've never even been arrested before." He lowered his voice, and Mark saw the desperation in his eyes. "I'm not like these guys in here."

"You're right," Mark said. "Most of them aren't murderers." He pulled a loaf of bread out of his bag, but didn't give it to Tharpe. Tharpe reached through the bars for it, but Mark held it out of reach. "Just tell me one thing, Tharpe. Tell me how you knew Beth was gonna be in the park that day."

"Give me the bread," Tharpe said. "I'm starving."

"Answer me," Mark bit out.

Tharpe stopped reaching and closed his fingers over the bars. "It's not what you think," he said finally.

Mark's disgust kicked up a notch. "What I *think* is that we found two bodies in your backyard, and that you attacked a girl I care about." His teeth came together. "So how did you know she was going to be there that day?"

"Because she came every day at the same time."

Mark frowned. That didn't even make sense. If Clay had seen her there every day, why hadn't he tried to shut her up before? Mark had assumed all along that Tharpe hadn't been able to find her—until the day he tried to kill her.

Tharpe reached through the bars again, trying to grab the bread. Mark backed away.

"Please," Tharpe said. "I'm starving."

Bluffing, Mark dropped the bread back into the bag and started to walk away.

"Please! I'm dying, here."

Mark turned back, his lips tight. "How did you know she went there every day?"

"Because I was told she did."

Mark froze. "Are you saying there was someone else?"

"That's what I'm saying. I didn't want to kill anybody. I just needed money."

Mark stared at him. "Did someone pay you to do it?"

Tharpe opened his mouth to speak, then seemed to change his mind. Beads of sweat sprang to the skin above his lip. Either he was bluffing, or Mark had just hit the target.

"Give me the bread."

Mark pulled the loaf back out of his bag and moved closer to the bars. "Tell me about this other person! Is that who saw Beth coming to the park? Is that who tipped you off that she went there every day?"

Tharpe snatched the bread out of his hands. "I'm not saying anything else," he said as he backed away with his food. "Just get me a lawyer."

seventy-three

THE NEXT DAY, MARK WAS STILL PUZZLING OVER THAT exchange with Tharpe. Tharpe had suggested he'd had an accomplice in Tomlin's death. If that was true, was it the same person who'd let him know he could find Beth at the park?

Tharpe would go to court today for his preliminary hearing, and Deni and Doug had decided to come watch. Kay chose to stay with Beth, too repulsed by Tharpe to face him again.

As one of the arresting officers, Mark would present the evidence the sheriff's department had gathered. He came in full uniform, ready to testify about the stolen car, Tharpe's flight to Huntsville, and the bodies they'd found in his backyard.

Mark knew Brad had already decided to recommend that the judge send the case to the Grand Jury. All they had to do was get the judge to agree to it.

Tharpe had managed to secure a lawyer, and according to Brad, the lawyer had been trying to cut a deal. But Brad wasn't backing down. He had every intention of charging Tharpe with first-degree murder, among other things. In Alabama, that meant the death penalty or life in prison.

Though he could have waited at the front of the court-room with the other deputies, Mark sat at in the gallery with Deni and Doug. He held Deni's hand and felt her pulse racing. Doug stared straight ahead, as if one movement might send him over the edge.

When the judge had been seated, silence fell over the courtroom. A side door opened, and several inmates dressed in orange prison garb shuffled inside, their shackles rattling on the tile floor.

It was the first time Deni had seen Tharpe, so Mark pointed him out. Again, he wondered about that second person Tharpe had mentioned. Someone who wanted Tomlin dead. Someone who perhaps had given him information about where Beth would be and when.

He saw Melissa Tomlin and her father, Scott Anthony, slip inside and sit on the other side. "That's the dead man's widow," Mark whispered to Deni and Doug. "And he's her dad."

They both looked where he pointed. Melissa looked like she hadn't slept in days. Her father appeared just as ragged. He kept his arm around her, comforting her as she looked toward the man who had murdered her husband.

Mark wished there were more light. The courthouse wasn't one of the buildings considered a priority, so they couldn't get gasoline to keep a generator running. The only light came from the windows, making the place seem dismal and gloomy. They went through the docket, hearing cases of several other inmates one by one. Finally, they got to Clay Tharpe.

Mark squeezed Deni's hand, then got up and joined the lawyers at the front. Tharpe stood and rattled to the judge's bench. They read the charges, and Mark testified to the evidence he and the others had found.

Finally, the judge looked at Tharpe. "Do you understand the charges against you?"

"It's not what you think, Judge. I'm not a killer."

Mark heard a sudden movement in the gallery. He looked back and saw Melissa Tomlin's father standing. Anthony pulled a pistol out of his belt, raised it, and pointed it toward the cluster of men at the front. In the time it took for what was happening to register in Mark's mind, Mr. Anthony pulled the trigger.

The gun blasted.

Clay Tharpe dropped to the floor.

Screams crescendoed as the scent of smoke filled the room. People dropped behind the benches, and the bailiff dove for the judge. The attorneys flung themselves under their tables. Mark drew his weapon and stooped to get out of the line of fire. "Drop it!" he shouted.

Melissa's father dropped the gun and put his hands in the air. Melissa cried, "Daddy!"

"Move away from the gun," Mark ordered.

Anthony took a step to the side.

Mark moved up the aisle, grabbed the gun. "I've got it," he yelled.

The bailiff came up from behind the judge's bench, his weapon drawn, and the other two deputies who'd been at the front of the room ran back and cuffed the shooter. Wiping the sweat out of his eyes, Mark glanced at Tharpe. He lay on the carpet in a circle of blood. Someone was taking his pulse.

Mark went back to Deni, and she came into his arms. "Is he dead?"

"I don't know." Mark could hardly catch his breath.

"Ambulance!" cried one of the people kneeling beside Tharpe. "Somebody get an ambulance!"

"I'll get them." Deni shouted. She pushed through the people and made her way outside.

DENI BURST OUT OF THE COURTROOM AND RAN AS FAST AS SHE could toward the place several blocks away where the ambulance was always parked. Since there was no way for people to call them, they stayed in a central part of town where they could usually be found when needed. Thankfully, they were there. She ran to George Mason's open window.

"George," she said, gasping for breath, "there was a shooting at the courthouse."

"Get in." He started the ambulance and turned on the siren. "What happened?"

Deni held on as they rounded a curve. "Someone shot the guy who attacked my sister."

They turned a corner, tires screeching. "Don't they check for weapons before you go in there?"

"They search your stuff and frisk you, but without metal detectors, that's all they can do."

"He must have been hiding it well."

At the courthouse, the paramedics jumped out and grabbed their gurney and their bags. Deni followed them in. The courtroom had emptied, and she saw her father pumping Tharpe's chest. Sweat dripped into his eyes as he looked up at the medics.

"I think it's too late."

George and Will took over, trying to revive him, but the man who'd shot him had been a good marksman. He'd shot him right through the heart.

Deni felt nothing as they pronounced Tharpe dead. Justice had been served.

She turned to see the man who'd pulled the trigger. The gray-haired man looked harmless as he stood placidly in a back corner, where Mark and his colleagues were shackling him and reading him his rights. They had handcuffed him, but he wasn't resisting. He looked fragile and broken, and filled with grief.

It could have been her or someone in her family with that gun in their hand. Her own mother could have done it. Pity for Scott Anthony swelled in her chest. His emotion had gotten the best of him.

Melissa Tomlin stood next to the group surrounding her father, clearly distraught. What a nightmare. She'd lost her husband to murder, and now she would lose her father to prison.

Mark was stooped in front of the man, shackling his feet. As they got him up and began escorting him out, Mr. Anthony turned toward his daughter. "I love you, sweetheart," he said as they took him away.

seventy-four

THE NEWS OF CLAY THARPE'S DEATH BROUGHT KAY A strange mixture of emotions. On one hand, she was not unhappy that he had come to a violent end. Whether it was God's vengeance or Scott Anthony's, she didn't know. But vengeance had come.

Still, shame plagued her over those feelings.

Maybe if Beth woke up, she would get past that burning feeling of hatred that threatened to smother her when she least expected it. Now that Tharpe had died, did it even matter how she felt about him? Was it a sin to hate someone who had done such a horrible thing, and never expressed remorse? Now that he was dead, was she accountable to forgive him?

"Mom, I've made a decision."

Kay turned to Deni. "What?"

"Mark says there's a second person who helped Tharpe pull this off. He thinks it's someone in the Tomlins' neighborhood, since it's across from Magnolia Park. Someone who lived there might have seen Beth on her route and alerted the killer." Kay was stunned. "Another killer? Someone else was that evil—that they would help Tharpe . . . ? I'm going to do one more story for the paper."

"Mark thinks so. And the sherrif's department hasn't made headway on finding that person. I want to help."

Kay knew where she was going with this. "Deni, isn't there some way you can do the story without going there?"

Deni shook her head. "Being a reporter can get me into places that the sheriff's department can't get. People are afraid to talk to cops. They aren't that afraid to talk to reporters. I want to go door-to-door and talk to the neighbors in Magnolia subdivision."

"About what? You think they'll tell you if they were Tharpe's accomplice?"

"No, but they might tell me something else that will blow their cover. If we have even a clue who it was, we might be able to dig deeper."

That was all Kay needed. Another daughter in a killer's line of fire. "No," Kay said. "I don't want another one of my children tangling with murderers."

Deni sighed. "What if I get Mark to come with me?"

"Just let Mark do it alone!"

"Mom, it'll take a lot longer. I can get things out of people. I'm really, really good at it. Don't you want the second person to be found?"

Kay let out a long breath. "Yes, but not at the cost of another child."

"I'm not a child, Mom. I'm a grown woman. A professional reporter."

"You quit your job."

"That's a technicality. I haven't been back to the recovery team since Beth's attack. I don't even know if I want to go anymore. Reporting is in my blood ... and I can use those skills to find Tharpe's accomplice. I have to do this, Mom. Maybe I shouldn't have told you."

Kay bit her lip, and started massaging Beth's legs again. "Maybe not." She looked back up at her. "Deni, please be careful. Go tell your father and listen to any advice he gives you about how to approach this."

"I will. Don't worry." Deni was out of the room in a flash.

Doug didn't like Deni's plan anymore than Kay did, but he felt better when Mark promised to go with her.

But as they left the hospital, Mark let her know that he wasn't crazy about the idea, either. "If it gets dangerous, Deni, I want you to promise me that you'll get out of the way."

She rode her bike beside him. "Don't worry, I will. I don't want trouble. I just want to probe a little."

She'd asked Mark to change into plain clothes for the visits, since people were more likely to talk to them if they didn't know he was a cop. He'd agreed, but still carried his weapon in an ankle holster under his jeans.

"I think we should start at the Tomlin house," Mark said. "You have an in there. You can bring condolences, as the sister of another victim. Maybe she's had time to think about who Blake's enemies were."

Deni dreaded facing the grieving woman. She'd lost so much even before her father was jailed. Deni hoped she'd be able to keep her emotions under control. The last thing she needed was to lose it right in front of the widow. Melissa shouldn't have to comfort *her*.

They passed the park where Beth had been injured. Deni saw children playing there now. Several moms clustered around the swing sets and slides. If only they'd been there that rainy day.

Deni's throat constricted as her gaze drifted to the trees where her parents had found Beth.

"You okay?"

She swallowed hard. "Yeah."

They reached Melissa's yard. Deni's gaze drifted to the park again, and she saw the swing set where Beth must have been sitting when Clay attacked her. She would have had a perfect view of the Tomlins' house from there.

Mark knocked on the door, then touched her back. She felt the reassurance in his hand and told herself she had a job to do.

The door opened. A woman a little older than her own mother appeared. Her eyes were red and sunken in, her skin pale and gaunt. She must be Melissa's mother. "Mrs. Tomlin?"

"Anthony," Mark corrected.

"Oh yes. Mrs. Anthony."

The woman just looked at Mark. "You've already locked my husband up. I don't know what else you want."

Mark started to answer, but Deni touched his arm, stopping him. "Ma'am, I asked him to come with me. I'm Beth Branning's sister. She's the girl who was attacked at the park. I just wanted to come by and talk to Melissa for a minute."

Her expression softened, and she let out a long, broken sigh. "I'm sorry about your sister." She shot another suspicious glance at Mark, then backed away from the door. "Come in. I'll see if Melissa is up."

Deni and Mark stepped inside. The house was stale, dark, cluttered, as if no one cared enough to straighten it up. A two-year-old played on the floor, his toys strewn across the carpet.

Mark stooped in front of him. "How's it going, buddy?"

The child smiled and slapped his hand.

"Don't touch my son."

Melissa came in, looking as if she hadn't been out of bed all day. She wore boxer shorts and a rumpled T-shirt, and her hair was disheveled.

Mark got to his feet. Deni stepped toward her. "Melissa, I'm Deni Branning."

"I know. The girl's sister."

"That's right. I just wanted to come by and tell you how sorry I am about your husband's death. And your father ..."

Melissa dropped into a chair.

"Please, sit down," Mrs. Anthony said.

Mark and Deni sat on the couch, realizing that this family's pain was even greater than that of Deni's own family. At least the Brannings still had hope that Beth would recover.

"What do you want?" Melissa asked wearily.

Deni's throat was dry. "Before Clay Tharpe was killed, he told Mark that he had an accomplice."

Melissa flinched at the news. "*What?*" She got up, backed away. "You don't believe him, do you?"

"We don't know," Mark said. "But if there's a possibility, we need to know."

"We were wondering if you knew of any enemies that your husband had," Deni said. "Particularly right here in this neighborhood. Someone who may have schemed with Tharpe to kill him."

Melissa was shaking. She brought her hand to her head, as if trying to think. "No, no enemies. I can't think of any."

She tried to sweep her frizzy hair behind her ears, but it wouldn't stay. "Listen, what's happening to my father is so unfair. The bond is too high; I can't bail him out. He was so angry about the murder ... but it wasn't premeditated. He didn't mean to do it. I know he didn't. Everyone carries a gun nowadays. It's a scary world out there. He forgot he couldn't take it into the courthouse."

That couldn't be true. Deni had been carefully searched before she'd gotten in. He couldn't have made it past security unless his gun had been deliberately, carefully hidden. "Do you have a lawyer?"

"Yes. He'll see him today."

"Maybe the lawyer can get his bond reduced. Melissa, I know you said no enemies. But can you think of anyone at all who might have had a dispute with your husband?"

"No!" She went to the child, picked him up. "I have to change his diaper."

Deni wasn't likely to get anywhere with them. They were too upset to think clearly. Maybe she would get more from the neighbors. "I understand. I'm really sorry for the intrusion. We'll go now."

Mrs. Anthony walked them to the door. "I hope your little sister will be all right," she said.

"I hope so too. It's all in God's hands." It felt like one of those churchy things to say. As Deni walked back to her bike, she wondered if Mrs. Anthony saw it that way. Was she a believer? Did she, too, see a purpose in the cruelest of events?

Or was she sick of the lip service people paid to the grieving?

Mark pulled her close as they walked and kissed her cheek. "You did good," he said.

"No, I didn't. We should have left them alone. Those poor women."

"Well, don't get discouraged now," Mark said, looking up the street. "We have lots more people to talk to."

Three houses away Deni saw a lady working in her garden. "Let's talk to her next, since she's outside."

Mark agreed, and they walked their bikes to her house. When Deni introduced herself, the woman gave her a boisterous hug. "Bless your heart! It's a shame that your sister got caught in this mess. But you know, what happened to Blake was bound to happen. That man was mean."

Deni frowned. "*Blake* was mean? In what way?"

"Smashin' furniture, beatin' that poor woman in the face. I've seen her eye so swole up she couldn't see out of it. And y'ask me, that little boy had his fair share of bruises, too."

Deni met Mark's stunned eyes. "Did others in the neighborhood ever witness that?" she asked.

"'Course they did. You couldn't help hear it. We talked about what to do about him."

Deni glanced at Mark. He had that look on his face that he had when he slammed against the crux of a case.

"Did anyone confront him about it?" Mark asked.

"You bet they did. One time a few weeks ago a couple of the men interrupted when Blake got too rough with his wife, and they escorted him out of the neighborhood. He came back, apologizin' up and down, and she took him right back in."

Deni was amazed no one had mentioned it before. "Could you point us to those people who escorted him out?"

She pointed. "Melissa's next-door neighbors. The ones on either side of them. Tell them Corinna sent you. They'll talk."

Deni could hardly wait to talk to them. As she and Mark stepped out into the street, Mark spoke quietly. "Let me do the talking from here on out, okay?"

She didn't argue. "Can you believe this? Blake Tomlin was a wife-beater? Why wouldn't Melissa have told us that?"

Mark sighed. "Maybe she knows her father was the accomplice. Maybe he wanted Blake dead for what he'd done to Melissa. Maybe he hired him. Maybe that's why he killed him—to shut him up."

"Wait." Deni stopped in the middle of the street. "He wouldn't kill Clay in front of the judge to keep him from telling him he's a killer!"

Mark had to chuckle. "That would be pretty dumb. But people who are emotional don't think."

"That's not it. That man didn't look like a killer."

"But he *was* a killer. We *saw* him kill Clay Tharpe."

She thought of the anguished look on Scott Anthony's face after he shot Clay Tharpe, and the submissive way he'd let them take him away. It seemed more an act of grief than an attempt to cover up a crime.

They found one of the men at home and questioned him about Corinna's story. "Yeah, it happened that way, all right. We intervened several times when they were fighting."

"Why didn't you tell the deputies that when they questioned you?" Mark asked.

"Because they weren't interviewing us about Blake. They were questioning us about that girl who was attacked in the park."

They interviewed the rest of the neighbors on the street one by one. All were more than willing to tell what they knew. Each had the same refrain. Blake Tomlin was a wife-beater, and everyone knew it.

Deni and Mark headed back to the hospital. "So we have a wife-beater who's even hurt his son," Deni said. "We have neighbors who've pulled him off his wife. Then on the day the bank opens, that same guy is murdered? There's some connection here that we're missing."

"Maybe God used Tharpe to bring Tomlin's crimes back on his own head."

"Maybe," Deni said. "But I'm more inclined to think that someone else used Tharpe."

Mark had to agree. "Mr. Anthony sure had a motive."

"But he'd have to be an idiot. Seems to me he'd be better off taking his chances that Tharpe would talk than he would gunning him down in cold blood right in front of the judge. Maybe we should go back to Tharpe's neighborhood and talk to *his* neighbors. Maybe we'll find another Corinna."

seventy-five

FATIGUE CLAWED THROUGH CRAIG LIKE A LIVING THING, making him long for sleep and a reprieve from the urgency in every area of his life. He was used to working on pure adrenaline. For the last year, working for Senator Crawford, everything had been an emergency, and there were no slow days. But at least then he'd been able to focus one hundred percent on work, and hadn't felt the heavy weight of responsibility for a dying child.

Among the hundreds of job applicants, his team had found a few war veterans and ham radio operators who were fluent in Morse code, making it possible to communicate by telegraph through a series of relay stations between here and Washington. The government also had communications experts building radios with vacuum tubes, which would be available sooner than transistors would.

Craig jotted the note that he wanted sent to Senator Crawford's office and bent over Horace Hancock, who had just finished receiving a message. "Hey, Horace," he said to the World War II veteran. "I have to get this to Senator Crawford ASAP."

The old man adjusted his glasses and read the note aloud. "Senator Crawford, please advise if you've been able to find MRI scanners or contacts with Hope Drug Manufacturer? Hoped to hear from you by now. Deni's sister is dying. Please respond. Craig Martin."

"That's a long one," Horace said.

"Where would I shorten it?"

Horace took his pencil and marked out a few words, and changed a few others. "Pls advise if u found whr MRI scanners r bing manufctrd r contact at Hope Drug Mnufctr stop Hoped 2 hr frm u by now stop Deni's sister dying stop Craig Martin."

Craig read back over it. "Is this some kind of telegraph shorthand?"

Horace shook his head. "No, I learned this from my grand-daughter who used to love to text-message me."

Craig grinned. "Should have known."

"Hey, it works."

"Could you get it out now?"

He waited as Horace sent the message. If things were working the way they should, Senator Crawford would have the message sometime in the next hour. He'd done a lot for Senator Crawford when he worked as his aid. Maybe the overworked legislator would want to return the favor.

Another of the telegraph operators threw down his headphones and jumped to his feet. "Hot dog!" the white-haired man shouted. "The Tennessee Valley Authority is back in business."

Craig dashed to his side and read the message. That meant that electricity would reach the distribution plants, and power would flow to the transmission lines in Crockett. If they could get the substations reconnected to those transmission lines, they could get power to the homes in Crockett—and to the hospital.

It all seemed doable now. "I've got to get word to our trans-mission engineers," he said, pulling his keys out of his pocket. Grabbing his hard hat, he bolted out to his car.

seventy-six

KAY GREW MORE DESPERATE AS BETH'S CONDITION declined. Her blood pressure had dropped, and her kidney function was failing. They cared for her with sponge baths and massages, as well as frequent repositioning to keep her from getting bedsores. But they were losing her.

Kay and Doug read Scripture aloud to her, as if the words themselves could speak life into her. But the book of James was more for them than for her.

" 'Everyone must be quick to hear, slow to speak and slow to anger; for the anger of man does not achieve the righteousness of God. Therefore, putting aside all filthiness and all that remains of wickedness, in humility receive the word implanted, which is able to save your souls.' "

The verses seemed to reflect the growing shame Kay harbored over her hatred for the dead Clay Tharpe. "Do you think that's why God hasn't answered our prayers for Beth's healing?" she asked.

Doug stopped reading and looked up. "What do you mean?"

"I mean my anger. My hatred. It said the anger of man doesn't achieve the righteousness of God. Do you think God would have healed her if I hadn't gone to the jail and tried to start a lynching that day?"

"No, I don't think that, Kay."

She sighed, not sure she believed him. "I talked to God about it." She looked at the IV bag. The slow drips continued.

"I've repented over and over. I really am sorry I did it. But there's nothing more I can do."

"Then he is faithful and just to forgive you, sweetheart."

"But he won't forgive us if *we* don't forgive, will he? I'm not sure I've forgiven. How can you forgive someone who's dead? How do you let it go when every day you have to watch your daughter die?"

"She's not dying. She's going to live." He turned his chair toward Kay's and set his hands on her knees. "Look at me, love."

She turned and met his eyes.

"You have to stop beating yourself up. You had human emotions, and you acted on them. But you're not the one who killed Clay Tharpe. And you're not the one who's keeping Beth from waking up."

"But we haven't done everything," she said. "In the book of James, it says to call the elders. Why haven't we done that?"

"Our little church doesn't have elders." Doug paused and looked at Beth. "But maybe I could get some of the more spiritually mature men to come and pray."

Kay wondered if God would honor that. They had to try. "We could send Jeff to ask them to come this afternoon. How many do we need?"

"I would think just a few devout men who believe in the power of prayer."

"What kind of oil do they need?"

"Olive oil would do, if anyone has any."

"Are you sure? We have to do it right."

Doug looked helpless. "If there's some other kind of holy oil, I don't know what it is. The oil's not magic, Kay. It's God who does the healing, not the oil."

They had no time to waste. Hope rose in her heart as she headed for the door. "I'm going to find Jeff and put him on it right away."

Maybe prayer from those men would be what they needed to unlock God's healing power.

seventy-seven

THE THARPES' NEIGHBORS WERE EAGER TO TALK TO DENI
and Mark, and all of them expressed shock at what had
been found in their backyard.

But they hit pay dirt with a neighbor six houses down
from Clay and Analee.

"We were in the Crockett High School Class of '95,"
Amanda Sellick said as she invited them in. "I have the yearbook if you'd like to see it."

Deni didn't know what good it would do, but she took
it anyway. As Mark asked Amanda questions about the
Tharpes' friends and enemies, Deni flipped through the
pages. She had graduated from the same school several years
behind them and recognized teachers and classmates. She
found Tharpe's senior portrait and slowly scanned the faces
of the others in his class. She didn't recognize any of the
names or faces. Then she turned the page.

One face with a frame of big, frizzy hair jumped out at
her. She caught her breath.

Melissa Anthony, who later became Melissa Tomlin.

"Mark, look."

Mark stopped midsentence and looked at the picture.
His face changed as he took it in. "So Amanda, did you
know Melissa Tomlin?"

"No, I don't think so."

"Melissa Anthony," Deni corrected, showing her the
picture.

"Oh, yeah," Amanda said. "*That* Melissa. I forgot her married name."

Deni looked at Mark. "Didn't Melissa tell you she didn't know Clay Tharpe?"

"That wouldn't be true at all," the woman said. "Melissa and Clay were really good friends in high school. They even dated for a while."

Deni's heart started pounding, and the puzzle pieces began to align themselves in her mind. Could Melissa have been involved with Clay?

Mark stared at the coffee table, the wheels clearly turning in his mind. "You're sure? She told me she didn't know him."

"I'm sure," Amanda said. "You don't forget your best friends from school. Especially when you live in the same town with them."

Why would Melissa lie? Wouldn't it have been natural and normal to tell them that she knew him? Express shock that he was the one? The fact that she'd denied it—when there was proof right here, on paper—made Deni suspicious.

Deni began to wonder if that innocent-seeming, distraught woman she'd talked to earlier had been in cahoots with her husband's murderer to kill him. Could she have been the accomplice? Was it even possible that *she* was the one who had told Tharpe where to find Beth?

She felt the heat of indignation flushing her cheeks, almost making her dizzy. She had sat in Melissa's living room, had felt sorry for her. Prayed for her.

She kept quiet as Mark finished questioning Amanda, but her pulse pounded in her temples. Her lungs grew tight, her breathing shallow. She got to her feet. "I'm sorry. I need some air."

She heard Mark asking if they could take the yearbook. Amanda agreed. Deni stumbled outside and propped herself against the brick wall.

The door closed as Mark came out. "Baby, are you all right?"

"No," she said. "Mark, could Melissa Tomlin be the accomplice?"

His lips were tight. "Possible. Maybe she confessed to her dad, and he decided to do what he could to keep Clay from exposing her."

"That's why he would shoot him in front of a judge. To keep the heat off his daughter. He decided to shut Tharpe up, and no one would ever figure it out. So he goes to prison for first-degree murder, while his murdering daughter gets off scot-free."

"But how do you prove it?" Mark asked. "All we have is some hearsay and anecdotal evidence. Just because Clay and Melissa knew each other in high school—"

"Dated," Deni cut in. "And it's not anecdotal. We have the yearbook to prove it."

"It proves they knew each other, not that they dated," Mark said. "But even if they did, it doesn't prove they were in this together. Maybe they were having an affair, and she lied about knowing him to keep it secret. It doesn't mean she's a killer. We need more. We need to find out if they had contact recently."

They got their bikes and headed out. "Think," Deni said as they rode. "Why would Clay do something like this for her?"

"For money," Mark said.

"Yeah, but don't you think she'd want the money, too? I mean, we were all so desperate for cash. I can't imagine she would set things up so that she didn't get any of her own money."

"Maybe Tharpe split it with her."

Deni nodded. "She might have thought losing some of the money was a small price to pay for getting her abusive husband out of the picture."

"If they had a relationship, maybe they planned to pool their resources."

Now they were getting somewhere. Deni felt her strength coming back. "If they were having an affair, somebody knows about it. We've got to find that somebody."

seventy-eight

IT WAS GETTING DARK AS CRAIG AND TWO OF HIS EMPLOY-ees—an electrical engineer and the PR person filling in for Deni until she got back—drove to the substation that would provide electricity to the eastern side of Crockett, the side that powered the hospital and Oak Hollow subdivision. The transmission engineer who was working to get the substation online had sent word that they would try it this afternoon.

"So could we feasibly have electricity today?" Warren Ames, the PR guy, asked. "Air conditioning? Refrigerators?"

"Maybe," Jim Sevrino said. "It won't be perfect. The lights will probably flicker. And air conditioning will draw too big a load."

Craig hoped the residents would heed the warnings they'd posted all over town, to keep their air conditioners off and their appliances unplugged.

"Why will the lights flicker?" Warren asked.

Craig didn't know much about electricity—only what he'd learned in the last few months. But he was able to answer that. "Because all of our semiconductors are fried from the Pulses. They regulate voltage. So where you might have been supposed to get 110 volts, without good regulation you'll get less."

"Right," Jim said. "Power without control. Electric clocks might not keep accurate time. Semiconductors make sure the frequency is 60 Hertz and not 58. But without them, that's not controllable. We won't be able to control that until we get all that fixed, and it's going to take time. But for now, I think people will be satisfied with flickering lights rather than no lights at all."

"Will people have to get the meters on their houses working before they can get power?"

Craig deferred to Jim on that one.

"Some meters will work—the mechanical ones with the disk that spins around. The solid state meters won't work, but that won't stop electricity from flowing into their homes. The meters are only for billing. If they don't work, we can't measure usage, so we can't charge users for it."

Craig glanced at Jim in his rearview mirror. "The government is keeping the power companies afloat until they can start measuring usage and get people paying for their electricity again. The reconstruction can't go forward until we have electricity."

As Jim continued explaining the situation to Warren, Craig's mind drifted to Deni. She should be the one asking these questions. She should be sitting beside him, taking all the technical details and putting them into user-friendly terms that could go out to the press. Her mind was able to grasp the million intricate details that had to be fed to the public. But until Beth woke up and was on the road to recovery, he knew Deni wouldn't come back to work.

He reached the substation and turned into the driveway. A sign on the tall chain-link fence said "High Voltage. Keep Out." There must be three dozen power company employees working there tonight, all intent on getting the local power grid up.

Craig got out of his car and stepped toward the gate. Lee Cowan, the transmission engineer, came toward him. "You men stay clear," Cowan said. "It could be dangerous."

Craig got the hardhats out of his trunk and handed them to the other two. Then they backed up, watching the activity inside the fence. "How dangerous?"

Cowan looked back at the intricate webbing of circuit breakers and transformers. "The distribution network hasn't been used in a year, so we're not sure of its condition." He pointed to the lines connected to the tall metal towers. "If there's a short anywhere in the line, it could cause problems."

He didn't elaborate further, just went back inside the fence, leaving Craig there to wonder what would cause a short. He didn't like sitting like this, watching all the activity and not being able to control it. But he had no choice.

Hours passed as the animated power employees bootstrapped the different generators, cheering when each one powered up.

Men came out of the fenced area and watched, rapt, as a handful began to engage the breaker that would connect the substation to the transmission lines.

As the power began flowing into the substation, a cheer went up again. Now the substation could distribute power over its grid. Craig pictured houses and businesses—Beth's hospital, even—getting the power they needed. It was like watching a miracle in the making.

He heard a boom as something flashed, and heat blasted his face as he ducked to the ground. Something sliced into his arm, and sludge hit him in the face as he ducked to the ground. The men began to yell as they rushed into action.

Quickly, they disconnected the station. Curses flew as men covered with oil began to go back in.

Lee, who'd hit the ground with Craig, got to his feet. He, too, was covered with sludge. "Anybody hurt?"

Craig checked his arm. A shard of metal had lodged in his biceps. He pulled it out, and blood soaked into his shirt, mingling with the oil. He wiped the oil off his face. "What in the blazes just happened?"

Jim's head was bleeding. "What we've got here, my friend, is an oil-filled circuit breaker that exploded. There must have been a short in one of the lines. If you ask me, there's going to be a lot more of that happening before we get everything back online."

"Are you all right? Do you need to get to a hospital?"

Jim laughed. "Are you kidding? I wouldn't miss this for the world."

Craig turned back to the rest of the men. No one seemed to be injured beyond a few cuts. His own injury wasn't deep. It probably needed stitches, but he didn't want to be the only one rushing for first aid when everyone else was shaking it off. He looked at the mess the barrel's explosion had caused. Dirty oil contaminated with carbon drenched the machinery around it. "What do we do now?" he asked.

Jim grinned. "We get out of here and let them get to work cleaning up the mess. They'll have to replace the breaker, clear the fault, then give it another go."

"So we're not going to have power tonight?"

"Not tonight."

seventy-nine

BECAUSE THE SHERIFF'S DEPARTMENT HAD NOT BEEN ABLE to establish a solid link between Clay Tharpe and Melissa Tomlin—at least not one more recent than high school—Deni and Mark decided to pay a visit to Analee Tharpe late that afternoon. Her parents had come to visit and comfort her through the funeral, but Analee looked as if she'd been grieving hard since before the death of her husband.

She met them at the door with a look of suspicion. "What are you doing here?"

Telling herself it was for Beth's sake, Deni spoke first. "Analee, we're so sorry about what happened to Clay."

"No, you're not! You're glad he's dead."

Deni knew better than to deny that. "Analee, my sister is still in a coma, and we want to talk to you about something really important."

"I have nothing to say to you."

"Please," Mark said. "We have reason to believe that your husband wasn't acting alone. If you could just answer a few questions."

Analee moved away from the doorway, and Deni realized she was letting them in. She and Mark stepped over the threshold. Star, the baby, sat in a high chair in front of a woman who Deni assumed was Analee's mother. She was feeding her, feigning smiles and talking to her softly.

Analee waved her hand toward the couch in an exaggerated gesture of acquiescence. "All right, say what you came to say. What new surprises do you have for me? More bodies in my yard?"

Deni's heart ached for her. She sat down on the couch, but Mark kept standing. "Analee, we're trying to figure out if there was a second person who wanted Blake Tomlin dead, and the fact that Melissa Tomlin's father is the one who silenced Clay makes us think there might have been a connection to Melissa."

"Brilliant assumption," Analee said. "Where do they train you guys? Idiot camp?"

Her mother came and put her arm around her. "Honey, calm down."

"I don't want to calm down," Analee said. "My whole life has fallen apart, and I don't even know why. I don't understand any of this. We're talking about my husband. Who was he? I didn't even know him! And out of the blue someone shoots him down before he even has the chance to explain why he would do such a thing!"

"I know this is difficult for you," Mark said, "but it's important. Did you ever have any reason to believe that your husband might be having an affair?"

She breathed a mirthless laugh. "Well, why not go there? An affair can't be worse than murder, can it?" She wiped her eyes and paced across the room. "The truth is, he might have been. There were a lot of nights that he said he worked late, and a few times I went by the plant just to tell him something, and he wasn't there. And then he'd come home in the wee hours and swear he'd been there all along."

"Did you know that your husband and Melissa Tomlin were friends in high school?"

She stared at them for a moment. "Yes."

"Do you think there's any possibility that they could have been seeing each other?"

She frowned. "*Seeing* each other? What are you saying? Do you think my husband killed her husband out of jealousy?"

"We're just trying to put a few puzzle pieces together," Mark said.

Deni wished they could stop pressing her. But they had to know.

"They were still friends. I knew that. He talked to her from time to time. But I really thought that was all it was."

"After we identified the bodies, and you heard it was Blake, didn't you wonder?"

Her eyes squeezed shut. "I haven't had time to wonder anything except why my husband killed two people and attacked a thirteen-year-old girl. Anyway, why would she want her husband dead? If she didn't like him, she could have left him."

Deni spoke up. "Analee, do you know what happened to the money that your husband got in the robbery?"

She hesitated. "It's here in the house. Please don't take it. I need it. It's all I have."

"And how much was it?"

"Five hundred dollars," she said.

Mark shifted in his seat. "The sheriff's department has learned that Blake Tomlin withdrew one thousand dollars from the bank that day. What do you think happened to the other five hundred dollars?"

"I have no idea. Maybe Clay wanted to keep it for himself."

But Deni wasn't buying that. No, Clay Tharpe had split it with Melissa. His half was the price for killing Blake.

Somehow they had to prove it.

DENI WENT HOME BEFORE GOING BACK TO THE HOSPITAL, TO make something for her family to eat. The hospital provided food for their patients, but the visitors were on their own. She fried up some quick tortillas, sliced some stale bread, and stuffed it all into a paper bag that had been recycled a few too many times.

She heard the key in the lock and went to see who was coming in.

Craig stood on the threshold, his white shirt covered in something brown, and his face streaked with what looked like mud. "Thank goodness you're home," he said. "I have to change, but I don't want to track this oil through the house."

"Oil? How'd you get covered with oil?"

"An oil-filled breaker at the substation exploded when we tried to get online."

She brought her hand to her chest. "Exploded? Are you all right?"

She could see that he was shaken. "I caught a piece of metal." He gestured toward the torn place on his shirt, and she saw the blood. "But I'm fine. I just need to wash and change. I'll go scrub down in the backyard if you have any water."

"We have a little. I'll get it and meet you back there."

She ran into the bathroom and got a bowl of water that had been sitting there for days. Grabbing a bar of soap and some towels, she carried them to where Craig stood on the back patio. He had taken off his shirt, but he still had oil sludge smeared across his chest and arms. "Guess I'll never wear that shirt again."

The cut on his arm was bigger than he'd implied. "You wash, and I'll get something for your arm."

She ran back in for some alcohol they'd managed to preserve through the outage and some antibiotic ointment. He had managed to scrub off most of the sludge by the time she got back out. "Here, let me clean that cut."

He held his arm out for her. She suppressed a grin when she realized he was flexing. "You could have been seriously injured, you know."

"Yeah, well, I didn't see it coming. The station was supposed to connect seamlessly to the transmission lines, electricity was supposed to flow through the grid, and you were supposed to have lights tonight. The best laid plans of mice and men ..."

She looked up at him. "So does that set us back another few months?"

"No, not necessarily. They're telling me they can replace the breaker and clean up the mess. They'll have to find the short, and then they can try it again. Next time I'm going to be standing farther back. Tomorrow we're going to try one of the other substations in Crockett. Maybe we'll have better luck with that one."

She frowned as she cleaned the cut, straining to see in the dusk. "You need stitches. It's a deep cut."

His chest seemed to puff up. "Yeah, well, in the infamous words of Clint Eastwood, 'I don't have time to bleed.'"

She started to laugh. "Tough guy."

He gazed down at her with a smile in his eyes, and for a moment, she remembered the way she used to feel about him. Adoring and admiring. She had been attracted to power, and he'd had more than any of the guys her friends dated. They'd all moaned about how good looking he was, how much money he made, and what a great future he had before him.

He was still that person. But she wasn't.

She stepped back and handed him the washcloth she was using. "You might still have a little oil in that cut. I'd wash it real well if I were you. I have to go back in now and finish fixing my family some food."

"If you wait, I'll give you a ride to the hospital on my way back to work."

She thought she'd better not, but the offer was tempting. What would it hurt to accept a ride from him? Mark would understand.

"Okay," she said. "I'll clean up here while you get changed."

eighty

FOUR OF THE IMPROMPTU ELDERS IN THEIR LITTLE LAWN chair church assembled at the hospital as evening fell. Kay got special permission from Dr. Overton, who was a believer, to let the men into the ICU to pray over Beth. The men suited up, then came in and gathered around Beth's bed, laying hands on her body. Kay stood back, focusing her prayers on faith, as one of the men put a thumbprint of oil on Beth's forehead and led the men in prayer for her healing.

Kay's faith took her forward, to that moment when Beth would wake up. When Kay would take her daughter's hand and help her slip off the bed. She pictured Beth complaining about the catheter and the IV, fussing about the worsened condition of her hair, asking about the progress of the play the children had been rehearsing without her.

As the prayers continued, she expected for Beth to open her eyes. It would be like when the disciples were praying for Peter's release from prison, and he showed up at the door. Beth would open her eyes and see them all with their eyes closed, and she would have to tap on someone to get their attention.

Delight at what God was going to do filtered through her. She was ready to take Beth home.

She opened her eyes, watching her daughter as they prayed. Beth still lay there unmoving. Doubt crept in, but Kay chased it back. There was no room for doubt. Only faith. She had enough to move this mountain.

When the men had left, Kay sat beside Beth with that expectation that she knew was pleasing to God. *Go ahead and work, Father,* she thought. *We're ready for your miracle.*

As the hours went by, and there was still no change, Kay tried to imagine God reknitting the tissues in Beth's brain. These things took time, she told herself. God would heal her when he saw fit.

She just had to be patient.

BUT TWO DAYS LATER, JUST WHEN KAY THOUGHT THINGS COULDN'T get worse, seizures began to rack Beth's body. Her legs and arms stiffened as her back arched and convulsed.

The nurse called the doctor, who sent the family out of the room. They circled in the waiting room and prayed that God would intervene and undo the damage.

When the doctor sent for them to meet him in the conference room, Kay's stomach tightened. She was sure he had bad news. She braced herself for it.

She had expected so much after the elders prayed. Now she wondered if the elders were *elder* enough. Maybe it hadn't worked because they weren't ordained deacons. Maybe they should borrow some elders from some other church. Or maybe that wasn't it at all. Maybe it was all *her* fault. Maybe her faith wasn't strong enough for her daughter's healing.

Kay tried to keep that picture in her mind of Beth getting up, whole and refreshed. But all those imaginary pictures kept morphing into the memory of Beth's body convulsing.

The conference room was still mostly dark, except for the light coming in the window. Though it was stiflingly hot, Kay shivered as she walked in.

The plush chairs were like executive office chairs—they swiveled and rocked. She was sure they were meant to lend a sense of comfort to families whose lives were shattering. She found no comfort in them as she sank into one.

Doug's chair squeaked as he sat down next to her, and she thought how someone had dropped the ball on the WD-40.

Somehow, the sound calmed the terror screaming through her mind. One little squeak could so easily be fixed. Maybe Beth's problems could be broken down into tiny squeaks and WD-40.

She felt like one of the losers who used to sit in the boardroom on *The Apprentice* as Dr. Overton walked in silently and sat across from them. Derek Morton, their neighbor who'd been their primary care physician for the last year, came in with him.

"Doug, Kay." He shook both of their hands, his expression grave. "I hope you guys don't mind if I sit in for this."

Kay's throat clenched. "Not at all, Derek." Her voice sounded distant and hollow, like it came from someone else.

Doug bypassed the greetings. "Doctor, let's cut to the chase. What's going on with Beth? What was the seizure about?"

Dr. Overton opened Beth's file and let out a long sigh. "I had really hoped Beth would wake up by now, but the truth is, her vital signs are not very stable. Her blood pressure is extremely low and her kidney function is a concern to me. Her breathing is labored and shallow, and blood tests are showing that she's not getting enough oxygen into her blood." He looked up at them. "In normal times, I would change her medication to deal with those seizures, but we don't have the ideal drugs we need."

Could this get any worse?

"Her intracranial pressure is way too high. I recommend that we do a ventriculostomy as soon as possible."

"What is *that?*" Doug asked.

Derek spoke up. "It's a procedure that drains her cerebrospinal fluid, to take some of the pressure off her brain."

"It sounds dangerous," Kay whispered.

"No more dangerous than what might happen if we don't do it. Meanwhile, we're going to try our best to get some of the steroids and antiseizure meds in here that we need."

"Craig Martin is working on getting them," Kay blurted.

Overton nodded. "I know he is. He talked to me about them. Maybe he'll get them soon. But in the meantime, we have some decisions to make."

"What decisions?" Kay whispered.

"Well, we can do the procedure to drain the fluid today. After that, if we don't get the drugs and the pressure comes back, we could try a very radical procedure that sometimes does save brain tissue."

Doug took Kay's hand. "What procedure?"

"It's called a decompressive craniectomy. We remove part of the skull so there won't be so much pressure. That way the brain can expand without squeezing tissue, and cerebral blood flow can normalize."

"You remove it? Do you mean her head would be open? Her brains exposed?"

"Yes, until the pressure goes down."

Kay's mouth came open, and she stared, incredulous. "You can't be serious."

Derek cleared his throat. "It sounds awful, I know. But we actually have very good results with it. In wars, when soldiers have head injuries, the doctors do this as a first course of action. It lessens the probability of damage to the brain tissue."

"Then why didn't you do that first?" Doug asked.

The question was accusatory, but Dr. Overton took it well. "It's not *our* first course of action. Besides, Beth's skull fractures provided some of the same effects. But it's not enough. First we tried the medications we do have, and we monitored the pressure. But now we need to drain the cerebrospinal fluid. If it doesn't help, then we'll make the decision about the craniectomy."

Kay's hands and feet were ice cold. She slid her chair back and got up. She couldn't sit here and listen to a matter-of-fact discussion about opening her child's skull. How would Beth survive it?

"What about infection?" Doug asked. "If her head is open—"

"The benefits outweigh the risks," Overton said. "We have been able to get the antibiotics we need, so we would be able to fight infection."

Doug seemed so calm, so engaged in this cruel conversation.

"What would you do with the bone you remove? Of the skull, I mean? Would you ever be able to put it back?"

"We implant it in the abdominal wall until we can replace it where it belongs."

The room seemed to be closing in on her. Kay staggered, backing up against the wall. Reality pressed down on her with smothering heat. Her hands still felt like ice cubes. Doug got up and steadied her.

"I'm afraid Beth's brain isn't her only problem," Dr. Overton said. "Her kidney function is diminishing."

"We're going to put her on dialysis," Derek said. "Doug, Kay, these are all problems with solutions."

"Solutions?" Kay managed to say. "These don't sound like solutions. This is a nightmare."

"I know it seems that way," Dr. Overton said.

Kay pushed off from the wall. "Is she suffering?"

"I don't think so. From all we can tell, she isn't aware of anything."

But they weren't sure, Kay thought. For all they knew Beth was screaming in agony. Would she be strong enough for anesthesia, or would they just saw away without it?

Doug put his arm around her, pulling her morbid, racing thoughts to a halt. She pressed her face into his chest.

"Why are her kidneys failing?" he asked. "Her brain was injured, not her kidneys."

"But you see, the brain controls the function of all of her organs."

Kay brought both hands to her face. "She's dying, isn't she?"

Dr. Overton folded his hands in front of his face. "I haven't lost hope, Kay, and I still believe in miracles—"

"Miracles?" Doug repeated. "Is it going to take a miracle to save her?"

"Right now, it is. If we had the diagnostic tools we need, if we had the right drugs ... even then we'd be walking on very thin ice. But without those things ..."

Anger fired like bottle rockets in Kay's brain, bringing blood to her face. She slammed her hand on the table. "Beth is going to wake up and she's going to be back to normal. God would not take her from us. Do you understand?"

Doug slowly sat back down, his eyes locked into the surgeon's. "God can do this. He doesn't need diagnostic machines and computers. But until he does, we want to use whatever is available to save our daughter's life. We're not giving up on her and we don't want you to, either."

"I understand, and I won't. That's why I've presented you with these seemingly drastic options. If she survives, we don't want her to have lasting consequences of this injury—"

"*If* she survives? Beth's death is not an option," Kay bit out. "And neither is being a vegetable. You have to save her, Doctor."

Dr. Overton stood up. "I'll get her prepped for the ventriculostomy."

DOUG AND KAY STAYED BEHIND IN THE CONFERENCE ROOM WHEN the doctors left. Doug wanted to hold Kay, to comfort her, but his muscles felt as if they'd petrified into stone. He couldn't seem to move.

Kay couldn't *stop* moving. She trembled as if she were freezing and hugged her arms as if she comforted a broken child.

When she spoke, her voice was cracked, hoarse. "Every day of my life ... every single day ... I have prayed for the protection, safety, and health of my children, naming them one by one. Why would God let this happen to her?"

Doug just stared at his hands. "I don't know, but we have to trust him. There is a reason."

She looked at him as if he'd betrayed her. "There's no reason! There's no reason for a child to be tormented by some maniac killer and left to die in a hospital bed without the equipment and medicines they need to save her!"

"Kay, this is when it matters. This is when everything we've ever believed is put to the test."

"I'm sick and tired of tests," Kay cried.

He looked at his hands. They were callused and hard from the work he'd done over the last year. He could do so many things now. But he had no power to save his daughter. He opened his hands. "What can we do? We have no choice but to trust God to save her. There's no one else who can. With all their tricks and solutions, there's still so little doctors can do." His mind groped for Scripture. "The Bible tells us to consider it all joy when we encounter various trials, knowing that the testing of our faith produces endurance."

"Endurance for what? So we can cope through more trials like this one? How could I even *think* of considering it joy? There's no joy in this."

She was right. There wasn't. And as deep as he dug inside himself, he couldn't find any. Some spiritual leader he was. Some preacher.

Second only to watching his daughter die, was watching his wife suffer. "Kay, we've come through severe trials before and God has been with us, hasn't he? We have to look back on all the times he came through for us."

She couldn't answer.

"Remember when Deni disappeared and all looked so hopeless? God didn't let us down that time, did he?"

She shook her head. He could tell from the look on her face that she wanted to hold on to her anger. It gave her energy, adrenaline. It made her feel alive. But it was also a cruel poison.

"And God didn't let us down when little Sarah was kidnapped. God answered our prayers then, didn't he?"

"Yes," she said. "He did."

"And when Mark was falsely accused, we prayed again and God answered."

He saw the fury draining from her face, but not the fear.

"Kay, he's going to answer our prayers this time too. He's doing a work in us, and we have to let him."

She met his eyes with a glassy, terrified stare. "What if he's asking us to give more than we can?"

"Then he'll give us the strength to do it," Doug whispered.

She clearly didn't like that answer. She shook her head. "Well, I'm not giving up. I'm going to fight and wrestle with God until he gives me what I want. I may walk with a limp for the rest of my life, but by God, as far as it depends on me he's going to answer this prayer!"

Doug pulled her into his arms and held her, and she weakened against him. Thankfully, no other agonizing families were brought into the room for fatal news of their loved ones. They sat there until she had no more tears to cry.

Spent, she pulled a tissue from the box by the door and blew her nose. As she wadded it up, she looked down at it and gave a bitter laugh. "A few weeks ago I made a list of all the things I wanted to buy with our money. Stupid stuff. Hair dye. Lip gloss. Sugar. Things that seemed so important then. Now I don't care if I ever see those things again. If we had a million dollars to save Beth, it wouldn't do any good. There's nothing we can buy to make her better."

"We can pray. That's the most heroic thing we can do for her now. And we're going to ask God to do in us whatever it is he's trying to do."

"Yes, and we have to do everything it takes to make sure our prayers are answered." Kay's gaze moved from side to side, searching. "I've been trying to think of my sins, to repent. But every day there are new sins. I was jealous this morning when that old man next-door to Beth got better and was moved out of the ICU. I actually complained to God about it. And those people in the waiting room ... so many people to share Christ with. But I'm so wrapped up in my own troubles ..." She scratched her head as she looked at the wall. "There are other sins. Help me think of them, Doug."

"If you have unconfessed sin, God will help you think of it."

She looked up at him. "What about you? Have you confessed your sins?"

"Yes, Kay, and if I've missed something, I'm sure you'll point it out to me."

Finally, she managed a weak smile. He smiled too, surprised he still could.

"I don't think we're being punished or ignored because we've done something wrong. God is listening. He's working. He knew the number of days Beth had before there was even one. Like the woman with the unrighteous judge, we're going to bang on the doors of heaven until we finally get our answer. And whatever happens, we're going to continue to trust God. Are you with me on that?"

She nodded, but he saw in her face that she wasn't so sure. Her faith seemed to balance on a thin fulcrum of outcomes.

And he wasn't sure that his was any stronger.

eighty-one

DENI'S NEWS ABOUT THE PROGRESS IN THE CASE RAMPED up Doug's anger to an unmanageable degree. Across town, a woman was getting away with murder. If what Deni believed was true, Melissa wasn't simply an accomplice—she was guilty of first-degree murder for hiring her husband's killer. And she had covered that guilt by trying to do away with Beth.

Frustration over her freedom almost did him in. "Why haven't they arrested her?" he asked Deni.

"Because Brad thinks the case isn't strong enough yet to present to a judge. He wants a rock-solid case, so he needs more evidence of an affair between Melissa and Clay—something other than the fact that they knew each other."

Doug rubbed his temples and let out a long sigh. "I should be there helping them."

"Dad, how could you be? No one expects that. They're working on it. It's just going to take time."

He didn't want it to take time. Melissa might realize she'd been found out and flee the county. He went to the waiting room window and gazed out on the parking lot. Something inside him felt that if he could just solve this crime, Beth would turn a corner. Maybe if he took a crack at finding the evidence, he could convince Brad to issue an arrest warrant.

He turned back to Deni. "I'm going to the conversion plant to talk to Tharpe's coworkers. If one of them knew he was involved with Melissa, maybe that'll be enough for Brad."

"I'll go with you."

He didn't argue. He'd seen Deni's investigative skills at work before.

They walked the few blocks to the conversion plant. Deni carried her notepad and the yearbook she'd gotten from Tharpe's neighbor, so she could show pictures of Melissa Tomlin to Tharpe's coworkers. They went in through the open bay. The noise level was high as engines roared and men yelled to communicate.

Doug saw Ned Emory as they walked in. He and Deni crossed the room to the plant director, who was also their neighbor.

"How's it going, Doug?"

"We're hanging in there," he said.

"Has Beth come out of the coma yet?"

"No, not yet." He didn't want to talk about Beth. "Listen, I need to talk to some of the guys who knew Clay Tharpe best."

Ned shrugged. "Why? Tharpe's dead. Isn't the case closed?"

"Actually, no. We believe there was a second person who hired him to kill Tomlin. A woman he might have been seeing."

Ned's thick eyebrows came together. "No kidding. You just never know about people."

He pointed to a group of men in a corner of the building. They had grease smeared up to their elbows and dirty perspiration on their faces. Two of them were under a car, and the other two stood over the engine. "Those guys over there were on his team. You can start with them."

Doug thanked him, and they headed over. The men noticed Deni before Doug, and as they moved closer, they stood straighter—almost strutting for her. He wondered if she realized it.

"Hey, guys," she said, "Ned Emory just told us you're the ones who worked most closely with Clay Tharpe."

The two under the car rolled out and sat up, wrists on their knees.

"Yeah, it's too bad what happened to him," a guy whose nametag said "Gordon" said.

"Must be hard for you guys," Doug said. "Having one of your friends die like that."

"And under such bizarre circumstances," Deni added.

"Tell you the truth, we don't know whether to be depressed or angry."

Doug looked at the hulking man leaning over the engine. His nametag said "Smitty."

"The guy was a pain in the neck," Smitty said, "but we never would have wanted him to be shot to death."

"Did he really kill those people?" someone else asked.

Doug felt someone come up behind him and glanced back. Ned had joined them.

"The little girl he tried to kill is this man's daughter and her little sister," Ned told them.

The men looked at them with new eyes. Doug didn't like being pitied.

"Sorry about that, man," Smitty said. "You work with a guy for a year, and you think you know him."

"Look, would you guys mind answering a few questions for us?" Doug asked.

"Sure, what do you want to know?"

"When the sheriff's deputies questioned you earlier, you told them that Clay Tharpe liked the women."

"That was me." Smitty lifted his hand.

Deni took over. "Were there times when you saw him with other women besides his wife?"

"Now and then, but not in the last few months. Mostly he was just always looking."

Deni opened the yearbook to the bookmarked page with Melissa's picture. "Did you ever see him with this woman? This picture was taken about ten years ago, but she hasn't changed that much."

The men studied the picture. "Yeah, we know her."

"You do? How?"

"She comes up here sometimes," Smitty said.

"To see Clay Tharpe?" Deni asked.

"She knew him, I know that. Only ..." Smitty stopped and glanced at Ned.

Doug looked at the plant director. Ned's eyes were locked on Smitty. Doug turned back to the man who'd stopped midsentence. "Only *what?*"

Ned took the book and looked at the picture. "Oh, yeah, the frizzy-haired blonde."

"Did she come here to see Clay?"

Everyone looked down, as though they didn't want to answer. It was as if the shutters over their eyes had closed. He glanced back at Ned again, saw the cool look in his eyes.

Something told him he was hitting a nerve.

He turned back to Smitty who seemed the most forthcoming. "Smitty, you were going to say something."

Smitty cleared his throat. "Why are you asking about her? What difference does it make, if Clay is dead? It's no crime to have a fling."

"So she *was* having a fling with him?" Deni asked.

Smitty backed off. "No, I'm not saying that."

"Can you just answer the question?" Doug asked. "Did you ever see Clay with her?"

Again, Smitty glanced at Ned. "It's just—I don't think she was up here to see Clay."

"Then who was she here to see?" Doug pressed.

"All of us," Ned cut in. "I think she just liked being around all the men. She seemed to need attention."

Deni's mouth came open. "So she just bopped up in here now and then to flirt with the guys?"

"Something like that."

Doug wasn't buying that. "She must have had a favorite. She didn't show any special attention to Clay?"

"Not really," Smitty said. "She'd speak to him. 'Hey, how ya doing,' that sort of thing. I mean, they were friends. But I think that was all."

"So she wasn't having an affair with anyone up here?"

Smitty glanced away again. Shrugging, he said, "Not so's anyone could tell."

"WHAT DO YOU MAKE OF THAT?" DOUG ASKED DENI AS THEY LEFT the conversion plant.

"I think they're hiding something."

"But when did the tide turn? They acted like they wanted to talk at first."

"It changed when we asked them about her."

Doug played the conversation back through his mind. Did he just imagine that they were being forthcoming until then? "Why would they want to protect her?"

Deni walked along silently, thinking. "What if they're telling the truth, and Melissa and Clay weren't having an affair? Maybe Mark and I just got it wrong. Or maybe they were hiding it well from the other guys."

"No, I didn't get the feeling that they were ignorant about an affair. It was more like they were shutting down. They sure weren't protecting Clay, so it had to be that they didn't want to implicate her."

Deni looked at him. "Maybe it was a mistake to tell Ned that you thought she was involved."

Doug drew in a deep breath. This was why he should stay at the hospital. He was too distracted to do good police work. Yes, he'd tipped Ned off, and if the guys at the plant had any affinity for the friendly, attention-seeking young woman, then Ned probably had signaled for them to shut up.

As they walked back through town toward the hospital, they passed Brad's office. The sign outside that said "City Prosecutor" beckoned him. "Let's go in and have a chat with Brad."

They found Brad in his sweltering office, buried in files. He greeted them with hugs.

"How is Beth?"

"She's having seizures. That increases her chances of irreversible brain damage. And to make matters worse, they can't get the antiseizure medications she needs *or* the drugs to fight the swelling in her brain."

Brad rubbed a rough brown hand over his face. "Man, I can't believe it. I wish there were something I could do."

"There is." Doug sat down across from his best friend. He got Deni to tell him what she and Mark had found. Brad listened attentively. When Deni was finished, he filled him in on the visit to the plant.

"They're hiding something, but there's not time to get to the bottom of it. If Melissa gets wind of our connecting her to Clay, she'll flee prosecution. We need to take her into custody now."

He recognized the pain on Brad's face. "Doug, if she hurt Beth, I want her arrested too, but if she's guilty, I want it to stick. An affair is not enough."

"But don't you see?" Deni said. "Her father may have killed Tharpe to protect his daughter."

"But his confession says that he did it for vengeance, for what Clay had done to his son-in-law."

"And you believe that?" Doug asked. "Brad, why would he do that? He could have waited and let justice do its work. Clay was in custody, and we had plenty of evidence. It makes more sense that Mr. Anthony knew his daughter was involved in her husband's killing. That he shot Clay Tharpe right in front of a judge because he thought Tharpe was about to talk. Think about it. He was going before the judge, about to speak. What better time to shoot him down and make sure she wasn't implicated?"

Brad just shook his head. "Everything you're saying might be right. But I have to prosecute it. A judge isn't going to send it to a Grand Jury even if you do prove she was having an affair. You have no proof that she hired Tharpe or told him to kill her husband. And I'm more inclined to believe that her father was the one who hired Tharpe. Think about it. Melissa's husband was beating her and the boy, right?"

"Right."

"And the dad gets wind of it and decides to take care of it."

Deni wasn't satisfied. "So what was his motivation for killing Tharpe? You don't *prove* you're a killer to keep somebody from *saying* you're a killer. He shot Clay in front of a judge for a very good reason. He smuggled a gun in past security, because he planned to shut Tharpe up. It clearly wasn't to save himself."

"Deni, I'm with you," Brad said. "But if we're gonna get Melissa, we have to have something more solid. Follow the money. See if you can prove she got any of it. See if you can find evidence that she and Tharpe met up after the murder. Give me something to work with, Doug, and I'll give you a warrant." He rubbed his jaw, then set his elbows on his desk.

Brad was right, but Doug didn't like it. Maybe he could get Mark to trace her spending habits, to see if she'd bought anything bigger than what a FEMA disbursement would give her.

"And find somebody who can connect her with Beth. If we can prove she saw Beth watching her house, then our ground will be a little less shaky."

Doug and Deni walked back to the hospital with a sense of hopelessness that anything would be done. Their only hope lay in Mark's desire to get Melissa Tomlin. If anyone could find that evidence, it would be him.

eighty-two

BECAUSE HER BROTHERS WERE GOING STIR-CRAZY SITTING in the hospital waiting room, Deni's parents decided that the boys should start sleeping at home. It looked as if the Brannings might be in this vigil-keeping mode for a long time, so they had to find ways to create some normalcy for the family—if for no other reason than to keep their strength up. Deni was sent home to supervise this first night home.

Brad and Judith brought them supper, which Deni appreciated since they had so little food in the house. After dinner, she cleaned up with no help from her brothers. They'd vanished as soon as their bellies were full. Now the chickens needed to be fed, and the eggs gathered, and it was the boys' turn to work.

She went upstairs to tell them. Deni found Logan in Beth's room, sitting on her carpet next to Craig's suitcase, looking at the books in Beth's bookcase.

As she stood in Beth's doorway, Deni watched the melancholy look on her little brother's face. At ten years old, he'd always been a rival to Beth. The two behaved like normal siblings, complete with name-calling and tattling. But on his face she could see his deep love for their sister.

"Hey," she said. "What are you doing?"

He glanced back at her. "Looking for something new to read to her."

She went into the room and sat on the bed. Craig had made it up, but one of his belts lay on it. She picked it up.

"We really ought to move him out of here," Logan said. "When she wakes up, she'll need her own bed."

"I know," she said. "With all that's been going on, nobody's had time to think about it. I'm sure he's looking for a place."

"Get real," Logan said. "He's not going anywhere until you marry him."

Deni grunted. "He knows I'm not going to."

"No, he doesn't. He's trying to make himself part of our family, and nobody even notices." Logan's cheeks reddened. He was taking this personally. Clearly, he didn't want anyone sleeping in Beth's bed.

"I'll talk to him about moving out, Logan. But don't worry. When Beth comes home, she'll have her room back."

He pulled out a book, opened it.

"Here's an old Dr. Seuss book that Mom used to read to us," Logan said. "*Green Eggs and Ham*. Do you think she's too old for that?"

"You're never too old for Dr. Seuss. I think she'd love to hear you read it to her."

He stared down at the cover. "Do you think it's like sleeping? Do you think she has dreams?"

Deni had wondered that herself. "I really can't say, but I think it probably is something like that."

"I hope they're good dreams. I hope she doesn't just dream about that man." Some unseen force pulled at the corners of his lips.

"I'll bet they're good dreams," she whispered. "Maybe when we read to her she dreams about the stories."

"That's what I was thinking," Logan said, managing a weak smile. "It'd be cool to make her dream about Sam I Am."

Jeff came to the door, wet with sweat. "I got water," he said, "so we can all wash up. I also weeded the garden. It rained yesterday, so I didn't have to water it."

Deni's jaw dropped. "Wow. I thought you were loafing in your room. I was coming to make you feed the chickens."

"That's what you get for thinking."

Deni smiled at her brother's familiar barb. It smacked of normalcy. She needed that.

"I took care of the chickens and got the eggs in. Jeremy and Drew are taking our turn feeding the rabbits."

She should go down and cook some eggs to take to the hospital to her parents. Tomorrow, if it was sunny enough, she could make a few loaves of bread to cook in the solar oven. Jeff could get them out when they were done. They could make enough loaves to eat for days.

But right now, she felt numb, useless, lethargic. She didn't want to do anything.

"Let's just all rest now. We've had a rough few days. No more chores to—"

Suddenly the lights overhead flickered.

Logan caught his breath and looked up. "Did you *see* that?"

Deni stared at the light bulb. Could it really be ... were the lights coming back on?

They all froze, wide-eyed, waiting ... The bulbs flickered again. All three of them let out a yell and came off the floor.

"The lights are on! The lights are on!"

They stared at the lightbulb as if it were a new invention. For a moment it would dim, then it would brighten. They ran from room to room, flicked on every light switch, saw the same thing. Their electricity was back on!

"Whoa!" Jeff yelled. "Is Craig the man or what?"

Craig had done as much as anyone toward getting their power back on. If he hadn't convinced the recovery team to set up their offices in Crockett, they might have been the last place instead of the first. It gave her hope that maybe he could also convince someone to give them the things Beth needed.

Suddenly Deni's lethargy lifted, and she had new energy.

Life seemed to be turning a corner.

eighty-three

NEWS THAT THE LIGHTS HAD COME ON GAVE KAY A NEW
sense of hope, as if the crises in her life might be coming to an
end. It sent the hospital staff into a frenzy of activity. They ran
from patient to patient, preparing them for the moment when
they would transition the hospital from the hardened gas-pow-
ered generators to the power grid. Kay prayed there wouldn't
be an interruption in the power, making the ventilator go off.
If it did, they said, it would only be a few seconds.

She held her breath as the lights went off. The hum of
the equipment in the ICU hushed. The ventilator powered
off. Kay touched Beth's chest, praying it wouldn't be long.
She held her breath with Beth, counting off the seconds. As
more time passed, she felt as if her lungs would explode. She
needed to let it out. Beth hadn't had the benefit of taking a
big breath. Was she smothering?

"Come on ..." Doug muttered.

It was too long. She had to breathe! Kay expelled her
breath and gasped for another. Panic shot through her.
Maybe they should pull out her tube and do mouth to
mouth. "Hurry, people!" she shouted, though she knew the
electricians were outside. But as dark silence stretched into
a hellish eternity, she heard the hissing of a breath.

Beth's chest fell as she breathed out through the tube.

"Doug, she's breathing! On her own!"

Doug bent and put his ear to her mouth. "She is. It's a
miracle!"

Kay came around the bed to hug him, and he took her in his arms. "She's breathing!" she sang.

"She's gonna wake up, Kay. I know it."

It wasn't until an hour later, after Dr. Overton ordered staff to pull the breathing tube out of Beth's throat and watched to make sure Beth could breathe without struggling, that Kay felt the full import of the restoration of electrical power.

They'd hardly noticed, they were so focused on Beth. The event they'd waited for for the past year had been relegated to an afterthought.

But now that Beth was breathing on her own, Kay basked in the light of that bulb over her head. She wondered if her children realized the power was back on. Surely they'd left a few light switches on, all those months ago. "I wish I could see the kids' faces," she told Doug.

"Go home and give them the good news about Beth. I'll stay here."

Kay hadn't left the hospital at all except to go to the jail. Now that Beth had improved, maybe she could stand to be away.

Kay's spirits soared. Now that they had electricity, they could rebuild things for which they had critical needs—MRIs, CT scanners, PET scanners. Drug companies could get back up and running. Medicines would be more available.

Beth would live.

She bent over the bed and stroked Beth's hair. "The lights are back on, sweetie. Things are going to get back to normal." Beth gave no sign that she heard—but her rhythmic breathing spoke volumes. Gently, Kay pressed her forehead against her daughter's. "I love you, honey. Wake up soon. I don't want you to miss it."

She kissed Doug, then went out and found the bike Mark had brought for her—among the tangle of bikes lined up on the rack. Then she rode home, anxious to see the thrill on her children's faces.

eighty-four

MARK WAS SURPRISED TO SEE DOUG AT THE SHERIFF'S department the day after the lights came back on, dressed in his uniform as though he expected to put in a full day's work.

Two of the other deputies greeted him and asked about Beth when he came in. Mark waited until the commotion had died down. When Doug crossed the room, Mark said, "Man, you don't seriously think you're gonna work today. Go back to the hospital."

It was good to see him smile. "I just came by to see the sheriff's department all lit up. I'm not sure I've ever seen this place well lit." He looked around. "Paint looks terrible. Look at the cobwebs in the corners. Never saw those before."

"You didn't need full uniform to come by and see that. What's really up?"

Doug's smile faded, and his eyes took on that intensity he'd worn for so many days. "I want to talk to Melissa Tomlin's father. He hasn't been moved to the county jail yet, has he?"

"No, he's still here. So far he's sticking to his story that he was just angry at his son-in-law's killer. But maybe talking to you would shake him up a bit."

While Doug waited in the kitchen, Mark went to get Scott Anthony out of his cell. With the lights on, the cell area was much more pleasant than it had been yesterday. The prisoners had been quieter since the lights came back on. Having been

326

incarcerated himself, Mark knew that the fear factor had decreased. There were few things worse than being crowded into a cell with killers and thieves when it was so dark that you couldn't see your hand in front of your face. Darkness seemed to breed more evil.

He found Scott Anthony sitting on his bunk, reading the Gideon Bible he'd been given when he was booked. Mark wished the man had read more of it before he decided to commit murder. Still, he almost felt sorry for him, since he seemed so out of place here. Wheaton had clearly had the same sentiment, since he'd assigned Anthony to a cell by himself.

Mark stopped at the bars to Anthony's cell. "Mr. Anthony, we need to see you in the interview room. Step up to the bars and I'll put your shackles on."

Anthony looked humiliated at the prospect. But it was county policy for those charged with violent crimes. He came to the bars. Mark stooped and locked the chains around the man's feet, then got up and unlocked the door. Anthony shuffled through. "Is something wrong? Is my family all right?"

"They're fine. We just want to ask you a few questions."

He was silent as Mark walked him through the squad room back into the kitchen area where Doug waited, standing with his hands in his pockets. He looked at Scott Anthony as he rattled in. "Have a seat, Mr. Anthony."

He kept standing for a moment. "Should I have my lawyer present?"

"It's up to you." Doug set both hands on the table, leaning over. "Do you know who I am?"

Anthony studied him for a moment. "I saw you in the courtroom."

"Beth Branning is my daughter."

Anthony swallowed and pulled out a chair. "The girl Clay Tharpe injured?"

"That's right."

Emotion dragged at his face. "I'm very sorry about your daughter. How is she?"

"Still in a coma," Doug said. "Please sit down."

The man who looked like he could have been a neighbor in Oak Hollow lowered to a chair.

Doug kept his voice soft. "The reason we want to talk to you, Mr. Anthony, is that we believe your daughter may have been having an affair with Clay Tharpe."

Mark didn't react to Doug's bluff. Instead he watched Anthony's face, expecting him to look shocked and deny it completely. But Anthony didn't. "I've already signed a confession. There were dozens of witnesses who saw me kill Clay Tharpe. Considering what he did to your daughter, you should be giving me a trophy."

Doug frowned. "That's what you have to say about your daughter's affair with her husband's killer? I'm sorry, but that wasn't quite the reaction I expected."

Anthony looked scared. "I don't know what you want from me."

"Did you know about the affair?"

Anthony looked pained. Finally, he hunched over and raked his hand through his gray hair. "You have to understand."

Mark uncrossed his arms and leaned forward. "Understand what?"

"You don't know what kind of man Blake was. He treated her horribly. She had broken bones, black eyes, bloody lips."

Doug sat straighter. "Are you justifying what you did ... or what *she* did?"

Anthony's face hardened. "My daughter did not kill her husband, and she had nothing to do with your daughter. She was a victim."

Mark decided to show another card. "Mr. Anthony, what if I told you that Clay Tharpe told us there was someone else who wanted Tomlin dead?"

He looked distraught, as if he'd been found out. "He meant that I hired him."

Doug stood up. "So you're changing your story about it being a crime of passion? That you just lost your head in the courtroom?"

"No ... yes. I don't know. I need my lawyer."

"We can send for him," Doug said. "He'll probably tell you to shut up, and you can. You can keep the truth to yourself. We'll build a case against your daughter anyway."

Anthony rubbed his face, clearly confused about what to do. "I'm stuck here. I committed murder in a courtroom. They're not going to let me out no matter what you think you've found."

"So you figure you can take a little more heat to protect your daughter?"

"I'm not protecting her! I did it. You *saw* me."

Doug leaned on the table again, his face inches from Anthony's. "Of all people to hire, why would you hire your daughter's lover to kill her husband?"

"Because I knew he'd do it!"

There it was. Confirmation that there was an affair.

"Why would you know that?" Doug asked. "Clay Tharpe had never been arrested before. There's no reason to believe he would kill."

"But he had problems. He was a gambling addict. He had a lot to hide. He took the job for the money," Anthony said. "Don't you see? There was nothing in it for her. She needed that money, but she didn't get any of it."

"I don't believe that," Mark said. "Tharpe only got home with five hundred dollars."

He got tears in his eyes, and couldn't meet Mark's gaze. "I don't care what you believe."

"Want to know what I think?" Doug asked through curling lips. "I think Melissa told you she did it, didn't she, Mr. Anthony? She told you about her affair and about how she planned this murder out with Clay Tharpe to get rid of the man who had abused her, and you realized she wasn't going to get away with it, that Clay wouldn't go down alone, that he was going to spill his guts, and your daughter was going to wind up spending the rest of her life in prison."

Anthony's face told them Doug had hit the mark. Doug lowered himself into his chair and softened his voice.

"You couldn't let that happen, could you, Scott? You'd do anything to save your daughter, so you killed Tharpe in front of the judge and a room full of witnesses, to keep Tharpe from implicating your daughter in her husband's murder."

Mark saw the twitch on Anthony's face, the stark truth he couldn't hide in his eyes. The man rubbed his stubbled jaw and brought his pained eyes to Mark's.

"I'm not proud of my daughter's affairs."

There, Mark thought. He'd admitted it. It was just what they needed.

"But she's not the one you need to be looking at."

"Then who do you think we should look at?" Doug asked.

"Ned Emory," he said. "That's all I have to say."

eighty-five

SCOTT ANTHONY'S BOMBSHELL ABOUT NED EMORY LEFT Doug reeling. Ned was his neighbor, and the father of his son's best friend. He'd been put in charge of the Alabaster Road Conversion Plant and had done a good job. While Doug sometimes questioned his judgment in raising kids, Doug couldn't imagine Ned being involved in murder. Especially not when it involved an attack on Beth.

Ned knew Beth. He'd come to her plays, laughed and clapped in all the right places, given her pats on the back.

Was Scott saying that Ned was having an affair with Melissa? What did that mean? That Ned was the one who'd hired Tharpe? That he'd tipped off the killer about Beth being at the park?

But that didn't square up. Scott Anthony wouldn't have killed Tharpe to protect Ned. And as Deni had suggested a couple of days ago, Anthony had premeditated Tharpe's murder when he smuggled a gun into the courtroom, so it clearly wasn't the crime of passion he wanted them to believe.

They summoned the sheriff, who was working that day in his Birmingham office. When he got to Crockett, the rest of the on-duty deputies showed up for the briefing.

"It's too far-fetched to believe," Doug said. "I just can't see it. Ned has too much to lose."

"People do strange things for love all the time," Wheaton said.

Doug thought back to his visit to the conversion plant. "You know, when I was at the plant, Ned did seem real interested in what I was asking Tharpe's coworkers. And when I asked about Melissa Tomlin . . ." He tried to play the scene back through his mind. "The guys said she came up there a lot, but not to see Clay. When I asked who she came to see, they all clammed up and looked at Ned. I knew something wasn't right, but I didn't think for a minute that they were covering for *him*."

"Those guys probably fear for their jobs," Wheaton said. "If the boss wants them to be quiet about an affair, they will."

"It's not like they can get fired," Mark said. "They were drafted by the government."

"Yeah, but they could get transferred somewhere else and have to leave their families. Besides, they probably don't realize that the affair could possibly implicate Ned in the murders."

"Wait a minute," London piped up. "Why are we believing what Scott Anthony says?"

"Because he's the guy next door," Wheaton said. "He doesn't fit the typical profile of a murderer."

"Neither does Melissa Tomlin, and we know she lied. She could just come from a long line of liars."

"It really doesn't matter if they're all lying," Doug said. "I want everyone who had any part in my daughter's attack to pay the consequences."

"So what do we do next?" Mark asked.

Wheaton thought that over for a moment. "We get Tharpe's coworkers in one at a time and interview them again. Find someone who can confirm that Ned and Melissa had a thing going. Interview the Tomlins' neighbors again and see if they ever saw Ned Emory coming or going. Eventually we'll get to the bottom of it."

eighty-six

THE INSTALLATION OF VACUUM-TUBE RADIOS IN CRAIG'S building caused a celebration among his employees. In his work, communication was almost as important as electricity. Before the end of the day, he hoped the emergency personnel in the area would have their own radios. Soon all the government buildings would be in communication with each other. After that, it was just a matter of time before they could restore telephone service.

Because they wouldn't need Morse code anymore, he moved Horace Hancock to the radio. The other World War II veterans were moved to jobs that fit their experience. Though they were in their eighties, he chose not to let them go. They needed the money, and he suspected their wisdom and skills might prove to be useful in the coming days. They knew more than he did about how to do things without technology.

Not long after they'd gotten the radio up and running, Horace yelled across the room. "Craig, Senator Crawford's on the line!"

Craig's heartbeat tripped. He cut across the room and almost slid to a stop on the polished linoleum. He grabbed the headphones and put them on. "Senator, how are you?"

"I'm better now that we can communicate!"

Craig laughed at the faint sound of his boss's voice. "We're all better, sir. Have you been able to find out about the things I asked for?"

The line was cluttered with static. "I've been checking around, Craig. It's going to be some time before the scanners you asked about are rebuilt. Not even the president has access to those. But I have my contact from Hope Drug Manufacturing here with me now. I'm putting Janice Goodwin on the radio."

This was too good to be true. Craig waited, breath held, as the woman took the radio. "Hi, Craig. What can I do for you?"

He swallowed the dryness in his throat. "I'm trying to help save the life of my fiancée's little sister." That wasn't quite true, but it was the simplest explanation. "We need Decadron or a generic version as soon as we can get it." He named the other drugs that Dr. Overton had listed for him.

"I do have those drugs available in generic form," she said. "I could send them by train if you could pay for it."

Craig tried to calculate how long it would take him to get them by train. It would be at least two days, maybe longer, with all the stops they made. They might not have that much time. He glanced at his watch. "I could come get them."

"Really? All the way from Alabama?"

"Yes. I could leave now."

"But isn't that about twelve hours each way?"

"Not if I drive eighty miles an hour." He checked his watch. It was ten a.m. now. "I could be there in eight and a half hours, maybe less, if I can get enough gas. Could you meet me at the Senate Building at seven tonight?"

"I'll be there," she said, chuckling. "But I'm betting you won't be. Oh, and don't forget the prescription."

CRAIG HOPED THE STATE DIRECTOR DIDN'T FIND OUT THAT HE'D ditched his job at such a critical time, nor about using the company car on personal business. He calculated that he would need eight tanks of gas to get there and back. His car held sixteen gallons. He went to the conversion plant next door and filled the car up, then filled thirteen ten-gallon containers. The plant employees assumed he needed it for government business, so no one objected. He lined the containers full of gas up on the floor of his backseat and in his trunk, knowing that if he had an accident his car would probably explode. He managed to store enough to get to Washington. Once he was there, he could fill them all up again to get back.

He ran by the hospital on his way out of town. "I'm on my way to get the drugs from Hope Manufacturing in Washington," he told Deni. "I'll be back by morning."

Deni just stared at him. "Craig, can you really do that?"

"Watch me." He took her shoulders and smacked a kiss on her lips. "Pray for me, babe."

Then he hurried out, intent on his mission, praying that God would clear the way to get Beth the help she needed.

eighty-seven

THAT NIGHT, DENI STAYED AT THE HOSPITAL WITH BETH so her parents could get some rest, since they didn't expect Craig back with the drugs until morning. She wished Mark could stay with her, but he'd been asked to work the night shift at the sheriff's department to fill in for her father.

She sat in the stiff chair next to Beth's bed, listening to the rhythmic rise and fall of her breath. It was a sweet sound. The room was hot; there were no windows in the ICU, and the building had gotten up to about ninety degrees. Summer was in full swing and there was no relief in sight.

She wet a washcloth and wiped Beth's face and neck, hoping she could keep her sister cool. The lights still flickered and dimmed, brightened and faded. But the electricity had enabled them to put Beth on a heart monitor and to put compression stockings on her legs. Every few seconds the machine hummed, inflating the stockings, to keep her from getting blood clots.

Since she no longer needed to massage Beth's legs, she found herself with little to do. It was going to be a long night.

Her friend Chris stopped in around midnight. "How are we doing in here?"

Deni hugged her. "I don't know. Check her chart and let me know."

"I already did. Dr. Overton left orders for her nurse to administer the drugs as soon as they arrive. Where are they coming from?"

She smiled. "Craig is driving to Washington to get them."

Chris's eyebrows arched. "Wow, what a guy. He's like a hero. First getting the power turned on and now this?"

Deni ignored her gushing. "Chris, do you think those drugs will help her wake up?"

Chris tugged at the mask over her face. "Getting the swelling down will keep them from having to do a craniectomy. And without the intracranial pressure, things could turn around. It might not happen tomorrow, but it would sure give her an advantage."

Chris went to the head of Beth's bed, checked her bandage.

"So are there parties going on everywhere around town, now that the lights are on?" Deni asked.

"There sure are. One on every block. It's like the end of World War II, when everybody was kissing in the streets. My parents have been firing up every appliance in our house, just to see if they'll still work. Some of them do."

"It's weird, being so detached from it all. If all this hadn't happened, we'd be doing the same things."

"So has Craig said when we're getting telephone service?"

"No, we really haven't had time to talk."

"Are you going back to work for him?"

She hesitated and looked down at her hands, remembering the kiss he'd laid on her before he left town. "I don't know. I'm thinking about going back to the newspaper."

"The newspaper? Why?"

Deni looked up at her. "It's just not the best idea to work with Craig. You know, with our history and all."

Chris seemed to understand. Deni was glad she didn't make her explain more. After a few minutes, Chris went back to work on another floor.

Deni tried to get comfortable in her chair. She slid it back against the wall, rested her head back, and tried to straighten out in the chair. There was no way to get comfortable. She longed to stretch out in her own bed with Beth next to her. She got up and stroked her sister's hair. Would she ever wake up?

Deni sat back down and prayed that Craig wasn't just talking—that he really could get the medications Beth needed. Then
she folded her arms on Beth's bed table, rested her head on them,
and tried to doze.

"I made it back, babe. Drugs and all."

Deni threw her head up. Craig stood in the doorway, suited up
in a fresh pair of scrubs and a mask over his face. She jumped up.
"You got them? You really did?"

His eyes were grinning. "I didn't think my car would go that
fast. I must have gone ninety all the way. Thank goodness it was
night or I might have run down a few dozen people."

She threw her arms around him, and he picked her up and
swung her around. "Told you I'd get them."

"He got them, all right." The nurse pushed past them into the
room, holding two syringes. "Dr. Overton told me to give them
to her as soon as they got here." She injected one into Beth's IV.
"You're a miracle worker, Mr. Martin."

"Just doing what I can."

Deni watched the nurse as she slowly injected the liquid. "God's
the miracle worker."

Craig nodded, as though he'd meant to say that.

The nurse administered the second drug, then checked Beth's
heart rate and blood pressure. "It's in God's hands. We've just got
to keep praying."

The nurse left the room, and Deni bent over Beth, watching for
any sign of a change even though she knew it was too soon. She
put her hand on Beth's soft head and began to pray out loud. She
felt Craig's hand on her back.

When they finished praying, they sat down. Deni wiped
her eyes. "I really appreciate you doing that, Craig. Driving to
Washington and back in one night. And it wasn't even government
work."

His eyes were red and tired, but they rounded as he looked at
her. "I did it because I love you, Deni. And I love your family."

She didn't know what to say to that. "Well, it was a really heroic
thing to do."

He took her hand, ran his thumb across her palm. "I'll stay with you until morning," he said.

She didn't pull her hand away. How could she, after all he'd done? "That's not necessary. You should go home and get some rest."

"I can't rest knowing you're here."

It was sweet, so unlike the apathetic Craig who had disappointed her so after the Pulses. This kind of behavior was what she'd yearned for, but she'd never gotten it from him. Had his newfound Christianity changed his personality as well as his spirit?

She swallowed and met his eyes. "Craig, I've been thinking. I know I said I'd come to work for the recovery team, but you've probably had to replace me by now."

"I'm holding your job, Deni. I hired another guy to help in PR, but your job is still there whenever you're ready to come back. We still have a lot of areas without electricity, and after we get all that fixed, there's still a ton of other things we have to do to rebuild the infrastructure. We'll need you for all of it."

"Well, I appreciate that. But I don't think I want it anymore."

Craig stiffened. "Why not?"

"Because ..." She got up, straightened Beth's blanket. "I love investigative reporting. I don't think I want to stop being a journalist."

"But Deni, the money. We can pay you so much more."

"I know, but that doesn't seem all that important to me now."

He looked at her as though she had just asked him to leave. He got up and touched her shoulder, pulled his mask down under his chin. "Deni, we were going to be a team. We had such big plans. I believe God sent me here to win you back. I wouldn't have come if I didn't have hope. I know you loved me once, but I was stupid then."

His sincerity touched her. "Craig, I can see that you've changed."

"When we broke up, I knew it had a lot to do with your faith. Remember, you told me we were unequally yoked? I got a Bible and looked that up, trying to understand what that meant, and finally I got it. I realized that you can't marry somebody who has different goals and different priorities. What kind of life would that be?"

"That wasn't the only reason I broke up, Craig."

"I know," he said. "I was a jerk when the Pulses started. I got so wrapped up in my work, so busy that I didn't take time to try to get in touch with you or come to get you. And I started to reflect on all the things you had done to get to me and how you'd risked your life. I was a sorry guy, and I knew I needed to change. So I started going to church."

"Which church?" she asked.

"Christ Fellowship. I'd walked by it a million times without even noticing it. Then one day I saw people going in. At first I just went and sat on the back row and listened every Sunday, and usually the preacher would cover something I'd never heard of. I would go home and look it up and read. I felt so helpless. At the Senate Building we were making all these plans, trying to get everything in place for the recovery. It finally occurred to me that all our efforts were worthless, because God is in total control. He'd caused the Pulses, and we had no way of stopping them or ending the crisis. It was all up to him."

Deni gazed up at him, captivated.

"And then I started going on Sunday nights, and one night the preacher asked us to come down for prayer, and I went down and told him I needed prayer because I wasn't a Christian. I had never surrendered my life to Christ and I wasn't really sure what it took. Brother Harris prayed with me, and the next thing I knew, I had turned my life over to Christ. And from that moment on, I knew I was different."

Deni blinked back tears. "I'm glad, Craig."

He took her hand again. His were still soft from office work and paper pushing, not hard and callused like Mark's.

But these hands did important work.

"Deni, I know when I came back and told you I'd become a Christian that you and your family thought it was just a ploy. But it's not. God's changed my life."

"I believe you."

"It means the world to me if you do. You were in love with me once, baby."

She looked away, but he touched her face and brought her gaze back to him. "With Christ at the center of our home, we can have a great marriage, Deni. We'll have beautiful children and a common purpose. Our careers are going the same direction. We have the same interests, the same intellect, the same drive. We'd be a power couple. You know we would."

She didn't say anything. The compressor hummed, and she looked at Beth's stockings as they inflated. He turned her face back to his.

"I can see why you're interested in Mark," he said. "He's a strong guy. You're right. He can do anything. But Deni, he's not right for you."

She smiled and sat back down. "Funny, he said the same thing about you a few months ago."

Craig stooped down in front of her. "He was right. The timing was wrong for us. But it's the right time now, Deni."

What was he doing? On his knees in front of her. She tried to pull him up. "Craig ..."

"No, don't." He set his fingertips over her lips, silencing her. "Please, just let me talk. My life these last few months has been miserable without you. I've had this gnawing in my gut like I'd had an organ removed or something. I can't stand the thought of living without you, and I know I can make you happy. I can give you everything you want."

"What are you doing?"

He slipped his hand into his pocket and pulled out the ring she'd worn for almost a year.

She sat up, rigid. "My ring ..."

His eyes filled with tears, and her heart softened. She remembered all the hopes she'd had for them, all the plans they'd made together. How excited she'd been, how honored, for him to want her for his wife.

"Listen to me, Deni. I want you to put this ring back on your finger, and I want us to set another date. I want to spend my life with you. Please don't say no."

Deni touched the ring, remembering all the pleasure it had brought her, all those months ago.

Suddenly, Beth's monitor began to beep. Deni sprang out of her chair, knocking the ring out of his hand.

Beth's face was pink, warm. Deni caught her breath as her eyes moved under the lids. "Beth!"

Beth opened her eyes and looked right at her. "Don't do it, Deni."

Beth had spoken! Deni's heart almost stopped, and she bent over her sister, tears rushing to her eyes, her nose. "Oh, sweetie!"

Her sister's eyes closed again as two nurses ran in. "What happened?"

"She woke up!" Deni cried. "She woke up and spoke to me!"

The nurse went to her bed and patted her cheek. "Beth? Beth, can you hear me?"

The other nurse was listening to her heart. "Heart rate has gone back up. Blood pressure is normal."

Deni swung around. "Craig, go get my parents. Hurry!"

"I'm on my way," he said, and ran for the door.

eighty-eight

THE POUNDING ON HER BEDROOM DOOR FRIGHTENED KAY from a deep sleep, and she bolted up. "Who is it?" She reached for the lamp and flicked it on as the door flew open.

Craig burst in. "Come to the hospital," he said, breathless. "Beth woke up."

Kay couldn't speak. He was supposed to be in Washington. Had she heard him right?

"Are you serious?" Doug launched out of bed and grabbed his pants.

"Yes. She opened her eyes and spoke. Deni sent me to get you."

Finally, reality penetrated her fog. Kay grabbed her robe. "She was aware? She *spoke?*"

The dim lamp light only deepened the shadows on Craig's face. "I only heard four words before I left, but yeah, she spoke."

Kay turned on the overhead light so she could look into his tired face. "Four words. What were they?"

Craig hesitated a moment. "She said, 'Don't do it, Deni.'"

Kay just stared at him. "Don't do what?"

He shrugged, looked at the floor. "It doesn't matter. The important thing is that she recognized her sister."

"Oh, Craig!" She threw her arms around him, almost knocking him back. "The drugs—you got them back already?"

"Yes. They gave them to her an hour or so ago."

Kay's arms came up in a show of victory. "That's why she woke up! Craig, how can we ever thank you?"

He gave her a lopsided grin. "You'll think of something."

She knew he referred to Deni. There wasn't time to think about that now. She looked around for something to wear. She hadn't done laundry in days. Grabbing up the clothes she'd taken off last night, she turned back to Craig. "We'll be ready in two minutes."

The door closed, and she ran toward her closet. Doug ran into her, and they both laughed. "She's awake!" Kay cried.

Doug picked her up and kissed her neck. "Hurry now!"

She threw on her clothes and grabbed her shoes. Doug was already out the door as she hurried through the house. She ran halfway up the stairs and called Logan and Jeff. "Beth woke up! Hurry, guys! Put on some clothes. Let's go."

The sleepy boys almost tumbled down the stairs, and they all piled into Craig's car. Kay wept all the way to the hospital, thanking God for this answer to prayer.

eighty-nine

BECAUSE HER SITUATION HAD BEEN SO DIRE AND THE NEWS was so good, the staff of the ICU allowed the whole family to come into Beth's room. Kay wrestled on her scrubs, thrusting her leg into the wrong hole. Frustrated, she pulled them off and tried again.

As the guys finished getting suited up, she flew into Beth's cubicle. Deni was bent low over Beth, talking softly to her.

"Is she still awake?" Kay asked.

Deni looked up, her eyes tired, but bright with hope. "No, Mom. She's out again."

"But she woke up? She recognized you?"

"Only for a second. But her blood pressure is stable now, and you can see the color in her face."

Kay touched Beth's face. "Oh, why wasn't I here?" Gently, she shook her. "Honey, can you hear me? Can you wake up? Please. Mom really wants to see that you're all right."

There was nothing.

"Sorry, Mom. I tried to keep her awake."

Kay fought her disappointment. "That's okay. If she woke up once, she'll do it again. The steroids obviously helped. We just have to be patient."

Doug swept past her to Beth's side. "Oh no. She's out again." He straightened and looked at Deni. "Tell me what happened. Don't leave anything out."

Logan and Jeff came in, and Deni looked past them to the door. "Where's Craig?"

"In the waiting room. He thought it would be too crowded."

Deni swallowed. "It was weird. Craig and I were talking … about us. And then he pulled out the ring and proposed again. And all of a sudden Beth said, 'Don't do it, Deni.' "

Logan laughed. "Way to go, sis!"

Kay threw her hands over her mouth and laughed. Doug kissed Beth's pink cheek. "That's my girl."

"That's it?" Jeff asked. "That's all she said?"

"That's it," Deni told them. "And then her eyes just fluttered shut again. But, Mom, Dad, she can hear us. I know she can. I've been talking to her ever since."

Logan came to the bed and shook his sister's arm. "Come on, Beth. We know you're faking now."

Kay set her hand on his shoulder. "She's not faking, honey."

Logan winked at her. He was trying to provoke an argument. If only that would work.

When there was no response, he tried again. "Jimmy has been up here to see you. He's about to give up on you if you don't hurry. He's sick of hospitals because of his dad and all."

Beth lay still and silent.

Hours went by, and they couldn't rouse her again. Finally, the nurses sent all but two of them out of the room. Kay and Doug kept talking to her, caressing her, but she didn't come to again.

Disappointed, Kay finally went to the waiting room and rounded up her family. "I'll stay with her. You guys go on home."

Deni refused. "No, Mom. I wanted you to rest. I'll stay with her."

"You couldn't force me to leave right now, Deni. I want to be here the next time she wakes up. Besides, I got several hours of sleep." She pointed to the window. "It's morning."

Deni looked surprised that daylight had broken. "What about Dad?"

"He's staying too. We've waited too long for this. We can feel a breakthrough coming."

ninety

MORNING SUN BLASTED DOWN ON TUNGSTEN ROAD AS Craig drove them home, stinging his tired eyes. He wished he could take time to sleep, but he had to go back to the office. There wasn't time for a day off.

Fatigue intensified his depression, magnifying the import of what Beth had said. He'd wanted her to wake up. That had been his goal in driving through the night to get the drugs. But he hadn't expected her to shoot him down. Not when he'd been on his knees proposing.

He was quiet as he drove, oblivious to the conversation between Deni's brothers in the backseat. Deni sat next to him, her head back against the seat, eyes closed. She was as exhausted as he. He wondered if she turned those words over in her head too, or if she'd dismissed them as disoriented muttering. He had to know.

Deni's eyes came back open as he pulled into her driveway. Wearily, she got out of the car and followed her brothers to the door. When they got inside, Logan and Jeff went upstairs.

Deni turned back to him. "Thanks for everything you did last night, Craig. Looks like it made a huge difference."

Not with you and me, he thought. It made no difference at all. If she'd wanted to marry him, she would have picked up the conversation. Her silence said more than he wanted to hear.

But he wouldn't be dismissed that way. He slid his hands into his pockets. "Deni, can we talk about what happened?"

She turned back to him, and it was clear she knew what he meant. "Craig, I'm really tired. Let's talk later."

That chafed him. "I'm tired too, Deni. I don't think I've slept in days. I got the power turned back on, for Pete's sake. I drove to Washington and back."

"I'm sorry. I didn't mean—"

"I had just proposed to you and offered you your ring back. I don't deserve to have that left hanging."

Deni lowered to the couch. "I'm sorry about the timing, Craig. I don't know what to say."

He breathed out a laugh. "Well, I guess that says it all."

Her eyes at least looked sad. "I don't want to hurt you. I really don't. I care a lot about you."

He let out a long, rugged sigh, and dropped into Doug's favorite chair. Rejection had a taste, he thought. Its bitterness brought a sting to his eyes.

"Has Mark even asked you to marry him?"

She looked at the floor. "Not in so many words. Things have been crazy lately."

He wanted to follow that trail, to make her think Mark had no intentions of asking. But he knew better than that, and so did she. He thought back over their time in the hospital, when she'd been so happy about the medication he'd gotten. When he'd offered her the ring, he'd seen the pleasure in her eyes. He'd had her in the palm of his hand. She might have said yes. But then Beth woke up.

He breathed a laugh. "Well, I've got to say this for your sister. She has perfect timing. She never has liked me."

Deni met his eyes. "That's not true. When we first got engaged, she adored you."

"She likes Mark better. She's rooting for him, even from a coma."

Irritation hardened her eyes. "Craig, be happy for Beth. This isn't about you."

Now he felt like a heel. "I know it's not. I didn't mean it was. You know I've prayed for her and I've done what I could."

"I do know that. We owe you a lot. We're going to get her back."

Maybe Mark had it right. It was no good proposing now, when Deni's every thought centered around Beth, and every conversation drifted back to her.

He stood and looked down at her, waiting for something she couldn't give him. He put his hand in his pocket, felt the ring, and slipped it onto his pinkie finger, wishing he'd been the kind of man to keep a woman like her happy. Then she would never have taken it off to begin with.

He rubbed his neck. "Guess I'd better head back to work."

"You can't sleep for even an hour?"

He shrugged. "I might find a place in the office to nap later on today. It'll be okay. Someone will have made coffee."

She got up and came toward him, then hugged him. He held her a moment too long, hating himself for seeming desperate. Then she kissed him on the cheek.

The platonic nature of it sliced like a knife through his heart. He let her go, and she went upstairs, leaving him to wonder why he was still here.

ninety-one

DENI WENT TO HER ROOM AND CLOSED THE DOOR. WEARILY, she lay on the bed fully clothed, staring up at the ceiling. The events of the night had been so confusing. Her heart had begun to soften toward Craig as he reminded her of their beginning.

But had God used Beth to speak to her?

With one foot in heaven and another on earth, did she have some special insight?

Deni tried to see things through Beth's eyes. Of course Beth wanted her to marry Mark. He was the one Beth loved, who'd given her a special nickname, who brought her unique gifts that he'd made with his own hands. He was the one who helped her with props for her plays and made her feel like a star. He was the one who treated her like a friend, not the little sister of his girlfriend.

Deni had no doubt that Beth's "Don't do it, Deni," had everything to do with Craig's proposal. She smiled.

She tried to imagine marriage to Craig. They'd live in the fast lane, no doubt about it. His work on the recovery team was a huge step in his career. If she stuck with him, she would rise to the top of her own career in no time. By the time she was thirty, the two of them would be known and respected for the power couple they would be.

Life with Mark would be so different. If she stayed with him, she would live here in Crockett and work for the paper.

He'd start his solar business, and she'd help him with that. She would raise children and stay close to her family.

Why did that sound better than what Craig could give her?

She heard a chime and sat up, wondering where it had come from. It rang again. Smiling, she realized it was the front doorbell. She hadn't heard it since the electricity had come back on.

Hoping it was more news of Beth, she went downstairs. Through the etched glass, she saw Mark on the front porch.

She flung the door open. "Mark, did you hear?"

"Yeah, I just went by the hospital," he said, throwing his arms around her. "Your mom told me. It's gonna be all right now, Deni. This is the beginning of her healing."

Something about his arms cut through her fatigue. She buried her face against his neck and breathed in his scent. "Are you as tired as I am?"

"Probably not. Come sit with me." He pulled her to the couch, dropped down at one end. She sat down and snuggled up in his arms, resting her head on his shoulder.

"Your mother also told me what happened with you and Craig."

She straightened and looked at him. "It's no big deal, Mark. Please don't worry about that." But the fragile look on his stubbled face broke her heart.

"So Craig offered you the ring back. I figured that was inevitable."

"I didn't take it."

"My understanding was that you got interrupted."

She smiled. "Yeah, interrupted by my sister who was in a coma. If that wasn't a message from God, I don't know what was."

He stroked her hair back from her face. "Did you need a message?"

The vulnerability on his face overrode her irritation. "You know I didn't."

"Well, he didn't just let the conversation drop after that, did he? You two came home together. He had to have brought it back up."

"He did," she whispered.

His gaze bored into hers. "And what did you say?"

"I kind of evaded the whole conversation."

His countenance fell. "So you didn't tell him no?"

"I was too tired to have a long, drawn-out talk."

He tried to smile. "Like the one you're having with me?"

"I like having long, drawn-out conversations with you. Anytime, anywhere." She kissed him, sliding her hand down the stubble on his face, to the dip of his neck. Her heart melted as she felt his racing pulse. "He got the message, Mark."

The concern left his face as he pulled her head back to his shoulder. She got comfortable in his arms and dozed into a gentle sleep.

MARK HELD DENI AS SHE SLEPT, THANKING GOD FOR THE PRIVIlege of knowing her. He tried to focus on Beth's victory, rather than his own pain. Deni had been through a lot lately, and she probably hadn't slept well in weeks. Craig's pressure on her had come after he'd driven to Washington for Beth's medication. That act, Mark had to admit, was sacrificial and heroic. If he'd been Craig, he would have taken the same opportunity.

As she slept, her head under his, he prayed. *I promise I'll make her happy, Lord. I'll spend the rest of my life trying.*

He'd been in love with her since high school, though she never knew it. Back then she'd seemed out of his league, so he'd masqueraded as her friend. When she went off to college, he forced himself to move on. But a year ago, when he saw her again, it had all come rushing back.

Of course he'd dated in the last few years, but there was no one else who played a starring role in his dreams. No one else.

Please, God.

After a while, he realized she was sound asleep. He loved the sound of her breathing. He could listen to it every night for the rest of his life and count himself privileged.

"I love you, Deni," he whispered, knowing she didn't hear. "You know Beth was right." He laid his head back, and drifted into his own shallow sleep.

ninety-two

DOUG'S HOPES PLUNGED WHEN, BY AFTERNOON, BETH hadn't awakened again. The steroids weren't helping. And when her blood pressure dropped to 60/40 and her breathing became uneven, Dr. Overton made the decision to put her back on the ventilator.

Doug tried to stay strong for Kay, who hadn't moved from Beth's bedside. But the disappointment tugged him down.

He left the ICU, depositing his scrubs in the laundry basket, and tried to find a private place to pray. He tried the chapel but found three or four others in there, sitting quietly in the three long pews, staring up at the cross hung on the wall or the open Bible on the podium. He didn't want to sit there among strangers, even if they were brothers and sisters in Christ. He wanted to talk aloud to God, to pour out his heart in uncensored honesty unbefitting a preacher of God's Word.

The stairwell was a traffic thoroughfare that presented no privacy, even though the elevators were now operational. Waiting rooms were breeding grounds for noise and anxiety. The courtyard outside was short on oxygen, since that was where the smokers clustered.

There was no place to be alone with God.

So Doug stood at the window in the corner of the ICU waiting room, whispering angry, desperate prayers against the windowpane. He practiced faith without doubting, ordering up a healing for his precious child, expecting it to come immediately like Lazarus coming out of the tomb.

Then he doubted his faith, wondering if it was strong enough to transport his prayers. Was there a hint of disbelief that would filter them out of heaven's gates?

So, like the father who came to Jesus on behalf of his tormented son, he whispered into the windowpane, "Lord, help my unbelief!"

Jesus had answered that father's prayers and healed the son. But Doug wondered if his own faith was somehow flawed and deformed. Was God using Beth to show him how flimsy it was?

Tears flooded his eyes and he wiped them away. "God, I'm begging you to save her," he whispered. "I'm dying, myself. Kay's dying. We can't stand this. We need your help. If this is my fault, if it's because of my failings, show me. Punish me, not Beth."

At once, he felt a peace come over him, filling him with the warmth of a father comforting a son—the immediate sense that Beth wasn't lying comatose because of anything he or Kay had done. The sudden, certain knowledge that it was about love.

Love? How could that be? If God loved them, wouldn't he give them their deepest heart's desire? Wouldn't he save their child?

His human mind searched for human answers, and dragged him to conclusions. Of course God would save her. Why wouldn't he? What would be served by her death? That wouldn't be love.

Someday, after she was healed, they would stand before congregations and tout God's goodness. They would tell how prayers prayed in faith are always answered. They would describe the miracle of her waking and walking. They would share their gratitude.

He would write a book to encourage others. Beth would write her own. And she would grow up to be an evangelist who taught of healing and brought glory to God. Everyone who knew them would be won to Christ by the miracle.

The thought of it lifted the heaviness on his heart.

But his daughter's condition hadn't changed. The reality of it settled over his heart like a lead blanket.

"Doug, can I talk to you for a minute?"

Doug wiped his eyes on his sleeve, then turned around. Craig stood there. "Hey, you're back. Did you get any sleep?"

Craig looked at Doug's teary eyes. "I'm sorry. I didn't realize you were ..."

"Praying," Doug said. "I'm fine. Sit down."

Craig sat down in one of the vinyl chairs, his concerned eyes on Doug. Doug pulled a handkerchief out of his pocket and quickly wiped his nose.

"Is everything okay? Beth hasn't gotten worse, has she?"

"Actually, yes. We had to put her back on the ventilator." He cleared his throat, banishing the dejection in his tone.

"I'm sorry. I thought things were looking up."

"Me too. But hey, she woke up this morning. She can wake up again." His voice was flat, tinny—revealing his flat, tinny faith. "So have you gotten any rest?"

"I napped an hour or so at the office. Then I had to go to Birmingham while they got another substation online." Craig sighed. "I came by to talk to you about Deni, but if it's a bad time ..."

Doug's chest tightened. Romance was the last thing he wanted to talk about. But Craig had done so much for them. "I'm listening."

Craig looked down at his hands. "I know she's been stressed about Beth, and I don't know how to help her. I'm sure you heard that I asked her to marry me last night before Beth woke up. I thought maybe if you gave her your blessing, it might change things."

His blessing? Doug hoped his surprise didn't translate to his face. He couldn't give his blessing for that. Again, he tried to spare Craig's feelings. "I don't feel comfortable talking to Deni about that."

"Well, you talked to her about Mark."

It was true. He'd talked to Deni many times about Mark. And Mark had talked to Doug about her. He had even asked for her hand. Craig never had.

"Look, Craig, I like you. I really do. You're a good guy, and I know you'll make someone a wonderful husband."

Craig bit the side of his lip. "Why do I sense a 'but' coming?"

"But ... before you came back, Deni and Mark were happy together. It was going somewhere, and Kay and I felt good about it. Deni had never been happier."

Craig clearly couldn't accept that. "Did you ever consider that God might have sent me back just in time to stop them from moving forward in their relationship?"

If there was providential intervention here, Doug thought, it was when Beth woke up and told Deni not to do it. But he didn't want to hurt Craig more. "I firmly believe that if God wants her to marry you, she will, and if he wants her to marry Mark, she will. And if there's someone else altogether, then he'll lead her to that person."

Craig leaned in, his eyes intent. Lowering his voice to a whisper, he said, "Doug, who can give her a better life? You know I can."

"Yes, if we're talking finances," Doug agreed. "There was a time in Deni's life when I used to think that was all that mattered. If somebody made a lot of money and could buy my daughter all the things she'd want, then he was the guy. But I've learned a lot over the last year. It's not money that buys happiness. I got nine hundred dollars the day the bank opened, and I've hardly thought about it at all. Money can't save my child right now. And money won't help me if we lose her." His voice broke and his face twisted. He paused and tried to compose himself. "I'd like to think that both you and Mark have what it takes to make Deni happy. But we're just going to have to let Deni make that decision."

Defiance colored Craig's face, and he looked across the people stirring around in the waiting room. Finally, he turned back to Doug. "You were all worked up for Mark to be your son-in-law, weren't you? You haven't forgiven me for coming back."

"Craig, we've provided you a place to live all this time. This isn't about a grudge. You've been a good help to my family, and I admire what you do. I've come to think of you as a friend."

"But not as a son-in-law?"

"Only if that's what Deni wants."

Craig's eyes softened as he gazed into his. "How can I prove to you what kind of man I am?"

"You already proved it," Doug said. "What you did for Beth was awesome. You have nothing else to prove."

"No, but I do." Craig's eyes were intense as he lowered his voice to a whisper. "I want to show you that I can make her happy. If she marries me, she won't have one day of trouble, not one day of sadness. I'll see to it."

Doug breathed a sad laugh. "You can't promise her that, Craig."

"Yes, I can."

Doug wished it were so. "I know you would try. But nobody can promise anybody that. Jesus said, 'In this world you'll have trouble.' We're sitting here in an ICU waiting room right now while my daughter is in here on life support. You can't promise Deni you can insulate her from trouble. You don't have that much power."

Craig leaned back against the wall. He looked at the ceiling, eyes glistening. "Just for the record, when she said, 'Deni, don't do it,' I think she was having a dream."

"You could be right."

"And even if Beth was fully conscious and was speaking from her own desires, that doesn't mean she's right. I can win her over when she wakes up. I just haven't had as much time as Mark has."

The pain on the young man's face touched Doug's heart. "Craig, even if Beth knew what she was saying—even if it was a word from God—it wasn't a testament to your character."

His forehead wrinkled as he looked at the ceiling again. "Yes, it was."

Doug touched Craig's shoulder. "Sometimes God just guides us into a different direction, because he loves us. Not because we're somehow less than anyone else."

Craig tried to laugh through his tears. "This is so strange. I rarely feel inferior."

Doug smiled. "I don't think there's anything more humbling than falling in love."

Craig looked down at his feet, and Doug patted his back. "Well, I guess I'd better get to work."

Doug shook his hand. "Trust God, Craig. If it's meant to be, Deni will be yours, and you'll have my blessing. But if it's not, there's someone better suited to you."

Craig's shoulders slumped as he walked from the room.

ninety-three

MARK ONLY SLEPT AN HOUR BEFORE HE WOKE UP. HE slipped his shoulder from under Deni's head and laid her down on the couch. He left her sleeping soundly, then stepped outside, trying to shake off his fatigue. There was work to do.

His individual interviews with Clay Tharpe's coworkers had brought no new information. At least none that he could put on paper. He'd had the sense with each of them that they weren't telling everything they knew. Something or someone was keeping them from talking. He suspected their boss had given them reason to stay quiet.

When they questioned Ned Emory again, they met with the same brick wall. He denied having any outside relationship with either Melissa or Clay Tharpe, and claimed he was happily married. Mark knew better. Ned's wife was half-crazy and suicidally depressed most of the time—not the makings of a happy marriage. Ned also denied knowing that Melissa's husband was abusive.

So why had Melissa's father put them on Ned's trail? Surely she hadn't told him about an affair, had she? Maybe he'd stumbled on it, along with the murder plot. And his mention of Ned's name had been intended to get them off Melissa's trail.

Mark had switched to the night shift so he could spend his daylight hours watching Melissa Tomlin, determined to make the connections he needed. So that he could watch her house without being noticed, he took his tools to Magnolia Park and tightened the bolts on all of the playground equipment, pretending to be working for the city of Crockett. With a baseball cap and sunglasses, he hoped he wouldn't call attention to himself.

He tightened bolts until he saw her garage door open. When she left, he followed her on his bike, keeping his distance and watching as she ran errands. The widow wasn't mourning. Instead, she seemed upbeat and happy. She walked with a bounce in her step, as if her life was smooth sailing. Never mind that her husband had been murdered, or that her father was headed for death row.

But that wasn't probable cause for arrest.

ninety-four

WHILE HE KEPT VIGIL BESIDE BETH'S BED, DOUG DEVOURED books on prayer that had collected dust at home. They were books he'd bought in his Christian growth spurts, titles recommended by friends, books he'd never found time to read. Now he soaked up the contents, thirsty as a sponge, searching for something that would enhance his prayer life and turn things around.

But no matter how sincerely or earnestly he prayed ... Beth got worse.

He had come to the end of himself, and exhaustion had made him despair. They'd sat at the hospital for days since her waking, waiting for another sign that she would come back to them.

On Tuesday night, Deni talked him and Kay into going home. Though they dreaded leaving Beth again, he needed a full night's sleep in his own bed, or he would be no good to anyone.

The bed was a luxury. He held Kay as she lay beside him.

"We're doing something wrong," she whispered. "Our prayers aren't being answered. What are we missing?"

Stroking her shoulder, he stared at the ceiling. "I've read everything I can find on prayer," he said. "Some books make me feel like a total and complete failure. That if my prayers aren't answered it's because I haven't worked hard enough at it. That I'm not doing it earnestly enough. But what more can we do besides turning ourselves inside out with our cries to heaven?"

"Maybe we shouldn't sleep. Maybe we should stay up all night and pray."

"We've stayed up *every* night and prayed," he said. "I don't think that's it." Weariness burned in his eyes, and all his muscles ached. "Some of the books I've read put Beth's life on our shoulders, like the energy spent in our prayers is the only thing that can save her. But there's just something that doesn't ring true about all that," he said. "Jesus said his yoke is easy and his burden is light. But this is crushing."

She sat up and looked down at him. "God must hear our prayers. He loves Beth more than we do."

"But what if—" His voice faltered. "What if it's just not his will to save her?"

Kay looked betrayed. "Doug, don't say that. Don't even think it."

"But I have to, Kay." He got up, walked across the room, looked out the window. "Jesus prayed for his cup to be removed, then he said, 'Not my will, but Thine.' Paul prayed for his thorn in the flesh, and when God said no, he accepted it. Job lost his family, all his possessions, his health—"

Kay slammed her fist into the pillow. "Don't you do that!" she said through her teeth. "Don't you give up on our daughter. We have to believe!"

His eyes burned as he turned back to her. "I believe that if Jesus wants to heal our child, he will. I have utmost faith that he can do that if he wants to."

She looked close to shattering. "Why *wouldn't* he want to?"

That despair that he'd been fighting rose up to choke him. He came to the bed, sat down facing her. "Kay, sometimes he takes his saints home."

She reared back and slapped him.

He caught her hand as she pulled it away, pressed it against the sting.

She jerked it away. "Are you saying that God's not going to answer our prayers?"

"No, Kay, that's not what I'm saying. I know he'll answer."

"But you think his answer will be no?"

"Honey, he might have a greater purpose. Maybe he's trying to do something in *us*."

"Well, he can stop!" she cried. "I'm *tired* of suffering, and I don't want to be that strong. I want to live a mediocre life with every day the same as the others. We had that once, and all our children were safe. Why can't we have that again?"

He wished he had answers. "Maybe we can. Maybe he's already healed her. Maybe we just haven't caught up to that place on the time line, when she gets up off that bed."

"Then pray that he moves the time line up. God has control over time, doesn't he? He created medical science. He can heal the tissue in Beth's brain."

"Of course he can."

She touched his chest, as if he were the one she had to convince. "Then why won't he? What on earth could be the reason for all this?"

"Maybe it's not a reason on earth. Maybe it's a reason in heaven."

She backed away from him. "I don't want to hear that, Doug."

"Neither do I." He wilted as tears overtook him. "Neither do I."

ninety-five

DAYS PASSED AND DESPITE THE USE OF THE DRUGS CRAIG had brought back from Washington, the pressure on Beth's brain grew. Dr. Overton took them into the dreaded conference room and presented their only option.

"Her brain has to have room to swell," he said. "As drastic as a craniectomy seems, it's saved a lot of lives."

Kay covered her face. "So you want to open up her head?"

Kay's pain seemed reflected on Dr. Overton's face. "Kay, Doug, I know this is hard for you, but if we're going to do it, we need to do it today." He looked at Doug, waiting for him to make the decision.

Doug's hands were clasped in front of his face. "Well, then, we have to do it."

Kay reigned her emotions in. "What do we have to sign?"

Dr. Overton gave them the consent forms for him to open Beth's skull. Kay's hands trembled as she signed.

"I'll go get her prepped for surgery." The doctor hesitated as they got to their feet, then came toward Kay and hugged her. It took her by surprise, but she clung to him, knowing that he would do whatever he could for Beth.

AS THEY TOOK BETH INTO SURGERY, KAY WALKED DOWN the hall. She passed the waiting room and saw that friends had gathered there to pray with them. Doug sat among them, talking softly. She didn't want to go in just yet. She wanted to be alone.

She wandered through the halls of death, sickness, and tragedy, hating the smell of antiseptic, the smiles on the nurses' faces as she passed their station, the detachment of the doctors scribbling in patients' charts.

She thought of going to the prayer room and sitting on one of the three pews, looking up to that cross on the wall and begging God to heal her child. But this time, she might pick up that Bible opened to the Twenty-third Psalm, rip out its pages, and hurl them against the wall. And then someone else, someone who hadn't yet prayed themselves empty, might come in and see how she'd lost it, intruding on her private anger ... her private grief.

People seemed to be everywhere. The building was too small for the community's needs. Where could she go to be alone?

She saw a janitor's closet up ahead. Opening the door, she slipped inside. The room was no bigger than ten by ten, with shelves along the walls filled with cleaning supplies. She saw a light switch but welcomed the darkness.

Closing the door behind her, she lowered herself to the floor. She sat cross-legged, the way she had done as a child at Sunday school, when Mrs. Nigel read them stories of Christ's miracles in the Bible. She thought of her wide-eyed wonder as she learned of Christ waking up a dead girl, healing a man with demons, restoring a woman who touched the hem of his garment.

All through her life, she had heard and read of those miracles, and she had believed solidly in them. Why wouldn't she? The Bible was true. Didn't it say that if you had faith as a mustard seed, anything you asked would be done? Didn't it say that a little bit of faith could move mountains?

Well, she had a mountain that wouldn't move. She had prayed for miracles before, and God had granted them. Deni had come home alive. Little Sarah had been found. They'd been protected and provided for. All, just as God promised. But this mountain wouldn't budge.

She stared up at the dark ceiling, hoping God knew she was looking for him. "*You* said it, Father! *You* promised! You said that if a child asks his father for a fish, he wouldn't give him a stone. 'How much more will your father in heaven do for you?'" The words were bitter on her tongue. "*You* said that. It's not just some doctrine that men made up. It's written in *your* Word!"

Her spirit broke then, and she pulled her knees up and dropped her face into them. "I have prayed and prayed and prayed, and she's still dying! I have more than the hem of your garment! I have the Holy Spirit. I have the rent veil. I can confidently enter your Holy Place!" The Scriptures she'd spent a lifetime memorizing poured out of her.

She realized she was almost yelling, her hands coiled into fists. The veins in her neck felt taut, ready to burst. "I don't want to believe the promises aren't true! I don't want to think you're ignoring my plea for a fish. I want to serve you, but how can I teach others about faith if my own has been shattered?"

She lowered herself to the floor, prostrate on her stomach, her face on the dirty tile. "Make me understand. I *have* believed, I have. But I can't make you do anything!"

She curled into a fetal position, weeping out her heart to four cold walls. "Doug's made all the excuses for you I know. That you have a bigger picture we can't see ... that you're trying to build our faith ... that you're doing something in us. But Beth is so frail. She doesn't have much more time! What are you trying to do in me? Give me a nervous breakdown? Debilitate me with grief?"

Her throat ripped with her cries. "My child is dying, and you *can* do something about it. Nothing is impossible with you. You said that."

She felt like Moses, pleading with God for the souls of the Israelites, begging him not to smite them. God had relented with Moses. But Beth still lay dying. And she had done nothing wrong.

Her anger racked through her. Was God angry too? Maybe he would strike Kay dead. Then it would be over.

But he didn't kill her. He did something far worse.

He remained silent.

So what would she do if he didn't answer? Would she stop believing? Would she declare the things she'd built her life around null and void?

There was no other Creator of the universe. There was no secret that bestowed magical powers on humans. There was no law of attraction that could bring Beth back, if God wasn't compelled to do it.

Whether he did her bidding or not—he was still who he was.

Her cries softened. "I need your strength, Jesus. I have to know that you're here with me. Don't make me face this if you're not with me. I still believe ... I'm still counting on your answering my prayers."

She felt as if God leaned down and put his arms around her, cradled her, and rocked her. He had wept himself, just like this. He had cried out for God to change the course of history. He had asked to be delivered.

And then he'd uttered those five frightening words: "Not my will, but Thine."

She couldn't make herself say those words, if it meant God taking Beth. But still she felt his presence, holding her like a father would hold his daughter. He wasn't giving her peeks over the horizon, or premonitions of Beth healed. He wasn't giving her words of knowledge or prophecies of good tidings.

He just held her and let her cry.

The door opened, and a janitor flicked on the light. Kay sat up quickly, wiping her face.

The man looked startled. "You okay, ma'am?"

She got to her feet and thought of making up a story about what she was doing in here. But he didn't look stupid. "Yes. I just wanted ... a quiet place to cry."

She saw compassion on his face. "I could come back later."

She shook her head and pushed past him. "No, I'm okay now. I have to get back to my family, anyway."

Leaving the man in the doorway, Kay walked away.

ninety-six

THE WAITING ROOM WAS A TERRIBLE PLACE TO WAIT. MARK wished someone would come in and order everyone to be quiet. A family across the room was celebrating after getting good news about their patient. Friends had poured in to join in the party.

In another corner, the family of a small child with pancreatic cancer hunkered together, their wet eyes shell-shocked and mournful.

And here, where the Brannings had staked out their territory, they sat with muscles so tense that they ached. Mark felt a headache starting behind his eyes. If they didn't bring news that Beth had survived surgery soon, he felt he might explode. And he wouldn't be the only one.

But if they did, then what? She would have to lie in a sterile room with her head open, giving her brain tissue room to swell. He couldn't even imagine it.

Next to him, Deni fidgeted, absently rubbing her hands together. He hoped she didn't rub the skin off. He lifted his arm to set it on the seat behind her—but Craig's arm was already there.

Their eyes met behind Deni's head. Mark was getting sick of this. He thought of knocking Craig's arm off Deni's chair, but this wasn't the time for an arm-wrestling match.

Finally, he got up and stepped outside to the balcony. There was no fresh air. A smoky haze hovered over the place as people smoked. He went to one side and leaned over the rail, looking into an unkempt courtyard below where more people clustered.

"You okay, man?"

Mark turned and saw that Deni's brother Jeff had followed him out.

"Yeah, I'm fine."

The sixteen-year-old backed up against the rail. "I saw the thing between you and Craig."

Mark breathed a laugh. "Yeah, well, what else is new?"

"It's your fault, you know."

Mark hadn't expected that. "What's my fault?"

"That Craig is still hitting on her. Dude, when are you gonna ask her to marry you?"

This was a first. Jeff had never indicated much interest at all in his sister's love life. Surprised that he would intervene now, Mark pulled the ring out of his pocket. "I was going to ask her one night—and it turned out to be the night Craig showed up in town. Then this happened with Beth. It's just never been the right time."

"Nice ring," Jeff said. "But Craig's probably carrying one too."

Mark couldn't help chuckling. "I'm sure you're right."

"Craig's not going anywhere, man. You'd better get used to it. He may be here to stay. You gotta do what you gotta do."

Mark turned back to the rail and looked out across the trees behind the courtyard. "I know."

"I'm just saying, don't wait another day, dude. He's pulling out all the stops, and I don't want to wind up with him as a brother-in-law. Not that she *wants* him, but he's asked her to marry him twice. You haven't asked her at all."

Appreciation warmed through him, melting the tension out of him. He turned and looked through the glass doors. He saw Deni standing up, looking toward the door to the hallway, as if expecting the surgeon to come in at any moment. Her mind was on Beth, not Craig. He saw Craig get up and whisper something in her ear. He touched her back in that proprietary way he had. Deni looked irritated and stepped away, putting distance between them.

Jeff was right. Maybe he didn't have to wait for the perfect time or set the stage for a romantic proposal. The moon and stars didn't have to be aligned. All he needed was a ring and a place to get down on one knee. If Beth came through surgery all right, maybe tonight should be the night.

He stepped back inside and Deni turned. Her eyes met his, and he saw pleasure there. Not irritation. She took another seat and patted the one next to her.

Mark glanced at Craig. His rival's eyes challenged him, warning him away. Unfazed, Mark pushed past him and sat down.

She took his hand, so naturally and intimately that he knew she was his. If he asked her to marry him, he had no doubt she would say yes. He made up his mind. He would take her to the hospital prayer room tonight, kneel with her at the altar, ask her to marry him before God, and put the ring on her finger. They would be bound together for the rest of their lives.

If Beth came through surgery alive.

ninety-seven

THE CONFERENCE ROOM WAS BRIGHT WITH LIGHTBULBS and lamps, giving it a homey feel that Kay hadn't noticed before. But it offered no relaxation. It was a place of verdicts, like God's courtroom, bringing down decisions that cut through the heart.

They'd heard a Code Blue half an hour ago, and though they couldn't tell which patient's heart had stopped, Kay had a burn in the pit of her stomach that told her it was Beth. The warmth and love she'd felt from God in the janitor's closet fled, and now she sat with her family waiting to be told whether Beth lived or died.

Dr. Overton opened the door, his mask pulled down to his neck. He had sweat rings around his armpits, down the front of his chest. His expression said it all.

"Oh, dear God, she's dead, isn't she?" Kay whispered.

His Adam's apple bobbed as he struggled to get the words out. "We tried to save her. We did everything we could."

It couldn't be true. Her Beth, who'd been so alive and vibrant just seventeen days ago, couldn't be gone. She *felt* her here, waiting just beyond these walls, crying for her mother. Whatever they'd done, it wasn't enough. Kay wasn't sure if she said it aloud. Her words echoed through her mind, bouncing off of walls, ramming into each other. She heard Doug sobbing next to her, saw Deni's red nose as she sniffed, saw Logan's calm, empty stare, and Jeff's anger.

"What?" Jeff asked. "No way. You were gonna save her!"

Deni got up and turned to Kay. "Mom!" She came around the table and fell into Kay's arms. Kay held her, her denial a living thing that made Beth alive in her mind. *God, make her get up. Make them marvel at your miracle. You've done it before.* But those cries from her spirit seemed to slam against the ceiling, unheard.

No one came to tell her of that miracle. Beth's life was done. As she held Deni, then Jeff and Logan and Doug, all in a tight, desperate family embrace, her body felt the crushing pain of that truth.

Her sweet Beth was dead, and no one could bring her back.

ninety-eight

KAY KNEW PEOPLE WHO DIDN'T WEAR BLACK TO FUNERALS. They chose to celebrate their loved one's life in color. But Kay found no joy nor celebration in the funeral of her child. There wasn't a dress in her closet black enough, and the tears that had once cleansed her now rubbed her eyes raw.

They had Beth's funeral five days after her death. Kay sat on the front row at the cemetery where they'd buried their friend Eloise. She watched with a cold detachment as Doug struggled through the eulogy that he'd insisted on giving. Summer heat burned down on them with no mercy, no summer breeze to give them a respite. The turnout was spectacular. Neighbors and friends from town had gathered at the graveyard to honor Beth. She'd touched so many lives. They'd had to make the funeral "Bring Your Own Lawn Chair," like they were coming to hear the Boston Pops play on a Saturday afternoon. People whose names she couldn't remember stared at her in pity, and whispered accolades about what a strong woman she was.

It was all a crock of lies. She wasn't strong at all. God knew it and she knew it. She was an empty, throbbing shell of someone she hardly knew anymore.

Her parents had come from Florida; they sat down the row, weeping openly. Logan sat on one side of her, holding her hand. He'd hardly said a word since Beth's passing, though she knew he cried in private. Jeff sat on the other side, wiping his nose with a wadded handkerchief. Down the row, Deni leaned into Mark, who'd kept them afloat as they'd drifted through the days since Beth's death, by bringing them food and water and attending to the details of life on which Kay couldn't focus. Craig, who sat on the other side of Deni, had helped by notifying family. He'd radioed government offices in the towns where the relatives lived and had them go to their homes to give them the news. Amazingly, they had all shown up by train. She'd had to become a hostess in her mourning, when all she wanted to do was be alone.

Doug's clothes hung on his thin body as he stood before them. He stumbled through his stories about Beth, trying to weave frayed threads that made sense out of the madness. But there was no sense to be made.

Kay sat stiff as a statue as betrayal permeated her thoughts. God had chosen not to answer her prayers. He was the God who had set a world into motion, full of curses and disease and violent men who inflicted their heartless cruelty on innocent children. The God who had raised Lazarus from the grave had left Beth dead.

She had no warm fuzzies for the Lord right now. No glory to give him. She couldn't sing praises to him or bow her knee to thank him for Beth's life. So she kept her mouth closed and sat rigid, railing at him in her heart and mind, demanding answers that she knew she might never get. As they lowered Beth's polished white casket into the hole prepared for it, she turned her rage in on herself.

She was a terrible mother. She'd done everything wrong. She had misread her child in her darkest moments. She had failed to protect her.

She deserved everything that had happened.

Her grief and anger imploded, collapsing her soul. She didn't hear a word as people whispered condolences and offered hugs.

She couldn't imagine there ever being comfort for her again.

ninety-nine

DOUG FOUND KAY IN THE DARK BEDROOM, SITTING ON THE
bed and staring into space. He turned on the lamp. The light
from the bulb deepened the shadows in her face.

He felt weak, hollow as he sat next to her. "You okay?"

Kay's eyes were dry, hard, colder than he'd ever seen
them. "We asked for a fish, and he gave us a stone. God
betrayed us. I believed, and my faith was *huge*."

He looked at his hands. She was waiting for answers.
Why couldn't he give them? He was the spiritual leader. The
stockbroker-turned-preacher. Doug had been asked biblical
questions many times since he'd started his little lakeside
church, and usually he answered calmly with the plumb line
of God's Word. But he had no proverb for Kay's question, no
scriptural band-aid for unanswered prayer. "I have all the
same questions you do."

Kay's face twisted now, as if he'd made it worse. "Then
how do we get back from here?"

He moved to his reading chair and set his elbows on
his knees. As he looked at the floor, his mind reached for
something that would ease Kay's pain. His voice cracked.
"When I was a kid, I had this friend named Joey. Joey had
been taking violin lessons since he was three years old. His
parents were accomplished musicians who played with the
symphony orchestra in my town. Sometimes they would
take us to rehearsal with them, and we'd run around the
building while they rehearsed. They made a record, and Joey

could play along flawlessly, in perfect harmony, as if he sat in that orchestra with them."

He saw the impatience in Kay's eyes, but he spoke as much for himself as her. "I envied him, so when I was about ten, I asked my parents if I could start taking violin lessons. They got me a violin. I practiced hard and learned 'Twinkle, Twinkle, Little Star.'" He chuckled softly. "When I got really good at it, I put on the record—Beethoven's Fifth. I tried to play along, but I didn't sound anything like them. My strings squeaked and my notes were off key. Eventually, I gravitated back to 'Twinkle, Twinkle' and played that instead. But the record kept playing. Beethoven's Fifth went on perfectly. They never missed a note."

"Where are you going with this, Doug? I'm not in the mood to talk about your failed career as a musician."

"Just listen." He got up and went back to the bed, sat on it facing Kay. "Praying in God's will is just like that. He tells us if we pray anything according to his will, it will be done. But our prayers aren't always in line with that symphony."

Her eyes flashed. "So you think my prayer for Beth was like playing 'Twinkle, Twinkle, Little Star'?"

His eyes rimmed with tears. "I think God was playing something much more beautiful."

She slammed her hand on the pillow. "The Holy Spirit helps us pray! Jesus intercedes with groanings too deep for words."

"But that's just it. Jesus knows the song, and we don't. The Father, Son, and Holy Spirit interpret our prayers according to *their* music, even if we're out of key and playing something else."

"Then what's the purpose in praying at all? Why even bother?"

"Our prayers matter, Kay. He listens to them. But his symphony is grander than ours." He pursed his lips, trying to go on. "He didn't neglect her. He knew the days that were numbered for her before there was even one."

Kay squeezed her eyes shut. "She was a child! How could he take children?"

"He takes everyone, Kay. It's what we humans do. We live and we die."

"Then don't tell me our prayers aren't useless!"

"Do you think Jesus' prayers were useless? He prayed, 'Not my will, but Thine.' He understood that there was a symphony playing. What if God had been compelled to answer Jesus' prayers to remove the cup? We'd still owe the debt of our sins. Instead, the Father saw the end from the beginning. His will was done. And thank God it was. Jesus' life wasn't wasted on that cross. And Beth's life wasn't wasted, either."

That just made her angrier. She slid off the bed and crossed the room. "Those were things that impacted the world. We're just one little family. She was one little girl! Why did he even *give* her to us? Why did he give us all those years to love her if he was going to rip her away ... *while* I prayed?" She thrust her angry face into his and ground her teeth together. "I was in the janitor's closet on my face, praying for her while she died! How does that make sense?"

Doug's chest tightened as his own sorrow overflowed. "It doesn't."

"Why would he take her and leave *me* here, when I *want* to die?"

"Don't say that, sweetheart."

"Why not, if this is all there is? Struggles and heartache and waste. I wish she'd never been born!"

"Kay, you don't mean that."

"Want to see?" With that, she threw open the door and stormed out.

Despair rendered him useless. He had no more arguments, no more defenses. He couldn't help his wife. He couldn't even help himself.

KAY BOLTED THROUGH THE KITCHEN AND LIVING ROOM and ran up the stairs. Beth's door was closed. Craig had been sleeping on a pallet in Doug's study since she died. The room hadn't been opened since that last night at the hospital. She turned the knob, threw the door open. It swung back and hit the wall. She stepped in, her chest rising and falling with the anguish that had driven her there.

It looked so serene, so pretty, and that fed her fury. She had decorated it herself when Beth was ten. She'd picked out the wallpaper, the colors, the curtains, the comforter. She remembered Beth bouncing with joy when they'd had the big reveal.

What was she to do with it now?

Livid, she pulled Beth's favorite childhood book off the shelf. Beth had memorized it before she could read. Now Kay hated the sight of it. She slammed it on the floor.

"What was it for?" she asked God through her teeth. "What good was any of it?"

One by one, she pulled the books out of their places, hurling them onto the floor. She tore the comforter off the bed. Pink flannel sheets lay underneath. She yanked them off, cushy mattress pad and all. They wouldn't be needing comfort in here anymore.

"Mom! What are you doing?" Deni came in and tried to stop her.

Kay flung the pillow to the ground. Then she attacked the drawers and began throwing Beth's clothes out, her socks, her yellow shorts, her favorite T-shirts. She dragged the top drawer out, let it crash to the floor. Barrettes and bows and hairbrushes scattered across the rug. Paper sacks, little boxes, Ziploc bags of Beth's treasures.

"Stop!" Deni said.

"I won't stop," Kay cried. "It was all a hoax!"

"What are you talking about?"

Jeff came to the door, and Logan peeked in, horror on his face.

"The pregnancy, the birth." She jerked out another drawer, let it crash to the floor. "Every single day of teaching her and loving her and caring for her. Worrying what she ate and who she was with."

She slid her arm across the top of Beth's dresser, knocking off trophies and framed pictures.

"You're wrecking all her stuff!" Logan flung himself to the floor. "Stop, Mom!"

Strengthened by adrenaline, she rolled up the area rug on Beth's floor, trapping all her things in it. "None of it mattered. Isn't this what you want from us, God? To amputate her from our lives?"

"It did matter!" Logan screamed. "It did!" He wrestled the edge of the rug out of her hands. "Dad!"

She heard Doug's footsteps pounding up the stairs, but she wasn't finished. She grabbed the pictures off the walls, tore down Beth's posters.

Doug grabbed her shoulders, pulling her back. "Kay, I won't let you do this."

"You can't stop me!" she cried. "I want it gone, every last bit of it!" She dragged the picture frames onto the rug and tried again to roll it.

Doug's face twisted as he got down on the floor with her, picking up the scattered things. "Please, Kay. Don't destroy what's left of her." He picked up a picture of Beth and her friends. The glass had shattered, but the memory could be saved. "I want to keep this." He grabbed the bows and Beth's hairbrush, and the paper sack that had fallen out of a drawer. He opened it and looked inside.

"Aw, dear God ..." He fell back against the wall, his hand covering his face.

Kay stopped her pillaging and took the sack. She reached in and pulled out a handful of Beth's hair. Trembling, she brought it to her face. She could almost catch the scent of her child. Almost feel her.

It knocked the wind out of her ... brought her to her knees. She fell into Doug. "Look what I did to all her stuff."

"It's okay," he whispered in a soft, soothing voice. "We'll just put it all back, okay? Until we're ready to let it go. All of us."

What had she just done to her children? She had ramped up their grief, intensified their mourning. What kind of mother was she? All these years, she'd been so careful to care for them, to protect them. Who would protect them from her?

Logan wiped his face with the back of his hand. "We'll help you, Mom."

Deni and Jeff got down on the floor, unrolled the rug, and opened the comforter.

Doug held her as tight as a swaddled baby while her children began to refold their sister's clothes. Kay watched, spent, as they put the clothes back in the drawers, the barrettes and bows back in the dresser, the books back on the shelves.

"Her veil." Deni's lips quivered as she picked up the veil that Beth had worn when she'd played Mary in the Christmas play. "She was a good Mary."

Thoughts of Mary, Jesus' mother, flooded Kay's mind as she remembered Beth's portrayal of the young girl not much older than she—perhaps even the same age—who had found herself with child by the Holy Spirit. Suddenly Kay felt an affinity with the woman who gave birth to the son she had later watched die on the cross. Mary had suffered as Kay was suffering. She had probably wondered what it was all for. All the love and heartache, all the years of teaching, nurturing, and worrying had seemed to end with three nails and a spear. Kay knew Mary's heartbreak. This woman who was remembered two thousand years later hadn't seen the whole picture when she surrendered her child to the cross.

The sacrifice was too great. Kay wasn't up to it. If all the suffering in the last year had been to make her stronger, it had failed miserably. She was as weak as a poisoned kitten.

But she laid her head against her husband's chest, accepting his strength.

When everything was back in its place, the room looked almost as it had before.

But it was different. Beth wasn't coming back, and Kay didn't know if she could ever forgive God for that.

THE DAY AFTER THE FUNERAL, CROCKETT CELEBRATED July Fourth at the soccer park. Tonight, fireworks would mark their freedom jubilee and the beginning of their recovery. But Mark wasn't interested. He stayed with Deni, trying to lend her his strength. When he left her that afternoon, he sank into depression. That sorrow took him back to Magnolia Park late that afternoon, and the swing where Beth had often sat. He watched Melissa Tomlin's house while she kept the killer's secret.

Had Melissa already left for the soccer field? Was she in a festive mood, or was her secret eating her alive? She hadn't been to the jail to see her father even once, but her mother came every day.

A few people sat on the park benches, their small children playing, but most of the neighbors had gone to the soccer fields. Mark sat alone, praying that God would bring resolution to Beth's case—and justice to Clay Tharpe's accomplice. Maybe it would comfort the Brannings.

He heard the clicking of bicycle wheels and glanced back at the man turning into the neighborhood. He rode by on his mountain bike, never looking in Mark's direction.

Mark's heart bolted as he realized that the man was Ned Emory. Leaving the swing, Mark stepped behind the monkey bars, watching as Ned turned into Melissa's driveway. The garage door came up, as though she'd been watching for him. Melissa stood in the shadows of the garage. Ned rode inside, got off his bike, and kissed her.

So Ned had lied, and all of his workers had covered for him. He had come here in broad daylight, probably thinking that the neighbors would be at the soccer field.

As the garage door closed, Mark's mind raced with thoughts of Ned's son Zach, still not fully recovered from his gunshot wound a few months ago. His other son Gary, his depressed wife, Ellen. Before his eyes, a family was being ripped apart.

Clay Tharpe had said there was another person who wanted Tomlin dead. Melissa's father had given them Ned Emory's name, implying that he was involved in the murders. But why had Scott Anthony gunned down Tharpe? He sure hadn't done it to protect Ned.

But here Melissa and Ned were, together in her house. Mark had to do something, but what? An affair wasn't enough to justify an arrest warrant.

"Hey, Mark. What are you doing here?"

Mark turned. Jimmy Scarbrough was walking his bike toward him. Mark managed a smile for the former sheriff's son. "Hi, Jimmy. I could ask you the same thing."

Jimmy just shrugged, but his gaze strayed to the trees where Beth was found. "I just keep thinking about her."

Mark messed up the fourteen-year-old's hair. "Yeah, me too."

"The last time I saw her was right here. I said something stupid about her haircut and she started crying."

Mark turned fully to the boy now. He vaguely remembered hearing about that. "When was that, exactly?"

Jimmy shrugged as though he couldn't remember. "After the banks opened. Sometime before ... it happened. I followed her to tell her I was sorry, and she kept crying and telling me about the lady whose husband died. She said she heard the lady sitting here in the park talking about how her husband had disappeared, and she felt bad for her."

Mark looked back at the Tomlins' house. So Melissa had been here when Beth was here. He turned and stepped toward the boy. "Jimmy, did she say if she talked to the lady?"

"I don't think so."

"Please, try to think. Could the lady have found out her name that day?"

Jimmy thought for a moment. "Well, I yelled her name when I saw her. She probably heard that. After I asked Beth what she did to her hair, I saw her look at them, like I'd embarrassed her."

Or like he'd just written her death warrant. Mark wiped the beads of perspiration from his lip. He tried to imagine what had happened that day. If Melissa was Clay Tharpe's accomplice in the murder, then Clay would have told her about his witness.

"She seemed scared, and said she couldn't talk because someone might get hurt. Then we got off the subject and started talking about Craig. I wish I'd listened better."

Mark's mind ran through the facts. Somehow the killer had learned her name and told his accomplice. If Melissa heard Beth identified in the park that day, she could have told Clay how she'd altered her appearance, and where he could find her. "Jimmy, you've helped me a lot today."

"Really, how?"

"Never mind that. I'll tell you all about it later. Right now, I need you to come with me to the sheriff's department to fill out an affidavit, with everything you can remember about that day."

Jimmy's chest puffed out a little. "Sure, I can do that."

At the station, Mark got the affidavit, then raced to Brad Caldwell's office. "I need a warrant so I can go arrest them both while they're still together, Brad. We've got probable cause. We've got Melissa Tomlin having an affair with Ned Emory. Melissa's husband was abusive. She and Ned could have planned his murder and hired Tharpe, who worked for Ned. Ned lied about having a relationship with her, and she lied about knowing Clay. And now Jimmy can connect Melissa to Beth and prove she could have been aware of Beth coming to the park every day at the same time."

Brad read the affidavit. "This is all soft, Mark. These things are all circumstantial. We need a smoking gun if we're going to get a conviction. And just because Ned is having an affair with her doesn't mean he's a murderer. I know the man. He doesn't strike me as a killer."

"If we wait for a smoking gun, it might be after they've turned it on the next person they want dead. Come on, Brad. Don't tell me they've committed the perfect crime. That they're going to get away with it. It's Beth we're talking about. Melissa set her up, and Ned's her lover. We have to catch them while they're together. We have to go now."

Brad studied the affidavit again. Finally, he let out a long sigh. "I hope I'm not gonna regret this." He wrote up the warrants. "Arrest Melissa for conspiracy to commit murder. We don't have anything solid on Ned right now, except that he lied to police, so bring him in on perjury. It'll buy us time to get evidence that either clears him or implicates him."

That was good enough for now. Mark's burden was a little lighter as he hurried away.

MARK STOPPED BY THE SHERIFF'S DEPARTMENT TO GATHER SOME backup. Sheriff Wheaton and two other deputies joined him in the van. They parked at Magnolia Park, so that Melissa and Ned wouldn't be tipped off by the sound of their engine. Using the same technique they'd used when they arrested Clay Tharpe, London went to the back to catch Ned when he made his escape. Wheaton banged on the door, hard enough to give anyone inside a heart attack. "Po-lice! Open up or we'll kick it in!"

The door swung open. Fear bleached the color from Melissa's face as they bolted inside and clamped the handcuffs on her wrists. "You're under arrest for conspiracy to commit the murders of your husband and Beth Branning. You have the right to remain silent—"

"What? Why would I do that? I didn't even know that girl!"

The back door opened and London pushed a very agitated Ned Emory in. He, too, was cuffed. His shirt was unbuttoned, his face burning. "Sheriff, I'm not involved. You don't understand!"

"You lied to a police officer, Ned!" Mark bit out. "Doug asked you point blank if you had a relationship with Melissa Tomlin and you said no."

"I'm a married man!" he cried. "I didn't want to admit to an affair!"

"We haven't broken any laws!" Melissa said. "You won't hold us fifteen minutes when my lawyer hears this! I never saw that girl in my life. And I was babysitting neighborhood kids the day my husband was killed. I can prove it."

Getting in her face, he said, "You hired Clay Tharpe! He gave you half the money he got from your husband." His teeth came together. "And you saw Beth at the park. You heard her name. You knew she came every day to load her newspaper boxes. You helped Tharpe plan her attack!"

"I didn't!" she screamed. "I'm innocent!"

Ned jerked out of London's grip and came toward them, his cuffed hands behind his back. "I didn't know anything about all this. All I did was cheat on my wife. I wouldn't have a relationship with someone who could come up with a scheme like that, especially against Beth."

The very utterance of her name sent Mark over the top. "We'll see if a judge and jury buy that."

"I'm telling you," Ned said. "I'm a father. I've sat in the ICU next to my son struggling for his life. I wouldn't put another family through that, believe me." He tossed his head toward Melissa. "She came up to the conversion plant every day, flirting with whoever would show her attention."

"Shut up, you moron!" she shouted.

Ignoring her, he went on. "She did have a thing with Clay, but she started coming on to me too. I figured, why not? After the stuff with Clay, I wouldn't have kept seeing her if I thought she was to blame. But she didn't mean enough to me to murder someone over her. She's a fling, that's all. A meaningless diversion."

Melissa's face went rabid. "A fling?" she cried. "You told me you loved me! You *should* have wanted Blake dead! He terrorized me and abused me! If you were half a man, you would have stepped up to the plate like Clay did, instead of making me come up with a solution of my own. *He* loved me enough to help me! You were just a coward!"

Mark's chest hurt as Melissa condemned herself in a fit of rage. Ironically, her ranting seemed to clear Ned. Maybe he hadn't been involved after all.

By the time they'd loaded the two of them into the van, neighbors were standing out in their yards. The affair had been exposed, along with Melissa's deadly schemes.

"My son!" Melissa cried. "I want to see my little boy!" She was sobbing, trying to get out of the van. She turned to Sharon, the next-door neighbor who stood on the edge of her lawn. "Sharon, please go to my mom's house and tell her what's going on. Tell her to get me a lawyer. Tell her to take care of Danny until I get out."

Mark's heart went out to Melissa's mother, who'd lost so much. Her husband, who had obviously been trying to save their murdering daughter. And now this.

Wisely, Ned was silent as they rode to the sheriff's department. Melissa didn't shut up, and every word she shouted would be used against her in court. Brad would recommend that the judge refuse to set bond. She'd be held in the county women's facility in Birmingham. Mark hoped she'd come to learn what real fear felt like—the kind that Beth had felt before she died.

OCTOBER USHERED COLOR INTO THE DARKNESS OF
Kay's life, and she found herself still among the living.
Civilization slowly bought back what it lost. Three television stations returned to the airwaves. Families who could
afford it replaced their flat screens with old vacuum-tubed
TVs—awaiting the day when solid-state sets would be man-
ufactured again.

Kay and her family didn't join the television rush. They
merely observed their neighbors' frenzy with a comfortable
detachment. Filling their lives back up with noise and chat-
ter didn't aid in their healing. Spending time with each other
did, even when that time was passed in hard work.

The charges against Ned were dropped, since there
was no evidence he'd been a part of the murder scheme.
Surprisingly, his wife took him back. The Brannings sat
through the trial of Melissa Tomlin from the first gavel to
the verdict. She was found guilty of two of the three counts
of conspiracy to commit murder and sentenced to spend
thirty years in prison. Melissa's father, Scott Anthony, was
given a life sentence without parole. After each verdict, Kay
found herself unable to celebrate. So many lives had been
trashed by greed and selfishness. She took no pleasure in
seeing two more destroyed.

Doug decided not to return to his job as a stockbroker
when Wall Street reopened, and as they replaced the force at
the sheriff's department, his volunteer hours fell off. Instead,

he and Mark began work on their solar energy store for the thousands who wanted to avoid dependence on the power grid.

Meanwhile, Doug was ordained by his former church, so he continued to preach, working through his grief fully exposed to their growing church body. It was after one of those sermons in late October that Brad's wife, Judith, took Kay aside.

"Kay, I don't know how you'll feel about this, but I wanted you to know. The neighborhood kids have been working on the last play Beth wrote. They're performing it Saturday night."

Kay stared at her. "How did they get the script?"

"Apparently Beth gave a draft of it to Cher and told her she could direct it. They quit working on it when she died. But a few weeks ago, Cher got the kids back together and they decided to do the play in honor of Beth. It made them feel better and helped them grieve."

That debilitating sadness raised its head again. But Kay was growing weary of it. The energy to maintain it was draining her. And the children hadn't done this out of dishonor or malicious intent—they wanted to feel closer to Beth.

"What a surprise. I don't know what to say."

"I was told to ask if you'd like to come."

"I don't know, Judith. I really don't think I can." They could have the play and perform it when they wanted, but they couldn't expect her to sit there on public display while they did.

Judith didn't press. "I understand. And so does everyone else. But if you change your mind, they'd like for you and your family to be the guests of honor." A slow grin crept across her face. "Kay, just so you know, Beth's title is *The History of the World.*"

Kay laughed. "Is it really? She named it that?"

"Girl, she had to," Judith said. "That's exactly what it's about."

That night, Kay shared the news with the family and told them they could go if they wanted to, but she planned to stay home.

"I'm going," Logan announced.

"Me too," Jeff said. "They went to all that trouble. We should at least show up."

Deni was more sensitive. "Mom, I know it would be hard. But they'll be saying Beth's words. I want to hear them. She would want us there. Don't you want to see what she considered to be the history of the world?" She chuckled softly. "Mom, the *entire world!*"

Kay had to admit that the title intrigued her. Still, her heart was a bruised and bleeding thing, and she wasn't sure she could hold herself together long enough to watch the play. But part of her yearned to see Beth's sense of humor and insight played out through the children who recited her words.

Maybe it was time to pull her attention from death to life and embrace the memories that Beth had left behind.

THE MOMENT MARK HEARD ABOUT THE PLAY, HE OFFERED to help the children with the stage and props, as he'd done with each of Beth's productions. The children were secretive about the contents of the play, but Cher, Beth's best friend, told him they would need Mark to paint three backdrops. One of a garden, one of an open field with trees, and another of stone walls.

The day before the play, he rushed to get it completed. Craig, who'd been working around the clock to get telephone service restored, took the day off to help. Mark and his nemesis worked side by side, painting and hammering and setting things up on the assembly lot by the lake. When they had the stage together and hung the three backdrops, the children were bouncing with glee.

"Good job, man." Mark raised his hand to slap Craig's. "You didn't have to help, but I appreciate it."

"No problem," Craig said. "I did it for Beth."

KAY BRACED HERSELF FOR A CRYING JAG THE DAY OF THE play, but she found herself laughing instead. The children had reserved a front row just for the family, and as they arrived, Kay struggled to keep her emotions in check.

The play began with a mother and daughter in a loveseat on a lower part of the stage. Chris Horton played the mother, her hair pulled up to make her look older than twenty-two.

Eight-year-old Olivia Huckabee, Hank and Stella's granddaughter, played the child curled up against her mother, listening as she read to her.

Kay's heart tightened as Beth's words came to life.

"In the beginning, God created the heavens and the earth. And then he created the man and the woman. Life was wonderful, and then they mucked the whole thing up."

The curtains opened to the backdrop of the garden, with Adam and Eve played by two of Beth's classmates, and a funny little boy named Matt who wore a snake costume and crawled around on his belly.

Eve spoke like a valley girl. "So, like, I'm sorry, okay? I only ate a stupid apple. It's not like I've brought a curse on mankind."

Adam crossed his arms and looked at the audience. "Um ... actually? You have."

Matt the serpent agreed. "Yep, you've done it, all right. Now my fun begins." The serpent laughed like a wicked scientist, rubbing his hands together.

Kay and Doug laughed through the depiction of Joseph being sold by his brothers, who talked like gang members and did a funny rap song while slave traders carried Joseph away.

Next came Daniel in the lions' den. The lions were played by four second graders whose moms had made them gigantic manes that dwarfed their small bodies. Daniel was a fifth grader with a painted mustache. As the lions came for him, he said, "Nice boys," threw a stick, and told them to fetch. The lions retrieved the stick like trained puppies.

The play followed all the major events of the Bible right through the nativity. Amber's youngest played Baby Jesus, and Cher and Jimmy Scarbrough played Mary and Joseph. The stage filled with the youngest boy actors—toddlers to preschoolers—who were told to scream as a mean King Herod came stomping through to kill the boy babies. Cher and Jimmy whisked the baby away. The children screamed with delightful smiles on their faces, lightening the heavy moment in the play.

Kay glanced back at their former sheriff, Ralph Scarbrough, who had finally been able to venture out in public after his long convalescence. He beamed with pride at Jimmy's star performance as Joseph.

In the depiction of Jesus' miracles, Ben Latham played a leper with spots all over his body, and Jesus healed him. Ben posed then, like a Mr. Universe, eliciting applause. Drew Caldwell played the demoniac in chains, ranting and hurting himself until Jesus healed him. Then he shook off the chains and did a hip-hop dance until the curtains closed again.

The mood grew serious as Chris read again of Jesus in the garden of Gethsemane, and the false accusations, and his betrayal by his friend.

As Chris read, a memory came to Kay: Beth coming outside as Kay stood over the fire, dripping with perspiration as she cooked.

"Mom, I'm having trouble with Jesus."

Kay's oil popped and bubbled, and she didn't have much time to look away. "What kind of trouble?"

"When I'm writing about him, it seems disrespectful to have some kid playing his part on the cross. People laugh when they see their children on the stage. How could I show Jesus on the cross in a way that he likes?"

Kay remembered smiling. "Just think about it for a while, honey. I'm sure Jesus will show you the right way." She hadn't known what Beth was writing and had never asked more about it. Until today it had fled from her mind.

Now, as the curtains opened, she saw two boys tied to crosses on the stage, with a larger pole in the middle. The boys looked toward the top of the middle pole, as though Jesus' cross were higher than the audience could see.

"If you're really Christ, save yourself and us!" one of them yelled.

"Shut up, you jerk!" the other one cried. "We're here for breaking the law. But he didn't do anything to deserve this!" The first boy looked up at the cross between them. "Jesus, remember me when you get to your kingdom, okay?" His face changed, and he started to smile. "Did you hear that? He said today I would be with him in paradise!"

The audience clapped as the curtain closed. Chris read of Christ's resurrection and his promises that "Where I am, there you will be also."

When the curtains opened again, the final backdrop returned them to the garden, a sweet depiction of Beth's idea of heaven. Beth had clearly come to the conclusion that it wouldn't be irreverent to show a heavenly Christ in the happiest place on earth. Jimmy had been recast to play that role. He wore a white robe and a long brown wig, and his face was painted with gold paint that seemed to glow.

A crowd of children in robes assembled there, dancing, pretending to fly and eating the apples from the Tree of Life. A blind boy arrived at the gate, and Jesus met him like a long-lost son, healing him as he came in.

"Wow, the colors are way cool!" the boy said as he joined the group.

A deaf girl came in, speaking frantically in sign language. "No need for that here," he said, and healed her.

"Oh, my goodness," the deaf girl cried. "I have *so* much to tell you!" And then she chattered on and on.

The next person to come in was played by Cher again. Beth's best friend wore a bandage on her head.

Kay's hand moved to her heart.

The crowd went quiet. Kay tried to hold the tears back as Jesus picked the girl up and whirled her around, like he'd been waiting for her. He set her down and pulled the bandage off, throwing it on the floor. "We don't need this anymore. Here, we don't have bandages or broken bones or sickness or tears."

Kay reached for Doug's hand. She saw him take Deni's, and Deni took Logan's, and Logan took Jeff's.

"You're safe here. Nothing can hurt you ever again. There's no Next Terrible Thing. Only good things. And soon your family will be here, too."

By the time the scene was over, Jimmy and Cher were as teary-eyed as Kay was. Her heart was full as the children came to the edge of the stage, one by one, and read lines from the last chapter of the Bible.

Olivia said, " 'And I heard a loud voice from the throne saying, "Look! God's dwelling is now among the people, and he will dwell with them." ' "

A lion stepped forward. " 'They will be his people, and God himself will be with them and be their God. He will wipe every tear from their eyes. There will be no more death or mourning or crying or pain, for the old order of things has passed away.' "

The gangster brothers of Joseph came out and spoke in unison. " 'He who was seated on the throne said, "I am making everything new!" ' "

One by one, the little performers came through to great applause, dancing and strutting and bowing.

Kay burst out of her chair for a standing ovation, as tears of joy ran down her face. Beth ... oh, Beth. She had single-handedly taught dozens of children the major events of the Bible, and had probably driven them and all their parents back to Scripture to read more. She had shared the gospel even from death.

Finally, Chris stepped back onto the stage. "At this point, we would normally applaud for the author," she said. "But since she's not here, we'll point you to heaven. Beth would want us to give those of you who don't know Jesus the chance to know him now. The men of our little lakeside church are coming forward now, to counsel anyone who wants to learn more about Christ."

The men came forward as music played—the ones Doug had shepherded and taught over these last grueling months—and met several children who came off the stage in response to the invitation.

And then Kay saw a miracle. Brad Caldwell, her next-door neighbor, the prosecutor who hadn't been able or willing to believe before, made his walk through the lawn chairs. Instead of going to the men waiting at the front, he came to Doug.

Doug let Kay's hand go and got to his feet, embraced his best friend.

"It wasn't all for nothing, was it?" Brad asked, weeping. "There's a pattern ... a plan ... a God."

"*The* God," Doug said.

Brad nodded. "I believe that Jesus died for my sins—and for the sins of all those I prosecute every day. And I believe that Beth is in heaven with him, just like she wrote, waiting to greet each one of us."

Kay got up and joined that hug. Her heart felt cleansed and lighter now. Beth's purpose had been fulfilled. Now she saw the privilege of being part of that.

Brad was so right. It wasn't for nothing.

LATER, WHEN SHE RETURNED HOME, KAY WENT TO HER BED-room to put her shoes away. Basking in the good memories that were coming back to her, she knelt in her closet. Gratitude washed through her. Beth had shown her that she *had* been healed. Her broken skull was whole, her bandages were gone. She wasn't mourning her family as they were mourning her. God was so good to have led Beth to write such a play ... a play that would be used to comfort her family when she was gone.

Wasn't that how he always worked? Intricately weaving a web of events throughout their lives, intersecting them with others, con-necting the dots in a way that no genius ever could.

Kay's sadness over Beth had lifted for a while. Now she could cling to memories of the joy Beth had brought to their family, and all they had to look forward to.

MARK'S HEART WAS FULL OF JOY AS THE CROWD BROKE UP and the parents began disassembling the stage. Craig hung around to help them.

But Mark didn't want to help right now. He saw Deni sitting at the end of the boat pier, her feet hanging in the water. He slid his hand in his pocket and felt the ring he'd been carrying for the last few months. After Beth's death, Deni had been too mired in grief for him to propose. But today he could see that the cloud of her mourning was lifting, and blue skies were beginning to break though.

He whispered in Chris's ear. "Keep Craig busy for a little while, okay?"

Her face lit up. "Is it time?"

Mark gave her a crooked smile. "We'll see, won't we?"

He drew in a deep breath and walked down the pier. Deni looked up and smiled as he sat next to her.

"You okay?" he asked.

"I'm great. I feel like I got to see Beth today. Like I got a glimpse of where she is. That she's all right, and she wants *us* to be. There were so many things she wanted for us. I hope she'll know when they all come true."

Mark suddenly felt as nervous as a kid on his first date. He slipped the ring on the tip of his index finger, pulled it out of his pocket. "Speaking of things Beth wanted ... I've been carrying this since the day Craig rode back into town. It's never been the right time."

She sucked in a breath, and joy rounded her eyes as he showed her the ring. Holding it up, he slid off the pier and into the four-foot deep water, and knelt on one knee. The water hit him up to his chin. The ring stayed dry.

He looked ridiculous, but he didn't care. "Deni, will you marry me?"

Deni laughed and fell in after him, pulling him to his feet. "Yes, I'll marry you! Of course I will!"

They laughed as he put the ring on her finger, then hugged and fell back into the water, splashing and gurgling and laughing some more. Deni got to her feet, soaking wet, and raised her left hand in the air. "He asked me to marry him, everybody!"

Mark lifted her like a bride over the threshold and carried her out of the water. Friends and neighbors crowded around to congratulate them. His dreams were finally coming true.

Deni was going to be his wife.

CRAIG DIDN'T NEED A NEON SIGN. HE COULD SEE THAT Mark had proposed, and Deni had accepted. She was in love with Mark, and there was nothing he could do about it. She'd given up a great future to be with a man who would trap her in mediocrity. It was her loss.

But it was his too. He clenched his jaw as he walked to his car.

He got behind the wheel and slammed his door. Chris came and leaned in his window. "You okay?"

He planted his hands firmly on his steering wheel. "I can't believe it. She's going to marry him. After all I've been through with her."

She gave him an apologetic smile. "I'm sorry, Craig. But it can't be a surprise, can it? She told you from the beginning."

"She was mine first." He looked back toward the happy couple. "Where'd he get money for a ring, anyway?"

Chris glanced back at her friends. "He has a little nest egg."

He swallowed and took a deep breath, wishing she didn't have to see him like this. He didn't like being a loser. "No, it's okay, really. You're right. I did see it coming. I was just in denial, I guess. But hey, I don't have time for a wife now anyway. I have important work to do."

"Yeah, you do. We're all counting on you." She looked down at her feet. "Where are you going now?"

He turned the key and the engine roared to life. "Back to work, I guess."

"It never ends, does it?"

"No, it never does."

"Have you eaten? My parents got hold of some sirloin steaks. They're throwing them on the grill as we speak. Want to come?"

He hesitated. "Sounds tempting."

"I'm a good listener too, if you want to unload."

He almost said yes. But wallowing in it would do him no good. He should get right back to work. That was the only thing that would get his mind off what he'd lost.

"Maybe a rain check?"

"Sure." She backed away from the car, and he drove away.

Maybe he would take her up on that someday.

DENI LIFTED HER WHITE SILK SKIRT AND STEPPED CARE-fully down her front porch steps. Two horse-drawn carriages waited in front of her house—one of polished black for her mother and brothers. The second one was painted white, with gold filigree, and two white stallions pulled it. Men in black tuxedos sat on the front benches, holding the reins.

Awestruck, she brought her hand to her mouth. "Where did that white one come from?"

"Your groom built it just for you," Kay said. "He's been working on it since you said yes."

Deni had known he was working on something secret, but when he put the gazebo together at the lake, she thought that was it. It was crafted just as perfectly, with the same painted gold filigree, and the skillful carvings that spoke of devoted love.

"You look beautiful, sweetie." Kay kissed her cheek, then with glossy eyes, pulled her veil down over her face. "It's a far cry from Vera Wang. But I like it better."

Deni whispered a laugh. The designer dress she'd had for her wedding to Craig had come to a bad end, but it was just as well. She wasn't the same debutante who had needed designer labels. She'd found no shortage of neighbors willing to loan her their wedding dresses. She'd settled on Judith's simple but elegant silk dress. With a few alterations, it fit her well.

When she'd been engaged to Craig, Deni had planned a wedding with ten bridesmaids from her sorority, ten groomsmen, a miniature bride and groom, five flower girls, and two ring bearers. But her dreams had changed. Now she had only Chris as her maid of honor, her two brothers, and Mark's stepdad to stand up with him.

"You couldn't look more beautiful," her mother said. "I'm so proud of you."

"Don't make me cry, Mom. I don't want to ruin my veil. I have to be beautiful when Mark sees me coming down the aisle."

It had been an emotional day. She'd gone from overwhelming joy that she would finally be Mark's wife, to crushing sorrow that her sister wouldn't be standing beside her. To compensate, they'd put an empty chair inside the gazebo, with the dress Beth would have worn, and a bouquet of burgundy and white roses. She wouldn't be forgotten as Deni and Mark exchanged vows.

"Come on, Mom! I wanna see how this thing rides." Logan had taken the seat next to the driver in the front carriage. Jeff stood on the ground, waiting to help Kay in.

"Don't let him drive," Jeff told the driver. "He'll run us off into a ditch."

"I'd better go." Kay squeezed her arm.

Deni watched from the steps as her mother climbed into the carriage. They waved as it pulled them away. Deni stepped across the lawn to her own.

Her dad stood beside it with tears rimming his eyes. "We can't go yet. We don't want anyone to see you until it's time for you to go down the aisle." Emotion pulled at his face. "We've come a long way, haven't we, sweetheart?"

"Yeah, from planes falling out of the sky, to this."

"You've changed."

She smiled. "So have you. Remember that day, when that guy stole our bike?"

"Oh, I remember. You practically called me a coward."

"You went from that to fighting criminals. Who would have thought?"

His amusement faded. "And you went from the prissy girl who stomped around in high heels, to a woman of real substance."

"Thank you, Daddy." Here came the tears. She would look like a scarecrow walking down the aisle. She pressed her mother's lace handkerchief to her eyes to catch the tears before they fell.

"Well, it's time to go."

His mouth trembled as he helped her into the carriage. The seat was burgundy velvet, one of her colors in the wedding. The thought of Mark making it with such care banished her tears, and laughter filled her throat. Her father stepped up and sat beside her.

"Ready, ma'am?" the driver asked.

"Yes," she said, "I'm ready."

He slapped the reins and the horses began to pull them. They turned off her street and went around the block. As the horses clomped closer to the site of the wedding, Deni's heart almost burst. Her parents had rented chairs for the occasion, so they wouldn't have to have lawn chairs.

There was a red carpet running up the aisle, and the gazebo, where Mark would be waiting, was covered with roses. She saw her mother already seated in the front row, and Mark's mother across the aisle. From her perch in the carriage, she could see Mark in the gazebo, his stepfather at his side. He looked stunning in his tux and tie, so tall and handsome.

"Sit back so he can't see you until it's time," her father whispered. "You're going to blow him away."

Her brothers walked the aisle together and lit the candles, then turned and went to their places, one on each side of the gazebo. Chris, her maid of honor, stepped down the aisle then. Her burgundy dress—one she'd bought for one of her sorority dances in college—looked lovely on her small frame. She took her place beside Beth's empty chair.

The violinists ceased playing. All got quiet as the small string quartet marked the hour with the sound of a gong: one ... two ... three ... four.

"It's time," her father said.

A swarm of butterflies rose up in her chest as her dad got out and came around the carriage. As the guests stood and watched, she got her bouquet, took her father's hand, and stepped out of the carriage.

The music began again, the soft violin rendition of "I Will Sing of My Redeemer." She stepped on the red carpet and took her father's arm. Her gaze came up, and through her veil, she saw Mark, biting his lip as tears ran down his face at the sight of her.

She had never felt more beautiful.

They walked slowly down the aisle, her father and her, and her mind sang along with the old hymn that spoke so eloquently of what Christ had done for her. They reached the gazebo, and the sweet look on Mark's face almost melted her. Doug lifted Deni's hand and gave it to Mark. Then Doug turned to the guests to conduct the ceremony.

He made the crowd laugh as he talked about Deni as a little girl, and his memories of Mark when he was in high school. Deni giggled and leaned into Mark, her heart full of gratitude that God had turned her from the path of emptiness and mediocrity, to pure, unadulterated joy.

When they'd exchanged rings, Doug pronounced them man and wife and told Mark to kiss his bride. She turned to him. He wore that teasing grin that sent fireworks through her heart.

"Ready?"

"Yes," she said as the crowd waited.

"Love me?"

"Bad," she said.

Mark lifted the veil, slid his arms around her, and dipped her back. She let out gales of laughter. As her neck arched, he kissed it first, then moved to her lips. She came back up as the crowd erupted in applause.

"Ladies and gentlemen, I now present to you, Mr. and Mrs. Mark Green."

She raised her bouquet and gave a victory shout. Mark swept her feet off the floor as he lifted her again, presenting his bride to everyone. Then he carried her back down the aisle.

She put her arms around his neck and kissed that jaw she loved so much. "You're full of surprises, aren't you?"

"Oh, baby, this is just the beginning."

THE RECEPTION WAS LOUD AND JOYFUL, AS THE BAND PLAYED AND people in dresses and suits danced in the cool November breeze. They feasted on the wedding cake Amber had made for them. When Deni threw the bouquet, she made sure that Chris would catch it.

As she congratulated Chris with a hug, George Mason, the paramedic, asked Chris to dance.

"You sure, George?" she asked with a teasing grin. "I'm next up for a wedding."

"You don't scare me," he said with a grin as he took her in his arms and danced away.

When it was time, the crowd parted and Deni and Mark ran through. He helped her back into the carriage, then stepped into it beside her. "Let's go home, Mrs. Green," he whispered.

Home. Her home with Mark would begin in Eloise's house, across the street from her parents. They'd spent the last month getting it ready. Though they couldn't afford to buy it yet, Eloise's son had allowed them to rent it at a price they could afford.

Twilight fell as the driver pulled them the long way around Oak Hollow, and Deni basked in her husband's arms and the gentle sound of the horses' clopping hooves. As they rode in their wedding carriage, an occasional car passed on the street. Lights came on in the open windows. They could hear television chattering in some of them, radios playing, rotary phones ringing. The waning sunlight glistened on the antennas reaching from the rooftops, and shone on the dull paint of reconditioned cars.

As they reached their street, Deni had the sense that much of the world had gone back to normal.

But she and her family hadn't. And neither had Mark.

He seemed to read her thoughts. "I don't want to go back to the way I was before."

She shook her head. "Neither do I. God got our attention with the Pulses. He had to empty our hands so we could finally reach for him."

Mark touched her face and pressed his forehead against hers. "And then he gave us more than we had before."

THAT EVENING, WHEN THE RECEPTION WAS OVER AND EVERY-thing had been cleaned up, Kay and Doug snuggled together, feeling the contentment and joy of having a child who had chosen well. Kay closed her eyes and saw a time line, stretching into eternity. Recorded on the line, she saw illnesses and healings, miracles and milestones, lives and deaths. And she saw heaven, stretched out in a long, glorious line, crossing farther into the future than she could see.

God was the keeper of that time line, the maestro of all that happened within it. The symphony played on—a song of love and hope and promises kept. A song that wouldn't end before they were all gathered together again.

As God's healing presence fell over her like a down blanket, Kay smiled. She could almost hear the music.

Afterword

TODAY I RAN ACROSS A VERSE IN ISAIAH 26 THAT JUMPED out at me. It says, "For when the earth experiences your judgments the inhabitants of the world learn righteousness" (v. 9b). As I've worked my way through this series, I've asked the question over and over: What might God do to get our nation's attention in order to bring righteousness? Will he use a supernova that knocks out all our technology? Will he use E-bombs, nuclear weapons, terrorist attacks? Or hurricanes, tornadoes, fires, tsunamis, earthquakes? We know that none of this is outside his control or ability, and it's not outside his sovereignty. He holds the world in his hand and wants what's best for us. "In their affliction they will earnestly seek Me," the Lord says in Hosea 5:15.

In our narcissistic society, we can't quite grasp why seeking him is good for us. Those who want life to be all about them can't understand why God wants it to be all about him. The truth is, God knows that when we focus on him as the Lord of our lives—not on some generic "higher power," and certainly not on ourselves—we will live safer, more peaceful lives. "Then your light will break out like the dawn, and your recovery will speedily spring forth; and your righteousness will go before you; the glory of the Lord will be your rear guard ... And the Lord will continually guide you, and satisfy your desire in scorched places, and give strength to your bones; and you will be like a watered garden, and like a spring of water whose waters do not fail" (Isaiah 58:8, 11).

We squabble over whether Christ's name can be proclaimed in public, to the point that the words "Merry Christmas" have become offensive to many. As a society, we've tried to erase the memory of our history and the Christian heritage that got us here, as well as the goodness of our God in blessing us so richly. We've allowed the singular voices in courthouses to determine how we acknowledge our Lord as a nation.

So, I ask you. What will God have to do to our country to get our attention? How will he choose to refine us, so that we'll finally seek him?

If you're a Christian, realize the impact that your witness has on those around you. Not only could it save their souls, but it could save our nation. Imagine if every Christian lived a life like Christ. Imagine if we walked in light of the Great Commission. Wouldn't those unbelievers around us begin to seek him? Wouldn't they want what we have? Wouldn't the fire of Christ sweep with its healing power across our world? Wouldn't it save us from catastrophe?

No, not every catastrophe is a disciplinary strike from the Lord. That's not what I'm saying at all. But God is a loving parent, longing to bless us. Imagine if you had a beloved child to whom you'd decided to give everything—a new car, a college education, a starter home, vacations, a trust fund, a gift of $20,000 a year for life, and ultimately everything you own when you pass on. But before you could fulfill your plans, he ran his car into a brick wall. Gambled away every cent he got. Got kicked out of school for cheating. Refused to return your calls. Would you continue blessing him the way you'd planned? While your heart broke, you would alter your plans until he straightened up. Though the blessings were meant to be his, you would be irresponsible to continue lavishing them on him until he turned around. You would devise ways of trying to get your child's attention, so you could bless him again.

God is a parent like that. And we are the children, fighting the goodness of a Father who loves us. He wants to bless us, but because of our choices, he sometimes can't.

One of the themes in all my books has been that the crisis is sometimes the blessing. If crisis causes us to seek him with all our hearts, or draw even closer than we already are, then it puts us in a position to receive abundant blessings. "Things which eye has not seen and ear has not heard, and which have not entered the heart of man, all that God has prepared for those who love him" (1 Corinthians 2:9).

I pray that this series has made you think, and that it has drawn you closer to Christ, the ultimate blessing the Father has bestowed on us—himself in human flesh, who came to take the punishment for our wrecked lives and our bankrupt, rebellious souls, so that we could walk in blessing again. All we have to do is cry out to him, admitting our guilt, and his grace will do the rest.

—Terri Blackstock

1. Beth is paralyzed with fear after witnessing the murders. Have you ever been that afraid of something? Where would you find comfort in such a situation?
2. Beth's erratic personality worries her mother, but Kay can't seem to find a solution. What would you do if you were in her position? How could you help your child?
3. Kay thinks Beth may be experiencing post-traumatic stress disorder (PTSD). What do you know about this disorder? Do you know anyone who has experienced PTSD?
4. Craig's arrival ruins Mark's plans to ask Deni to marry him. How does he react? What does he do well or poorly? How do his interactions with Craig evolve during the course of the book?
5. Do you think it was wise for the Brannings to allow Craig to stay at their house? Should there be a limit to our hospitality? If so, what is it?
6. Mark's anger at Beth's attacker drives him to pursue Clay Tharpe. Is this anger healthy and appropriate? What are the advantages and disadvantages to letting anger drive our actions?
7. Discuss the scene in which Kay confronts Clay Tharpe in the jail. What does she do and why does she do it? Can you sympathize with her?

8. Discuss the hope the Brannings had for Beth's recovery. Were they right to have such hope? Is it unrealistic to expect a miracle?

9. The Oak Hollow church shows great support to the Brannings when they hold a prayer service for them and Beth. Would your community do the same for you and your family? What can you do to foster community where you live?

10. How do you explain Kay's actions in Beth's room? Why does she want to throw away Beth's things? What effect does seeing Beth's hair have on her, and why?

11. Consider the play the neighborhood kids produce. What is it about seeing the play that allows Kay to heal and come to terms, at least partially, with the death of her daughter? Why is she able to do this? What other events have helped her get to this point?

12. Deni eventually chooses Mark instead of Craig, but what does she sacrifice in doing so? Are these sacrifices worth it? What would you sacrifice for love?

13. Throughout the Restoration Series, the Brannings have tried to adapt to the problems brought on by the Pulses and still maintain their integrity as Christian witnesses. Did they succeed? Do you think you and your family could do the same? What would you do differently?

Cape Refuge Series

This bestselling series follows the lives of the people of the small seaside community of Cape Refuge, as two sisters struggle to continue the ministry their parents began helping the troubled souls who come to Hanover House for solace.

Cape Refuge
Softcover: 978-0-310-23592-7

Southern Storm
Softcover: 978-0-310-23593-4

River's Edge
Softcover: 978-0-310-23594-1

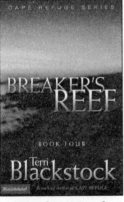

Breaker's Reef
Softcover: 978-0-310-23595-8

ZONDERVAN®
.com

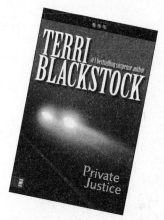
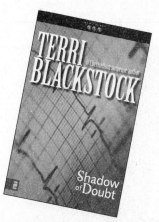

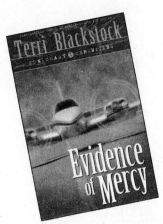

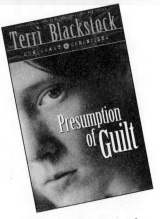

ABOUT THE AUTHOR

Terri Blackstock is an award-winning novelist who has written for several major publishers including HarperCollins, Dell, Harlequin, and Silhouette. Her books have sold over 6 million copies worldwide.

With her success in secular publishing at its peak, Blackstock had what she calls "a spiritual awakening." A Christian since the age of fourteen, she realized she had not been using her gift as God intended. It was at that point that she recommitted her life to Christ, gave up her secular career, and made the decision to write only books that would point her readers to him.

"I wanted to be able to tell the truth in my stories," she said, "and not just be politically correct. It doesn't matter how many readers I have if I can't tell them what I know about the roots of their problems and the solutions that have literally saved my own life."

Her books are about flawed Christians in crisis and God's provisions for their mistakes and wrong choices. She claims to be extremely qualified to write such books, since she's had years of personal experience.

A native of nowhere, since she was raised in the Air Force, Blackstock makes Mississippi her home. She and her husband are the parents of three adult children—a blended family which she considers one more of God's provisions.

Terri Blackstock (www.terriblackstock.com) is the #1 bestselling author of the Cape Refuge, Sun Coast Chronicles, Second Chances, and Newpointe 911 suspense series, and other books. With Beverly LaHaye, she wrote *Seasons Under Heaven*, *Times and Seasons*, *Showers in Season*, and *Season of Blessing*.